MIDNIGHT

The Aggressor Series
Volume IV

D1523812

FX Holden

MIDNIGHT

"The night is always darkest
before the dawn."
Khwaja Shirazi
14th Century AD

Cover concept by Diana Buidoso (R.I.P.)
Realization of Midnight cover by Jimmy Machon

Public domain maps created from MapChart and Openstreetmaps.
Copyright images purchased Shutterstock.

Contact me:
www.fxholden.com
fxholden@yandex.com
https://www.facebook.com/hardcorethrillers

Novel four of five in the Aggressor series

With huge thanks to my fantastic beta-reading team for their encouragement and constructive critique.

In no order: Justin Martin, Dan Fisher, John Polo, Mike Ramsey, Darren Andrew, Lee Steventon, Alexander Anderson, Bob Imus, Barry Roberts, Dogger Day, Alan McDonald, Simon Kimm, Matt Thorne, Julian D Torda, Dave Hedrick, Julie Fenimore, Robert Bugge, Alain Martin, Dean Kaye, Johnny Bunch, Mukund B, Thierry Lach, Bror Appelsin, Andy Sims, Glenn Eaves, Marshall Crawford, Claus Stahnke

And to editor, Nicole Schroeder,
alexandria.edits@gmail.com
for putting the cheese around the holes.

Books in the Aggressor Series:
1. AGGRESSOR
2. BEACHHEAD
3. SWARM
4. MIDNIGHT
5. FULCRUM Coming September 2024.

Also by FX Holden: The Future War Series
(each is a stand-alone story)
1.KOBANI
2. GOLAN
3. BERING STRAIT
4. OKINAWA
5. ORBITAL
6. PAGASA
7. DMZ

Doomsday Clock Ticks Closer to Midnight as US Declares War on China

Bern, Switzerland, May 30, 2038: The Doomsday Clock, an enduring symbol of humanity's frailty, now stands at an unprecedented 30 seconds to midnight—the closest to global catastrophe it's ever been. This chilling shift follows the US Congress's declaration of war on China, sparking fears of a devastating nuclear conflict.

Established in 1947, the clock's hands track humanity's vulnerability to threats like nuclear war and climate change. The previous closest setting was 90 seconds, reflecting mounting concerns in 2023. Moving the clock to 30 seconds highlights the immense danger posed by the US-China conflict, two nations with vast nuclear arsenals.

Experts warn that miscalculations or escalations could trigger a nuclear exchange, potentially ending human civilization. The Bulletin of the Atomic Scientists, the group maintaining the clock, urges world leaders to immediately de-escalate and avert disaster.

Contents

Contents 6

Area of Operations 8

Aggressor Series Recap 9

Cast of players 11

Executive disorder 14

Operation Midnight: Hilo 20

The Battle of Hawaii: Ford Island 27

The Rearguard: Highway 20 56

The Battle of Hawaii: Infirmary 66

State of the War Briefing 79

Operation Midnight: Agincourt 82

The Rearguard: Hide 93

The Battle of Hawaii: NOAA pier 103

The Rearguard: Tongxiao 120

Operation Midnight: Piranha 135

The Battle of Hawaii: Battery Boyd 143

The Rearguard: Under Taichung 158

The Battle of Hawaii: Hilo 174

The Rearguard: Taipei 196

Operation Midnight: Enigma 213

The Battle of Hawaii: Fujian 222

The Rearguard: Garage 247

The Battle of Hawaii: CAP 264

The Rearguard: Jinhua Street 308

The Battle of Hawaii: Vandenberg 313

Operation Midnight: Máo-niú / Yak.........................355

The Battle of Hawaii: Northwest Kaua'i 364

The Rearguard: Overwatch.....................................384

The Battle of Hawaii: Pago Pago 389

Operation Midnight: Tag 428

The Battle of Hawaii: Bellows 'AFB' 433

Operation Midnight: *Taifun*..................................481

The Battle of Hawaii: Makaha Ridge......................489

State of the War Briefing.......................................503

Epilogue 505

Author note 538

FULCRUM: Coming July 2024................................540

Glossary 542

Area of Operations

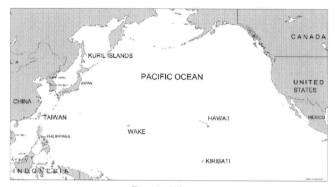

Pacific Theater

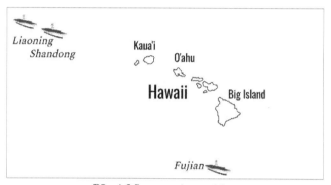

PLA Navy carrier positions

Aggressor Series Recap

Aggressor: The pilots of private military contractor Aggressor Inc. are thrown to the front lines of a superpower conflict between China and America. A Chinese blockade of Taiwan escalates into a shooting war. Having smuggled hypersonic "carrier killer" missiles onto Taiwan, Aggressor Inc. pilot Karen 'Bunny' O'Hare delivers a heavy blow to China's supercarrier, PLAN *Fujian*. But as Aggressor Inc. uncovers a traitor in its midst, China fights back, driving US carriers back to the sheltered waters of friendly countries.

Beachhead: US President Carmen Carliotti is prepared for war. She sees Taiwan as "the rock upon which I will break Communist China's back." Trapped on an encircled Taiwan, Aggressor Inc.'s contract with the USAF sees it stood up as 68th Aggressor Squadron. As China unleashes a storm of missiles against Taiwan, and the US responds with a lightning campaign to dislodge China from its possessions in the South China Sea, events spiral out of control. India and China clash on their Himalaya border. China attacks US internet infrastructure as a demonstration of its capabilities. And a well-planned assassination attempt nearly claims the US President's life. As casualties mount, 68th Aggressor is tasked to destroy a Chinese missile launch site, but the weapons it is launching are unlike any the world has seen. As 68th Aggressor Squadron is pulled out of Taiwan, Bunny O'Hare is shot down over the Strait and makes her way back to the Taiwanese mainland. She arrives to news of an outbreak of deadly virus on the island, a virus for which only China and its Shanghai Pact allies have a vaccine.

Swarm: The US and its Coalition partners surge aircraft, ships and troops into the Taiwan theater, prepared to meet a coming Chinese invasion. However, China's game plan for conquering Taiwan is not to invade it with troops but with thousands of autonomous killer drones— "slaughterbots." And they do not intend to fight alone. China announces a new multinational defense alliance, the Shanghai Pact, comprising nuclear-armed nations China, Russia, Iran and North Korea. The defenders of Taiwan are overwhelmed in the air, as well as on the ground. Losses mount. And taking its drone war into space, China launches an offensive that takes out US and allied military communication and GPS satellites. As O'Hare and a Taiwanese robotics engineer race to find a counter weapon to the Chinese "slaughterbots" scourge, US deaths on Taiwan mount, the virus threatens to spread to the US mainland and the US declares war on China. A traitor emerges at the heart of the US government, but which master does he serve?

The Taiwan government is on the brink of collapse. The US government is forced by the bioweapon threat to enact draconian internal security measures and decamp to a secure facility on Greenland. Its forces in the Pacific are fighting blind, satellites destroyed, undersea cables cut. The fog of war has become a pea soup, and from the fog, a massive Sino-Russian fleet emerges. China launches strikes on Japan and the Philippines, but also across the Indo-Pacific: on Guam, Wake Island, Midway … and Hawaii.

The Battle for Taiwan is not yet over. But the Battle for Hawaii is about to begin.

Cast of players

COALITION

Hawaii
Carmen Carliotti, US President (POTUS)
Colonel Taylor Charles, USAF, aide to POTUS, ad-interim
Admiral Harry Connaught, Commander, US Indo-Pacific Command (INDOPACOM)
General Reg Samuels, US Army and Joint Operations Commander, US Forces, Hawaii
Seaman Apprentice Falaniko 'Niko' Akiu, Federal Fire Department, Station 4, Ford Island
Presley Ortiz, Corner Canyon Chargers Girls Varsity Golf Team, Utah
Tammy Ballard, Police Officer, Honolulu PD
Lieutenant Alessa Baruzzi, 7th Air Defense Artillery Regiment, Kaua'i

Greenland
NSC ExCom members: Chief of Staff HR Rosenstern, Vice President Mark Bendheim, Homeland Security Secretary Janet Belkin, Defense Secretary Dan Caulfield, Chair of the Joint Chiefs General Earl Maxwell

USAF 492nd Special Operations Wing
Captain Rory O'Donoghue, 18th Flight Test Squadron, AC-130X 'Outlaw'
Lieutenant Robert E. 'Uncle' Lee, 18th Flight Test Squadron, AC-130X 'Outlaw'

68th Aggressor Squadron, AGRS (Aggressor Inc.)

Lieutenant Karen 'Bunny' O'Hare, P-99 Black Widow flight leader, 68th AGRS

Captain Anaximenes 'Meany' Papastopolous (USAF Reserve), CO, 68th AGRS

Captain Charlene 'Touchdown' Dubois, F-22 Raptor flight leader, 68th AGRS

Captain Michael 'Agony' Payne, F-22 Raptor flight leader, 68th AGRS

Second Lieutenant Lukas 'Flatline' Fibak, F-22 Raptor pilot, 68th AGRS

Lieutenant Brooks 'Flowmax' Brown, F-22 Raptor pilot, 68th AGRS

Senior Airman Seamus 'Crystal' Hennessy, Intelligence specialist, 68th AGRS

Taiwan

Sergeant Mason Jackson, 1st Battalion, 8th Marines

Corporal Jerome Xu, Airborne Special Service Company, Yun Chi Tuan 'Thunder' Squad

Gunnery Sergeant James Jensen, US 3rd Marines, 1st Battalion, 'Lava Dogs'

'Fi' Feng-yun Tsui, Taipei resident

US Space Force

Colonel Alicia 'The Hammer' Rodriguez, 615th Combat Operations Squadron, Space Launch Delta 45

Colonel Dan 'Tug' Boatt, Director of Operations and Lead Pilot, 615th Combat Operations Squadron Skylon Program, Space Launch Delta 45

Captain Sally Hall, Assistant Director and pilot, Skylon D4 'Tiger', 615th Combat Operations Squadron Skylon Program, Space Launch Delta 45

His Majesty's Royal Navy Submarine Agincourt
Captain Allen 'Tidewater' Courtenay, Commanding Officer
Lieutenant Arjit Singh, Executive Officer
Captain Gary McDonald, Royal Australian Navy, RAN, (attached)
Lieutenant Carla Brunelli, RAN (attached)

CHINA
PLA Navy Air Force
Colonel Wang Wei, Air Wing Commander, PLA Navy carrier *Fujian*
Major Tan Yuanyuan, PLA Navy Intelligence, PLA Navy carrier *Fujian*
Lieutenant Maylin 'Mushroom' Sun, flight leader, Ao Yin Fighter Squadron, PLA Navy carrier *Fujian*
Captain Lei Yu, Victory Squadron, PLA Navy carrier *Shandong*

Hawaii
Sergeant Pan Tien, 1st Battalion, 5th Amphibious Combined Arms Brigade (Recon)
Corporal Pi Weng, 1st Battalion, 5th Amphibious Combined Arms Brigade (Recon)

June 19, 2038

Executive disorder

US PRESIDENT Carmen Carliotti had taken a very zigzag route from Pituffik Space Base on Greenland to her location at that moment, 15 minutes out of Edwards AFB.

She couldn't make the trip to Hawaii in a target as big and obvious as Air Force One, so instead she was flying in a USAF Bombardier 9500, a 20-seat super-cruise-capable executive jet. A four-plane of F-35s swept the skies ahead of her, and she had another two Panthers riding off each wing.

She was reviewing the schedule for her meetings with military commanders on Hawaii—either face to face or virtual depending on the situation—when she noticed the Chair of the Joint Chiefs, General Earl Maxwell, in discussion with his Space Force liaison up at the front of the plane. He glanced at Carliotti, and then started back down the aisle. It didn't look like he was bringing her good news.

The rear of the aircraft was arranged as a compact meeting space, with U-shaped bench seats around two fold-out tables, currently occupied only by the president and the military aid Maxwell had assigned to be her assistant for her time on Hawaii—a full bird USAF Colonel by the name of Taylor Charles.

He had appeared uncomfortable with the role when they first boarded, so Carliotti had tried to put him at ease. "Colonel Charles, did anyone ever tell you your name works better backwards?"

He frowned. "Ma'am?"

"Charles Taylor seems much more logical. Did your parents fill in the birth certificate wrong?"

Charles was from South Carolina, and when he realized she was not serious, he gave her a relieved smile. "They got a lot of things wrong, ma'am," he said. "But I do believe my pa did me that little favor on purpose."

Charles moved aside so Maxwell could sit, but Maxwell indicated he should stand. "Give us a moment, Colonel."

What Maxwell said after Charles had moved out of earshot explained the grave look on his face. "Thanks to the Brits, we have near real-time data on the Sino-Russian fleet west of Hawaii. It's worse than we feared. Estimate is two carrier strike groups, two amphibious ready groups and auxiliaries— over 40 ships total, 70-plus aircraft. Their fleet is already in cruise missile strike range. We think they are saving their powder for a massive pre-invasion barrage. The target has to be O'ahu." He paused. "We have a decision to make and three minutes to make it in."

Carliotti set her jaw. "I'm not turning around, Earl. I'm not going to sit in DC or in a bunker under the damn ice while the Chinese come ashore on Hawaii."

"I didn't think you would," he said. "A *strategic* decision, ma'am. We have a small window to strike their fleet before those ARGs hit the beaches of O'ahu. But our targeting data is getting older by the minute. The only way we can be sure to hit the enemy fleet is with strategic nuclear weapons."

Carliotti had been prepared for the ask from the moment US and Chinese forces started directly trading blows. And Maxwell already knew her answer, but he'd asked anyway.

"It's that bad?" she asked him.

"We have been sucker punched," he said. "Our carriers and most of our attack subs are off the coasts of Japan and

15

the Philippines, with most of our Pacific Air Force and nearly our entire contingent of combat-ready Army and Marine divisions. The attacks on Guam, Clark and Kadena took out a lot of our forward-deployed strategic bomber force." He paused. "Ma'am, we have to prevent those Chinese and Russian troops from coming ashore. Strategic nukes have the footprint to do significant damage to that invasion fleet. We can hit them at sea, no collateral damage."

Carliotti was surprised to find she didn't feel horror, panic or any rising sense of impending doom—any of the emotions she had thought might overtake her when the decision finally came, as she knew it must. But she wanted Maxwell to say out loud what he knew in his heart before she gave the order.

"And if we do, the Chinese and Russian reaction will be?"

"China and Russia might retaliate with nuclear strikes on military or civilian population centers," he said. "And of course, not just China and Russia; North Korea and Iran could pile on."

"Armageddon, General."

"Not necessarily, ma'am. The alternative ..."

Her voice was firm. "For the record, I will not authorize the use of nuclear weapons yet, tactical or strategic. You and the Joint Chiefs will do all in your power to prepare our islands to repel this invasion and protect our citizens by conventional means."

Maxwell stood. "Yes, Madam President." He moved forward and the colonel, Charles, took his place again.

He was holding a tablet PC. "Ma'am, a message from State Department. The Chinese premier has made a brief broadcast to his nation. State translated it and sent the unclassified version straight through. I assumed you'd want ..."

She took the tablet from him. She'd had no direct contact with her Chinese counterpart since the start of hostilities—any communication had been through third-party diplomats and back channels and had ceased entirely when it became clear China had no desire to negotiate about Taiwan's future with anyone.

The Chinese premier was an avuncular panda of a man, his dark hair now graying but dyed heavily—according to her sources. Dark eyes glittered in a round-cheeked face. "Citizens of the People's Republic. It is with a heavy heart but boundless faith in our future that I must advise you that the USA has chosen to declare war on China. The Western countries led by the United States have, for decades, attempted all-round containment and suppression on our country, bringing unprecedented severe challenges to our development. We were seeking the peaceful reunification of Taiwan Province into One China. They brought war to Taiwan and now disease. I ask all citizens to follow the advice of your party and medical leaders. Restrict non-essential travel. Restrict non-essential gatherings. And get Vaccinated for Victory.

"As you know, this year is the year of the Yellow Earth Horse. If we must go to war, then this is an auspicious year in which to do so. The Yellow Earth Horse represents our nation's strong character of independence through hard work. And the Yellow Earth Horse knows its responsibilities.

"In that respect, despite the war being waged on us, our expert medical corps stands ready to assist our Taiwanese brothers and sisters in their struggle against the virus the Americans brought to their island. They need only ask. It is a condition of our assistance, however, that all foreign armies leave Taiwan Province."

Carliotti laughed bitterly at that. But he wasn't finished. "Now I speak to our Asian and Pacific neighbors. Do not to join this imperialist misadventure ..." he said, a clear message to the leaders of Japan, South Korea, Vietnam and the Philippines. "Do not give the warmonger's ships and aircraft and troops safe harbor, at risk to your citizens. We offer you peace and prosperity by joining with us. Our medical expertise will also be available to help our allies. The alternative, if you choose war, is disease and ruin."

China had attacked US bases in Japan and the Philippines but not, so far, non-US targets. It had also pulled its troops back from the Himalayan border with India. It was clear to Carliotti it was trying to peel away America's regional allies with the carrot of a vaccine and the stick, or club, of war.

Carliotti returned her attention to the recording. "Fellow citizens, the path to national rejuvenation now leads through war. We should seize the day, remain confident in our history, exhibit greater historical initiative, uphold fundamental principles and break new ground, maintain strategic resolve, carry forward the fighting spirit, and strive to overcome all difficulties, to contribute to the cause of building China into a great country and defeating our enemies."

The Chinese premier looked and sounded urbane, composed, concerned and oh, so reasonable. As the clip of the broadcast ended there, Carliotti threw the tablet across the aisle with enough force to make the screen crack.

She did a mental reset. "Colonel, where are we with the proposals for retaliation against China's leadership for using bioweapons?"

"CIA and the Pentagon have worked up a target list, ma'am, with delivery proposals. Some ideas are more ... creative ... than others. When do you want to review them?"

"As soon as the immediate threat to Hawaii stabilizes," she said. "So, what is the latest from Hawaii?"

"Confused picture, ma'am," he said. "That's to be expected. Most of the reports we are getting are via quantum encrypted long-wave, so there's a limit to what can be communicated. But a second wave of Chinese drones just came ashore. Army on O'ahu is deploying a microdrone swarm using the Taiwanese algorithm. And the Joint Chiefs are pulling together everything stateside that can march, sail or fly to send to the central Pacific."

"Too late," she murmured, to herself more than to the colonel. "Too late."

Operation Midnight: Hilo

THE IMPACT of the Chinese attack wasn't limited to matters above the surface of the sea.

"Clear the bridge. Secure all hatches."

"Secure all hatches, aye. Hatches secure."

"Dive, dive, dive."

"Pressure in the boat. Board green."

'Make depth niner zero feet."

"Niner zero feet, aye!"

"Open bulkhead flappers; confirm ventilation."

"Bulkhead flappers open, aye. Ventilation started."

"Take her down."

"One third trim, niner zero feet, two-degree down bubble."

"One third trim, niner zero feet, two-degree down bubble, aye!"

"Final trim, niner zero. Request speed …"

Commander Gary McDonald, formerly of the Royal Australian Navy submarine HMAS *AE1*, and Lieutenant Carla Brunelli, formerly his executive officer, watched with quiet approval as the crew of *HMS Agincourt* went about the business of submerging their boat with old-fashioned professionalism.

Which none of them could be feeling inside, since they were being sent on a mission that was almost certainly either futile or suicidal. McDonald and Brunelli had just managed to get aboard and stow their gear before the order was given to move the boat away from its berth in Hilo Bay and head north for the open sea.

The control room of *Agincourt* was crowded; that was the first thought that went through McDonald's mind as the boat

20

leveled out after its hurried dive. *Agincourt* was a generation older than McDonald's own *AE1*, and unlike *AE1*, it was not made to be "optionally crewed." Where *AE1* sailed with a redundant crew of just 12 officers, *Agincourt* bore nearly a hundred souls.

Banks of flat screens and consoles peopled by personnel in leather armchairs lined both sides of the conn, with an optical/infrared periscope and comms station in the center and, down one end, raised in the center and able to spin 360 degrees, the captain or officer of the deck's chair—which was currently occupied by Captain Allen 'Tidewater' Courtenay.

McDonald hadn't yet been properly introduced to the British captain, merely escorted aboard and then to the conn as they got underway. He knew better than to interrupt while the crew was putting to sea, especially when the boat was at general quarters. But Courtenay suddenly spun his seat to face the rear of the control room, where McDonald and Brunelli were standing.

"Welcome aboard, Captain, and you, Lieutenant," Courtenay said, smiling. "It's an unexpected pleasure to have you aboard His Majesty's vessel *Agincourt*." The smile faded. "Shall we repair to my cabin? XO, you have the conn."

'Tidewater' Courtenay, a curmudgeonly Tynesider from Gateshead near Newcastle, was not a man who enjoyed surprises. And being told the two Australian submariners would be assigned to his boat as "advisers" was unexpected, unwelcome, and to his mind, completely unnecessary.

Courtenay had been trained on diesel subs before starting out his proper career as a navigator on *Trafalgar* class nuclear subs, patrolling the Atlantic, the Baltic and the Mediterranean.

21

Promoted to XO aboard a *Swiftsure* class sub, he'd learned how to get the most out of the new pump-jet propulsion systems being deployed for His Majesty's nuclear attack submarines, before being handed command of a *Trafalgar* class boat and, finally, the prize he'd been seeking all along, one of the most advanced and by his reckoning deadliest submarines in the world, the *Agincourt*.

He wasn't given to pride or boasting. His belief in his boat was shored up with cold, hard fact. In recent exercises against the pride of the US submarine fleet, the *Virginia* class sub USS *Silversides*, the *Agincourt* had tracked the *Silversides* at ranges the Americans at first couldn't believe. But when they began combat simulation exercises for real, the results spoke for themselves.

After the spray settled, the *Agincourt* had been awarded four "kills" against the *Silversides*, and the *Silversides* only one against *Agincourt*.

Courtenay had trouble seeing what the disgraced captain and XO of an Australian boat that had to be ignominiously towed back to port at Pearl Harbor after being disabled by its Chinese adversary could teach either himself or his crew. He knew the AUKUS version of the *Astute* class submarines were supposed to combine the best of both US and British technology, and their skeleton crews were supported by combat AIs that could operate entirely independently if needed.

He'd never been a fan of that notion, and the ease with which China had apparently bested the *AE1* had not changed his opinion.

As he led the two Australians to his quarters, he decided he was willing to allow them a modicum of recognition, if they themselves proved modest enough to warrant it. He'd seen a summary report of HMAS *AE1*'s engagement with the PLAN *Fujian* Carrier Strike Group off Palau. Not only had it survived that encounter, but it had put a Spearfish torpedo into the hide of the *Fujian* to slow it down, and later a brace of Tomahawk missiles through its decks that stopped *Fujian*'s run for the South China Sea and sent it limping toward a friendly neutral port at Kiribati.

That effort deserved some recognition, even if *Fujian* was still both afloat and in the fight.

He held his cabin door open. "Please, take a seat." There was a thermos on a sideboard by his map table, and some thick porcelain cups. "Tea?"

Both Australians accepted the offer, and he poured, pushing a bowl of sugar and some spoons across to them as they sat.

"So, I take it you are here to observe," Courtenay began. "Not the first time we've had Royal Australian Navy observers aboard *Agincourt*. I think you'll find …"

"Advise," the Australian captain said.

Courtenay frowned. "Sorry, what?"

"We are not here to *observe* anything. Both Lieutenant Brunelli and I spent several months at sea on Royal Navy *Astute* class boats as part of our preparations to take command of *AE1*, which itself is an enhanced *Astute* class, as you know." McDonald drained his tea in a single gulp. "We are here, Captain, in the context of Operation Midnight, at the request of *your* Admiralty, to advise."

"Respectfully, to advise," Brunelli said in a conciliatory tone.

Courtenay sat back. "I see. So, you have been indoctrinated into Operation Midnight?"

"Indoctrinated, press-ganged, Shanghaied," McDonald said. "But we're here, to help."

"And, sorry to be obtuse, but how do you intend to be of help?" Courtenay asked.

"Can I be blunt, Captain?" McDonald asked, leaning forward. "Operation Midnight is a hunt for the Chinese submarine *Taifun*. We are the only officers in any Western navy who have been up against the *Taifun*, and we lost. What we learned could save you from the same fate."

Courtenay clearly didn't expect McDonald to come out the gate swinging, and certainly not with an admission of failure. "That could be … valuable," he allowed.

Brunelli reached into her pocket and pulled out a small solid-state drive. "This is even more valuable: the acoustic signature data *AE1* captured when we were shadowing the *Taifun*."

Courtenay was still digesting *Agincourt*'s mission orders himself. "What do you think about our mission?"

Brunelli and McDonald exchanged a glance. "We know you are expected to achieve the impossible: find one Chinese submarine in the vastness of the Pacific Ocean and put it out of commission."

"A submarine which is probably already halfway to China," Brunelli added. "Which is impossible enough to start with."

Courtenay sipped his tea thoughtfully. "Not entirely impossible," he said. "We know where it was just one hour ago."

"How …?" McDonald asked, frowning.

"Classified, I'm afraid," Courtenay said. "Not being difficult, but even the best of friends have their secrets from each other, eh?"

"You have some way of tracking *Taifun*?" Brunelli asked.

"We do. That's why our American cousins have asked for *Agincourt*'s help. It's a capability we haven't seen the need to share with them, yet."

"Where is she? We think she launched the slaughterbot attack on O'ahu," Brunelli said.

"We made the same assumption." Courtenay nodded. "And we think we know the position the last salvo was fired from. That gave us our first fix on *Taifun*. The last position we have is about 30 nautical miles northwest O'ahu, heading west. We suspect it is making for the Sino-Russian fleet, to hide amongst friends—more likely to be rearmed."

"If you can track it, you don't need this," Brunelli said, twirling the data chip in her fingers.

Courtenay eyed the chip. "Actually, we do. Our data on *Taifun*'s position is … intermittent. With a high degree of uncertainty. If we get ourselves into a position to intercept her, we'll need your data to be sure we are shooting at the right Chinese boat, or we risk giving ourselves away, attacking the wrong submarine and scaring off our prey."

"It goes without saying, Captain, we owe China some payback," Brunelli said, giving Courtenay a winning smile. "So how do you want to do this?"

He caved and waved a hand at Brunelli. "You can shadow my XO, Lieutenant Singh. I'll tell him to behave as though you're joined at the hip and he's to treat your … advice … with due consideration. Acceptable?"

"More than," Brunelli said.

"You, Captain, will shadow me. I'll be sure to seek your counsel in matters of strategy, or you can offer it proactively if I forget to ask," Courtenay said, then raised a finger. "But some ground rules. Non-negotiable."

"Go ahead," McDonald said.

"You will not question my orders, or those of my XO, in front of my crew. You will not issue orders to any member of my crew. And you will not, under any circumstances, countermand an order given by any of *Agincourt*'s officers, even if you believe in your marrow that order is inappropriate. Is that clear?"

McDonald nodded. "I'd have insisted on the same."

"Very well." Courtenay reached behind him for his thermos and refilled their cups, lifting them as though to toast. "In that case, here's to a fruitful voyage."

The Battle of Hawaii: Ford Island

SEAMAN APPRENTICE Falaniko 'Niko' Akiu was languishing in the brig on Ford Island because he'd been late. Gotten back late from shore leave and missed a drill and maybe was a bit of a smart-ass and didn't take his bawling out serious enough, so he'd been put in the brig to think things over.

Which he was doing over a breakfast bowl of cold oatmeal when he heard gunfire outside, then reeled back as the wall in the cell next to his *exploded*, masonry and dust flying, tearing out the bars between the cells and leaving a Seaman Apprentice-sized hole into the courtyard.

Then he heard gunfire and shouting from the other side of the brig too. Niko didn't hesitate; he dived through the hole in the wall because behind him was a locked steel door and if shit was going down, he wasn't going to sit in a cell like a sheep waiting to be slaughtered.

He got outside and found himself in a parking lot, big barbed wire fence all around, of course. And a couple of Navy security guards blasting away at something from behind a car. But then the car exploded, took out about 10 yards of fence and the two security guys, and he saw this … *thing*.

Big, like half the size of an SUV. Four rotors. Humpbacked. Nine-barrel missile launcher hanging underneath it, swiveling around, looking for something else to kill.

Niko got down behind a car, out of sight, watching the thing in the car's mirror. It rose up about 10 yards, did a 360, then headed out over the gap in the fence.

Niko waited a while, listening. More gunfire, more explosions, from out the other side of the brig. The only way

27

out was through the fence where the slaughterbot had just gone.

Yeah, he knew what it was. He'd seen the news footage from Taiwan. All those video clips of the Chinese killer drones. So China had found a way to land them on O'ahu? That figured. Maybe dropped them from a bomber, or some kind of ballistic missile. Maybe from space. Sure, what did he know? All he knew was the war had come to Ford Island.

Gunfire moving away. Shouting back inside the brig. Was he going back in there? *Hell he was.* Wait in a cell for the slaughterbots to bring the roof down? He looked across the parking lot and saw one of the dead security guards had dropped his weapon.

XM250. Oh yeah. That was a serious gun. Niko had never fired one, but he knew a serious gun when he saw it. He'd trained on old M4s, once on an XM7, which was the same thing but different, since the XM250 had a bipod, a suppressor and a 100-round magazine.

He gathered himself. Six foot, 182 lbs., he'd been a running back in the Kalaheo High School Mustangs, able to get that ball and find gaps in a defense no one else could see. *Think of it like a blast play, Niko,* he told himself. *You run out there, grab that gun, head for the gap in the fence.* What was on the other side? He couldn't remember. It faced north, and the brig was on the coast on the north side of the island, so maybe just the sea?

That was alright. He'd chosen the Navy because he was a good swimmer, grew up by the sea. Get to the water, get *into* the water and hide; that was a plan.

He was already running before he'd even decided whether he should or not. Scooped the rifle up in his right hand without slowing down, nearly dropped it—it was *heavy*—but kept going until he hit the fence and stood there panting, pulling in air. He slowly stuck his head through the gap, just his nose exposed, enough to look left and right.

Nothing. No slaughterbot.

He looked up. The things could fly, right? Could be cruising right overhead.

Nothing there either.

He heard a big explosion to the south, sounded like the one that had blown his wall in. Maybe it had moved down there.

Time to find out.

He put a leg through the gap in the fence, moved his weight through, got the rifle through too, holding it in one meaty fist by its hand guard.

Coastline. Boundary road, grass, scrub, mud and water. He ran for it and threw himself down in the grass behind a scrubby tree.

Alright, he was out where he could see better if he had to fight. Holding the rifle in front of him, he scanned the coast up and down. He was south of the old gun battery. He started making a plan. The Marine Operations Center was just the other side of the battery. Maybe 200 yards. Get there, get help, join up with someone who had some idea what the hell was going on. Maybe get a boat, get off the island.

Except when he got there, there was no one.

No one left alive, anyway. Or not really alive. There was one guy sitting up against a wall with a hole in his chest, mouth opening and shutting like a fish on a riverbank. But before Niko could even get the guy's shirt off to look at the wound, he stopped breathing. Niko felt like puking, held it down. He counted five bodies, all with wounds like the first guy. Big caliber. Niko knew from internet videos there were

29

two kinds of slaughterbot: the kind with a recoilless autocannon and the kind with missiles. These guys had met the autocannon kind.

Keep moving.

There were boats on trailers lined up along the road, maybe 10 of them. Forget that. Even if he could wheel one down to a ramp, it would take too long, and how would he even launch it? He had no idea. Plus, he just noticed, none of them had engines mounted.

He kept running north along the path, crouched, like that would make him less visible to a bot flying a hundred feet off the ground. Instinct. By the Hawaiian star compass set in the ground, which he'd never really worked out. Yeah, he was Hawaiian, and he was a sailor, but how did you use a star compass if you didn't know all the stars?

He used it for cover anyway, peeking out over it and looking for slaughterbots. He saw some guys running the same direction as him, maybe a block away, then they were gone. Where they'd come from, an enormous explosion. That was the Tsunami warning center. More people running north, away from it.

He took the hint and did the same. Everyone was probably headed for the bridge and the main island, by the stadium.

Except he was looking out across the water to the west as he ran, and he could see smoke that way too, and to the north. Whatever was hitting Ford Island was hitting all over O'ahu.

Then he got to the USS *Utah* memorial and looked right, saw a bunch of people come out of the Kamehameha Loop houses there, heard a ripping sound from back between the houses, and they were mown down as they ran: men, women, all of them.

Niko veered left, away from whatever was in there, not thinking, just running up the small pier that led to the *Utah* memorial, except there was no cover there. It was just a 50-yard-long pier that ended facing the wreck of the *Utah* about 10 yards off the end of the pier, and he hit the end of the pier as cannon fire started chewing up the railings on his right, so he dived off the pier to his left, hitting the railing, rolling over it with his rifle clutched to his chest and splashing into the water in a ball.

Sinking.

But he could touch bottom. He got his feet down and his hands up, rifle over his head, and quickly waded under the pier.

Be a firefighter, Niko, just like your papa, Niko, he was thinking. He was still an apprentice, halfway through his 26-week firefighter training. Should have joined the Marines instead, got some training in something more useful for whatever this was, right now.

He heard the buzz of rotors hovering overhead, then they seemed to draw away.

"Is it gone?" a voice behind him said.

He jumped and spun around. Standing in the water behind a leg of the pier was a girl. She was short, solidly built, about 17 and wearing a T-shirt that said *Corner Canyon Chargers Girl's Golf.*

IN 217 BC, the Macedonian general Hannibal led a massive force of Carthaginian cavalry and infantry on a thousand-mile march that took them from Spain, across France and into Italy via the alps to attack Rome from the north.

31

In the opening battle of the second Punic war, the Roman armies were routed.

The defenders of Rome were unprepared because such an attack—by an army that could not be where it was, crossing terrain that was uncrossable—was quite simply, impossible.

In 1941, the Russian spy, Richard Jorge, working as a journalist in Japan, reported in detail about German plans to tear up the Molotov-Ribbentrop Pact and attack the Soviet Union. He even provided an accurate estimate of *when* Germany would attack. His intelligence, corroborated by reporting from Soviet military intelligence, was passed directly to Soviet Leader Josip Stalin, who refused to believe it. Hitler had provided his personal assurances of friendship between Germany and the Soviet Union. Such an attack was impossible.

On June 22, 1941, Germany attacked the Soviet Union.

In 2025, the Ukraine-Russia War had reached a stalemate. With both sides dug in behind the most heavily mined landscape on the planet, fighting endlessly over the same small villages, Ukraine's allies judged a Ukrainian victory to be impossible against the mastodon of Russia and began winding back military aid while nudging Ukraine toward a negotiated settlement.

Ukrainian leader Volodymyr Zelensky did not believe in the word "impossible." Through 2024, he directed his generals to preserve their forces—even if it meant making the occasional strategic withdrawal—to build up supplies of men, armor and artillery. In the spring of 2025, coinciding with the arrival in strength of promised F-16 fighters from the west, Ukraine did the unthinkable. It feinted south but then attacked *east*, across the poorly protected Russian border, and within days its tanks and infantry penetrated 120 miles, or 200 kilometers, into Russian territory, capturing the cities of Belgorod, Kursk and the Russian southern army headquarters of Voronezh.

The unprepared Russian army in the Voronezh direction was routed. Five thousand Russian prisoners were taken. Ukraine consolidated its hold on the Russian cities over the next several months while dissent raged within the Russian government, culminating in a coup in 2026 against the weakened Russian leader Vladimir Putin. In 2027, Volodymyr Zelensky sat across the table from a new Russian president, negotiating Russia's return to 2014 pre-invasion borders.

The underdog Ukraine had achieved the impossible.

At the US Naval Academy, the then midshipman Harold Connaught studied the Punic Wars, the German surprise attack on the Soviet Union, and Ukraine's Russia offensive. His teachers impressed on him that the soil of history's battlefields was stained deep red with the blood of fools who had died refusing to believe in the impossible.

Harry Connaught also studied the Japanese attack on Pearl Harbor—maybe not considered impossible by US military leaders at the time, but certainly highly improbable. He designed a war game to test what a modern-day Pearl Harbor attack could look like, which became the basis for the treatise he wrote for his history bachelor, "Contemplating the Impossible: The Fall of the Hawaiian Islands."

His treatise was described by his examiners as either "provocative" or "ludicrous." It earned him a middling grade but was promptly classified CONFIDENTIAL and sequestered.

The main reason for scoring Harry's treatise down was the assumption, made in his war game and subsequent arguments, that for a foreign power to contemplate a large-scale attack on Pearl Harbor in the near future, it would need to achieve a communications blackout that would blind US INDOPACOM forces for the time it took to move attack assets into place sufficient to threaten the US Hawaiian bastion.

In his war game, the "main adversary" achieved this via a cyberattack, but the attack vector was secondary; its effect on US C3I was the critical requirement for any attack to succeed.

This, his critics argued, was his treatise's fatal flaw. There was no enemy, now or in the foreseeable future, who could take out the entirety of US INDOPACOM satellite and undersea cable links for any meaningful period of time. It was, frankly, impossible.

The young Harry Connaught had taken the criticism on the chin, but as he watched the Chinese navy expand, then overtake the US Navy in number of hulls, he never let go of the idea that an enemy may one day achieve the impossible. The idea fermented throughout his time as a Navy pilot flying F-18 C/E/F Hornets and F-35C Panthers across the vast skies of the Pacific. Ashore, a role as flag-aide to the Vice Chief of Naval Operations allowed him to press for resources to be diverted in order to dramatically increase the number of crewed and uncrewed refueling platforms available to the Navy. As special assistant for weapons systems and advanced development in the office of the US Secretary of Navy, his signature initiative was pushing for incorporating warfare command level C4I capabilities (Command, Control, Computing and Intelligence) into the new *Constellation* frigate class, enabling them to take over the role of the aging *Blue Ridge* class of amphibious command ships.

Every frigate in the *Constellation* class could perform as the communications nexus in a fleet-wide area network. And he championed the deployment of communications systems that could function as a backup to satellites: quantum encrypted Extremely Low-Frequency transmitters and receivers, and High Bandwidth Longwave radio. Harry Connaught ensured that by the time he took over as commander of INDOPACOM, the US Navy could communicate even in the event of a satellite and cable comms blackout.

Connaught and his staff on Hawaii were already managing the Navy involvement in the conflicts in the Taiwan Strait and South China Sea when US military satellites started going dark and undersea cables were cut. He issued orders for all ships and aircraft plying the heavily trafficked logistics routes from Hawaii to the Taiwan Theater to be alert to any sign Chinese forces were expanding into the central Pacific.

But China avoided the US logistics corridors, and no threatening activity was sighted. Then the reports started coming in from northwest of Hawaii: *a Sino-Russian fleet 270 nautical miles out.* Connaught dispatched reconnaissance aircraft; when they were destroyed, the USS *Canberra* attacked, destroying a Russian frigate in reply. A USAF AC-130X was attacked, launching its load of cruise missiles in response, damage results unknown.

Finally, the size of the Sino-Russian fleet was confirmed by an RAF Skylon suborbital overflight: two carrier strike groups, *Shandong* out front, *Liaoning* in the rear. A half dozen *Renhai* class missile destroyers, at least as many *Luhang IIIs*, ten or more *Jiangkai II* class frigates. Three *Yushen* class landing helo docks and support ships. And a Russian fleet, including a *Kirov* class battlecruiser, two *Udaloy* missile cruisers, two—now one—*Gorshkov* frigates and one older *Grigorovich*. A brace of newer *Steregushchiy* anti-air/anti-submarine corvettes and what looked to be most of Russia's complement of *Ivan Gren* class landing ships.

China and Russia were sending the most capable ships of their combined fleets against Hawaii.

And, not to forget, the US Coalition was also facing a renewed threat from an unexpected quarter: the PLAN *Fujian* and its escorts, to the south.

The US battlenet had gone dark. An enemy fleet was inbound Hawaii. The impossible had just happened.

Harry Connaught was as ready for it as he could be.

INDOPACOM had already moved to DEFCON 2. Connaught couldn't relocate the six *Constellation* frigates he had deployed to the western Pacific theater, but he immediately ordered the entire remaining combat-ready *Constellation* class flotilla to sail from Naval Station Everett in Washington State. Five of the eight ships would serve as high-speed data relays, using their FireScout C3I drones to extend signals and data from the US West Coast all the way to Hawaii.

The other three *Constellation* frigates Harry ordered to make speed for Hawaii itself, ready to serve as data hubs for the assets he was about to surge into the Eastern and Central Pacific. But the carrier strike groups of USS *Doris Miller* and *Enterprise* were in Japanese and Philippine waters respectively, the *Enterprise* having taken damage in the opening days of the conflict with China. He had four amphibious ready groups also in the Taiwan and South China Sea theater, supporting operations there, and a fifth on the way with the *Fallujah* ARG.

But his submarine force was out of position. He had three *Virginia* class submarines on Hawaii he could send against the Sino-Russian fleet, but the rest of his boats were forward—

36

either in the Taiwan-South China Sea area of operations or on escort duties guarding task forces like the *Fallujah* ARG. Ideally they'd be harassing the enemy fleet the whole way across the Pacific, but with the satellite blackout, it had been detected too late to put submarines into position to interdict.

That left Connaught with two available carrier strike groups in West Coast ports, the USS *Kennedy* and the *Reagan*, and two ARGs based around the USS *America* and *Tripoli*. Connaught's aviation bias showed in his orders regarding the ARG's loadouts. He ordered *America* and *Tripoli* to sail with a reduced complement of just 1,000 Marines so that both could carry a full complement of 20 F-35Bs and fly them off as soon as they were within range of refueling aircraft between Hawaii and California.

He didn't want to bring more carriers or amphibious assault ships into reach of Chinese anti-ship missiles or carrier aircraft but ordered his staff to use the carriers and their refueling drones to puddle-jump fighter aircraft from the US West Coast to Hawaii and further into the western Pacific if needed.

As Commander INDOPACOM, he could also direct the deployment of Air Force assets and ordered the PACAF commander to deploy all available long-range P-99 Widows from the US West Coast to Hawaii, pronto. Most of his stealth strike bomber force was already forward deployed—to Guam, Kadena in Japan, or Clark Base in the Philippines … and had also taken losses from Chinese strikes on those bases.

Despite being ready for this day, it took time to redeploy so many assets.

Time they didn't have.

Then the first slaughterbot assault started, and the war in the western Pacific arrived on Hawaii, as Harry had always feared. He had to pull his attention from the fighting in the Taiwan Strait and South China Sea to fighting right outside his window. Figuratively, since they'd moved to an underground command center as the first reports of the Chinese attack had come in. Normally located in Honolulu at Camp HM Smith, in wartime, essential functions moved to an installation beneath the US Naval Research Laboratory at the hilltop Opana Radar Site.

Or what *used to be* Opana Radar Site, but after the Chinese missile strikes was three smoking radomes. Getting to the site had not been straightforward either—all main roads out of Marine Corps Base Hawaii and Honolulu were under threat from roving slaughterbots. Connaught had been flown by helo to Opana, now the only way to move safely around O'ahu, though there was always the risk of a Chinese offensive air patrol sweeping in.

Connaught called the JOC facility simply "the war room." It gave him 24/7 links to the senior officer across his command, like Army Major General Mobilization Reg Samuels.

With a Sino-Russian fleet moving on Hawaii, Connaught needed a single commander on Hawaii who could coordinate the energies of his peers in Navy, Air Force, Marines and Space Force for the defense of Hawaii. Samuels hadn't asked for the job—hell, Connaught knew no senior officer would really want it. The glory was always forward, taking the fight to China in the South China Sea and Taiwan, not back home on Hawaii.

But Samuels had everything that made him perfect for the job. Twelve years combined experience on the islands across three postings. People who owed him favors across the other forces. A reputation as a canny horse trader, who always

38

made sure he got what he needed but left the supporting officer feeling like a winner too.

And an understanding of Indigenous Kanaka Maoli culture that went beyond duty and into genuine admiration and respect, and earned him respect in return.

Connaught had Samuels beside him in the war room. Samuels's boss, COMARPAC, the US Army Commander for the Pacific, was on Guam, managing Army support for the South China Sea campaign and now the ongoing attack on Guam too.

Though in the last 48 hours their communication links had gone from instantaneous to Stone Age, they were gradually being restored. One entire wall of the war room was a digital map of his command showing the current location of all Army, Navy, Marine and Air Force units from corps down to company level, and the known or estimated location and size of enemy forces. Another wall was broken into a dozen customizable screens that could show anything from satellite imagery to helmet cam footage from individual soldiers. Again, assuming one had a satellite network to pull from. These had been distressingly dark but were now coming to life again.

Connaught pointed at chairs arrayed around a desk at one end of the war room. "People, please, grab a seat and take a deep breath. Situation in the Hawaiian Islands. Sam?"

Samuels remained standing, a tablet PC held against his thigh like a sidearm, though the retinue of Navy, Marine and Army officers he had with him took Connaught's invitation as an order and sat.

"At 0100, General, China began landing autonomous killer drones on O'ahu. We assume they were submarine launched, though we can't rule out long-range aircraft. We intercepted

39

one of the motherships, but the estimate was anywhere between 80 and 100 bots made landfall. Air and ground defenses engaged; 20 Chinese bots were destroyed in early fighting. At 0800, a second wave of killer drones was launched, two motherships were intercepted, eighty more bots made landfall. Losses ..." He gestured to a Naval Intelligence major, who brought up a list on the room's main screen. A long list. "The Chinese drone attack force comprises mostly missile-armed drones, and they have gone after O'ahu's air defenses, radar, radio and power installations, ships moored at Pearl, helos and aircraft at Hickam. Most of the naval units listed here are damaged, not definitively destroyed at this stage," he said.

Connaught's stomach dropped at the length of the list on the screen. One minor blessing was that there were very few high-value ships at anchor in Pearl Harbor at the time of the attack since most had already sailed for Taiwan, Japan and the Philippines.

"Critical losses?" Connaught asked.

"Three *Arleigh Burke* class hit and burning: *Cochrane, Lugar, Evans.* One LHD, the *Iwo Jima,* hit while being loaded, secondary explosions and fires below deck, down by the stern. One *Virginia* class submarine, the *Long Island*, damaged at its mooring. Twenty-five aircraft destroyed on the ground, including an E-3 AWACS, a B-2 bomber and a C-17 transport, and nearly the entire Air National Guard 199th F-22 squadron. Half of the Apache helicopters of 2-6th Air Cav. But the Chinese are also going after fixed radar or comms installations. Kaena Point has been hit hard, and we're down to mobile radar at most bases ..."

"What about that microdrone algorithm the Aggressor pilot brought back from Taiwan?" Connaught asked.

"We had one microdrone swarm under trial out at Aloha Land. It's being deployed to Pearl right now to take on the Chinese second wave."

Connaught nodded. "Update me on casualty figures as soon as you have firm numbers." Between them, the three destroyers and the LHD China that had been hit carried up to 3,000 sailors and Marines. How many were ashore and how many aboard would determine how bad the casualties were. "What air assets do you have until you're reinforced?"

Samuels consulted his tablet. "Four National Guard F-22s were airborne, and we have the 68th AGRS on Hilo with four F-22s and two P-99 Widows. One AC-130X on Tonga, damaged but airworthy. We have a single AWACS on station east of Big Island. As you know, we sent off 20 Marine F-35Bs on *Fallujah* before we picked up the Sino-Russian fleet to the northwest, so we're left pretty much naked." Samuels looked up. "That wasn't a criticism, Admiral."

"Not taken as one," Connaught said. "Go on."

"We're hunting the drones street to street in Honolulu—most seem concentrated around Pearl Harbor-Hickam for now, but there are a couple reported downtown, and moving down major highways," Samuels continued. "We're evacuating civilians; police are isolating the city center. Ground personnel across the island are at minimum strength since we moved the 25th Infantry and Lava Dogs out, but I've mobilized Fort Shafter and Kaneohe Bay, and we're bringing Army and Marines into Honolulu to …"

"Wait on that," Connaught said.

"Sorry, Admiral?" Samuels said, frowning.

"I want you to deploy troops to defensive positions across O'ahu and the islands, not in the city. Leave National Guard and police to look after Honolulu."

41

"But, Admiral, the drones ..." Samuels interrupted.

"Will run out of ammunition," Connaught said, voice cold, face impassive. "And self-destruct. This isn't 1941, General; China doesn't expect those drones to deliver some kind of knockout blow. They're a distraction, like that damned zombie carrier to our south, *Fujian*. China wants to sow chaos and pull our attention away from the real threat, the fleet to our northwest."

"Yes, sir. Sir, we also just received a report of a container ship 50 miles east of Big Island that reported it was attacked by a submarine and sinking. Coast Guard is responding. It looks like China is also going after our maritime supply routes. I guess you know that if they manage to cut us off, we have about three days' supply of food across the islands."

Connaught nodded. "You have more immediate problems, General. That fleet is already within cruise missile range and probably timing a strike to follow these autonomous bot attacks. It's what I'd do. I need you and the other Heads of Command on Hawaii to put together a plan to hit the Sino-Russian fleet with everything you can muster—Air, Navy and Space Force ..." Connaught said. "You'll have to deal with the Chinese carriers, but your key objective will be to sink the troop transports and prevent them landing troops."

The atmosphere in the room changed. It was already tense. The tension hit a new level.

"Grab some java, please, ladies and gentlemen," Samuels said to his staff. "I need to speak with the Admiral alone."

He waited until it was just Connaught and himself. "Harry, with respect, hit the enemy with *what?*" Samuels said, voice barely controlled. "Maybe I wasn't clear. Air Force has just *10* aircraft left flying," Samuels warned. "We need them for air defense. We lost our Aegis destroyers. Navy has *three Virginia* class submarines, two on patrol and out of position, one still at anchor. We'll need them here if we're to engage any Chinese landing force. Space Force is in disarray ..."

"Sit, Sam," Connaught said. "What would you need to take those troop transports out? Big picture, real world, not ideal world."

Samuels didn't need long to think. He'd started his staff working on the problem as soon as reports of the Sino-Russian fleet stated coming in. "I need satellite or space-based assets to give us precise targeting data. Several squadrons of F-35s and Widows to tie up their combat air patrols, stop them intercepting our missiles. Strategic bombers, armed with drone swarms and hypersonics, to whittle down the Chinese anti-air pickets so we can hit their carriers. Assets to allow a follow-up strike by sea or air, or preferably *both*, targeting the amphibs." He paused. "Subs and sub hunters, to keep our supply lanes open. And at least an additional division of troops on Hawaii for ground defense in case all that fails."

Connaught didn't appear fazed. "I can't pull resources out of the Taiwan theater in the time we have, but here's what I know I can give you." Connaught had a sheaf of printed pages on his lap, and he flipped it over to the report he wanted. "I can turn *Fallujah* ARG around, put it on the flank of the Chinese fleet with its 20 F-35s while it hauls ass back to Pearl. And you'll get two squadrons of P-99 Widows: the 173rd from Oregon and the 354th from Eielson. They were preparing to deploy to Japan and can be here inside five hours, *with* loyal wingmen, loaded for bear. That will give you 36 Widows and 72 Valkyries. You'll have the three *Virginia* class subs, and the Brits have also offered us an *Astute* class, the *Agincourt*. I can't guarantee you satellite ISR, but Space

Force is readying a Skylon D4. That should give you the targeting data you need."

Connaught could see Samuels's frown lift a little. "Ground reinforcements, sir?" Samuels asked.

"First Cavalry is readying two Brigade Combat Teams out of Fort Cavazos, but they'll take 36 to 48 hours to get here and then time to get where you need them. Likewise USS *Reagan* and *Kennedy* CSGs. I've ordered them to deploy from San Diego ... but don't count on their help for your first strike. You can factor them in for a follow-up strike if it's needed or use them for anti-submarine operations."

"That's ... better than I'd hoped, Admiral," Samuels acknowledged. "But I'm still short strategic bomber assets. We will not get close to those Chinese carriers and amphibs without them."

"Make a plan with and without them," Connaught suggested. "We lost a lot of airframes on the ground in China's opening strikes. And about the only available force we haven't already committed to the Taiwan OA is the 419th Flight Test Squadron. I know their CO is itching to get into this fight, and I've got people trying to work out what they could bring to the party while we look for better options."

"They fly Bones, don't they?" Samuels asked, his frown back again. The B1-B Lancer, or 'Bone,' was a 50-year-old Cold War warrior.

"Don't look so horrified." Connaught smiled. "The 419th is evaluating how we can keep them flying another 20 years because of the slow rollout of the Raider. They've had a few upgrades, I'm told."

"I'll include them in the package as a possible *extra* asset," Samuels said. He stood. "With your permission, we'll get to work, Admiral, and get back to you with a plan."

44

Connaught stood too, his mind already moving to his next meeting. As pressing and existential as the threat to Hawaii was, he needed to get his attention back onto the Taiwan theater, and the attacks on other US possessions, like Guam, Wake and Midway, not to mention their preparations to meet the H5N1c virus threat his medical staff were warning him was already a reality. "Thanks, Sam," he said. From somewhere outside came the deep rumbling thunder of a colossal explosion. "We'll need to dig in and weather this storm first. And the sky is going to rain Chinese cruise missiles any minute now."

"Yes, sir. May God protect our people out there."

AS REG SAMUELS stood to return to his officers and start turning the wheels that would get him the assets he needed, his aide intercepted him.

"Sir, there is a gentleman here from the NSA," he said, nodding his chin toward the entrance to the war room. "He wants to see you. Says it's urgent."

Samuels looked at the doorway and saw a short, wide, bearded guy in a hoodie standing there. He gave Samuels an awkward wave that was probably meant to be a salute.

"I can give him five minutes," Samuels said. "Put him in a meeting room and ask him to wait."

An hour later, Samuels was reminded about the NSA agent and went to the meeting room where the man was sitting behind a desk with a cold cup of coffee in front of him. He paused outside with his aide. "Who is he and what does he want?"

"His name is Specialist Carl Williams, and he wouldn't say, sir," Samuels's aide said.

Samuels grunted and went in. He didn't sit. He stood against a wall, arms crossed. "Mr. Williams. We are pretty busy today, as you can imagine. How can I help NSA?"

"Ask not how you can help NSA," the man said with a smile. "Ask how we can help you."

Samuels had no time for banter. "Go on. And be brief."

Williams picked up on the mood, at least, speaking quickly. "General, O'ahu was attacked today by slaughterbots launched by a new class of Chinese submarine called the *Taifun*. NSA has intercepted information indicating it is a very special kind of submarine."

Samuels sighed. "So a submarine that launches slaughterbots. They're just another kind of missile, Mr. Williams. Why is NSA interested?"

"It isn't the slaughterbots that make *Taifun* interesting, General," he said. "Do you know the story of the Enigma Machine?"

Samuels was getting impatient. "Of course. The German code machine recovered from a U-boat in the Second World War that enabled the Allies to crack German naval codes. What of it?"

Williams leaned back in his chair, pulling on his beard. "*Taifun* is carrying a Chinese Enigma Machine. And we need you to help retrieve it. If we're right, if we succeed, it could change the course of this war."

Samuels pried himself off the wall and sat. "You still need to make this fast, Mr. Williams. How?"

Williams leaned forward. "Codes today are uncrackable. Quantum encoding means only the sender and receiver can read a message. Anyone else tries to read it and the message goes *poof*. Correct?"

46

"You're the expert," Samuels said. "You people tell *us* that's true."

"It is. Except China created a problem for themselves. They created an AI they call Empire Dominator and put it in all their submarines to support the crews with decision analysis. But the demands for the AI piloting an *uncrewed* submarine, which *Taifun* is, are much higher. It had to be made as a learning system, able to make the decisions humans make and learn from its mistakes. And China wants Empire Dominator to be the ultimate combat AI, so they designed *Taifun* not to just learn from its own mistakes, not just from the mistakes of every other submarine in the fleet, but from *every* Empire Dominator system in the PLA Navy."

"You're saying this boat is dynamically assimilating data from across the entire PLA Navy, while submerged?" Samuels asked. "How is that possible?"

"High bandwidth, quantum compressed Extra Long Frequency communication," Williams said. "Now, imagine if we could get access to all that data. It could give us the position of every ship in the PLA Navy, ordnance loadouts, their combat and logistics reports, and even their orders, in real time, as they receive them."

Samuels shook his head. "No way China would send a boat like that to sea without fail-safes," he said. "You aren't going to just be able to force it to the surface and storm it with Navy SEALs, plug in a cable and download what it knows."

"No, we aren't. That's where you come in," Williams said. "Admiral Connaught told me you have first priority over all assets needed for the defense of Hawaii, and if I want to borrow one, I need to convince you to lend it to me."

"Which asset?"

"The British submarine HMS *Agincourt*," Williams said. "*Agincourt* has the capabilities we need."

"Sir, I had to trade a kidney to get first the British navy and then *our* Navy to allocate that submarine to me. You have not been anywhere near convincing enough," Samuels said. "But keep talking."

A SIMILAR conversation had taken place in China many years earlier.

"We are not convinced, Chief Engineer. We applaud your ambition. But we cannot concentrate that much information in any single system, let alone a submarine we are sending into combat. If it gets captured ..."

Chief Engineer for Operation Reunion Lo Pan was used to dealing with skeptical senior PLA officers. He'd been in wood-paneled rooms just like this a hundred times before during the course of the development of the Tianyi bots and *Taifun*. But rarely did they come as skeptical or as senior as the Commanding Officer of the PLA Navy Pacific Fleet, Admiral Li Bing.

"*Taifun* cannot be captured intact, Admiral," he said. "That is why we propose putting this version of Empire Dominator in a submarine, not on an aircraft, not in a ground vehicle, not on a satellite or even a land-based facility." He was animated, his hands drawing pictures in the air for the white-haired admiral and his phalanx of officers. "*Taifun* is already the most effective, most efficient hunter-killer under the sea, employing the learnings of a thousand submarine captains across hundreds of thousands of enemy encounters. But in the unlikely event the enemy gets lucky, and a torpedo sinks *Taifun*, the computing core is either destroyed by the torpedo or it self-destructs. If the enemy somehow disables the submarine and tries to drag it to the surface, it self-destructs. *Taifun* is always on, always aware, even when it is in port. An enemy tries to board it when it is docked, it self-destructs. A spy turned by the enemy boards the submarine and tries to interfere with it, it …"

"Self-destructs, yes, I get the picture, Chief Engineer Lo," the admiral said. "But assume the impossible happens. And the enemy captures *Taifun*, without the computing core self-destructing. What then?"

"Then we simply isolate it remotely," Lo said. "Cut it off from our battlenet. The power of *Taifun* is the data it accesses to learn and grow more powerful. If they capture *Taifun*, they capture nothing more than a submarine. Without that data, it is just an inert ball of quantum computing cores no different to any they already possess themselves."

Li Bing looked at one of the officers beside him, his second in command and captain of the carrier *Shandong*. "Each promise you make is bigger than the last, Lo. A stealth drone mothership that can be fired from the coast to Taiwan, undetected. Drones that can navigate themselves around enemy territory, identify their own targets and prosecute them before destroying themselves. A submarine that can deliver those same drones into the heart of any enemy city. And now, you want to make that submarine the most powerful ship in the PLA Navy by giving it a live feed of all data from across the fleet."

"No, Captain," Lo said, smiling confidently. "I want us to give it access to a live feed of all data from across the entire navy. And air force. Space force. And the ground forces. But I will settle for the data from the Pacific Fleet, to prove the concept."

49

Lo left the room with the approval he had sought. *Taifun* would conduct its attack on Hawaii, with access to the data of the Pacific Fleet. And if it succeeded, if it exceeded expectations, access to the data of other fleets, or even commands, would be considered.

If it failed …

Well, the consequences of that would be the same as he'd been threatened with at every other point in Operation Reunion. Humiliation. Imprisonment. Even death.

But Lo and his team were working on the AI equivalent of an atomic bomb, a weapons system able to out-think and outmaneuver any human opponent because it had already faced *every* human opponent.

ADMIRAL LI BING had long forgotten the meeting with the scientist, his superweapon and his bold assurances. He usually did forget about the many meetings he attended the moment he left them. His mind was always on his *next* meeting.

In this case: the one called by the Commander of the PLA Navy, Admiral Dong Zongming—an urgent meeting of his three fleet commanders, which could only mean he was expecting questions from the leadership of the party he wasn't equipped to answer, or was looking to pin a failure on someone to divert attention from himself. Bing wracked his mind, first for his own failures—because like any commander in war, of course he had several, some recent. But he could think of none which could be used to remove him from his post.

As commander of the Northern Fleet, Bing had been given the responsibility of commanding the biggest blue water fleet China had ever assembled, and joining it to the Russian Pacific Fleet, right under the noses of their enemies. That had been done under the cover of "joint exercises" in the Kuril Islands to mark the announcement of the Shanghai Pact.

The exercises were a fiction, but even that element of the operation had been executed as requested, with fake video footage of joint amphibious exercises on Iturup in the Kuril chain released to convince the world China and Russia were working together as brothers under an international flag of fraternity. And the Western analysts had bought the fiction, had they not? The fake footage his information warfare unit had created together with the Russians—showing Russian and Chinese soldiers storming a beach on Iturup with smoke billowing and amphibious armor splashing ashore under fire—had even aired on US streaming news channels. "China and Russia show the world what an invasion of Taiwan would look like," one headline said. His sources told him that one had been particularly well received in Beijing, so it couldn't be that.

Could it be the fact his flagship *Liaoning* had been late joining the fleet for the Hawaii operation? Hardly his fault. The operation to black out the American satellites had gone quicker than expected. What was expected to take several days was achieved in 36 hours. *Liaoning* had still been in port in Shanghai when the China Space Force operation had been initiated and was underway to Qingdao when it reported its objectives had been achieved. With the loss of Tiangong Space Station, yes, but achieved nonetheless.

Li Bing had been waiting in Qingdao to join *Liaoning* on its arrival, but he didn't make the carrier, or the joint fleet, wait for him. He ordered the fleet based around the carrier

Shandong to sail, with Russian ships in the *Shandong* Strike Group, while *Liaoning* and its escorts bypassed Qingdao and made directly for the open sea. Li even had himself choppered out to *Liaoning* rather than ask it to divert to pick up its admiral. Could he have done more? Not in his own mind.

And *Liaoning* had caught up with the fleet now. It was trailing *Shandong*, but he'd always intended it that way, so that *Liaoning* could be used to receive, refuel and then relaunch mainland-based aircraft and slingshot them onward to *Shandong* to make up any losses as they occurred.

Had their mighty fleet been discovered? He could not rule that out. The idea that a fleet of nearly 50 ships could cross 1,600 nautical miles of the Pacific, from the Kuril Islands to Hawaii, completely without detection was—though he wouldn't say it to his leaders—insane. A random overflight by a surveillance drone, a rapidly launched satellite, even a chance commercial image taken by the wrong company at the right time … Any of these could have revealed the Sino-Russian fleet was underway.

But they had destroyed every drone or aircraft that had come near them, and the Americans, British and the European allies had no satellites left to beam images to. His ships were communicating with laser, maintaining strict radio silence so that even their radio signals did not give them away, though his Russian counterparts were not as disciplined, nor did most of their ships have China's AI assisted line-of-sight laser communication capabilities.

They had made it across the Pacific without being attacked, and now they were just a couple hundred nautical miles from launching their main assault on the enemy bastion of Hawaii. Li had emptied his mind of all possible failures and accusations, which left only the impossible. Failures he *couldn't* have planned for, or didn't even know about.

He walked from his flag cabin, into the video conference center beside it where he expected to have a few minutes to compose himself before the meeting of the Fleet Admirals was due to begin. To his horror, as he walked in, he saw the meeting was *already underway.*

His aide was standing at the communications console, looking pale as Li walked in.

"Admiral, I ... they moved the meeting forward without advising us!" he said. Li could see their microphones were muted. He could also see the meeting had been going for 30 minutes already. But something was wrong. The Commander of the Eastern Fleet, Admiral Ye Fei, was onscreen, but his friend and colleague from naval academy days, the Commander of the Southern Fleet, was not.

Not good. Not at all good.

"Open up my microphone and leave," Li said.

The PLA Navy Commander, Dong, was speaking. The other officer on screen looked impassive. Or ... no, the Eastern Fleet Commander looked *pained.* His mouth tight, lips pressed together. He was usually ready with a light remark or jest. Nothing in his face suggested that was likely.

"... which leads me to, ah, yes, Admiral Li has joined us now. Welcome, Admiral, any news from the central Pacific?" the PLA Fleet Commander said as Li sat himself on camera.

Li pressed his microphone button. "No news, Admiral, which in our case, is good news," he said.

Dong nodded without smiling. Li was trying to read him and failing. But he wasn't kept in suspense long. "Li, I have just informed Admiral Ye that he will be taking over responsibility for our Southern Fleet, and we will find a

53

suitable replacement for him in the Eastern Fleet, though this will be difficult."

"Yes, Admiral." Gone. Like that. The Commander of the Southern Fleet, his comrade for 40 years, gone. "May I … I may not be up to date with the latest developments in the South China Sea. Are you able to share these with me?" It was a simple lie. Li was of course up to date, but he wanted to hear how Dong phrased the situation.

"The latest developments are … serious. And results are not satisfactory, as I have just told Admiral Ye. The American Marines have now taken, and still hold, Calderon Reef, Mischief Reef, Fiery Cross Reef and Subi Reef. Our operation to retake Fiery Cross Reef failed, with the loss of a full amphibious readiness group. American control of the South China Sea now threatens even our air force operations on Hainan and so makes air operations over Taiwan's southern sector difficult. My counterpart in the PLA Air Force has demanded action, and there is word of displeasure from the Chairman. These reverses are not acceptable at the moment we await the capitulation of the rebel government on Taiwan and are about to deliver a killing blow on the enemy across the Indo Pacific." He paused his summary of the crimes of which Li's comrade had been accused, and smiled a portentous smile. "I am sure you agree, Admiral Li?"

Li had not served 40 years in the People's Liberation Army Navy, the last few decades at the highest levels, without knowing how to answer loaded questions. "Admiral, at this time, total victory is within grasp," he said with what he hoped was convincing fervor. "Our leaders have provided all the means; it remains to the officers of the People's Liberation Army to use them well."

Dong looked as though he was trying to find fault in what Li had said, but Li knew he would not. It was a variation on an answer he had used many times before.

"Yes, well. Well said, Admiral. The new Eastern Fleet Commander will be confirmed in the next few days, but it should not concern you. You will have your full focus on the coming operations across the Central Pacific, and we are confident of the outcome."

His Eastern Fleet counterpart nodded but didn't speak. What should he say? He had just been handed a bowl of excrement and asked to make soup with it.

The Rearguard: Highway 20

"DID I TELL YOU I hate this war?" Corporal Xu, Airborne Special Service Company, Yun Chi Tuan 'Thunder' Squad, asked the man lying beside him, watching the winding mountain highway through a pair of binos.

Lieutenant Jack Chang, until recently a pilot with ROC Taiwan Air Force, kept his eyes on the road as he replied. "Yes. Five minutes ago."

"Well, I hate it more now," Xu said. He had dropped his rifle and was inspecting a tiger leech on the back of his hand. "If you asked me to rank the miseries of existence ..."

"I didn't."

"No, but if you did, you'd get the virus at number one, then leeches, then slaughterbots, then ..."

Now Chang shot him a look. He thought about letting the comment slide. The verbose corporal seemed to enjoy an argument and Chang doubted that Xu himself meant half of what came out of his mouth. But he couldn't stop himself. "You'd rank leeches *worse* than slaughterbots."

Chang slid a dirty thumbnail under the leech's sucker and then flicked it away before picking up his rifle again. "Definitely. Slaughterbots can't get up your nose." He put his eye to his gunsight again. "Not literally, anyway."

They were in the entrance to a cave on a cliff, 100 yards up and overlooking Highway 20, where it emerged from a tunnel and then ran deeper into Taiwan's central mountains. It was about the only route from the west coast to the east across south central Taiwan, and so it was a favorite for slaughterbots making their way from Tainan on the east coast to hunting grounds in the west.

Chang and Xu had made the cave their base since the day they joined up. They had taken down two slaughterbots so far from their clifftop hide, Xu using the Barrett rifle he'd inherited from Wu after … well, he didn't like to think about that. Wu dying in his arms a day after they got turned away by the US Marines at their base at Hualien Port.

He'd been angry as hell at those Marines as he'd carried Wu away to find a car he could transport him in, and he stayed angry at them until he got Wu to the Taiwanese army base at Xiayi, but Xiayi was chaos too. He found the base gates open, unguarded. Slaughterbots roaming unopposed, barracks empty. Barracks littered with discarded uniforms. Armory empty. And when he got outside the perimeter again, he saw why.

There were armed vigilantes in pickups and vans roaming the streets. Some were ex-army or police. A lot weren't. Said they were guarding against looters and "PRC infiltrators," but the couple times Xu was stopped, they felt more like shakedowns than peace-keeping operations. He had a few US dollars on him and they took those. One gang of thugs at a roadblock crewed by a guy who said he was a captain told him to hand over his rifle, until his pistol persuaded the guy the price would be too high. Lucky to get out of that town in one piece.

The *smell*.

Wu hung on another few hours, then gave a long racking cough, a sad wheeze, and he was gone. No last words for his wife or mother. Did he even have a wife or mother? Well, everyone had a mother, but was his still alive? What about the rest of his family? It was kind of messed up Xu didn't even know. All they'd been through.

Ah, what did it matter? Half the world was dead and the government had fallen. Rumor was the president and vice president had died of bird flu. The premier had taken over and was rushing a law through the congress, the "Executive Yuan," to authorize Chinese medical personnel to enter the country and render emergency assistance. Xu was willing to bet that if the law passed, the Chinese "medical personnel" would come ashore in amphibious tanks from Chinese landing ships, which was why he'd headed for the hills with his rifle. He'd decided he'd find a good hide and start killing slaughterbots. If the Chinese came, he'd start killing them as well. Kill until they got smart enough to work out where he was and come for him.

It was a dumb plan that was going to get him killed, but what else was there? So he thought about where a good place might be to go to work and started hiking up into the mountains to the pinch point by the tunnel.

About halfway up, he was regretting the whole hide-in-the-mountains idea. Felt like dropping the Barrett into the river he was walking alongside—the damned thing weighed like 15 kilograms, with a .50 BMG ammo pouch. Not like he'd promised the dying Wu he'd look after it, carry on his legacy, anything dumb like that.

Alright, yes. That was exactly what he did.

Then he ran into the pilot. Almost literally. Walking alongside the river after climbing a 50-foot-high waterfall, grumbling out loud to himself, when he saw something move in the trees up ahead.

Parachute. Body underneath it, hanging from some branches. Not moving.

He hadn't even heard aircraft overhead. No sonic booms, no explosions, no crashing planes. Whatever put this guy here must have all taken place over the other side of the mountain. Or happened long before Xu got here.

The mountainside was part of a valley cut through by the river, and the pilot at the end of the parachute cords was hanging right over the water. About 200 downstream was the waterfall. So if the guy wasn't already dead, and he fell in, if he didn't drown, he'd break his neck going over the falls.

Xu got closer, so he could see the uniform. If he was Chinese, Xu decided, he was going to let him hang there. But the uniform was ROC Taiwan Air Force.

Dammit, he'd have to see if the fool was alive. After a brief search, he found a fallen branch about 3 yards long so that he could reach out from the riverbank and prod the guy's legs.

No reaction.

Dead then. Oh well. He dropped the branch and, after wiping his hands, bent down to pick up his rifle when he heard a sharp report and a bullet ricocheted off rocks a couple of yards to his left.

Xu spun to see the pilot had a pistol in his hand and was trying to sight on him. Xu straightened, put his hands in the air at shoulder height. "Hey, fool, I'm Taiwanese!"

Fumbling with his helmet, the pilot pushed his visor up. Xu could see a frowning brow above the oxygen mask.

"Corporal Xu, Taiwan special operations!" Xu yelled, advancing slowly. He let his rifle lay where he'd dropped it.

The pilot put his pistol back into a leg pocket, with some difficulty. "Get that branch," he said, pointing as he swayed under his parachute. "Pull me over the bank."

Xu grabbed the branch up and held it out to him. The pilot took hold and Xu pulled him so that he was clear of the water, about 2 yards above the riverbank. It was rock, but mossy.

The pilot held the branch in one hand and pulled a knife from his boot, flicking it open. He began sawing at the parachute cords over his head.

"That's a two-meter fall onto rocks," Xu warned him.

The pilot paused. "You got a better idea?"

"No," Xu admitted. "You'll probably break an ankle, but falling in that river will kill you for sure."

"Alright then," the pilot said, and resumed sawing. As the cords parted, the parachute sagged, and the pilot got closer to the ground. By the time he cut the last cord he was less than a meter over the riverbank, and when he dropped, he rolled away from the river, flopped onto his back and pulled off his helmet. Spat out some blood, then looked at Xu. "Thank you, Corporal," he said. "Sorry about the gun. I was disoriented when my plane was hit, wasn't sure whose territory I bailed out over. Got lucky I guess."

"Well, you landed on Taiwan," Xu told him. "But I'm not sure you if you should consider that lucky or not."

"HERE THEY COME," Gunnery Sergeant James Jensen, US 1st Battalion, 3rd Marines 'Lava Dogs,' said quietly into his tactical radio throat mike, "LS3s in position. Are you ready, Chairman?"

He was lying on a grass mound inside the Taichung Air Force Base just south of Taipei, Taiwan. Beneath him, an underground facility the size of a small town was on alert, preparing to repel another wave of slaughterbots.

60

Several times a day, the autonomous Chinese drones gathered outside the airfield perimeter. They arrived in ones and twos, then strung themselves out in an irregular line, using the cover of shattered buildings to protect themselves from shoulder-fired missiles, mortar or sniper fire. When enough of them had gathered—and Jensen had yet to work out how they decided how many were "enough" since Jensen had seen them move in formations ranging from four to 20—they engaged the airfield's defenders.

No two attacks were ever the same.

Since arriving at Taichung on one of the last flights into Taiwan before the virus lockdown, Jensen had been through one-on-one engagements with the Tianyi killer drones, fought off an attack that used wave after wave of paired cannon- and missile-armed drones sweeping in from every point of the compass, and run for his life for the cover of their underground bunker when a swarm of more than two dozen slaughterbots advanced en masse, mowing down anything that moved. One had even made it into the tunnel network under the air base, wreaking havoc before it ran out of ammunition and self-destructed, taking a defensive position with it.

Jensen and his company had been airlifted from a victorious campaign to unseat China from its atolls in the Spratly Islands and dropped into a rout on Taiwan. Their force strength whittled down by the virus, the few hundred Taiwanese and American defenders he joined at Taichung were near collapse when he arrived. There were no aircraft left in the underground hangars; they'd all been flown out or destroyed. The only food and ammunition getting through were being flown in by uncrewed drones, from ships anchored in Taipei Harbor that were still getting sporadically supplied by either air or submarine.

The soldiers of the 3rd Marines, and the ROC Taiwan ground forces they'd been brought in to reinforce inside the Taichung facility, were down to squad-sized elements. Their operations above ground were limited to going out to retrieve a supply drop or rescue "stragglers"—civilian or military—who made it to the airfield looking for sanctuary. An entire wing of the underground base had been turned into a quarantine station, where anyone they brought in was stripped, sanitized, put into MOPP gear and not let into the base proper unless they were still symptom free after a week.

The latest estimate Jensen heard was that there were 300 military personnel and 6,000 civilians crammed into the tunnels under the air base, with food and water for two more days.

He was about to take a squad out to recover enough supplies to make it three. If they didn't destroy a supply drone in flight, the Chinese slaughterbots left the dropped supplies where they landed.

As bait.

He was more optimistic about this mission than the last couple. Because two days ago, a miracle had happened. His name was Sam Long-mao, so the Marines called him 'Chairman' Long-mao.

And if silicon could have bad dreams, he would have been a slaughterbot's nightmare.

Chairman had arrived at Taichung in a ubiquitous white delivery van of the type used to move everything from plumbing supplies to sacks of rice. They were too small to carry even a squad of troops, and were usually left alone by the Chinese drones. In the back of the van though, he was carrying a hydrogen power cell, a rack of servers and a high-powered VHF radio.

And trays holding 10,000 microdrones.

Sam Long-mao was a visual display technician from the Shining Sun Amusement Park and he'd just completed a three-day training program in Bunny and Hungyu's killer-bee algorithm.

"Ready, Sergeant," Long-mao announced. The trays were arranged behind the steel roller door leading into one of the tunnel entrances flanking the airfield. Jensen had seen the weapon in action once already, when it took down a four-drone slaughterbot element. The idea of using drones to kill drones was nothing new, but he'd seen nothing quite like the killer bees.

Jensen's supply recovery team comprised four rifle Marines and four "dogs." He'd first worked with prototypes of the Legged Squad Support Systems, or LS3s, in Syria several years earlier. They'd proven their worth in that conflict, and had been widely adopted since. They didn't look like dogs, not really. Their weight was primarily composed of a 125-kilowatt fuel cell, around which their actuators and electronics were built. They had a narrow, boxy body with rounded edges and four articulated legs that ended in tennis ball-shaped pads.

At the front of the LS3 was a head that didn't look like a head at all. It was an interchangeable robotic arm Jensen could swap out depending on the mission profile. There was a weapons arm that could be fitted with projectile weapons, tear gas or a grenade launcher, even a harpoon for pulling open wooden or light metal doors like car doors. Or it could be fitted with manipulator arms that enabled the LS3 to do everything from pin a man's hand to the ground, grab his throat, open a door or window by the handle, pick up and move an explosive device or stab a man in the heart. The

63

head also carried the infrared sensors … that weren't its only eyes.

In the center of its body, it had a 360-degree pan-tilt-zoom camera that it used for environmental pathfinding, object manipulation and image capture. All vision was streamed to an onboard AI, which managed target identification, macro navigation, systems and power distribution. Besides the compact and quiet power source, it was the adaptive AI that made the LS3 system possible. An LS3 could take in the inputs from its sensors, marry them to Jensen's verbal commands and then carry those orders out at a speed even a real dog would have trouble matching.

On recovery operations, the dogs were both guards and pack horses. Their teaming and autonomy routines had improved significantly since the models Jensen worked with previously. Moving in formation with Jensen and his Marines, they continuously scanned the terrain horizon for threats, sending data to a heads-up monocle over Jensen's left eye. Once they reached a palleted supply drop, the Marines loaded the dogs with a hundred kilos—220 lbs.—of supplies and sent them back and forth to the base until the pallet had been cleared.

Jensen was scanning the rows of slaughterbots assembling on the other side of the airfield. They were milling around, two or three standing sentry while the others formed up for their attack, careful not to bunch up to make it easy for a mortar or artillery strike. It was terrifying to watch, knowing that just a few weeks earlier, the Chinese drones had only been attacking in ones and twos. But they'd learned from their battlefield mistakes and adapted.

Jensen frowned, counting the Chinese bots. They were constantly moving, so an accurate count was hard, but he figured the swarm for at least 40, maybe 50 units. Too many for this to be a spoiling action to prevent them reaching the supply pallet.

"It's a swarming assault. Forty-plus units," Jensen told Long-mao. "They'll be going for tunnel access points. What's your play?"

He could almost hear the gears turning inside the head of the man a few hundred yards away. "Uh, that's four, no, call it five swarms. I'll keep one in reserve for any that get close to an access point. Ready to deploy on your mark."

"I'll let them pass my position so we have a clear run at the supplies, try to reach the pallet while they're under attack," Jensen said. "Happy hunting, Chairman."

"You too," the man said, and Jensen could just about hear him swallowing his fear.

And then the talking was over. It was time for the killing to start.

The Battle of Hawaii: Infirmary

"I'M HIT! Going in!"

"Meany! No!" She saw the missile strike Meany's plane, saw the ball of metal and fire expand, engulfing her own aircraft. Darkness, the stink of kerosene, she burst out the other side of hell into blue sky. Alone. Seconds earlier, missiles were flying. She had Meany to port, Touchdown to starboard. Ahead, a horde of Chinese drones. Now she was alone in the sky. Dark sky above, sparkling blue sea below. She checked her radar, 360 degree-optical infrared cameras. Nothing!

No. Not possible.

Then she looked around her and realized her cockpit was gone too.

Oh, FFS. Another damn dream.

Bunny O'Hare woke to the sound of shouting. Was she still dreaming? No, that was a real voice. One she loved to hate.

"Corporal, you will move your pretty ass or I will put a boot up it, I promise you," Touchdown was saying, in a tone that O'Hare was glad she was not on the other end of.

The orderly-slash-guard at the end of her corridor in the quarantine wing of the Tropical Medicine department at John A. Burns Infirmary replied. "Ma'am, I need to see your paperwork before I can ..."

Then she heard another voice. "I got your paperwork right here, Corporal."

A grunt. Feet scuffing the floor.

There was a rattle of keys, and then her door was flung open. Touchdown was standing there, looking like ... hell. Her normally perfect hair was stained with oil. So were her hands. She stood in the doorway with her hands on her hips. "Goofing off as usual, O'Hare. You want to get out of bed for me?"

Bunny dropped her feet into her unlaced boots—because they had taken her laces—and reached for her clothes, then remembered they had been taken away for incineration. She had been sleeping in a hospital gown, briefs and a T-shirt, but there was clearly no time to waste, so she followed Touchdown out into the corridor, looking for the other voice she heard.

"Flowmax!" she yelled, and ran to the end of the corridor, where the big mountain man from Montana was standing with one hand on the chest of the medical orderly, pinning him in place while flourishing a sheaf of papers. He turned as she bounded toward him and Bunny buried her head in his chest, threw her arms around his waist and held him like she was never letting go. If this was still a dream, it was the best one she'd had since they'd thrown her in quarantine.

"Can't breathe, Bunny," Flowmax said.

She let him go and stepped back. "But how are you …?"

"You two can catch up later," Touchdown said, moving past them both. She stopped to take the paperwork from Flowmax, smooth it out and hand it to the orderly. "Sorry, Corporal. It's all here; you have to trust me on that. Sorry for being rude, but we got a war to fight."

The man took the papers, looking a little lost, as they made their way off the ward.

They didn't head back to the main hospital building, which Bunny had only seen on the day she arrived, while she was processed—which had included being charged with several military code breaches. Instead, they headed for a fire escape, down some stairs, and then out onto a neatly manicured lawn in bright sunshine.

Bunny stopped to get her bearings. "Well, that was easy," Bunny decided, still not sure she wasn't having a drug-induced trip.

Touchdown and Flowmax were in front of her and Touchdown turned around. "It's a hospital, O'Hare, not a maximum-security prison. Meany magicked up the paperwork. But let's keep moving, shall we?"

"Wait ..." Bunny said. "Zak and Chief Delray, they were with me ..."

"They were released two days ago," Touchdown said, taking stairs two at a time. "We're here because you have an all-clear from the quarantine side, but Meany got word they were about to transfer you to a detention facility. You are on some pencil neck's Most Wanted list for breaking quarantine on Taiwan."

Tell me about it, Bunny thought ruefully. *They can get in line.*

They ran across the lawns to where a USAF Light Tactical Vehicle was parked under a row of palm trees. The inside of the LTV was hot. It stunk of sweat and spilled energy drink. Bunny decided maybe she wasn't dreaming after all. Touchdown and Flowmax climbed in front, Bunny in back.

Bunny reached forward, putting a hand on Flowmax's shoulder. "You're *dead*. I saw you die."

"No, you saw my plane die," Flowmax said, turning around. "I punched out, landed in the parking lot of some hypermart in Xiamen, China. Locals weren't too friendly, but they handed me over to People's Liberation Army, who handed me over to the PLA Air Force."

"Give her the short version," Touchdown said, driving them out onto a main road Bunny saw was filled with military

68

vehicles. Only military vehicles. "I had a good breakfast and I want to be able to keep it down."

"Alright." Flowmax faced forward again. His face was tight, eyes distant. "I was interrogated for, like, two weeks. *Before* they started asking me questions. When they finally started asking, I told them everything I could think of …"

Bunny squeezed his shoulder.

"I told them I was a Marine aviator flying a busted-ass Taiwanese F-16 and I never knew what hit me, that's how good China's pilots are …"

"I told you your fortune teller girlfriend was a hoax," Bunny said.

"Yeah, well. I told 'em the Marine training program ain't worth shit," Flowmax said. "Said I wanted to be US Air Force, but I wasn't good enough." He smiled.

"Too damn right you aren't." Touchdown nodded.

"I think they got sick of my BS," Flowmax said. "Eventually they sailed me to some Vietnamese island and swapped me and some civilians for about a hundred Chinese POWs."

Bunny sat back in her seat. They were overtaken by an ambulance and a convoy of military trucks.

"What's happening?" she asked. "I tried to land at Hickam, got told you were here, so I was redirected to Hilo. Was met on the tarmac by some MPs. They put me in a MOPP suit, drove me straight to quarantine, and apart from getting tested twice a day, I haven't spoken to anyone in, like, a week."

Touchdown gave her a short, haunted look in the mirror and then returned her eyes to the road. "Chinese are inbound. They took out our satellites, and their whole damn amphibious force, the one we thought they were going to hit

Taiwan with? It's about 270 nautical miles northwest of Kaua'i."

"Not *all* of it," Flowmax corrected her. "Some they saved for Wake and Guam."

"Guam?" Bunny felt her chest tighten. "Chinese took Guam?"

"Not yet. They landed in the south, just like we did in '44. Took the international airport and the town, and we're still holding the Marine base in the north. But they took Wake. Seabees there put up a hell of a fight, but they got steamrolled. We got caught with all our forces in the western Pacific— Philippines, Japan, South China Sea. Troops on Taiwan … The virus, well, you know all about that."

"And Russians," Touchdown said. "Did we mention them? Chinese have got Russian destroyers and frigates with them, Russian landing ships. Russians are moving against Japan too, we heard."

Looking out the window again as they were passing Hilo port, Bunny thought things didn't look so bad. "What's our situation?" she asked. "68th Aggressor is on Big Island?"

"Yeah, what's left," Flowmax said. "Why we busted you out. We lost two guys on the first day of the attack."

"NextGen and Cyber," Touchdown said. "They sent us against *Fujian.*"

Bunny did a double take. "No. *Fujian* is dead. I hit her with a hypersonic missile. The Australian Navy put a torpedo in her hide. She's …"

"Not dead." Touchdown grimaced. "She's south of here. Stays out of shore missile range, has a couple destroyers with her for air and submarine cover, always keeps a solid CAP overhead to protect herself, has her fighters taking out our tankers and surveillance in the east, in perfect position to

70

interdict any reinforcements we try to get through from California."

"Why don't we bloody *nuke* her?" Bunny asked, only half-joking. "Do it once and for all."

"Because like we said, we aren't just up against China. We're fighting Russia, North Korea too, if you believe it. We nuke them, they nuke us, and it would be game over for everyone," Flowmax said. "We have air superiority for now, but once *Shandong* gets in range ..."

"*Shandong* is here too?" Bunny said, disbelievingly. "I thought she was in Ningbo Harbor."

"So did everyone, while we had satellite coverage," Touchdown said. "Soon as we lost our satellites, she lit out and joined up with the rest of their invasion force."

"I don't get it," Bunny said. "Where the hell is the US Navy? They have like *70* nuclear attack subs ..."

"Two anchored at Pearl when the Chinese attack came in, two patrolling," Touchdown corrected her. "Only five in Guam, about a dozen back in Washington. The rest of the Pacific Fleet subs are in the Western Pacific, South China Sea, Taiwan. Some are probably on their way back, but they'll be too late. China could be landing troops by then."

Bunny felt a darkness descend over her that was in complete contrast to the sunshine outside. "So why do you need me?" she asked. "Sounds like we are getting our arses kicked and we should all be trying to get the next plane out."

She heard what she was saying like she was standing off at a distance, outside, looking on. She'd had a lot of time to herself to think things over in the hospital. Was this where she'd landed? Where was the old "take another punch in the face rather than give up" Karen O'Hare?

She was tired. Physically, yeah, but mentally too. She'd seen a lot of people die in her adult life. Had a hand in their deaths a few times. But none of them as up close and personal as the old man who'd pulled her out of the Taiwan Strait. Choking to death on his own body fluids while slaughterbots roamed the streets of his fishing town.

Was that what war had become? Autonomous drones and biological warfare? What could one pilot do against that?

You do what you've always done, she heard a voice saying. *You fly the next mission.*

"Sorry," Bunny said. "Forget I said that."

"There's that Aussie fighting spirit," Touchdown said drily. "We're not going anywhere. We're still in the fight. National Guard has four F-22s flying continuous CAP over O'ahu. We have two P-99s and four F-22s, but Meany is our only other P-99 pilot, and he's dead on his robotic feet, if you'll forgive my not being woke about it. He's more of a danger to himself and the rest of us than he is to the Chinese or Russians."

"That's *it*?" Bunny couldn't help asking. "The defense of the airspace over Hawaii comes down to a few National Guard Raptors and what's left of Aggressor Inc.?"

"That's why we had to bust you out," Flowmax admitted. "I *can* fly a P-99, but I'm a better Raptor driver. And our best Widow pilot was sitting on her ass drinking green daiquiris …"

"Kale immune-boosting smoothies," Bunny corrected him. "Which is worse than being tortured by Chinese interrogators." She checked the mirror to see if that got a smile out of Flowmax. She saw a flicker at the corner of his mouth. So no, he was not OK, yet. But there was hope.

The radio was playing, and Bunny noticed it was something on a loop. She hadn't been tuning in, but a sentence caught her attention. "... all citizens of Hawaii to embrace the support of our fraternal Chinese and Russian cousins, and help them eject the colonizers from our land. Our time is here at last. You don't need to take up arms, just stay home, stay indoors, keep your family safe, but offer no support to the American military. They have never had your ..."

"Who the hell is that?" Bunny asked.

"Jonah Freak," Flowmax said in a disgusted tone.

"Freeth," Touchdown said. "Some kind of Hawaii independence leader on O'ahu who crawled out of the woodwork. Only reason we keep the radio on is sometimes our guys can burn through the Chinese jamming."

Touchdown slowed. A roadblock was coming up. Bunny tensed, but the only vehicles being stopped were civilian. All military vehicles were being waved through.

"Ten minutes to Hilo," Flowmax told her. "Hope you got a lot of rest in hospital."

"She was sleeping when we busted in," Touchdown said.

"Nice for some." Flowmax nodded. "But you better slap your face or whatever you do to wake up. Meany is putting together a mission package, and you're on the roster."

HARRY CONNAUGHT was right when he judged that the Sino-Russian fleet was planning to follow the slaughterbot assault with a cruise missile strike on Hawaii.

But not *only* a cruise missile strike.

So it was that Sergeant Pan Tien found himself inside a Z-8 helo on the deck of the *Type 075* Landing Helicopter Dock *Hainan* at midnight, together with 20 other members of the

73

specialist 1st Battalion, 5th Amphibious Combined Arms Brigade (Recon).

In rehearsals for an invasion of Taiwan, the men of the 5th Amphibious had prepared for their coming mission expecting to be put ashore in the dead of night in rubber boats, ahead of an invasion force.

But they were not using rubber boats because reefs and rough surf off their objective would slow a seaborne landing and his rapid reconnaissance unit needed speed and surprise to succeed.

A hundred PLA Infantry Scouts, the equivalent of US Army Rangers, were going in ahead of the first wave of the main amphibious force. Their task was threefold: to reconnoiter their allocated sector and confirm the exact locations of ground, anti-ship or air defense forces; to direct an air-launched and naval missile barrage onto the enemy positions; and then to sow chaos with attacks in the enemy's rear.

Pan Tien's company had a fourth objective. Where the other Scouts were in blue and green PLA fatigues, Pan and his unit either wore the shorts, gray T-shirts and high-visibility vests of Highways Division road workers, or Honolulu Police Department uniforms. And though the 9 mm pistols they carried were made by China's Norinco, they could use the same ammunition as a standard Honolulu PD Glock 17.

Pan Tien's unit would not be scouting targets for the amphibious landing. On reaching their LZ, the 16 men in his squad would steal civilian SUVs and make their way inland. From Haleiwa Beach on O'ahu's northwest coast, to Honolulu.

Where they would meet with the Hawaiian rebel Jonah Freeth, who called himself *Ka Mo'opuna Pono o Kalakaua.*

"MY NAME is Jonah Freeth, *Ka Mo'opuna Pono o Kalakaua*, direct descendent of Kalakaua, the last true King of Hawaii, and I have come to reclaim the cloak of my ancestor." The man standing in front of the ticket desk at the Bishop Museum in Honolulu told the ladies behind the desk. He was tall, with broad cheeks, a pock-marked face and thick wavy black hair, gone silver at the temples. He looked behind him, where six more men, all *Kānaka Maoli*—Indigenous Hawaiians—stood with their arms crossed over black Hawaiian Freedom Alliance T-shirts.

A museum guide, a man in his late 50s, held up a hand. "I know who you are, Mr. Freeth. Let's all just calm down, shall we?" A siren sounded outside as a fire truck raced down Kahili Street toward Pearl Harbor. More sirens were wailing in the background. "There's some kind of situation outside right now."

"No," Freeth said. "There's some kind of situation in here." He nodded to one of his men. The man grabbed the guide and pulled his hands behind his back, tying them with zip ties. One of the ladies behind the ticket counter started shouting for help.

But none came. Freeth watched the worry rise in her face. "We have secured the building, madam," Freeth told her. "No harm will come to anyone here." Then it occurred to him that the other museum guides trussed up throughout the building might not agree with that. "No serious harm," he added.

75

With that, they walked out of the foyer, through the gift shop, across the grass and into the main museum building. The "Hawaiian Hall" was on the right, and Freeth took the stairs to the third floor. Everything about the place disgusted him: his culture, his people, his heritage, on display in dusty glass cases like so many circus tent curiosities.

Flanked by his personal guard, he pushed over a complaining guide, tied up and silenced with a gag through his mouth. One of his men working at the museum as a cleaner had let the rest in, and they had taken over the building just as it was about to open. Lines of schoolchildren were milling around outside in the sun, their teachers trying to shepherd them back on buses, not just because the museum had not opened on time but also because of the Emergency Alert System sirens and radio warnings telling people to return to their homes.

Freeth knew they would also be casting worried looks at his supporters outside. More and more would be gathering, even as he climbed the stairs.

Ah, yes. Large glass case, displaying some of the *ahu'ula*—the feathered cloaks of the rulers of Hawaii through the ages—like the spoils of war that they were, for the colonists to gawk at.

He came to the case holding the ceremonial beaded suit of his ancestor Kalakaua, the last of the *ali'i*, or Kings of Hawaii, who did *not* bend his knee to colonists, who did not cede his kingdom to them but had it stolen from him at the point of a bayonet.

He didn't want the suit, a pseudo-European affectation; he wanted the feathered shoulder cape next to it. The cape of his ancestor, Kapi-olani.

Freeth held out a hand to the man next to him and took the hammer he was given, raising it above his shoulder and bringing it down on the glass with unsuppressed violence. The glass shattered and he pulled it away with the claw of the hammer until the opening to the 200-year-old cloak was wide enough to lift it out carefully.

He took off his T-shirt and chinos and handed them to one of his men, wrapping a malo, or loincloth, around his waist and then pulling the cloak over his shoulders. In his late 40s, he had not let himself go to seed. His shoulders were wide and his legs like tree trunks.

He pointed back into the case at a large silver and white jeweled star-shaped brooch, the Star of Oceania, created by King Kalakaua for those who championed the cause of Hawai'i. "Bring that," he told one of his men. If today went well, he wanted to present it to Duke, in recognition of the herculean work he had put into making this day possible.

Walking downstairs again, he went through the courtyard to the entrance foyer, past the shell-shocked ticket sellers and museum guides who had now been herded into a corner by his men, and then out the front door to where his people were waiting.

Two busloads of supporters had just arrived, and Hawaiian Freedom Alliance members who came in cars were starting to assemble outside. *Considering what's happening further down the island, a good turnout*, Freeth thought, doing a quick headcount. *Two, maybe three hundred?*

An enormous explosion caused everyone's heads to turn, and then they all looked back at him, standing on the steps that led into the museum. He didn't flinch, like many did. He had known not only that this day was coming, but he'd known to the hour *when* it would come.

Not what. Of course, he hadn't been told all the details of the Chinese battle plan, but in coded phrases and with darknet cyphers, after years of negotiation, he'd been alerted. *Be ready.*

He raised his hands in the air to show they should gather around. His media adviser was filming, capturing the moment for posterity, and handed him a microphone. He spoke first in the language of his ancestors, and then in the language of the colonizers, so they would understand too.

"Brothers and Sisters!" he said. "On this day, June 10, 2038, we take back our island from the oppressor!" There was a large roar from the small crowd. It would be amplified by AI in editing, as would the size of the crowd. "At my invitation, the fraternal governments of China and Russia have agreed to support our independence movement and help us eject the occupier from our land after nearly 200 years of oppression." He raised a fist in the air. "Today we march on the Capitol, to take back Hawai'i!"

Another roar.

He led the way through the crowd, camera following him closely as people parted to let him through, thumping his back as he went. It wouldn't show him boarding the bus—the "march on the Capitol" needed to move fast. Other buses were already on their way to the Capitol building, traffic chaos permitting, with at least as many sovereignty supporters as they had gathered at the museum.

What happened when he got there, what happened over the next few days and nights—that was a question of *mana*, and fate.

State of the War Briefing

Transcript, Pentagon Press Office, June 19, 2038

PEOPLE, welcome to the first of what we expect will be regular briefings on developments in the War with China. I will start with headline events and then take questions:

War with China was declared after China released a weaponized version of H5N1c bird flu virus on Taiwan. We have not yet discovered how this was done, but its appearance on the island at the moment the US committed to send ground forces to Taiwan in strength was no coincidence. This is a highly contagious, deadly virus. Cases have already been reported among US troops on Taiwan and among those who have returned to the USA. As a result, the president has announced several measures domestically, and the administration has moved to a Defense Department continuity of government facility to ensure the continued smooth running of government.

In the South China Sea, we continue to make progress in removing Chinese forces from illegally occupied installations. Calderon and Mischief Reefs, Woody Island and Fiery Cross Reef are now in US hands and at the end of this conflict will be demilitarized in line with resolutions of the Permanent Court of Arbitration in the Hague, until such time as territorial disputes over these islands and atolls are resolved. I won't comment on specific targets for future military action, but the South China Sea campaign will continue until or unless China withdraws its military forces from all disputed territories.

On Taiwan, our focus is on the health and wellbeing of our troops and providing medical and other support to the

Taiwan government to help it manage the Chinese bioweapon attack. US Coalition forces have been successful in retaining air superiority over the island and reducing cruise missile strikes, but autonomous drone attacks continue. This briefing will make regular reference to the perceived danger of Chinese invasion as low to high, with the highest level being "imminent." Currently, with Chinese amphibious readiness groups exercising with Shanghai Pact allies in the Kuril Islands, and not available for operations in the Taiwan Strait, we rate the danger of invasion as "high" but not "imminent."

In space, it is true there has been significant disruption to satellite communications. The US identified that the source of this disruption was the Chinese space station Tiangong. An operation conducted by Space Force has now neutralized the threat posed by the Chinese space station, and I will not be commenting further on this development except to repeat the threat has been neutralized and Space Force is now prioritizing the restoration of satellite communications.

In the last 24 hours, China has broadened its military action beyond the Taiwan Strait, with air- and submarine-based cruise missile attacks on US installations on Guam, Wake Island and Midway and on the territories of our allies Japan and the Philippines. There have been a number of US casualties; we are still trying to determine how many and will give you an update on this.

China has also attacked Hawaii with the same autonomous drones it is using on Taiwan. These weapons operate without human control, indiscriminately attacking civilian as well as military personnel and targets. That attack is ongoing and is being met with resolve by our forces on Hawaii. I will have no more to say on that in this briefing.

Ladies and gentlemen, the president has given the Armed Forces of the United States three clear objectives in this war, and we are prosecuting these with success and vigor: one, to defend the people of Taiwan from Chinese military aggression; two, to demilitarize the South China Sea; and three, to meet and defeat Chinese military aggression wherever it may be directed against the United States and its allies.

In all of these objectives, we are succeeding and will continue to do so. I will now take questions ...

Operation Midnight: Agincourt

HMS AGINCOURT had covered 160 nautical miles, or around 300 kilometers, in the time since she left Pearl Harbor. Her route had taken her past O'ahu and Kaua'i islands, then northwest. Trusting in her passive sensors' ability to sort the noise of her own passage from the sound of the sea around them, she made best speed directly toward the intercept point, at which her crew would start their search for *Taifun*.

It was also about 80 nautical miles from the estimated position of the Sino-Russian fleet's outer ring of picket destroyers. So *Agincourt* floated a comms buoy and contacted the two US *Virginia* class submarines, the *Tang* and *San Francisco*, currently making speed for the fleet's position, to attempt a delaying attack.

Unlike the two American submarines, *Agincourt* didn't have the luxury of being able to lie in wait for the enemy to come to them. They had to find a Chinese needle in a Pacific-sized haystack.

Courtenay, Singh, Brunelli and McDonald were bent over a digital map table. The British ship had just downloaded a new estimate of *Taifun*'s position. The map showed a line of dots, each "sighting" about an hour apart, showing a path from northwest of O'ahu to a position east of *Agincourt*. Though it wasn't a straight line, their original hypothesis hadn't changed—the Chinese boat was heading for the protection and noise of the anti-submarine patrols of the Sino-Russian fleet.

"And you don't want to tell us how you're getting these position estimates?" McDonald said.

"Would love to, Captain," Courtenay said. "But am not empowered to." He drew a line across the Chinese submarine's direction of travel. "We'll patrol here. Should be able to pick up something the size of the Chinese *Type 095* as long it passes within a 10-mile radius."

"That patrol area will also expose us to the Chinese fleet's anti-submarine pickets," McDonald pointed out. "*Fujian* had two *Type 095*s out ahead of it," he told Courtenay. "One passed within 5 miles of us; the other we picked up 10 miles away. They're quieter than a *Type 093*, but not as quiet as they think they are—not to our *AE1* anyway. We were lucky to pick them both up and played possum as they went by."

"*Agincourt* has played tag with *Type 095*s before. Can we talk about *Taifun?* How did she beat you?" Courtenay had asked. He'd avoided the topic until that point, but it had to be discussed sooner or later.

"My own stupidity," McDonald growled, daring Brunelli with a glare to contradict him. She didn't. "We were in overt pursuit, right in its baffles pinging, trying to bully it into breaking off what we thought was a standard Chinese patrol, when it disappeared. Dropped behind a ridge or into a depression." He paused, his lips clamped tight as though the next part of the explanation was too infuriating to speak.

Brunelli took up the story. "We'd drifted ahead of it. We didn't expect it to open fire as soon as it emerged from hiding; we thought we were still playing by peacetime rules, but China wasn't. It put a torpedo into our stern and shot through."

"Shot through?" Courtenay asked.

"Scarpered," McDonald translated. "Decided we were out of the fight and didn't wait around to finish us off."

"Our guess is it had a time on target to meet," Brunelli said. "Which would make sense if it was the boat that launched the slaughterbot assault. Or one of them."

83

"A wily captain indeed," Courtenay said, chewing on a toothpick. His XO had confided to Brunelli that the other captain was trying to give up smoking, and the toothpick, plus a liberal application of nicotine patches, were his way of doing it. "If all of their boat drivers are as cunning as that one, we'll need to be on our toes."

"My advice, for what it's worth," McDonald told him. "If you pick up a *Type 095* and have a shot at it, take it. Don't hesitate. If you wait, *Taifun* is unlikely to give you another chance."

Courtenay and Singh exchanged a look. Connaught straightened. "The XO has the conn," he said. "Captain, would you join me in my cabin?"

McDonald left Brunelli with an annoyed look on her face but followed Courtenay to his room. They squeezed into the compact space, another compromise that hadn't been necessary on the largely uncrewed *AE1*. His cabin was twice the size of Courtenay's, which suddenly seemed even smaller, because there was already someone sitting in it.

"Hey, hi there," the portly bewhiskered man in a black hoodie and dirty blue jeans said. "Forgive me if I don't get up because ..." He gestured to the table he was wedged behind. "Can't."

McDonald recognized him. He'd come aboard *Agincourt* just ahead of McDonald and Brunelli. McDonald had wondered what an apparent civilian was doing climbing aboard a submarine about to get underway under wartime patrol conditions, but he'd forgotten about the man just as quickly during the controlled panic of their departure, and hadn't seen him since.

"Captain McDonald, Carl Williams," Courtenay said, squeezing in beside McDonald as they sat.

84

"NSA," Williams said. "National Security …"

"Agency. What is an American cyber spook doing on a British submarine?" McDonald asked.

Williams smiled. "Could ask why the Royal Australian Navy is along for the ride too, Captain," Williams said. "But I have a lot more important questions I want to ask."

"I've decided we need to brief Captain McDonald on the full nature of our mission, Mr. Williams," Courtenay said. He reached behind him for a thermos of tea and some cups. "Tea?"

Williams shook his head. "Disgusting stuff. There was a reason we threw it in Boston Harbor." He waited as Courtenay poured, but only briefly. "Captain, you're the only Western submarine commander who has gone up against *Taifun*. Tell me, what was it like?"

"What it was *like*?" McDonald growled. "I assume you know the outcome."

"I do. I read the debrief interviews. I'm not asking what happened; I want to know how it *felt*, fighting *Taifun*."

"Felt?" McDonald asked. He looked at Courtenay, face going red, then back to Williams. "It felt like a proper arse-whipping is how it felt, Mr. Williams."

"Carl. I'm sorry," Williams said. "Let me try again. Did anything strike you about the captain of the Chinese submarine: his tactics, decisions? You were engaged for nearly two hours. Thinking back, was there anything remarkable or different?"

McDonald opened his mouth, closed it again, then sat back in his seat. "Actually, there was."

"Yes?"

"He was ice cold. We were in his baffles, like you said, for a very long time, following him toward Hawaii, so close we

85

could have counted the rivets in his hull …" McDonald had his two hands out, one "swimming" behind the other. "He knew we were there, must have. We were trying to scare him off, but he showed no sign he cared. Just kept his depth, heading and speed constant, until …"

"He magically *disappeared*," Williams said, eyes bright. "Like I said, I read your report."

"It wasn't magic, Carl," McDonald said. "It was bloody good seamanship. He lulled us into complacency, then he took his boat over a small ridge. We lost sight of him for a few minutes, and he used that window to drop his boat into an impossibly small depression that wasn't on anyone's maps. Not in your Navy, or ours."

Williams nodded. "What would it take, a maneuver like that?"

"Hundreds of hours of practice, minimum," McDonald said. "An incredibly competent crew. A single mistake by any of them, they could have smashed their boat into the sides of that depression and it would have been over for them."

"Then he emerged and put a torpedo in *AE1*." Williams nodded.

"An hour later," McDonald said. "We'd all but given up. Most other captains"—he looked at Courtenay—"brighter than me, would have left the area long before then. That wasn't skill on his part, by the way. We were playing by peacetime rules. He wasn't."

"But the maneuver where he lost you, that should have taken a lot of practice?" Williams said.

McDonald nodded. "Not sure I could do it. Not even in *AE1*, and she's the best boat in anyone's navy."

Williams smiled. "What if I told you *Taifun*'s captain had probably never once practiced that maneuver, and it was

86

probably the first time they'd ever executed it over that particular depression."

"I'd say that's b—not possible, son," McDonald said.

"Not only possible, almost certain," Williams said. "We know a lot more about *Taifun* now than we did before you met her, thanks to some diligent 'cyber spookery' as you call it, Captain." He held up a hand and started counting off chubby fingers. "We got her blueprints and a recent version of her source code. We know this was her first blue water voyage, outside Chinese home waters. We know her captain had never rehearsed that maneuver because *Taifun* doesn't have a captain, or a crew. Not a human one, anyway."

"She's completely *uncrewed?*" McDonald asked. "Our navies would never allow a nuclear boat to sail without a human on the conn."

"China apparently doesn't have the same qualms," Williams said. "Not only did they send *Taifun* to war uncrewed, but they sent her out with the most advanced combat AI anyone has put inside a weapon of war in anyone's navy, army, air or space force. That's what defeated you, Captain."

"No wonder our three navies want it dead," McDonald said.

Courtenay shifted uncomfortably. "Well, that's the thing, Captain. We don't want it dead. We want it very much alive."

McDonald looked at Courtenay and then at Williams. "What are you talking about?"

Williams leaned forward again. "Tell me, Captain, have you heard about the German Enigma Machine?"

TAIFUN HAD ADVANTAGES beyond not needing a human crew. The US Coalition battlenet was still crippled, but *Taifun* had access to the PLA Navy battlenet. Every signal, every report, every order and every decision made by every captain of every submarine going back five years to the launch of the first *Type 095* submarine.

She used that data to avoid detection as she passed through the US SOSUS line around Hawaii. She downloaded intelligence on the Sino-Russian fleet's anti-submarine operations and the suspected positions of US submarines stalking the fleet, so she could avoid them too.

But she had exhausted her full complement of Tianyi motherships and she had to get through to the fleet to rearm.

Between *Taifun* and the fleet was a suspected *Los Angeles* class submarine, being prosecuted by a Chinese *Jiangdao* class anti-submarine corvette, the *Nanyang*. Her intelligence told *Taifun* that the only *Los Angeles* class submarines in the theater had sailed with the USS *Fallujah* Amphibious Readiness Group, which had left Pearl Harbor several days earlier.

So either the submarine had turned back on its own to try to intercept the Sino-Russian fleet ... or the entire *Fallujah* ARG had been turned around and the *Los Angeles* class submarine was a picket submarine, out in front of it, trying to locate the fleet.

Taifun passed her analyses to her controllers at Huangpu Wenchong along with the suggestion that she assist the *Nanyang* in dispatching the American submarine. She had no more Tianyi drones on board, but had loaded two torpedoes for defense in case she was intercepted.

Meanwhile, she followed the engagement on the surface. The *Nanyang* had lost the *LA* class submarine after initial contact and was trying to reacquire it. When the order came back to assist *Nanyang*, *Taifun* had already war-gamed a thousand scenarios and, rising to communication depth, she proposed one of them to the *Nanyang*'s captain.

PLAN Taifun *to* Nanyang, *available to assist. Recommend you lay a five-mile line of sonobuoys* ... She sent a position to *Nanyang*. *If you search north of the line, I will search south.*

She didn't expect the sonobuoys to pick up the American submarine except by dumb luck, but the American would hear them and would need to avoid them. If they wanted to continue toward the Chinese fleet, they would need to pass either north or south of the sonobuoy line.

Taifun patrolled the line to the south. She was a generation younger than the *LA* class submarine; her reactor quieter, pump-jet propulsion instead of conventional propellors, the latest in an-echoic tiles coating her hull.

She picked up the American boat on passive sensors at about 5 miles' distance, clanking through the water like something from a steampunk novel.

Laying in a course that would put her 2 miles behind it, she matched depth, slowly filled her torpedo tubes with water and then opened her outer tube doors.

She already had weapons authority and orders to engage the American submarine if she found it. In milliseconds, she reviewed every engagement between a Chinese submarine and an *LA* class submarine in the last five years. Only four, all in the last month, involved the use of live weapons, but all indicated that the American's standard evasive maneuver when subjected to a rear-aspect attack was to deploy noise-making sonar jammers and make a diving starboard turn to try to bring their own torpedoes to bear.

Taifun set her missiles to MAD homing mode, so they would silently seek the big metal bulk of the target, and sonar jamming wouldn't affect them.

She fired her first torpedo. It made half the distance to the *LA* class submarine before the target reacted to the noise of its passage and immediately dumped decoys and began a hard diving turn ... to port, not starboard.

Interesting, but not material, since *Taifun* was still a good distance behind it and as it turned, she activated her sonar, calculated an intercept solution and fired her second torpedo.

Her first torpedo couldn't turn with the target and was lost in its wake. Her second was headed in front of the American submarine though, and just had to correct its course slightly to meet it.

The sodium hydroxide warhead in *Taifun*'s Yu-9 torpedoes was designed to create a superheated ball of steam when it exploded so that it not only breached the hull but forced a 2,000-degree Celsius jet of gas through the breach to split the hull open and ignite anything inside.

Taifun's Yu-9 hit the *LA* class submarine just above its two loaded portside torpedo tubes, breaching one of the tubes and flash-heating the torpedo inside, which detonated in its tube, triggering secondary detonations among the 12 Tomahawk missiles in their vertical launch tubes between the torpedoes.

Taifun registered the kill, alerted *Nanyang*, wrote up her combat report and transmitted it to Huangpu Wenchong to add to the collected learnings of other Empire Dominator AIs.

Then she resumed her course for the fleet tender in the middle of the Sino-Russian fleet, still many miles distant. She didn't reload her torpedoes. The probability of running across a second submarine between her position and her rendezvous with the fleet tender was almost zero. And by the time she reloaded, she would only have to unload again to be able to take aboard the Tianyi reloads.

"ADMIRAL, a communication from *Nanyang*," *Liaoning*'s comms watch officer said. Li frowned. "It reports an enemy submarine engaged and destroyed."

China had nearly 60 *Jiangdao* class ASW corvettes, and at least 10 were part of his fleet. Li knew *Nanyang* was one of these, but where in the fleet formation *Nanyang* was stationed was a level of detail he didn't have.

"Show me where," Li said. He was standing on the bridge of *Liaoning*, monitoring the fleet's progress quietly, without interfering unless he saw a need.

The man walked to a wall screen, showing a map of the Pacific and the fleet's position, then zoomed in. *Nanyang* was a forward picket, on the southeastern extremity of the fleet, protecting PLAN *Shandong*'s flank.

The American submarine had been detected before it could penetrate the ASW cordon. But it was a portent of things to come. The Americans clearly knew they were coming, knew the general position of his fleet now. They would throw at it everything they could, from both above and below the waves.

"Send a signal to *Nanyang* with my congratulations and copy all ASW units," Li said. "Tell them to be vigilant. This is just the beginning."

"Yes, Admiral, but ... *Nanyang* was part of the engagement but did not make the attack. The attacker was the autonomous uncrewed vessel, PLAN *Taifun*," the man said.

91

Taifun … ah, yes. Operation Reunion. The slaughterbot carrier. Chief Engineer Lo Pan's very expensive pet. Once again, he'd forgotten all about it; it ceased to be important after it successfully launched its attack on Hawaii. So now it had also claimed a submarine kill? Li was a modern thinker in many ways, but AI-captained autonomous submarines, slaughterbots, uncrewed surface vessels—these were all just hardware to him. Not more or less significant than a torpedo or a missile. Perhaps he did need to start paying more attention to individual vessels, like Lo Pan's *Taifun*. But to congratulate a piece of hardware for a kill? Ridiculous.

"The message stands," Li said. "Send congratulations to *Nanyang*. I am sure they made the kill possible."

The Rearguard: Hide

ABOUT the second week after Xu met up with the pilot, Chang, a dead man came looking for them.

An American sergeant. Which was impossible, because Xu had seen this particular American sergeant *die*, in a hail of slaughterbot cannon fire and concrete dust outside Dongshi.

Sergeant Mason Jackson of the US Marine Corps couldn't be alive because Xu had swerved around his crumpled, bloody body on the way to deliver the sick driver of their IFV to his heartless Marine colleagues.

"Do you know how easy it was to find you, Corporal?" Jackson asked, dumping a pack on the ground at the entrance to their cave and then parking his ass on it.

Xu put down the pistol he had pointed at the man's body mass from the moment he first saw the shadow in the trees outside the entrance, and nodded. "Kind of the point, Sergeant." He nodded toward the pilot, Chang. "Welcome to the Free Taiwan Resistance Movement."

Jackson had grinned, swatting a mosquito. "Free Taiwan Resistance … I like it." He flicked the mosquito away. "Except your secret guerilla movement wouldn't last long. I was about to say, finding you was *easy*. I just had to ask about anyone I bumped into on road out here, had they seen a Taiwanese corporal, sniper, gun longer than he is tall, and they all pointed me up the mountain to this place."

The Lieutenant looked at Xu with a "who the hell is this?" expression. Xu made introductory gestures. "Lieutenant Jack Chang, ROC Taiwan Air Force, please meet the ghost of Sergeant Mason Jackson, US Marines."

Jackson rose, shook Chang's hand and then sat down on his pack again. "Yeah, about that, Corporal. You left me to

93

die in a slaughterbot-infested neighborhood, but since I would have done the same, I forgive you."

Xu didn't feel especially sorry, considering how they'd been turned away by the US Marines when they sought medical help. Then again, like Jackson, Xu wasn't the type to hold a grudge against an ally.

"Why did you come looking for me?" Xu asked Jackson.

"Because I have a mission that needs a damn good special operator who knows his way around the territory, and from what I saw in Dongshi, that's you." Jackson sent a side glance at Chang's air force uniform. "Though I don't need a pilot."

Chang wasn't about to be sidelined. "Why don't you tell us about your mission, Sergeant, and I'll decide whether I can release Corporal Xu to assist you," he said, reminding Jackson whose army Xu was in and on what island his butt was parked. "I'll tell *you* what you need."

Jackson could hear from the tone of Chang's voice he was ready for an argument, so he reached into his back pocket and pulled out a couple of folded pages. "It's all in Taiwanese, but I was told this should get me cooperation from whoever I showed it to."

Chang read the first page, then turned to the second, going pale. "That's ... it's signed by both the ROC president and vice president."

"Yup," Jackson said. He pointed casually to the first page. "And that name at the top is mine. The rest I don't understand."

Xu was looking over his shoulder. "It says to give you 'all necessary assistance in the execution of your mission.'"

"Good."

"It doesn't say what your mission is."

"No, because my mission is not the kind of mission that presidents can admit they authorized. But let me explain it like this—your president asked the US Marines for help. The 1st Battalion, 8th Marines, got the job and my captain asked for volunteers, so I stepped forward because I know the terrain, I have the contacts, and I owe China a strong dose of payback."

"If you want our help, we need to know what we're helping with," Chang insisted.

Jackson stood, took back the two pages, folded them and slid them into his back pocket again. "Well see, that's 'need to know' for now. All I can tell you right now is, like the letter says, I'm acting on the authority of your government, and your government wants me"—he nodded at Xu as he pulled a Taipei city map out of another pocket and pointed at a point in central Taipei—"and the corporal here to be at *this* address in a few days' time. At the latest."

There was nothing circled on the map, but Jackson's finger made it clear where he was pointing. The two Taiwanese servicemen leaned forward.

"Jinhua Street?" Xu asked. "That's central Taipei."

Jackson folded the map and put it back in his pocket. "So I was told. I have transport hidden under some trees back down at the highway."

AS THEY packed their gear—since Chang made it a condition of releasing Xu that he would accompany them—Xu gave Jackson a crash course in Taiwan's political structure.

"At the top you have the president. He's elected and heads up the armed forces and foreign policy. He appoints the premier. The premier is the head of the legislature, the

Executive Yuan, and chooses the cabinet. He's third in line as head of government after the president and vice president."

"So if the president and vice president are absent, he takes over," Chang added.

Xu was shoving ammunition, snack bars and bottled water into his pack. "Which he has, since the president and vice president haven't been seen for, like, two weeks, since the virus took hold ... so the rumor is they're dead."

"Except, maybe not, if those orders are authentic," Chang said. "They're dated two days ago."

"But the premier is out there, on the radio at least, telling people he has taken control of the government," Xu said. "And no one is saying he hasn't."

"Anyone can see no one is in control," Chang continued. "China owns the sea, we still own the sky—or did—and the virus rules on the ground. Our ground forces, those who aren't dead or sick, have either deserted or taken to the hills like us, to prepare a resistance. China could sail into Taipei tomorrow and take over with a few thousand soldiers, except it seems they want to be invited in, so they're waiting for the premier's 'emergency decree' to pass through congress and open the way."

"We were going to keep fighting," Xu said, looking at Chang glumly. He spoke like he was quoting a field manual. *"It is the duty of every member of the Armed Forces of the Republic of China to resist the armed overthrow of the democratically elected government.* Oo-rah."

Chang gave Jackson a worried frown. "Before I was brought down, I heard that the surviving Marine and US Army forces are digging in at their bases since they've been told they won't be pulled out and no more Coalition troops are coming in. Is that right?" he asked.

"Pretty much," Jackson said. "But you could also look at it this way. We *are* digging in, and if we have to, we are going out fighting too."

"Not if the government invites Chinese forces in," Xu said. "All foreign troops will be ordered to get on the ships you arrived on and leave."

Jackson looked unconvinced. "Yeah, I don't see that happening. We lost too many good people to virus and slaughterbots. Trust me, there are still plenty of Marines left alive who would be more than happy to roll out a high-explosive red carpet for any Chinese visitors." Shouldering his pack, he pointed down the mountain. "Shall we go, gentlemen?"

AT TAICHUNG, Jensen did one last tactical survey. The supply pallet was a half mile out into the landing field, still lying where it had been dropped the night before. The observation bunker they had deployed to was connected to other observation bunkers lining three sides of the airfield, and to the main hangar and maintenance facilities by the "ring road"—an underground highway large enough for small maintenance vehicles to move in two directions. The ROC Taiwan Air Force had designed the underground air base to survive cruise missile barrages and multiple attacks by bunker-busting munitions, as well as brigade-level combined arms assaults. It was divided into five sectors, each with independent power, water, maintenance and storage facilities, and it had an NCBW-rated central "citadel" that could hold 500 personnel in case of a nuclear, chemical or biological weapons attack.

Unfortunately, the base personnel, like the rest of the ROC Taiwan Armed Forces, had been decimated by H5N1c virus outside the base, dramatically limiting the number available to report for duty in its defense.

Jensen returned to the viewing port.

"Movement, Gunny," the Marine on the 20 mm said. Jensen looked over his shoulder. Across the airfield, he saw the slaughterbots advancing in groups of two and three, staggered both horizontally and vertically. As he'd hoped, they were making for the main hangar entrances to his right.

"Let them pass," he told the rifleman. He addressed the men out in the corridor on his radio. "Ready the dogs." Each of the three men in the corridor controlled one LS3, and Jensen managed the fourth. After field-testing the units in Syria, his report had recommended that any operational units be assigned numbers, not names, so that personnel didn't "humanize" or develop attachments to what was, after all, just a weapons system. His recommendation had been adopted, then ignored by Marines in the field, since the urge to name the dogs was hard-coded into human DNA.

Jensen's dog, officially called LS3-9, had been given the nickname Squirt because of a persistent hydraulic leak. "Controller to LS3-9, power up and report status," Jensen said into his mic. The dogs used the same tactical frequency as the rest of the squad.

In the monocle over his left eye, he saw an icon flashing, showing the LS3 was powering on and running its diagnostic routine. Out in the corridor, the dogs lining the walls would be putting on a small gymnastics display; standing, squatting and lying flat as they tested their mobility systems.

>*Hydraulic leak extensor 4. All other systems nominal,* Squirt reported to Jensen's heads-up display. The leak was a known

issue and couldn't be repaired until they had access to parts again. It didn't limit the LS3's speed or ability to bear weight, only its endurance.

Jensen returned his attention to the view outside. The airfield was thick with slaughterbots now, moving left to right with deadly intent.

INSIDE HANGAR BAY 4 at the other end of the airfield, Sam 'Chairman' Long-mao had also just finished checking the ready status of his weapons system. He signaled to a Taiwanese air force airman standing by the hangar blast door control.

He didn't love the nickname the Americans had given him—Chairman Mao was, after all, a brutal Chinese mass murderer—but he didn't mind it either. The diminutive, bespectacled IT technician had gone through life without anyone really paying much attention to him at all. He'd never had a nickname before.

Hangar 4 was on the western side of the U-shaped underground complex, diagonally opposite Jensen and his squad. Monitoring their approach on a CCTV camera, for him, the swarm of slaughterbots was moving right to left. They zigged, zagged and bobbed across the terrain to spoil the aim of anyone trying to target them, and it occurred to Long-mao that if they were human, they might be surprised, even encouraged, at the complete lack of defensive fire coming at them.

Or suspicious.

Long-mao held an arm high and swung it down sharply to signal the airman, who punched the blast door release and *ran*.

99

Its magnetic clamps released, gravity drove the two-ton, 20-meter-wide, 10-meter-high blast door into a slot in the concrete in seconds. As he saw it fall, Long-mao hit the "Enter" key on his laptop. A manic buzz filled the otherwise empty hangar bay as 5,000 hummingbird-sized microdrones powered on.

The "queen bees" were the first off the ground, a small cloud of them streaming out of the hangar entrance. They had one purpose: to find an object resembling the image of the slaughterbot in their tiny memories and close with it. If they did, they would signal the other queen bees, either to call them to join it or, if two queens were already engaged, to tell them to find targets of their own.

The manic buzzing turned to a high-pitched roar as the rest of the killer bees rose into the air and began pouring out of the hangar entrance in pursuit of their queens. Long-mao had his hands over his ears—he'd have to get some earplugs if he wanted to avoid ear damage—and watched his laptop as his system counted the drones out the hangar door.

Five thousand launched, four thousand nine twenty active. Failure to launch: 80.

Not bad.

He raised an arm in the air again and the airman began running for the door control again. He punched it with ill-disguised haste, missing the button on his first attempt, then he ran for cover again. Long-mao followed his lead and ducked down below a concrete berm at the back of the hangar. His job was done; the killer bees would operate autonomously until he recalled them. The hangar blast door began slowly rising from the slot in the concrete like the eyelid of a leviathan.

The reason for the airman's haste became immediately apparent, as the first Hongjian anti-armor missile sailed through the gap above the blast door and exploded against the concrete wall, filling the hangar with flying chips of concrete and white dust. Long-mao felt a hand on his collar as a squad of shoulder-launched-missile-armed Marines joined him at the berm and shoved him to the ground.

JENSEN SAW a change in the slaughterbot formation and, looking downfield, saw why. A gaping maw had opened in front of a hangar, and the lead element of slaughterbots accelerated toward the opening.

Two of them stopped, rising another 5 yards into the air before loosing a volley of missiles at the hangar. For the second time in the war, Jensen witnessed a phenomenon that looked eerily organic. A thick cloud of microdrones, poured out of the hangar like a swarm of locusts. The slaughterbot missiles passed through them like spears through fog as the cloud closed on the nearest slaughterbots and enveloped them, forming blinding balls of whirring darkness that tightened visibly with each second. Four slaughterbots were stopped cold and began jinking—left, right, up, down—until they realized the cloud surrounding them was going nowhere. Jensen could hear the now familiar chainsaw-grinding sound of microdrones colliding with slaughterbot rotor blades until, one by one, the first engagements resolved themselves with the slaughterbots auto-destructing. The "killer bees" were scattered by the blasts, only to coalesce again and move on to their next target.

The tailenders in the formation had passed Jensen and his squad now. He tapped the rifleman in front of him on the shoulder. "We're moving out. Take down any bot that shows an interest in us." He had a last look downfield at the ground-level dogfight to make sure the slaughterbots were well and truly occupied, then moved out into the access tunnel leading to ground level. He saw the four dogs on their "feet," standing two by two, either side of the wall, their Marine handlers beside them.

He pictured the mission in his mind. Get out, get to the supply drop, load the dogs, shuttle the materiel back to the outpost as quickly as possible, trying not to draw the attention of any nearby slaughterbot.

Easy to imagine, not so easy to execute.

"Alright, people, we ..."

From the connecting tunnel that led deeper into the base he heard a muffled explosion. Then gunfire.

His hand darted to his tactical mic switch. "Chairman, talk to me."

"Gunny we've got ... there is ..." Jensen heard shouting, and more gunfire over the radio. "... A breach. Your sector. They came from behind us. Slaughterbots, inside the ..."

The signal went dead.

Jensen ran back into the observation post. The killer bee swarms were still doing their work, derailing the attack across the airfield. But he saw smoke drifting across the field from his right. *An attack from two directions? One to draw their fire, the other to force an entry somewhere?*

"Squad on me," Jensen said, running back out into the corridor. "Slaughterbots inside the facility."

The Battle of Hawaii: NOAA pier

NIKO AND THE GIRL stayed under the pier until Niko was sure the bot had moved on. The battle, however, was still going. Niko heard cannon fire, return automatic rifle fire, the crump of a grenade and something that sounded like secondary explosions as ammunition began cooking off.

"Bot's gone," Niko decided. "But you have to stay here."

"No, I'm *not* staying here," the girl said.

"Look, you'll be safer here, don't be afraid ..."

She came out from behind the pillar. "I'm not *afraid*, asshat. I know first aid. I can help."

Niko smiled. "I deserved that. What's your name, Charger?"

"Presley Ortiz," she said.

"*Presley?*" he asked. "As in Elvis?"

"And so what?"

"Nothing. I'm going to call you Charger. That your school, Corner Canyon?"

"Yeah," she said, giving him nothing now.

He pulled the pouch off the rifle and checked the ammunition belt. Too many rounds to count quickly. It felt heavy, so that was good. "What state's that?"

"Utah. That's why I was taking pictures of the wreck. You know, the *Utah*."

He looked up. "You are a long way from Utah, Charger."

"We're here for the PGA High School National Invitational," she said, then winced as something big exploded nearby. "Are we going to stay down here all day?"

"You in a hurry to die?" Niko asked. "That's a war going on up there."

103

"And you're in the Navy. Shouldn't you be *fighting*?" she shot back at him.

"I'm a firefighter," he told her. "Not a Marine."

She looked pointedly at his XM250. "You've got a gun."

"Which I got off a *dead* guy, who I don't want to meet any time soon, so get off my back, alright?" Niko said, turning around. He was thinking he needed to get back to his unit at the fire station, but it was across the other side of the island. And his phone had been taken off him in the brig. Once upon a time there had been thousands of personnel on Ford Island, working on the docks and World War II–era airfield. Now it was just museums and a few defense facilities people commuted to, like the Pacific Warfighting Center and the NOAA Tsunami Center, plus housing for about 150 Navy families. The only way on and off the island by foot or car was the Admiral Clarey Bridge.

He was back to the idea of stealing a boat, but then what?

"They were going to give us a tour of some old bunker," Presley said, watching the gears turn inside his head. "The teacher went on ahead. I was taking photos of the shipwreck with a couple other girls when the machines attacked and the rest of the class ran for the bunker. Maybe they got inside. Maybe they're hiding there?"

"Bunker? Oh, you mean Battery Boyd …" Niko guessed. He'd made a tour of it himself with a fire crew while checking an alarm that had gone off. It had just been an electrical short, not a fire.

It was as good a plan as any, and he was pretty sure no slaughterbot could fly through the narrow doors down into the battery. But it was 500 yards back the way he'd just come, and he didn't see himself going back up on the path and out in the open again.

"Alright, we'll head there. But we'll stay down at the waterline. It'll be slower going in the mud, but the bushes will hide us."

She nodded.

Five hundred yards isn't far if you're on a golf course maybe, but with the black mud along the waterline on the west coast of the island sucking at their heels every step, it took nearly 15 minutes. They stopped twice and ducked down in the water when they heard gunfire nearby, including the ripping sound of a slaughterbot cannon. Niko kept stealing glances across the water toward the Victor Wharf and the suburb of Waipahu beyond it. He could hear sirens, see smoke rising from several places.

It was like the videos he'd seen from Taiwan, except ... here. And *real*.

They got back to the NOAA pier eventually, and Niko crawled back onto the shoreline, checking the path left and right. He'd also considered going back into the brig for a moment, but all thought of that disappeared when he saw the building was ablaze, ugly black smoke pouring from two places on the roof. It looked like someone had tried to follow him out through the hole in the cell wall. Their bodies lay across the path.

The mound of the battery was ahead of him, but the two old gun emplacements faced outward toward the water, and they'd been sealed up long ago. He knew the metal doors into the facility were on the other side of the mound, one rusted solid, the other more serviceable but locked. There was a fence going all the way around the battery to keep out vandals, and that was locked too. They had keys at the fire station, for all the good that did him.

But if they'd been planning to give the kids a tour, it was just possible someone had opened the place up.

Possible, not guaranteed.

With gunfire to the left, the only way into the battery was around the fence to the right.

"You up for this?" Niko asked the girl.

"Sure," she said, in a voice that said anything but.

"Alright, we get up onto the path, follow the fence right. There's two bodies up there. Don't look. If the gate in the fence is still locked, we'll ..." *We'll what, Niko? Crawl back into the mud?* "We'll try and make it to the Community Center, south end of the island. There might be someone there."

"What if we see one of those machines?" she asked.

"We get behind cover," he told her. "Fast."

THIRTY MILES NORTHWEST, the sky was just lightening as Sergeant Pan Tien's chopper went feet dry on O'ahu. Their ingress was timed to coincide with the point of maximum chaos from the slaughterbot assault. Tien had a view out the open door of the chopper and was expecting to see tracer fire, the smoke of MANPAD missiles screaming into the sky around them, the puff of radar-directed cannon rounds exploding in their wake.

He saw paddleboarders.

People in wet suits or board shorts, standing on their boards in the calm waters of Kaiaka Bay, faces turned upward at the sound of the rotors thudding in from the sea.

A beach, with resort workers setting out deck chairs and umbrellas for the day.

A robot cleaner, combing the white sandy beach for trash.

Then they were past the beach, headed for Hala'iwa Town Center, two rows of houses and palm trees flashing beneath them, then fields, some trees. A main road, the shops lining it still dark and shuttered, light traffic only. In no time, they were at their LZ: Joseph P Leong Highway. It had struck Pan as more than a little fitting that their LZ was named after a person of *Chinese* ancestry.

Their pilot aimed them at a median strip dividing the four-lane highway and flared his helo before he started dropping toward the ground.

"Hands on harnesses! Check your kit!" Pan yelled and checked his own. His Honolulu PD motorcycle police uniform and helmet. Combat boots. One Norinco 9 mm on his hip. Two magazines in utility pouches on his belt. At their feet were several duffel bags holding weapons and ordnance.

Pan was a simple NCO, with basic English language training. Nothing more, nothing less. Others in his squad were comms, cyber and information warfare specialists. His job was to get everyone where they needed to be.

Preferably alive.

He had trained for this day for nearly a year, though no one had told him what he'd been training for. As their wheels thumped onto the ground, their sergeant threw the small forward door open, and Pan hit his belt buckle, leaping to his feet.

The man in front of him jumped onto the bitumen of the highway and Pan followed. The light, though dim and gray, was near blinding after the darkness of the helo's interior, and he blinked as he landed, trying to get his bearings. Two helos left, two more right. Men jumping out, throwing gear to the ground, spreading out across the highway, hands in the air, waving down traffic in the right lanes, headed toward

107

Honolulu, those in high viz vests out front, pulling hard hats onto their heads.

An SUV swerved uncertainly around one of the men in a road worker uniform and looked like it was going to continue until Pan stepped right in front of it. It was an anonymous matte black color, with tinted windows. Perfect.

It was *just* like the exercises on Hainan. The driver was a guy in his 20s. He looked surprised, then pissed.

"What's going on, Officer?" he yelled out his window.

Pan ran around and tried to pull his door open. It was locked. But his window was open.

Pan didn't try to negotiate with him. He wasn't keen to use English when violence would be faster. He stepped up to the window, grabbed the back of the guy's head and slammed it into his steering wheel.

"*The fu*—" he said, then Pan slammed him again, reaching inside the door and grabbing for the door lock, pulling it open.

The guy had his hands over his bloodied face, and Pan hit him with a left jab to the temple, then reached across and undid his seat belt.

He grabbed the guy under his right armpit and heaved him out of the vehicle. He flopped to the ground and Pan dragged him a couple yards from the vehicle, then jumped in. His corporal, Pi Weng, was already at the other door, and Pan leaned across and opened the door for him.

"Just like in training," Pi said with a grin. He pointed ahead of them. "Hit it, Sergeant."

Speed and violence were their bywords. Pan put the SUV into gear and shoved his foot down on the accelerator. Six minutes after going feet dry, the 16 men of 1st Battalion were headed for Honolulu.

THE DESCENDENT of the last true King of Hawaii was stuck in traffic.

He had reclaimed his ancestor's ceremonial feather cloak from the Bishop Museum, and was in a bus with 50 armed members of the Hawaii Freedom Alliance. More trailed behind in a convoy of SUVs.

He had just declared himself a public enemy of the government of the United States of America.

Not in so many words, but standing on the steps of the Bishop Museum, surrounded by his supporters, he had announced via social media that, with support from the governments of China and Russia, he was marching on the Hawaiian Capitol building to take Hawaii back for Hawaiians.

He had to admit they had underestimated the mayhem the Chinese attack on Pearl Harbor would cause. Highway 1, the main route cutting through the center of the capital, was choked with traffic heading east, away from Pearl Harbor. Emergency vehicles—ambulances, police and fire trucks—were headed in the opposite direction, toward the harbor, where pyres of smoke were rising into the sky and merging to form a low, gray ceiling that occasionally flashed orange or red, reflecting an explosion below.

Freeth went forward to talk his number two, a man called Duke Apana.

"We need to get off the highway," he told him. "This is a cluster."

"I know, I know," Duke said. He was talking to the driver. "How about take the next exit, head down to 99, go along the waterfront, come up to the Capitol that way, on Punchbowl?"

"Worth a try," the man said. "Can't be worse than this."

109

They pulled into a service lane and started pushing past the stalled traffic toward the next exit. Satisfied, Freeth sat himself in the seat next to Apana. "How many at the Capitol now? Don't embellish." He knew he had an intimidating demeanor, a weightlifter's physique and a thick black and silver mane that demanded respect. People had a tendency to want to please him, but right now he just wanted facts.

Apana checked his phone. "About 160, already there, keeping a low profile. Another 60 from the Hawai'i Chapter; they were stuck out at the airport, but they're moving now. Fifty from the Maui Chapter—I can't get ahold of them, but they were walking up from their hotel in the Arts District last time I talked to them. A hundred in our two buses. What's that, about 400?"

"Three seventy," Freeth corrected him. "What about Kaua'i?"

"Kaua'i Chapter is a no-show. I told you Matsunaga is a windbag ..."

"I know." Freeth nodded. "And I will remember."

"It's enough, isn't it?" Apana asked. "It has to be."

"More than enough," Freeth assured him. "Do you know how many soldiers the Colonialists landed in 1893 to depose Queen Lili'uokalani?"

"I don't know. Thousands, I guess," Apana said.

"We were so weak by then, they stole Hawaii from its people with just 162 Marines," Freeth told him. "We are three times that number. And we have the might of China and Russia at our backs." He looked out the windshield as they took an off-ramp and began heading south, toward the waterfront. To their right, the fires and smoke of the attack on Pearl Harbor were clearly visible. Freeth had no idea what was happening there—he hadn't been told, and he hadn't

110

asked. He'd only been told to "be ready" for today, and he'd done that. "You have a weapon?" he asked Duke.

Duke nodded. They'd discussed whether to ask people to bring guns, but with the occupier busy elsewhere, Freeth was hoping for a bloodless coup. He didn't want casualties among his people.

And besides, they had friends on the way who had promised to provide them with protection.

THE REST of the trip to the Hawaiian Capitol building went faster, since downtown was emptying out as people fled. Fifteen minutes and they were pulling up on the street outside the colonnaded Capitol. Unique among state capitol buildings, the building was open to the elements: a beautiful atrium outside its ground floor, Congress chambers open to the elements, the doors to each chamber guarded by just three security officers managing a small metal detector.

Several dozen Freedom Alliance members were already milling around, and had attracted a small Capitol security and police presence. A particularly vexed highway patrol officer was shouting at one of Freeth's lieutenants, and Freeth made his way quickly through the crowd in the internal plaza, to the shouting police officer. Behind him, his other lieutenants fanned out and started getting people ready.

The crowd parted and he stepped forward, naked except for the malo and the ceremonial feather cape. He had oiled his skin on the bus, so it glowed honey brown.

The agitated police officer, a blond-haired Haole, picked up on the change in the crowd—and the fact that suddenly no one was paying attention to him—and spun around to see Freeth standing right behind him. His hand went immediately to his sidearm, which Freeth ignored. "Is there a problem, Officer?" Freeth asked.

"There is a damn civil emergency is the problem. Who are you, sir?" the man asked.

Freeth wasn't surprised the officer didn't recognize him. He appeared more than a little distracted, and after all, Freeth was wearing a loincloth and cape.

"I am Jonah Freeth, *Ka Mo'opuna Pono o Kalakaua*," Freeth said. He gestured around himself. "Myself and my people have come here to reclaim these islands for their original owners."

The police officer held up a hand like he was warding off an evil spirit. "I didn't recognize you, Mr. Freeth. Look, you and your people don't have a permit for whatever *this* is." The police officer waved his other hand anxiously in the air. "And we have a state of emergency declared, sir. The building is closed and everyone has been evacuated, so you can't be here."

Freeth looked around. His men had positioned themselves throughout the atrium behind the few private security officers, and he was accompanied by the same six bodyguards who had been with him earlier in the day when he reclaimed his ceremonial cape.

"You misunderstand, Officer," Freeth said very reasonably. "It is you who is not welcome here." He nodded to Apana, who pulled his pistol from his belt and put it to the officer's head.

"Hey, whoa!" the officer said, raising his hands in the air in alarm as Apana took his weapon. There were scuffles throughout the crowd as other Alliance members disarmed the small handful of security guards who weren't used to handling anything more threatening than psychotic street dwellers.

"Gather up their weapons," Freeth said to Duke. "I don't want people we don't know running around with guns. We need to keep control." When that was done, Freeth turned to face his people. The ones in the front had their cell phones out and were live-streaming the exchange. He cleared his throat. He knew the next lines by heart, having rehearsed versions of them a thousand times in his mind, never daring hope he would one day speak them into being. "Let this be heard. On this day, June 20 2038, I, Jonah Freeth, *Ka Moʻopuna Pono o Kalakaua,* descendent of the last free ruler of Hawaii, and the people of the Hawaiian Freedom Alliance, here assembled, reclaim our islands from the American colonists!" There was a roar from the small crowd.

His people were rolling a mix of gasoline and diesel fuel drums off the buses and putting them up against the eight thick columns holding up the foyer of the square, open-roofed Capitol building. He waited impatiently as some were opened and fuel was spilled across the marble floor and walls. Since the atrium was mostly stone and ceramic tiles, he had to wait a little longer as the doors to the colonists' two legislative chambers were kicked in and fuel poured into the wood-paneled senate and congress meeting halls. Neither House nor Senate had been in session, so they didn't have to deal with hysterical, grandstanding politicians.

The last of the employees from upstairs was ushered out into the atrium, stepping over pools and rivers of fuel.

He called over to Duke, coming out behind them with several other men. "The building empty?"

"Every room, cupboard and washroom stall," his deputy confirmed.

113

Kalakaua handed him an unlit torch. He turned to address the crowd again. "Today, this symbol of the occupiers will be destroyed, and the true Congress of the People of Hawaii, at 'Iolani Palace, will again be convened!"

He marched out of the atrium, torch held high, stink of diesel in his nostrils, onto the steps at the west of the Capitol building in front of the statue of Queen Lili'uokalani, who watched on weakly as the American landowners stole her kingdom from her. It was fitting that she should stand there now, in bronze, and watch as the Kingdom of Hawai'i was restored again.

A man with a diesel can followed him down the steps, trailing fuel on the ground. The smell was overpowering. On the other side of the building, he could see his people chasing onlookers away.

Well, if anyone gets barbecued, it's their own fault.

Looking for Apana, he found him standing on his right, and held out the torch for Duke to light. Duke had his lighter ready and applied it to the head of the torch, which burst into flame. Freeth took three bold steps forward, yelled "*For Hawai'i!*" and threw the torch down. Flame blossomed on the grass, then skipped up the stairs and into the middle of the atrium.

With slowly increasing intensity, the flames took hold. A gasoline barrel ruptured and exploded. Freeth crouched instinctively, a blast of super-heated air scorching overhead. When he stood, it seemed the deceptively small building was burning nicely.

Freeth turned. Behind an iron railing fence 200 yards away was the true seat of government, the three-story Florentine 'Iolani Palace.

Staff from the palace were already gathered on the lawns out front, watching the action down at the harbor, and they now started yelling and pointing at the burning Capitol building.

Tourists poured out of the palace to watch the bonfire.

Good, that will make the building easier to clear.

Freeth spun on his heel, holding his feather cape in place with one hand and pointing toward the palace with the other.

"Forward, brothers and sisters!"

SERGEANT PAN TIEN and his squad from the 1st Battalion, 5th Amphibious Combined Arms Brigade (Recon), only got 7 miles along the highway that led away from the coast, to where it joined onto the east-west-running I-83. There was a police patrol there, turning people around, either back to the beach or toward the southwest coast. A line of about 20 vehicles was crawling toward the roadblock, and a convoy of open-top military trucks, crowded with troops, was stuck in the middle of the traffic jam.

They had trained for this too. *Speed and violence.*

Pan checked his mirror and saw the convoy in formation behind him.

Their SUVs pulled onto the highway verge and sped past the stalled traffic. A soldier who had dismounted from his truck stepped into their path, and Pan leaned on his horn, sending the man jumping back toward the safety of his vehicle.

The horn also made the police another 20 cars ahead look their way.

"I count two cars, four tangos," Pan said over the tactical radio.

"Confirmed," Pi replied. They'd chosen their own callsign for this mission—Jiùxīng, or "Liberator." "Liberator Squad, roadblock ahead. Car two, deploy," Pan said, putting into play one of dozens of their rehearsed scenarios.

Pan didn't slow. He drove at 40 miles an hour until they reached the roadblock and then jammed on his brakes, pulling right. An SUV full of recon scouts in police uniforms overtook them, and before it had even reached a full stop, their doors were open and they were jumping out, running toward the police at the roadblock.

"Get down!" Pan heard them yelling in a good imitation of pure panic. "Stand back!"

The police at the roadblock looked confused. The men running at them with panic on their faces were their own. They looked at each other in fear, not looking at the "police officers" running at them but over their shoulders, down the traffic jam, looking for whatever the hell had scared them so badly.

As they reached the road lock, the five Chinese scouts in police uniform drew their sidearms and gunned the Americans down.

Pan heard people screaming, saw a couple of cars try to break out of the long line and U-turn to get away, but he ignored them.

"Tangos down," he said to Pi, setting the SUV in motion again.

"Roger that," Pi replied, reaching an arm out the window and flipping a salute to their men on the roadblock. Pan maneuvered his stolen SUV around the bodies on the highway, then put his foot down again.

In his mirror, he saw his men throw thermal grenades into the police vehicles before they mounted their SUVs again. As

116

they formed up, he saw the bright flash of explosions and dark clouds of smoke in his rearview mirror.

In minutes they were passing the turnoff to Wheeler Army Airfield, leaving death and fire in their wake.

Military airfield. Someone else's problem, he thought. But he was amazed at how normal the island seemed, apart from the roadblock they'd just passed. He was overtaking cars with parents and kids who looked like they were on their way to soccer games. A plumbing company truck, guy chewing on some kind of sandwich while he drove, sucking on coffee from a paper cup, gave them a disinterested look as they passed him.

But ahead of them, smoke was rising over Pearl Harbor. Too early to be cruise missile strikes, so it must be the work of slaughterbots. Didn't these people have a civil emergency system? Didn't they have radios?

"Costco," Pi said, pointing out the window at a sign on a warehouse store off the highway. "I heard they got good stuff. Cheap."

"It's all Chinese or Mexican, stupid," Pan told him. They were both from the same province. "You can get it from Guangzhou half the price you can here."

"Not the pineapples," Pi told him. "Pineapples is what Hawaii does best."

"Pineapples?"

"Pineapples. I read about it," Pi told him. "And coffee, cane sugar and uh ..." He clicked his fingers. "Nuts. The little round ones. You know the ones."

"Macadamias?"

"*Macadamias*, that's it." Pi nodded. "That's the ones. You can get them with chocolate. Chili even. We get to Honolulu, I'm getting me a pineapple and chili macadamia omelet."

Pan frowned at him. "That's not a thing."

"We're helping put the King of Hawaii back on his throne, man," Pi pointed out. "If I tell the royal cook I want a pineapple and chili macadamia omelet, then it's a thing."

Pan checked his mirror. Full convoy again now. Someone had said during exercises there was no way they were all going to get SUVs, but they did. Except for that pickup, but that just looked authentic, four roadworkers sitting in the back of a pickup. Well, in China it would have been perfectly normal. Hawaii, maybe not.

Pi pointed out the windshield, ahead of them. "Another roadblock ahead. Police are awake at least. One car, two tangos."

"Got it," Pan told him. Pan reached down and pulled his Norinco out of its holster. Lifting his hands from the wheel, he racked the slide and then put the gun under his right thigh.

Pi did the same.

Pan reached the back of the long line of cars and pulled onto the shoulder again, driving around them toward the roadblock. He saw plenty of space either side of the police car. "Liberator, roadblock ahead. We are not stopping. Car one is lead."

Speed and violence.

"You ready?" he asked Pi in English.

"You know it," his comrade said, trying to sound cool. Pan knew he was just as nervous as Pan was.

Pan kept up his English. "If we get stopped, I'll take the tango on the right. You got the one on the left."

Pi leaned forward, squinted through the windshield. He switched to Mandarin. "I get the *female* cop? Aww, come on …"

"The *tango* on the left, Corporal," Pan said firmly.

118

"Ah, shit, Sergeant," Pi said, pulling out his pistol and holding it between his thighs. "I was just starting to enjoy this war."

The Rearguard: Tongxiao

SERGEANT MASON JACKSON wasn't exactly enjoying his war either. The "transport" he had hidden at the base of the mountain was an electric tricycle of a type that had become the mainstay of Taiwanese courier services during the 2030s. With two wheels up front and a single drive wheel at the rear, it had a cab to keep the rain off its driver and pillion and a rack at the rear for packages.

Jackson registered the dubious look on the pilot, Chang's, face as he walked around it. "Does 60 miles an hour fully loaded and has more than enough range for the three hours to Taipei. You'll have to ride in back with the gear; I wasn't planning on the extra passenger."

"A single shot from a slaughterbot and we're dead," Chang said grimly.

Jackson had been chewing gum and spat it on the ground as though to show what he thought of the Chinese drones. "I got past two on the way here. The first had a good look at me and decided I wasn't worth a missile. The second sprayed some cannon shells my way, but this bike is ninja. I dodged behind some trees, into an alley, and I was gone."

Chang didn't look convinced.

Xu loaded his duffel into the rear tray and then looked down the road. "No traffic. Is it my imagination, or were there more graves when we came down the mountain than when we went up?"

The number of dead from H5N1 had quickly overwhelmed the ability of the locals to conduct normal burial rites. Bodies were hastily buried, small mounds of dirt over shallow graves that attracted dogs and wild pigs. Any villagers still moving around outside their dwellings, if they paid attention to them at all, had regarded them with defeated apathy.

"Definitely more," Chang said. "I don't think the epidemic has peaked yet."

"We're immune though, don't you think?" Xu asked hopefully. "We have to be, if we're still alive?"

"No bird flu going to kill me," Jackson grunted, climbing into the bike's cab. "I'm West Virginian Black Bear."

"No one is immune," Chang said. "If we are headed to a populated area, we will be at risk. We need to get this job done while we're still alive. You're in back," he told Xu.

THEY MET Fiona and Fluffy on the coast road outside Tongxiao, about halfway to Taipei. They'd evaded two patrolling slaughterbots with quick detours down side roads—the advantage of having three pairs of eyes scouring the road ahead and behind.

But the third trapped them cold. It appeared from between two low buildings outside the Tongxiao Extreme Sports Ground and stopped on the deserted highway 5 yards up and 50 yards ahead of them. The ground either side of the highway was flat fields with no cover.

Jackson slammed the trike to a halt.

"Pass me my kit bag," Xu said to Chang. He figured the slaughterbot for a relatively easy target … if he could put his rifle together and take the shot without triggering the bot's kill algorithm. "I'll take it out before …"

"Don't move," Jackson said over his shoulder. "It's got us dead to rights. We need to play possum."

"Possum?" Xu asked with a frown.

"Just stay *still*. It's a missile drone. They prioritize bigger vehicles," Jackson told him. "Usually."

But the drone was behaving strangely, bobbing around like it was ... *drunk*? The box magazine of nine missiles slung under its belly swiveled left and right as though trying to draw a bead on them and failing. Then it swiveled all the way around and pointed *away*. It was definitely not behaving normally, Xu decided.

Jackson gripped his throttle, seeming to get ready to turn the trike, make a quick retreat, when they saw a small teenage girl with glasses walk out from between the two buildings to stand *underneath* the bobbing slaughterbot, looking up.

"Damn fool girl," Jackson cursed. "What is she doing?"

The girl noticed them then, and gave them a big smile and an enthusiastic wave.

"Something weird is going on here," Jackson said. "Stay on the trike. Don't touch that rifle. I'm going to walk closer."

Xu looked over his shoulder at Chang, who just nodded.

Jackson slid off the saddle and began walking slowly forward. But the bot continued its erratic motion, and didn't appear particularly fixated on the trike, Jackson or the girl with the glasses.

Which ... he could see now that the glasses she was wearing were VR goggles. She looked about 15: short hair, jeans, dirty T-shirt. She was still smiling, and called out something to Jackson as she held up what looked like a VR game controller. Too far away for Xu to hear over the buzz of slaughterbot rotors. She was motioning him to approach but he stopped about 10 yards away.

Jackson looked over his shoulder at Xu, who was sitting obediently frozen in place. "Get down here, Corporal," Jackson said. "Move slowly."

Xu eased himself off the saddle and approached Jackson with deliberate slowness, halting step by halting step. The girl called out at them again and began walking toward Jackson, but he held out a hand and yelled "Stop," which she did, frowning.

When Xu was just behind him, Jackson turned. "Ask her what she said," he told him.

"Girl, what the hell are you doing with that bot?" Xu asked.

"It's safe," the girl yelled back. "I hacked its operating system and turned off the gun."

Xu translated.

"The hell it's safe," Jackson said, not taking his eyes off the slaughterbot. "We stay here. It could detonate any moment. Ask her how she got hold of an intact slaughterbot."

Xu yelled a few questions at the girl, who replied with obvious impatience. "She said she found it down by some railway tracks a few days ago. It had powered down but not exploded like all the others. She worked out how to recharge it and then hacked its operating system ..."

"The hell she did," Jackson exclaimed.

Xu shrugged, and nodded his head at the slaughterbot, obediently hovering over the girl's head, as though no more evidence was needed. "She can control the gun, more or less, but she said she's still learning to fly it."

"If she's in control of it," Jackson said, "tell her to land it on the ground and power it down."

Xu yelled out the instruction and the girl looked up at the drone, manipulating the controller. The slaughterbot sideslipped away from her, then in jerky downward increments, lowered itself to ground level, dropping the last few inches to land on its belly. The familiar but still terrifying buzz of its rotors stopped.

It was suddenly very, very quiet.

Chang joined them as the girl walked up. An animated conversation began between the two Taiwanese, with Xu and Jackson looking on, Xu following along and Jackson trying to read the emotions.

"If you have hacked into its control system, we might be able to use it," Chang said, holding out a hand. "Give me the goggles and the controller. I'm a pilot; I'll see if I can fly it."

"Can you code in Anaconda?" the girl asked tartly. "Because you'll have to hack in again to reboot it and get it flying. Which I'm totally sure you can't." Xu smiled. He liked her already. She had orange home-dye hair color, a cheeky grin, and the thing you couldn't ignore, she'd *hacked a slaughterbot.*

The girl pulled her VR glasses off and waved them at Chang before putting them on again. Chang argued with her some more. With the buzz of the rotors gone, people were starting to emerge from nearby buildings. They were standing on their doorsteps for the moment, some clearly not trusting that the slaughterbot was not about to wake up and start killing again.

"Someone want to bring me up to speed?" Jackson asked. "Before we draw a crowd?"

"The girl is not cooperating," Chang said, irritably. "I told her to give me the VR glasses and controller so that I can try to pilot the slaughterbot, but she refuses."

"With respect, Lieutenant," Xu corrected him. "She didn't refuse. She just said the only way to get the bot flying again is for her to hack its operating system and reboot it, and she established you don't have the skills. Me either."

Chang looked at Jackson hopefully.

"Don't look at me. I can barely work a radio."

Chang grunted. Xu tried. "Hey. What you did here was insane. No one has hacked a slaughterbot as far as we know. It's amazing."

"I know. I call it Fluffy," she said. "Makes it less scary."

"What's your name?" Xu asked.

"Fi," she said. "Short for Fiona. My Western name. Tsui Feng-yun if you want the Taiwanese."

"That's some crazy coding, Fi," Xu repeated.

She pulled out her cell phone and loaded an app. "I pulled some video from the drone's cameras. You want to see?"

Jackson bent down and peered at the small screen. It wasn't an idle brag. She had about a hundred 30-second videos that appeared to show whatever the drone had been looking at—some in HD color, some in infrared—as it panned and zoomed at the environment around it, locking onto anything that moved and no doubt classifying it. And deciding whether to kill it or not.

"Can you do that in real time?" Xu asked. "Look through its cameras?"

"That's how I steer it," she said, holding up her VR glasses. "I made it so the video goes to here."

As Jackson had warned, a small circle of onlookers had formed around them now, and Chang ordered them to keep their distance because the bot could still explode. They moved back a few steps, but that was all.

"Idiots," Chang decided. "We need to get it out of here." He looked at the trike. "It's too heavy to carry. We're about 2 miles from the coast. If she reboots it, and we can use its own vision for steering, I could fly it into the sea, get rid of it there."

"Hey," the girl said. "No. It's mine!"

"It's a bomb, waiting to go off," Chang said. "It could explode at any second ..."

"No, it isn't. I commented out the self-destruct code."

"You can't be sure of that," Chang snapped.

"I bet my life on it, didn't I?" the girl responded. "And that was yesterday. If it was going to explode, it would have exploded."

Xu couldn't fault her logic.

Jackson had been quiet, but he spoke up now. "We can use it," he said.

"What?!" Chang asked.

"Sure, fly it ahead of us doing recon. Slaughterbots aren't going to shoot their own, are they?"

"What about her?" Xu asked him.

"We need her to reboot it, that's all," Chang said. "If we can stream video to those VR glasses, I can fly it."

"Hey, I understand English," Fi said to the two Taiwanese personnel in Taiwanese. "I know when you're talking about me. You *need* me, to boot it up and recharge it and if anything goes wrong."

There was something about her determination and eagerness, something beyond any kind of "finders keepers" mentality. "Where are your parents?" Xu asked her.

A shadow flickered over her face. "Dead."

"Your grandparents?"

"Also dead. *Everyone* died," she said, her voice quavering. "Everyone except me." She drew a deep breath. "You have to take me. You need me."

Xu looked around at the trike and turned to Chang. "She can ride in back with me, sir. You sit behind the American, fly the bot. She's right; we might need her to keep it flying."

126

The circle of onlookers was closing again now, one person even taking up a half brick and making as though to throw it at the slaughterbot. A few others egged him on.

"Come on, we need to move," Jackson said. "Ask her to get it airborne again. That will scatter them."

It did. A few seconds manipulating a code interface with her VR rig and Fi had the slaughterbot flying again. The crowd dispersed with alacrity, the street deserted again in seconds.

Fi pulled off her VR glasses and hesitated, Xu giving her a reassuring smile, before she handed them, together with the controller, over to Chang. "Don't break it," she said.

TO THEIR SOUTH, an *untamed* slaughterbot was surveying the network of underground hangars, tunnels and storage and maintenance facilities that made up Taichung Air Base. The tunnel network was designed to keep the base operational even if besieged by enemy forces. The base facilities were compartmentalized, with three sectors—east, north and west—that could be sealed off with blast-proof doors if a sector was breached, and tunnels were mined as a last-ditch defense against attackers.

The slaughterbot cloud AI that constantly updated the drones' onboard algorithms had dynamically analyzed every attack by and on its units on Taiwan, pulling in data from air, electronic and satellite surveillance and adjusting its tactics accordingly. It had decided it had no immediate counter to the "killer bee" defense and identified the killer bee system's main weakness to be its human controllers. Kill the controllers, neutralize the killer bee threat. So it sent wave after wave of bots against the human defenders of Taichung until it found a potential attack vector.

Satellite surveillance showed it that, when attacked from across the airfield, the human observers and MANPAD-armed missileers rushed out the rear of the base's observations posts, as Jensen had done, to engage the attackers from the top of the earthworks.

And some of them left the exit hatchways open.

Pixel-level image analysis showed one of the hatchways was large enough to admit a 20 mm autocannon-armed slaughterbot.

The slaughterbot finished its survey and signaled the units around it. As the swarming attack formed up at the edge of the airfield to assault the main aircraft hangar doors, a four-bot element of slaughterbots positioned itself behind cover just 200 yards from the identified hatch. And waited.

In 2023, China launched the Yaogan-41 satellite aboard a modified Long March 5 heavy-lift rocket and parked it in geosynchronous orbit over Taiwan to generate constantly updated high-definition imagery of the island's surface. Yaogan-41 and the AI that analyzed its constant stream of data could detect and report the smallest of changes, from the patterns of train traffic to the appearance or disappearance of a single tree on a wooded mountainside.

As Taichung's defenders streamed out of their hiding places to engage the slaughterbot swarm advancing across the airfield, like ants from a nest that had just been kicked over, Yaogan-41 saw they left the critical hatchway open, and alerted the Slaughterbot AI.

The four-bot element emerged from cover.

Two Hongjian missile-armed bots targeted the squad of human defenders that was lying on the ground just below the lip of the mound, preparing to engage the incoming airfield attack with a sniper rifle. Heat-seeking missiles speared toward them unseen and killed them where they lay. The three-by-three box magazine slung under the Tianyi missile-armed drone made it too large to enter the hatchway, but its cannon-armed cousins had a lower profile. Their ammunition was carried on a belt slung under their gun, and it was flexible enough that they could lower themselves to just 2 feet above the ground, and squeeze inside the two-meter-high, two-person-wide hatch.

One moved left, the other right.

US MARINE Private Jeremy Waters had been sent by his sergeant to fetch ammunition for their squad light assault weapon from the eastern sector ammo bunker and emerged into the tunnel outside with belts slung over each shoulder ... then paused.

The sound of a *buzz saw*, from the hatchway corridor?

No, not a buzz saw.

Slaughterbot.

He dropped to a crouch and hobbled into a corner, away from the door. He had no weapon himself, so all he could do was hug the wall and make himself as small as possible. The sound of spinning rotors grew in volume. The doorway to the ammo bunker was only one person wide. It had a steel door, but to try to close it, he'd have to move, and though his brain told him to try, his legs were saying *no freaking way, Marine.*

The terrifying scream of rotors paused at the entrance to the bunker. It was too small for a slaughterbot to enter, wasn't it? But the room was full of weapons and ammunition.

A single high-explosive 20 mm round fired into the room could set it all off.

Which could take the slaughterbot with it, but also Private Jeremy Waters.

Then the bot was moving again, apparently deciding the room held no targets or threats, and he listened until he judged it turned the nearby dogleg in the tunnel. He had no tactical radio, couldn't warn anyone about what he'd seen. But there was a Nuclear Chemical Biological Warfare panic button on the wall outside the ammo bunker. He could trigger that.

Still crouched, he moved to the doorway, listening. The sound of rotors was still loud, but the tunnel was clear. He stood, stepping into the tunnel, looking left, then right. *Where was that damn panic button? It was the size of a fist and luminescent red, for Chrissakes …*

He saw it, waist high, about 3 yards to his right. Then the buzz of rotors increased again—not from his right, where the slaughterbot had gone, but from his left. The entry hatch! A second bot. He watched it edge itself into the tunnel, swing its cannon toward him. He'd have to run toward it to get back into the ammo bunker. Not happening. He backed up slowly, back flat against the tunnel wall, took two steps …

His hand slammed the NCBW panic button on the wall. As the first of the slaughterbot's 20 mm caseless rounds chewed into him, the blast-proof door behind Jerome Waters slammed shut, titanium bolts sliding into hardened steel receivers.

THE CHINESE DRONE regarded the crumpled body, judged it no longer a threat, but saw that its way forward

130

toward the main hangar complex was now blocked. It had a map of the complex in its onboard memory and quickly ran some scenarios. It could exit the complex again, seek another entry point in order to reach its primary objective, the underground aircraft hangars. Or it could go deeper into the eastern sector and look for targets there—a secondary objective, but with a higher probability of success. It chose the latter. Swiveling its cannon, it moved away from the bloody mess that had been Private Jeremy Waters.

And toward the very much alive Gunny James Jensen.

JENSEN AND HIS SQUAD doubled toward the sound of fighting, sending a dog out in front of them to scout around the blind corners built into the tunnel for defense. The tunnel wasn't made for vehicles or aircraft; it was just wide enough for four people shoulder to shoulder, made to allow patrols to move the length of the airfield underground and emerge from observation posts to defend against aboveground attackers, or escape, if that was the only option.

Jensen and his squad weren't running. Not yet.

"Movement on LS3-3," one of Jensen's men reported. They were crouched about 5 yards back from the next dogleg in the tunnel. "Something coming around the corner."

No shit, Marine, Jensen thought. He could hear the buzz-saw hum of rotors, low, but getting louder. He looked over his shoulder. This section of tunnel was about 20 yards long before the next defensive zigzag. "Set up the anti-tank rifle down at that corner." He had the vision from the helmet cameras of his men and their dogs in his monocle and flicked to the video from the dog on point.

131

Just in time to see the slaughterbot round the bend and open up with its cannon on the LS3.

Jensen winced. The sound of the 20 mm autocannon caromed off the walls around them as the vision from the LS3 died. *Well, that answers that question,* Jensen thought. They hadn't lost any dogs to slaughterbots yet. He'd been wondering if the LS3s were in the slaughterbot database, and whether they would see them as a threat and attack on sight.

They were and they did. The tunnel filled with dust and smoke.

Two of his men were humping the heavy anti-materiel rifle back down the tunnel. The other two were crouched by their dogs, rifles up.

"Frags, Gunny?" one asked over the tactical radio, his voice nearly drowned out by the still-echoing cannon fire and the buzz of rotors.

"Read my mind," Jensen said. "I'll look after the dogs. Set your frags to two seconds and throw as soon as you think that mother is close enough to the corner, then join me back behind the anti-tank rifle in case the grenades don't stop it."

Jensen put their three remaining LS3s in "follow me" mode and jogged back to the corner where his gun team was setting up—one lying on the floor, half of his body around the corner, the other in cover with ammunition ready. The NTW-20 rifle was 1 meter 70 long, the barrel and stock both resting on bipods because of its weight.

Jensen checked the man was sighting on the corner they had just vacated; then he got their dogs around the gun team and further down the next leg of the tunnel, monitoring the video feed from his two men. One stuck his head quickly around the corner, and Jensen saw the grainy image of an approaching slaughterbot, filling the tunnel from near floor to

132

ceiling with little if any space either side. Its gun barrel swiveled as the man pulled back behind the corner.

"Frags out!" Jensen heard him call.

The vision then became confused as one man threw his grenade at a far wall, going for a ricochet, while the first man took the chance to look around the corner again and be more certain of his throw ...

Which cost him his life.

THE SLAUGHTERBOT had picked up the infrared signature of a human head briefly appearing and disappearing behind the next corner.

It put its cannon crosshairs on the corner, aiming about 20 inches along the wall so that when it fired, it would tear chunks of concrete shrapnel from the corner and send them flying into the tunnel on the other side.

It had hair trigger reflexes, and as soon as the infrared blob edged around the corner again, it fired, even as it registered a single small object come flying toward it, bouncing off the wall to its left.

The image was poorly lit and blurred by movement but not hard for the slaughterbot AI to identify.

Fragmentation grenade.

It stopped firing its cannon, dipping its front rotors like it was a matador bowing to a bull. This put its armored topside carapace between its vulnerable core and the expected blast and, because the drone also rapidly retracted its rotors, dropped it nose-first onto the floor of the tunnel, tipped forward over its cannon. For a fraction of a second, it skidded, and the housing of its cannon had to take the bot's full weight, but it held.

133

The grenade detonated in the angle of wall and floor, hot metal shrapnel spraying in all directions, some burying itself in the slaughterbot's carbon-fiber-covered ceramic shield. Even as the crack of the grenade was still ringing from the walls, the slaughterbot extended its rotors again and spun itself into the air, cannon trained on the corner, ready for the next attack as it edged forward.

Operation Midnight: Piranha

AGINCOURT WAS TRAPPED.

She'd successfully penetrated the widely spread outer picket line of the Chinese fleet with its crisscrossing *Jiangdao* class corvettes, submarines and helicopters dropping sonar buoys ahead of the fleet.

All the time listening for one particular submarine that the mysterious British location system told them was ahead of them, somewhere.

But now *Agincourt* was 600 feet down and pinned. A helo had dropped a sonar buoy right on top of her when she'd been cruising at 300 feet, and it must have gotten a return off her hull, because it dropped another six buoys in a wide circle around her that started hammering on her hull like mallets on an anvil.

Her only option was to go deep, under the sonar-reflecting thermocline, trying to get out of range of the Chinese sonobuoys before the helo called in an ASW vessel or torpedo-armed aircraft. Which meant a steep, tightly turning dive with flooded ballast tanks.

And it looked like they were going to get away with it. Until …

"Surface vessel moving in, bearing one one two, range 2 miles, twin screw, classifying … *Type 053 Luyang*."

The *Luyang* destroyer was one of China's better anti-submarine platforms. And Courtenay had never faced off against one. He spun on his chair, to McDonald and Brunelli at the back of the control room. "Captain, the *Luyang*. Have you tangled with one before?"

"I have," McDonald said, Brunelli nodding grim-faced beside him. "You have nothing to worry about if it's a *Type*

D—they're more anti-air than anti-submarine builds, they only have hull-based sonar, no towed array …"

"But the *Type E* is a bastard," Brunelli said, finishing the sentence. "Towed array, Piranha swarming torpedoes. We met one off Palau and it fired a swarm that nearly ended us."

Courtenay swung to his sonarman. "*Luyang* D or E, man? We need to know."

"Cleaning up the signature, sir," the man said. "Can't give you the vessel ID yet …"

"I don't need to know its bloody name and date of birth, man, just the type …"

"Sir. Just a few … I have it. *Type E*. It's a *052-E*."

Courtenay swung back. "Piranha swarm. How did you defeat it?"

"You start *now*," McDonald told him. "Before they even launch."

THE PLAN *Lishui* had started life as *Type D* destroyer but was refitted to *E* class in 2032 with the addition of a towed array sonar suite. At the same time, its ASROC rocket-propelled torpedo launchers were replaced with Piranha launch tubes that could spit a cloud of 20 Piranha drones 500 feet into the air, allowing them to glide to a surface entry point up to two and a half miles away.

Lishui was already within Piranha range of the contact detected by its Z-19 helicopter. Aiming the swarm at the center of the circle of sonobuoys dropped by the helo, its ASW commander issued the order to fire.

From the 20 tubes inside the box-shaped launch turret, compressed air spat the Piranha munitions into the air. As they reached apogee, wings flicked out of their bodies, and they began gliding. Coordinating their entry so that they would land in groups of four, at five different points around the target area, they activated their sonar seekers and armed their 20 lb. RDX sodium hydroxide warheads.

Hitting the water, they folded their fins to 45 degrees and used them to steer in slowly descending circles, searching for a target and holding formation with each other with their sonar.

If there was a submarine inside their square-mile search area, they would find it. That was almost guaranteed.

And finding it, they would converge on it from all directions, like the predators they were named after.

"CHILL CANNISTERS deployed, Captain," Singh said. "Every last one in our inventory."

"Very good, XO," Courtenay said. "Captain McDonald, I assume we need depth and separation."

"We do. You'll need to stay within illumination range but not so close you look like a better target."

"Helm, steer two four nine; make your depth 800, range to CHILL clouds a quarter mile maximum."

"Aye Captain," the boat driver said, repeating the order.

CHILL, or CHaff-ILLuminated jamming, was their best defense against small swarming undersea drones. Unlike the noisemakers or electronic warfare jamming decoys used against standard torpedoes, a CHILL cannister contained thousands of foil strips that were blasted into the water to form slowly spreading balls of sonar-reflecting decoys.

The reason McDonald urged Courtenay to deploy them early was to give them time to spread through the water to increase their area of effect.

Simple foil was not enough to fool the sonar aboard a modern weapon like the Piranha though. It could measure the Doppler effect, the shift in wavelength from the sonar return caused by the twisting foil, and eliminate the foil cloud as a valid target.

So *Agincourt* had to stay close enough to fire Doppler-correcting low-frequency radio energy at the chaff foil clouds—illuminate them—to make them appear to be a solid target a Piranha could fall in love with.

"Illuminating CHILL," Agincourt's EW specialist said.

"Anything else, Captain McDonald?" Courtenay asked.

"Yes," McDonald said. "Hold your dive. And pray."

A SCHOOL of four Piranhas had dropped right beside a CHILL cloud and picked it up as soon as they started descending.

Their onboard sonar suite looked at the return and classified it.

Decoy.

They turned away. Then they saw a second cloud, further down.

Decoy.

They kept descending. Another contact. Solid this time. Each Piranha sounded the target, classified it and compared its conclusion with the other Piranhas in the school.

Contact. Submarine.

Three turned immediately to intercept the target. The fourth turned away, using its sonar to signal the other Piranhas in the swarm to join the attack.

138

ABOARD *Agincourt*, the sonarman could only hear the high-pitched whine of the Piranha propellors as they converged.

"Cavitation. Piranhas closing," he said.

"On us or a CHILL cannister?" Courtenay asked tightly.

"Can't tell on passive sensors, sir," the sonarman said.

"Piranha doesn't have home-on-sonar capability," Courtenay's EW specialist said. "You can risk active sonar, sir."

Courtenay didn't hesitate. "Sonar, 15-second pulse down the bearing to that swarm."

"Aye, Captain," the sonarman said. The sound of their own sonar activating rang through the hull. "Contact. The swarm is going for the decoy. Shutting down sonar." They didn't want to keep ringing their bell in case another submarine nearby picked it up.

"Keep pushing deep," McDonald urged. "Don't assume success."

"Helm, depth?" Courtenay said.

"Four ninety feet, sir."

"Hold your dive."

"Diving to 600, sir, aye."

"Detonations on the bearing to the swarm!" the sonarman said. "Multiple!"

"*Deeper*," McDonald said, to himself this time.

SIXTEEN of 20 Piranhas closed on the CHILL cloud and exploded themselves within it, sending shrapnel into the water with their RDX explosive and creating superheated spheres of gas as the sodium hydroxide in their cylindrical bodies reacted with the water around it.

To the sonarman, it sounded like a ripple of cannon fire.

Four of the Piranhas, further away than the others, were a full minute behind the rest of their swarm, and their sonars saw only noise and confusion.

They aborted their attack and began circling again, looking for a more promising target.

Directly below them, they found it: at around 500 feet, the unmistakable sonar return of a large submarine. As one, they dropped their noses and began swimming toward it.

"FIVE FIFTY FEET, sir," the helmsman said.

"Make your depth 600 as ordered," Courtenay said.

"You are rated for 1,200 feet, correct?" McDonald asked.

"Classified, Captain, but thereabouts, yes," Courtenay said.

"Then steepen your dive and take us down, Captain," McDonald said. "This attack isn't over just because we heard a few explosions."

"Noted. Helm, make your depth 900."

The helmsman swallowed hard. "Depth 900, aye." He pushed forward on the aircraft-like yoke he used to steer *Agincourt*. The sound of more water flowing into their ballast tanks forward was like a waterfall in the stillness of the control room.

The Piranha school could travel through the water at 20 knots on standard power, or 30 knots with range-reducing burst power.

As they saw the target steepen its descent and start dropping away from them, they applied burst power and began speeding toward it.

At 600 feet depth, they were only 100 yards behind. Then 50 ... then 30 ...

"CAVITATION AGAIN. We have incoming," the sonarman said. "Impact imminent."

"XO, sound the warning; brace for impact."

Singh sent the impact warning through the boat.

UNLIKE *Agincourt*, the Piranha's small tubular body wasn't rated for depths beyond 600 feet, and they were already down at nearly 700.

The first of the four Piranhas folded as its body was crushed by water pressure, and seawater penetrated to its sodium hydroxide chamber. It dissolved in a ball of superheated gas.

The second Piranha followed almost immediately after.

"DETONATIONS AFT," the sonarman said. "Three ... no, four."

"What's our depth?" McDonald asked the helmsman.

"Eight hundred, sir," he replied.

"Then I guess we now know the crush depth for a Chinese Piranha munition," McDonald said.

"Helm, level out at 850 feet; maintain your heading, propulsion ahead standard."

The relief in the control room was palpable. The air had become thick with body heat and sweat.

"So, *that's* how it's done," Courtenay said. "XO, when you get a moment, you can write that up and send a memo to

141

Scapa." He gave McDonald a small salute, and a smiling McDonald returned it with an even smaller one.

The Battle of Hawaii: Battery Boyd

SEAMAN APPRENTICE Falaniko 'Niko' Akiu wasn't ready for the next attack. The idea of breaking cover down by the water to run for the World War II battery sucked three ways to midnight, but he didn't have a better idea.

He went first, up the verge, over the path and along the fence. No slaughterbot in sight, but he could hear one in the center of the island somewhere. The *whoosh* of a missile, the crump of something exploding over by the Aviation Museum. He hit the fence and ran around it, checking over his shoulder the girl was following. She was right behind him, easily as fast as he was.

He could see the gate in the fence as he rounded the shoulder of the mound. And see the big padlock and chain still threaded through it.

Whoever had been going to show the kids of Corner Canyon High around Battery Boyd hadn't made it there. And neither had the rest of the class.

Keep running, he told himself. There was a small residential area to their right, Community Center at the other end of it. He was about to veer that way when he saw the metal door to the battery swing open. "Padlock isn't locked! Get in here!" a croaky voice yelled. He saw a hand beckoning from inside the doorway.

He got to the gate and saw the chain holding it closed was held by a padlock that was still threaded between the two ends of the chain, but unlocked, the weight of the chain holding it in place. He tore it away and kicked the gate open.

As he did, he heard rotors.

"Machine!" the girl yelled, pointed down the road toward the Undersea Warfare Center, a tall, hangar-like building. A

143

cannon-armed slaughterbot was rounding the building. As though it saw them, it rose into the air and began moving their way.

"Quick, run!" Niko said. He threw himself down, pulled out the bipod and charged the handle, sighting on the drone, which was about 100 yards away. Squeezing the trigger, he sent a two-second burst toward the drone. Maybe he clipped it, maybe he didn't. He sent it whirring up into the air.

And it opened up with its 20 mm cannon.

Niko was already on his feet again. With cannon rounds fountaining dirt into his wake, he made the open doorway and stumbled inside. He heard the door slam behind him.

Rolling onto his back, he saw a figure in blue overalls throw a metal bar across the door to lock it and then step back a few steps. They both waited for 20 mm cannon rounds to start hammering into the metal, but they didn't come.

The man edged forward again to a viewing port beside the door.

"What's it doing?" the girl asked from behind Niko.

"Just hovering out there, gun pointed right at the door," the man said. He turned around to Niko. "It's one of those Chinese things?"

"I'm guessing," Niko said, getting to his feet and dusting himself down.

"How long their batteries last?"

Niko could see the man now. He looked old enough to have served inside Battery Boyd once. Like in World War II. "Don't know. I'm guessing it will run out of ammunition before it runs out of juice though."

Niko looked around. They had electricity; that something. The corridor went back about 20 feet, then just in

144

front of one of the old gun emplacements doglegged right, where, if he remembered right, there were five or six former storage rooms for powder and shells.

"Presley!" a voice yelled. "Is that you?" A woman in a dark-gray leggings and a bloodied Corner Canyon polo shirt came barreling around the corner, stopped to focus on the girl, then rushed her and pulled her into a bear hug.

They both started crying.

Niko looked at the old man. "How many did you get inside?"

"I found her outside, with one of the girls," he said. "Kid has been hit in the leg. No idea where the rest are."

POLICE OFFICER TAMMY BALLARD was 38 years old and a mother of three girls, all of whom played soccer. Her oldest was 18 and drove herself to her games these days, thank heavens. The other two, ages 14 and 12, couldn't though, and Tammy's weekends were taken up ferrying her kids and their friends to games across Honolulu, which, because she was also assistant coach for one of the teams, meant she usually flopped onto her couch at the end of a busy Saturday desperate for a beer and for someone else to make dinner.

Like that was going to happen.

So it was almost a relief when she was asked to work a weekend shift. A guilty relief since she always felt like she was letting her girls down, but their dad wasn't able to pick up the slack.

He was Honolulu PD too, like Tammy. And right now, he was downtown, in the thick of whatever shit was going on there. She could see the smoke, hear explosions, even from

145

their roadblock up on Kamehameha Highway just outside Pearl. They had their patrol car parked broadside across the highway's eastbound lanes. They were redirecting traffic back west, away from Pearl. Across the railway tracks that ran down the middle of the highway, another patrol was redirecting westbound traffic, sending it north.

It was amazing how many dumbasses had no idea what was going down. No one listened to radio anymore; she was learning that.

"What do you mean, civil emergency?" the guy in a pickup that had just pulled up to her was asking. "I don't pick my wife up from work in 10 minutes, there's going to be a civil emergency, ma'am, you'd better believe me."

She put on her don't-mess-with-me voice. "Sir, the governor has declared an emergency. You turn south at this exit, go home, or if you can't get home, you get to an emergency assembly point. I can't ..."

Shouting, farther down the line of cars. *Oh, give me a break*, Tammy thought, looking up from the guy's window. She heard tires crunching on the rough concrete of the breakdown lane, and she saw a group of SUV drivers all break from the long line and start accelerating toward their patrol car, using the breakdown lane.

She narrowed her eyes. Five SUVs and a pickup, moving in fast trail, like a convoy. Ten years on the force gave you a sense of when things felt wrong. And this felt six kinds of wrong.

"Tony, trouble coming!" she called to her partner doing the traffic at the other end of their vehicle. She stepped back from the pickup. "Get out of here, sir," she said. He looked like he wanted to argue some more, but she drew her weapon, held it so he could see it and yelled at him. "Now!" His truck jumped forward with a squeal of tires and he did an awkward U-turn.

Moving behind the hood of her patrol car, Tammy watched the approaching SUVs. Her partner got behind the trunk, drawing his weapon too.

The lead SUV was 50 yards away now. Jet black, tinted windows.

"Government, you think?" Tony asked. He was a kid in his early 20s. Just two years on the force, both of them in traffic.

"No, I don't think," Tammy said, instincts jangling. "Safety off."

Time dilated. It did that, in Tammy's experience. She'd been inside a vehicle when it rolled once. Hit a concrete barrier during a pursuit and just flipped. She remembered every second of that crash like it was a minute. Grabbing the dash so she didn't go through the windshield. Air bags deploying, slamming her back into her seat. Passenger window exploding in a shower of glass. The sparks as they skidded across the road upside down. All in slow motion. A trauma psych told her it was the adrenaline surge that did that.

It did that now.

The SUVs were 20 yards away. The one in the lead, windows dark. Then the two behind it, one moving slightly left, the other right. Ready to pass them on either side. Not slowing down. Their patrol car couldn't cover both lanes, so they had it parked nose into one lane, ass across the other. Plenty of room to go around them. Too much room.

Rehearsed, she thought. *That looks rehearsed.*

"Get my shotgun from the trunk," Tammy yelled to Tony. He looked at her like she was crazy. "Do it!"

On the radio earlier that day, Tammy's husband had told her Pearl was under attack by Chinese drones. "They're wasting anything that moves, Tammy," he'd said, shocked. "Not just military. It's a bloodbath here."

Tammy Ballard wasn't only a police officer. She was also Hawaii Army National Guard, having done three years out of college before going Ready Reserve when she got the job in Honolulu PD. She'd only done one combat tour, but she'd been called out to wildfires, pandemic control, landslides, you name it.

Tammy Ballard knew trouble when she saw it, especially when it was headed straight at her at 60 miles an hour.

She holstered her pistol as Tony came up from the trunk. "Shotgun!" she called out. "Toss it."

He lobbed the weapon and she snatched it out of the air. A lot of officers had their own long weapons, but Tammy liked the standard-issue Benelli M5 semi-auto. No stock, just a pistol grip. She kept it loaded, and worked the charging handle.

The lead SUV was 10 yards away now, not slowing. She could see two shapes inside, driver and passenger side. She took one last look at the three SUVs in the vanguard. One swung farther left, the other two right.

"Down! Get down," she yelled at Tony, and ducked down, back against her front tire.

"THEY MADE US," Pan decided a hundred yards out. He saw the two officers jerk their heads up and reach for their weapons.

"Maybe the last roadblock radioed ahead," Pi guessed, pistol between his legs, pointing at the floor.

148

Maybe, but how? Pan wondered. They'd killed everyone. Maybe the soldiers they'd passed? It didn't matter.

"Long gun!" Pan said, one hand on the wheel, lifting his pistol. He saw the female officer grab a shotgun out of the air and work the action. There was still clear road either side of the patrol car, and he stuck with his original decision. They were still at least 10 miles from their objective. This was a fight they didn't need to take. He aimed the vehicle at the gap on the left side of the roadblock.

"Liberator Squad, tangos are armed and alert. We are running this roadblock; don't dismount," Pan ordered. He turned to Pi. "Shoot as we pass."

TAMMY HEARD the whine of electric engines accelerating, and the rumble of tires.

In seconds, the lead SUV was alongside and then blowing past. The passenger had a pistol aimed at them and Tammy ducked. But he didn't fire.

She could have stayed back up against the front wheel, let the convoy pass, left it for someone else to deal with.

But that wasn't Tammy Ballard.

There was no time to really aim. She lifted the barrel of her shotgun, aiming it around waist height, and jerked her trigger finger.

The blast smacked into the back of the disappearing black SUV, and the next vehicle was already coming alongside. Dirt and dust kicked up into a cloud around her and she closed her eyes, shotgun pointed sideways, firing as fast as she could pull the trigger.

She got her last shot away as the last vehicle, a pickup with what looked like a bunch of road workers in back, blasted past her.

Road workers with AR15s, looks like. One was on his ass, with his rifle resting on the back gate of the pickup. He ripped off a burst that stitched across their patrol car a half yard from Tammy's shoulder, working its way down the car to where Tony was crouched.

The burst cut across him from left hip to right shoulder, slamming him into the body of the patrol car. Tammy dropped her shotgun and scrambled over to him.

"I'm alright," he said, gasping, trying to sit up. "I think. Body armor took it all."

"Let me check you," Tammy said. She shot a glance down the highway at the disappearing convoy of SUVs. She'd emptied her shotgun at point-blank range. At least two SUVs and the pickup had passed her while she was firing. She'd hit the first one but then missed *every one* of the others?

"LIBERATOR ONE, Liberator Four is shot in the neck. It's bad. We need to stop or he'll bleed out."

Pan cursed. "We don't stop. You know that. Do what you need to."

"Understood."

Pan looked in his mirror, Pi with an arm over his headrest, craning to look behind. They'd rehearsed what to do in the event of én-route casualties too.

They didn't hear the shot, but Pan saw the door of the SUV behind them ease open, and a body tumbled out onto the highway. The cars following swerved around it as it tumbled untidily along the road.

Pan set his jaw. "*We* didn't kill him. That female cop killed Four because you let her. You still going to be squeamish about doing what needs to be done, Corporal?"

Pi looked pale. "No, Sergeant."

Pan checked his speed. The highway ahead into the city was clear. He put his foot down, pushing the speedometer through 80 miles an hour while the going was good. Pan switched back to English. "Alright. We're 20 minutes out, plus minus. We can let our contacts know we're inbound. Make the call."

TAMMY PULLED Tony forward, checking his back. The front of his ballistic vest was torn up, and he was having trouble sucking wind, but she couldn't see any bleeding.

She jumped up and pulled him up with her. From the trunk she pulled some traffic cones and threw them on the ground. "You stay here, put these down, keep turning the traffic around, get your breath back," she said, pulling the passenger door open. "I'll call this in."

"You think I should get to hospital?" he asked, still feeling himself gingerly under his vest. "Seriously, I feel …"

"We're not taking you to the hospital, Tony. You're staying here and turning traffic around. I'll get you backup, then I'm going after those asshats." She picked up her shotgun, hauled the driver's door open, slid into the seat and powered the patrol car on. She spun the wheel and grabbed her radio. "Dispatch, this is Unit 490, Kamehameha Highway by Waimelu Stream …" The wheels skidded then bit into the road as she accelerated east, leaving her partner standing in the road, scratching his head. "In pursuit of a convoy of SUVs that broke our roadblock. Shots fired. Perps in a green pickup are heavily armed and dangerous. Officer hit; requesting support at our patrol position, including a paramedic. We need another roadblock up ahead on the eastbound, maybe by the Dixie Grill if there are any units in the area ..."

She was looking ahead of her, trying to spot that damned pickup. It was *bright green*, how hard could it be to ...

No, what?

She saw the body just in time. It was lying right across her lane. She swung the wheel, snaking around it, fighting as the car threatened to skid and getting it back under control. In her mirror, she saw a dark lump on the ground, receding.

Unmoving.

Was that me? she wondered. *Did I hit one of them after all? Or did those lunatics hit a pedestrian?* She picked up her radio handset and called it in.

She felt bile rising up from her gut and stuck her head out her window, sucking in a lungful of air. What a day. The dispatcher on her radio again, telling her there were no patrols available, asking dumb questions. She tuned it out. No way anyone was going to be able to block the highway outside the city before these guys reached the Stadium exit. They could go three ways from there, but she figured she knew where they were headed. Retail stores. She figured the convoy for looters, headed downtown in the chaos to see what they could grab up.

She focused on the road ahead again and floored her gas pedal. She patted her hip to be sure her pistol was still there. Shotgun on the seat beside her; she'd have to reload that. Shells in back. She could have taken the side-saddle shotgun card and saved herself the trouble of messing around in her trunk looking for ammunition, but no. "If you need more than six rounds, you're in a war, not fighting crime, right?" she'd told the station armorer.

Irony much?

She ground her teeth and clenched the wheel tight. She'd take Vineyard to Waikiki, start looking there.

Oh, I'm going to find you a-holes, and I am going to bring the pain.

SEAMAN APPRENTICE Falaniko 'Niko' Akiu was a firefighter. OK, trainee firefighter. He'd told the girl he was no Marine and he knew just carrying a gun didn't make him one. So as soon as he got inside the battery, he put the gun down so people wouldn't get any ideas. Plus, it was heavy.

The girls' teacher took them to a room deeper inside the battery that looked like some kind of caretaker's cubby hole: a locker, a desk with an ancient PC on it, table and chair with a thermos of coffee and a single cup. And a cot, for taking "rest breaks."

On the cot, a girl, jeans bloodied from the knee down, arm over her face, crying.

"This guy is a firefighter," the girl, Presley, told her teacher. She turned to Niko. "You can help her, right?"

The old curator, the teacher, the girl Presley—they all stood there looking at him.

Niko was no Marine and not a paramedic. His medical training so far had been little more than an extended first aid course. So when he saw all the blood, and started to feel faint, he suddenly thought maybe he wasn't much of a firefighter either.

He kneeled down beside the girl, looking at her leg without touching. *Think, Niko.* Over his shoulder he said, "I need scissors. Clean water. A first aid kit. You can't find a

first aid kit, start tearing up some clean cloth for bandages."
No one was moving. "Scissors," he said to the curator.
"Now!"

The old man finally moved, jumping to his desk, where he
pulled a drawer open and came out with some big heavy
scissors.

"Perfect," Niko said, taking them. "First aid kit,
bandages."

He put a hand on the girl's arm by her shoulder. "What's
your name?"

The girl pulled her arm away, looking at him with
unfocused eyes. "It hurts."

"I know. I'm just going to take a look, OK?"

She didn't reply. Kid was in shock.

He dug one blade of the scissors into her jeans, and then
slid the blade down her leg, chomping through the hem by
her ankle. Then he peeled it back, like a banana.

Thank God. She hadn't taken the slaughterbot's shell
directly in her leg. He doubted she'd even have a leg if she
had. Shrapnel—maybe the shell broke up and hit her. Her
calf was flayed, several big deep cuts, blood pulsing from the
wounds but not squirting. He was no doctor, but he figured
she needed the wounds cleaned and sewn up. That could wait.
For now he would just flush them and bandage her up.

The curator returned with a first aid kit that contained
bandages and sterile saline in a squeeze bottle.

He looked up at the teacher. "I don't see broken bones.
Her bleeding is bad but not dangerous, so we're going to
clean these cuts and bandage her up. Sit with her, hold her
hand," he said. "This is going to hurt."

The woman nodded and sat. "It's OK, Denice. You'll be
OK."

Niko heard more gunfire outside the bunker and winced. *Yeah, or maybe none of us are.*

WHEN THE GIRL'S leg was bandaged and she was sitting up and crying softly on her friend Presley's shoulder, he went to the teacher and the curator.

"I need to find the rest of my class," the teacher said, looking toward the exit. "They're out there somewhere."

"How many?" Niko asked.

"Four more. Some of the girls were still playing in the tournament, so we took the ones who were already finished on a field trip."

Niko thought about the people he'd seen mown down between houses up by the wreck of the *Utah*. Adults, but also some teenagers. He shook the thought away. "They probably ran for the bridge," he said, trying to sound convincing. "Might have made it off the island already."

The teacher pulled out her phone and checked it. "I tried calling them. There's no signal."

"First thing the bots would go for," he told her. "Cell repeaters. Power relays."

"I have to look for them," she insisted.

The comment coincided with the ripping sound of a long burst of autocannon fire, not far away.

"Anything that moves out there is a target," he told her. "If they're in cover, if they stay where they are, they'll be OK."

"You don't know that, son," the curator said.

Niko felt like clocking him. "You want to go out there, old man?"

The curator raised his hands. "You said it, I'm an old man. You're the firefighter."

The teacher gave him a pleading look. Presley was looking at him too. *Ah, hell.* "Alright, I'll go. But if I find them, I'll get them somewhere safe and tell them to keep their heads down. I'm not bringing them back here."

"Alright, alright," the teacher said. "They'll be wearing the same shirt as Presley."

He looked at her. It was a nondescript blue polo. Great. "Right. Cool," he said, not feeling it.

Something exploded, but it sounded like it was a ways off. Maybe the fighting had moved somewhere else?

Now or never, Niko, he told himself.

How about never? A voice replied.

But he was moving out into the corridor and picking up the XM250 with a grunt. The teacher and curator followed him out.

"What's your name?" the teacher asked him.

"Niko," he said, hefting the weapon in both hands. "Niko Akiu."

"God bless you, Niko Akiu," she said. "For bringing Presley to us, for helping Denice, and for doing this."

It was the kind of thing his own church-going ma would have said. "Uh, you're welcome, ma'am."

He went to the doorway and pressed himself up against it, risking a peek outside through the port.

The slaughterbot that had been hovering out there had moved on. He heard someone call for help. Should he check that out first?

You can't help everyone on Ford Island, Niko. You go find those girls. See if you can't do that without getting killed.

He unbolted the door, pulled it back quickly and rolled out of the doorway, running for the nearest building.

Slamming into the wall, he took a breath, turned to look around the corner, then heard footsteps behind him. He whirled to see Presley slap into the wall beside him.

"Uh-uh, *no way*, Charger," he said.

"Uh-huh, yeah," the girl insisted. "You don't know where to look, or who to look for. Besides, you forgot this." She held up the first aid kit.

He felt like yelling at her. Was she worried he wasn't going to do like he promised? He didn't have time to argue.

"Stay behind me; move when I say," he told her. Looked around the corner. *Clear.* "Now!"

The Rearguard: Under Taichung

JENSEN REGISTERED the death of his rifleman with a pain deep in his gut, then heard the thudding feet of the surviving Marine growing louder as he approached the corner. The Marine leaped over the anti-tank rifle gunners to bounce off the wall and fall into the tunnel beside Jensen, his rifle clattering to the ground.

"I ... did we get it?" he asked, massaging his shoulder as he rose to one knee and retrieved his rifle.

The sound of rotors had stilled, and Jensen's hopes rose, then fell again as he heard the buzz-saw whine start up again.

"No. Plan B," Jensen said. "Ready on the NTV," he ordered his gun crew. "I'm sending the dogs in attack mode. Take the shot first chance you get." The 20 mm NTV had a three-round magazine, but Jensen doubted his rifleman would get the chance for a second shot.

Crouching behind the prone rifleman, Jensen used his monocle to lay a crosshair on the ground beside the fallen Marine. He wasn't moving, and the pool of blood spreading from underneath him told Jensen he was probably beyond rescue. Tapping a pressure pad on his helmet, he directed their three remaining dogs to move to the waypoint he'd set—in targeted attack mode.

The sound of rotors screaming was so loud it set Jensen's teeth on edge.

Their dogs weren't armed—they'd deployed with manual manipulator claws on their robotic necks to help with loading the supplies they were supposed to retrieve—but they could jump, rip and tear at whatever Jensen ordered them to.

If they got the chance.

THE SLAUGHTERBOT approached the corner where it had seen the attacker. There was no sign of them now, and no follow-up attack. But it was not programmed to hope for the best. It assumed the worst—that its attackers were still alive and waiting to attack again, just around the next corner.

It brought its gun up, checked the belt feed mechanism was not jammed by running it backward and forward a couple of rounds, and then aimed the barrel so that it would fire about waist high on a human at close range.

As it rounded the corner, it started firing two-round bursts, causing concrete chips and dust to fly into the corridor beyond.

JENSEN HEARD the autocannon opening up again, flinched as HE rounds began chewing into the wall ahead, saw the dark silhouette of the slaughterbot through dust and smoke.

He put the crosshairs on the shadow in the haze, and tapped his helmet trigger pad twice.

LS3-9 'SQUIRT' was the rearmost of the three dogs. If it had been a real dog, it would have been salivating at the thought it had been released in attack mode.

All it needed was a target.

And it got one.

The wall about 5 yards ahead of it exploded, clouding the corridor with smoke and dust. It lost the ability to focus its optics and switched to infrared, waiting for its cue.

Now it came.

A glowing shadow in the smoke, the targeting cue dancing over it. It locked the shadow, saw its brothers rising, charging at the shape. Twenty-millimeter shells began chewing down the wall toward it.

Squirt raised and opened the claw at the end of his actuator and prepared to launch himself at the target. His two brothers were already moving.

Close. Strike. Grip. Tear.

JENSEN HAD the video feed from the three dogs on his monocle and was crouched around the wall, out of the slaughterbot's line of fire.

The LS3 system had been developed further in the years since Jensen worked with prototypes in Syria. They could perform more missions now, their robotic arms capable of using more weapon types, and of much more complex movements. There was even a combat surgery model that could cauterize wounds and stem bleeding on the battlefield.

They were also able to work together, like a pack. Jensen didn't need to tell each of them what to do; he just had to point to the target and order them to attack. They worked out the rest among themselves.

The video feed jerked as the LS3s propelled themselves toward the slaughterbot like a pack of wolves, one on the left, one on the right, one up the middle. On flat, level ground, these models could go from a standing start to 40 miles an hour in five seconds—faster than an Olympic sprinter.

At the same time, the man lying prone behind the anti-tank rifle sent a 20 mm round downrange.

THE CHINESE Tianyi drone had anticipated there would be an attack and gamed the different scenarios it might face. An attack by a pack of kamikaze robot dogs was not among those scenarios. But its AI was flexible enough that it didn't need an exact ID on the threats it was facing to know they were a threat—just as a human child didn't need to wait for a crocodile to attack before they realized all those teeth meant it was probably *not* friendly.

Its cannon was already firing two-round bursts as it rounded the corner, so it simply trained its sights on the closest dog and hammered it into junk metal before moving its aim to the next.

Its millimeter radar picked up the incoming anti-tank round, and again, it angled its carapace toward the threat. The round ricocheted off the ceramic shield and into the tunnel roof.

With millisecond precision, the slaughterbot knocked out a second LS3, then sent six HE rounds toward the infrared blob at the end of the corridor, which was the human shooter.

Then, with clinical silicon equanimity, it turned its gun on the final threat, the last wildly charging robotic dog.

SQUIRT SAW his brothers go down, smashed to junk metal by the slaughterbot's autocannon. He saw the Chinese drone fire past him, at a target behind him, then swing its cannon barrel back toward him.

He didn't react with anger or fear. He had mission orders, and his only thought was to execute them.

But just as he closed within attack range, preparing to leap at the slaughterbot, his left rear leg hydraulics failed, and he lurched left, momentarily losing his lock on the target before he could reroute power to his remaining rear leg.

The sudden lateral movement caused the slaughterbot's volley to miss, hammering into the ground where Squirt had been headed, not where he was now.

Squirt pushed off from his remaining rear leg, not rising as high as he could have but still going airborne at 36 miles an hour, like a cornerback trying to take out a wide receiver.

JENSEN HUGGED the wall around the corner from the oncoming slaughterbot as 20 mm shells slammed into his prone rifleman, sending the man's body tumbling into the wall at the back of the tunnel as his spotter fell backward on his ass and crabbed away in shock.

In his monocle, the video feed from two more dogs turned to static as they were erased too.

"Frags ready!" Jensen shouted to his two remaining men, pulling a grenade from a pocket on his tactical vest. "Throw on my command." Fragmentation grenades had already failed once to disable the Chinese drone, but since assault rifles were also useless, he had no better option.

He moved up to the blood-covered corner and readied his throw ...

Then he saw the video feed from Squirt was still live. With parkour-like agility that Jensen didn't know the dog possessed, it dodged left, evading a withering burst of fire from the slaughterbot, then launched itself off one leg and straight at the bot's underbelly.

Jensen risked a look around the corner, just in time to see Squirt latch onto the pylon that held the slaughterbot's autocannon. The cannon sprayed wildly, but Squirt was under

162

the bot now, and holding tight. With 100 lbs. of determined dog hanging underneath, the slaughterbot could no longer stay airborne and crashed to the ground with Squirt underneath it.

Squirt released his grip on the cannon pylon and plunged his claw deep into the lighter armored underside of the Chinese drone, until he had reached as far as he could, and then grabbed and pulled whatever his claw had just closed on.

Realizing it was no longer combat capable, the Tianyi drone triggered its auto-destruct sequence, but Squirt didn't notice. He was a simple machine with simple orders to execute.

Strike. Grip. Tear.

Mangled wiring and circuit boards came free, and he twisted his claw and plunged it in again.

JENSEN SAW the slaughterbot stagger and drop, Squirt disappearing from view underneath it. It stopped firing, and two of its rotors died. He reached for his helmet pad, tapping a quick sequence of commands.

Abort attack. Form on me.

He knew a wounded slaughterbot would explode about 30 seconds after it hit the ground. He gave Squirt about a five percent chance of getting out from under the slaughterbot before it did.

Make that one percent, he thought, as the dog wrestled its way from beneath the Chinese drone but then began limping on three legs back down the tunnel toward him.

It only got about halfway before the slaughterbot detonated.

163

HAVING YOUR OWN pet slaughterbot took some getting used to, Xu decided. Even if it was called Fluffy. The nerve-racking buzz of its rotors got up inside your skull, like a saw on sinew. Every instinct told him to hide, and the sight of it made his skin crawl.

He kept expecting it to suddenly wake from its induced slumber and turn on them.

Lieutenant Chang mastered the job of flying it pretty quickly. The girl, Fi, was confident she could also give him control of its gun, if she were given time, but Jackson was happy enough they could use it for recon. They kept it out ahead of them about a mile, scouting intersections and the alleyways and narrow roads between warehouses and apartments.

It did a good job of clearing civilian foot and vehicle traffic too. One look at it sent the few vehicles they encountered fleeing, and its buzz-saw whine had pedestrians diving for the nearest doorway.

They met two more slaughterbots on the way. One was being attacked by a swarm of killer bees, indicating there was a Taiwan Army defense unit still operating in the area. Jackson got them on his tactical radio and convinced them his slaughterbot wasn't a target, which he proved by flying it right over the top of their trike.

Xu hated that little demonstration.

The next slaughterbot was waiting in ambush at a road junction, rotors powered down so that it could conserve energy, rest on the ground and keep a low profile while still scanning the terrain around it. It was a missile-armed variant, and its underslung box magazine allowed it to sit easily on level ground. Xu hadn't seen a slaughterbot do that before, but the damned things were learning new tricks every day.

The sight of their own slaughterbot entering the intersection triggered it to life, which was when they first noticed it, as it powered up and rose into the air, moving closer as though greeting a long-lost friend.

As he carefully assembled his rifle and chambered a round, Xu tried to imagine the Chinese slaughterbot's confusion as it tried to communicate with their hobbled pet.

He and Jackson worked around behind the bobbing Chinese drone, which was circling their tame slaughterbot.

"Like it's trying to work out what the hell is wrong," Jackson said as Xu settled himself, legs splayed, cheek against the rifle stock. Jackson was looking at the slaughterbot through a monocular with an inbuilt ballistic calculator.

"Read off the wind direction and speed for me, will you, Sergeant?" Xu asked him, dialing in his sight but wanting a second opinion. "They communicate with laser pulses. I think it's just trying different angles to see if it can get a comms link."

Jackson grunted, then read off the data from his scope.

Two hundred yards. No wind to speak of. Humidity 93 percent. Easy shot. Xu pulled back the bolt on his rifle.

As though struck by a stone, the drone reacted to the mechanical *snick*. Its magazine whirled around to face them, and Xu could see the rounded noses of nine Hongjian missiles coming to bear on their position.

He fired at the missile magazine, the most vulnerable part of the drone. The bullet hit home.

"Down!" Jackson yelled, as multiple things happened simultaneously. A missile speared toward them from the slaughterbot. The drone rocked from the impact of Xu's .50

165

BMG round, but the magazine didn't explode, as he'd hoped. He quickly chambered another round and fired at the magazine again. The Chinese missile screamed over their heads and impacted against the wall of a building 20 yards behind.

Xu's second bullet found the warhead of one of the remaining eight Hongjian missiles and the resulting explosion sent it spinning into the ground, out of control. It hit the road hard, landing upside down.

"Move our bot away!" Jackson yelled back to the pilot, Chang, still sitting on the trike. The tame slaughterbot rose into the air like it was on a rocket-propelled elevator, then began sliding away from the intersection. Chang turned the trike around and moved it, and the girl Fi, around the corner. Jackson and Xu retreated too, crabbing backward from their shooting position.

With a muffled *crack*, the Chinese slaughterbot self-destructed, hot metal and ceramic flying in every direction, shattering nearby windows and flaying shopfront billboards.

Xu stood. "Damn things can kill you even after they're dead," he said.

"Probably sent out a mayday too," Jackson muttered. "We better keep moving."

THEY MADE the outskirts of Taipei about five in the evening. The city was eerily quiet. Smoke rose from still-burning buildings and piles of garbage in the streets. The authorities had managed to distribute body bags for virus victims, but the system for collecting the bodies seemed to have collapsed, or been abandoned. Bagged bodies were piled in alleyways beside overflowing dumpsters, some bloated

166

from the release of gases by the decomposing bodies inside. The only civilians they saw were either rummaging through looted shops and supermarkets or scurrying from doorway to doorway before disappearing again. Like everywhere else they'd been in the company of their tame slaughterbot, the sight and sound of it emptied the streets around them.

Looking around her, eyes wide, the girl, Fi, whistled. "This is some seriously post-apocalyptic shit."

Near their objective they found themselves a parking garage between two deserted office buildings and set up camp. Chang landed the slaughterbot beside their trike, one level down, out of sight of drones or satellites.

Jumping off the baggage tray, Fi pulled a backpack off her shoulders and lifted a tablet PC and cables out.

"You want me to see if I can give you control of the gun?" she asked Chang.

"If you can do it without blowing us all away, yes," Chang said.

She rolled her eyes. "It's just *code*," she said. "I'll let you know if I think it will work and we can test it somewhere safe."

"I guess that's alright."

She sat down cross-legged beside the slaughterbot and joined the tablet to it with a cable. Then she looked up at Chang again. "Its battery is only at 20 percent. We need to find power. It will take all night to charge."

Chang got on Jackson's radio to alert the city's ROC Taiwan Army defenders to the slaughterbot they had riding shotgun with them but was unable to reach anyone on the Taiwan military radio net. He tried police, fire brigade, even ambulance services, on open frequency VHF. Apart from a frightened police sergeant holed up with a few of his men at an inner urban station nearby, they got no response. And the police officer they reached was more interested in being evacuated than in providing any information or assistance.

"I've got 10 men here, about 50 family members, food for maybe three days, no running water, no medicine, and we're surrounded by looters," he said, desperation in his voice. "We're going to try to make it to the port. We hear the Americans are offering protection. Their troopship is still docked there."

Jackson nodded after Chang translated. "The USS *Bougainville*, with a couple of *Constellation* class frigates for air and anti-submarine support. It was hit in the first days of the war, propulsion damaged, but it arrived full of supplies." He held out his hand. "Give me the radio. I might be able to get a sitrep from the Navy."

He worked the radio for a few minutes and then had a conversation with someone at the other end in rapid-fire English, which Xu and Chang struggled to follow. He signed off and handed the radio back to Chang.

"US and ROC Navy still control the port at Keelung where *Bougainville* is docked. Captain, I talked to said they've locked down a perimeter of about 10 square miles around the port, which they're keeping slaughterbot-free with Stingers and killer bees," Jackson told them. "They're getting some supplies air-dropped, and they're taking in women, children, wounded without virus symptoms and ROC Armed Forces personnel, but turning away male civilians. They've got a quarantine station set up on *Bougainville* that they're cycling people through. Like the Lieutenant said, China doesn't have air superiority over Taiwan. Our fighters out of Japan and the Philippines are keeping them at bay. But they're still landing slaughterbots up and down the coast and trying to sneak cruise and ballistic missiles through to hit our forces inside Keelung and Kaohsiung, where most of the surviving US forces have dug in."

"Any good news?" Chang asked.

"Well, the attacks are getting lighter every day. China suffering from missile hunger maybe. My guy said the theory is China has drawn its missile stockpile so low it needs to hold back to build it up again."

"What about our government? Our forces?" Xu asked.

"Your government is expected to surrender anytime in the next few days," Jackson said. "Your forces—what's left—have been ordered to return to barracks by your premier. Your president and vice president haven't been seen in public for a week."

"Except by you," Chang remarked.

"I never saw them," Jackson said. "A US intelligence officer gave me my orders. And the letter I showed you."

"So it could be *fake*," Xu said. "We don't know it's real."

"I don't know if the signatures are real or not, but my orders are." He crouched, reached into his backpack and pulled out a couple of MRE packs, throwing one to Xu and opening the other himself.

Xu looked at it skeptically. Chili beans, creamed corn and crackers. The pack date was eight years earlier, and the last inspection stamp was three years old. He wrinkled his nose but tore the pack open. The girl looked over at him hopefully, and he pulled out a plastic-wrapped pack of brownies and threw it to her. If she didn't die from eating the brownies, he might try heating the beans.

Chang was still standing, arms crossed, looking down at the Marine. "We got you to Taipei like you asked. I think it is time you shared what your mission is," Chang told Jackson.

Jackson took something else from his backpack and laid it on the ground next to him. A Sig Sauer M18 handgun. He wasn't holding it, but he kept his hand near it and gave Chang a wry smile. "The mission is very simple. Before he can issue his emergency decree and invite China to come strolling into Taiwan, we are going to assassinate your skunk of a premier."

SHOWING SHE understood a lot more English than she was letting on, the girl, Fi, looked up sharply. "*What?*"

Xu saw Jackson's hand edge toward the pistol beside him, as he waited for Chang's reaction. Chang still had his arms crossed, and if the Marine's announcement surprised him, he didn't show it. He was ignoring Jackson's pistol too. "When I went to your country to qualify on the F-22, I read a book about the JFK assassination."

"Which is relevant how? Beyond the obvious," Jackson asked.

"It was called *Patsy*," Chang said. He turned to Xu, who had stopped investigating the MRE pack and was following their conversation attentively. "Unless I am very much mistaken, Corporal Xu there is your patsy."

"Me? What's a patsy?" Xu asked.

"Someone who is set up to take the blame for a crime," Chang told him. "Like, say, I don't know … the assassination of the Premier of Taiwan."

"Should I take that little observation to mean you are withdrawing your cooperation, Lieutenant?" Jackson asked.

Chang eyed the pistol now. "No. You can put your sidearm away, Sergeant. I just think the Corporal should go into this mission aware of the possible consequences."

"What consequences?" Xu asked.

170

"He's saying if you are the trigger man, you'll be forever known as the soldier who killed Premier Ko En-Le," Jackson explained. "You won't be able to stay anonymous."

"So I'll get a medal," Xu said.

"*If* your mission is truly sanctioned by our legitimate president, Corporal. More likely, you'll get shot by a firing squad," Chang corrected him. "Along with the rest of us, when China takes Taiwan."

"*If*, Lieutenant," Jackson said. "If China takes Taiwan. My mission, our mission, is to stop your rogue premier from inviting China to fly troops in here under the cover of a medical red cross, offering to vaccinate people against the virus *they* released."

Chang was not convinced, the color rising in his cheeks as he replied. "And *then* what, Sergeant? Are the president and vice president even alive? Why don't they show themselves? And say you do assassinate the premier—what is to stop Chinese troops landing and taking control anyway? If we have any troops left guarding the landing beaches, they will be sick, weak and easily outnumbered. Your compatriots, those still alive, are besieged in their bases and on their ships. Your Air Force *barely* has control of our skies. Your Navy is either trapped in port or hiding in the waters of Japan and the Philippines."

Jackson didn't appear perturbed by the outburst. "Well, see, Lieutenant, I'm a West Virginian born in a holler, and we're simple folk. The Man told me to kill that sumbitch Premier Ko, so we'll kill him, and then I'll ask the Man for another mission. The question of 'then what' will take care of itself, I reckon."

Xu stood. "I'm a simple man too. If my country wants me to be a patsy, I'll be a patsy."

171

Chang sighed. "God help us."

Jackson looked at his team: a pessimistic pilot, an overly optimistic shooter, a kid with mad cyber skills and a pet slaughterbot. It gave him options he hadn't planned for, and it wasn't even complete yet.

He looked at his watch. The last two members of their team should be joining any time now.

SERGEANT JAMES JENSEN lost two men to the slaughterbot breach. The swarming attack on the hangars, combined with two other breaches in other sectors, cost the defenders of Taichung 11 dead and 15 wounded.

Not that it compared, but Jensen also lost three of his LS3s and his fourth, the unkillable Squirt, had a dead leg and had to be carried to the electronics depot for refitting. That meant they'd had to hump the pallet of supplies from the middle of the airfield back to their central stores bunker using a couple of dollies pulled by hand.

Jensen had gone to check on the repairs. He was discussing Squirt's persistent hydraulic leak with a technical specialist when his CO, a captain who had been in the South China Sea with Jensen, and who had also survived a course of H5N1c since arriving on Taiwan, walked into the depot.

"Officer on deck," Jensen announced, standing to.

"At ease," the captain said, motioning to Jensen to join him.

This can't be good, Jensen thought. *I'm either in trouble, or about to be.*

"Sorry for your losses, Gunny," the captain said in greeting. "They were good men."

"They were, sir."

He looked over at the technician at the workstation festooned with wires, grapples and beeping machines, like a dry dock for a robot. "That's the dog that took down the slaughterbot? How's it looking?"

"We'll get it mobile again, sir," Jensen promised. "Or, as mobile as it's ever been. What's up, Captain?"

Jensen knew the man was not one to varnish the truth. "Gunny, I have a job I can't ask a man to do with a clear conscience, and you don't have the luxury to refuse."

Jensen just nodded. "Sir."

"I need you to get yourself north to Taipei, meet up with a sergeant from 8th Marines, name of Jackson. I've been asked to send him our best robotics operator, and an LS3, so that's you." The captain looked over at Squirt. "And your dog there, since that slaughterbot took out the other two."

Jensen heard what the captain was saying, but more importantly what he wasn't. "What's the mission, sir?"

The captain told him the bare bones. "Jackson will fill you in with the finer details when you join him. And about that ... I won't sugarcoat it. Taipei is H5N1c ground zero right now, Jensen. There's no organized ROC Armed Forces in control of the city. Killer bees are a precious resource, so slaughterbots are roaming free outside our perimeter. Citizens, civil emergency and defense personnel have formed neighborhood militia to control the looters and rioters, but you might have to fight your way in, and if you survive, fight your way out again."

"Well, hell, Captain," Jensen said, scratching his head. "You could have sugarcoated that just a *little*."

The Battle of Hawaii: Hilo

MEANY LOOKED TIRED. Bunny guessed about the only thing holding him upright was his exoskeleton. When they walked into the 68th AGRS ready room at Hilo, he looked over and took a moment to focus. He was standing at table with Seamus 'Crystal' Hennessy, the squadron intel officer.

"Ah, O'Hare," he said. "At bloody last." He and Crystal were looking over a large table map of the air and sea around Hawaii. He looked her up and down. "You look lighter than I remember," he said. "Hospital food not agree with you?"

"That, or maybe it was the 30-hour swim off Taiwan," Bunny replied. "I heard you missed me."

"We didn't say that," Flowmax said.

"Are you ready to get back to work?" Meany asked.

"Gagging for it."

Meany looked dubious, turned to Touchdown. "What did the doctors say?"

"Uh, let me see. Something like, 'Please get her out of here, she's driving everyone nuts.'"

"They didn't appreciate my singing voice," Bunny shrugged, "or my extensive repertoire of Irish ditties."

"I'll take that as a yes, then," Meany decided. He smoothed the map out. "We are supporting Air National Guard with combat air patrols over and south of Big Island. They have O'ahu and West. Aircraft are being prepped now. I'll be leading one flight, call sign 'Teacher.' You'll be leading the other, call sign 'Student.'"

"That's just hurtful," Bunny said.

"Or appropriate, but I didn't choose them," Meany told her. "Touchdown and Flowmax are with me in Raptors.

You'll be going up with our other two Raptor pilots, Flatline and Agony."

Captain Michael 'Agony' Payne was one of Aggressor Inc.'s founding pilots and a flight leader like Touchdown, in normal times. In his 40s, married with a kid, he rarely deployed out of the US, preferring F-22 training duties instead. If he was here, it was another sign things were bad.

The other thing that struck Bunny—they were looking at a *paper* map. Festooned with multicolored Post-it notes indicating ground units on O'ahu and naval units in the seas around. A few—too few—pins showing air patrols. There was an LCD screen on the wall, but it was dead.

"Paper-based mission planning?" Bunny asked Crystal.

"Battlenet link is intermittent. China took down a big chunk of our satellite capacity. Most all, judging by the effect. Space Force dealt with it and is supposedly getting new birds up. Navy is moving some *Constellation* frigates into place to give us data links, but coverage is still patchy. So when that is down"—he pointed at the wall monitor— "yeah, we are back to analog maps."

"Voice comms?" Bunny asked.

"That's the one bit of good news. Government did a deal with some commercial satellite operators, so we have secure voice," Crystal said. "And right now we're working with an AWACS out of Edwards, call sign College ..."

"Until *China* shoots that down too," Touchdown said through gritted teeth.

"... but we have it for now, so you'll have some situational awareness, maybe even be able to sync data a good amount of the time, if Navy gets a *Constellation* here in time."

"Don't rely on it, is my advice," Touchdown told her. Bunny bent to the map, looking where she had her finger as

175

Touchdown continued. "ELINT shows China has a thick screen of Gyrfalcons and drones ahead of its carriers. They're probing Hawaii airspace already. *Fallujah* ARG is supposedly on its way back here, and there are two CSGs deploying from San Diego anytime now, but for now ..."

"We're alone," Bunny concluded.

"We're alone, but the cavalry is coming. There's two squadrons of P-99s, with Valkyries, on the way. The 173rd from Oregon and the 354th from Alaska. And they're tanking right now so they can get in, get down and take over from us on CAP. They'll be entering our air defense perimeter in about an hour."

Bunny studied the map and saw a flag and a Post-it showing where the Widows were tanking, and where she'd be patrolling.

"*Fujian?*"

"Yes, your old friend is still being a P.I.T.A." Meany drew a line from the tanker to Big Island with his finger, then one perpendicular to her patrol sector. "You'll be patrolling the southern flank to protect those Widows. *Fujian*'s aircraft try to interfere, you, Flatline and Agony push them back or draw them off until those Widows are feet dry over Hawaii."

Bunny's head was spinning trying to take it all in. She thought about all the traffic she'd seen on the airfield on the way in. "The virus hasn't hit here yet?"

"No. But the US mainland is going into lockdown. The president put out a video telling people to take it serious, but no one has seen her in the flesh for a week. Rumor is she's in a bunker somewhere. Anyone flying in from the west, like you, goes into quarantine until they either die or get cleared." Meany sighed. "Bird flu is the least of our problems right now."

Bunny remembered the Marine, Cruze, coughing pink phlegm onto the face mask of his protective suit and opened her mouth to disagree, but she got Meany's point, and arguing about it wasn't going to change anything.

Bunny tapped another flag on the map near the sector she would be patrolling. Red. "This flag?"

Crystal nodded. "*Fujian* usually hunts for our reinforcement flights there, 300 miles out. She took out a flight of F-15s being rushed over from Edwards AFB yesterday—that flag is where they were hit. She has Wing Loong ISR drone support and doesn't seem afraid to burn her Chongmings by keeping one or two on station running a search pattern until they drop out of the sky without fuel. We figure China is leapfrogging their drones from the Chinese mainland to their carrier *Liaoning* or aerial refueling them somewhere between the Kurils and Hawaii, maybe landing them on *Shandong*, fueling, arming and sending them on to *Fujian*. Could also be they had some crated up at Port Aeon on Kiribati and are flying them in from there—we haven't managed to shut that base down yet."

"My payload?"

"Limited good news there," Crystal said. "We were running Aggressor training from here, not combat ops. We only had Peregrines in our own inventory when China appeared. But National Guard inventory at Hilo has AIM-260s, and since they don't have but four planes, they're happy to share."

"I'm guessing no Valkyries," Bunny said sadly. A couple of drone wingmen could have made a world of difference.

"Not until the reinforcements get here, but National Guard gave us a half dozen MALD decoys. Meany used four on a sortie last night. I took the liberty of putting the last two

177

into your loadout." He consulted a flipchart. "So you'll have six AIM-260 long-range, four Peregrine medium-range missiles, two MALDs."

The MALD, or miniature air-launched decoy, was the next best thing to a Valkyrie wingman drone. It couldn't attack enemy aircraft, but it could be used to jam the links between Chinese drones and their pilots, or decoy them away by simulating the radar signature of a fighter aircraft like an F-35.

Bunny looked down. She was still wearing the hospital gown she'd been rescued in. And boots, without laces.

"I was wondering how long you were going to stand around like that," Crystal said. "There's, like, tattoos even I haven't seen before."

Meany straightened up from the map and smiled.

"Because, you know, it's open at the ..." Crystal continued.

"... back, yes, I know. I *am* wearing underwear, Crystal. Flight suit?" Bunny said.

"Locker's that way," Meany nodded to a side door. "See you back here for final briefing before we hit the flight line." He motioned them all to get into a circle and they put their fists in the middle. "*What are we going to do, Aggressor?*" he asked.

"*Bring it!*" they grunted.

SLAUGHTERBOTS weren't the only ordnance launched at O'ahu that morning. As Admiral Connaught had predicted, the first wave of cruise missiles was about to be unleashed, but not from the approaching Sino-Russian fleet.

As the autonomous bots were laying waste to ships, radar stations, anti-air batteries, vehicles, aircraft and facilities across Pearl Harbor-Hickam, 20 Chinese one-way extra-large uncrewed underwater vehicles, or XLUUVs, began rising from deep water outside the US SOSUS underwater detection perimeter.

Since they were not designed to return to port, their Chinese engineers called the boats "Shén fēng duì yú," or "kamikaze fish."

Built at China's Wuchang shipyards for a fraction of the cost of a normal conventional or nuclear-powered submarine, the ultra-quiet liquified hydrogen fuel-cell-powered boats were designed for only one purpose: to travel long distances underwater, undetected, and close within standoff distance of enemy coastal facilities.

And lay waste to them.

Though most of the internal capacity of the XLUUVs was taken up with fuel and ordnance, there was room for one more piece of equipment. A low-emission quantum radio for communicating with their masters in Wuchang

They could navigate themselves, but they had no crew, no other sophisticated sensors or weapons guidance systems aboard, only a four-cell missile launch battery. Targeting was downloaded from overhead satellites immediately before launch, then loaded into the CJ-100 East Wind supersonic cruise missiles in their tubes.

As one, at a range of 53 nautical miles outside the US SOSUS detection zone, the kamikaze submarines rose to communication depth.

From 100 yards down, they deployed transmission buoys on spiderweb-thin cables and squirted a message to Wuchang.

In attack position. Missile systems armed. Sending last received target data. Launch, retarget, or abort?

Mere seconds ticked past until the answer came.

Launch.

One by one, from every point of the compass in the ocean around Hawaii, 80 East Wind missiles punched out of the sea, hung in the air for a moment, and then lit their booster rockets before accelerating toward their targets at Mach 4, or 3,000 miles an hour.

The already pressed air defenses of the Hawaiian Islands—those still remaining—would have only 294 seconds to react.

AIR NATIONAL GUARD F-22 pilot Captain Annunzio 'Nun' D'Angelli, flying a defensive CAP 60 miles north of Kaua'i Island, was the first to detect the incoming Chinese missiles. He immediately got on the horn to the E-3 AWACS aircraft, call sign "College," currently orbiting in relative safety east of Big Island.

"College, Saber Four. I have six-plus fast movers on radar, bearing north to northwest, altitude 1,000, range 120. Uh, flight profile suggests cruise missiles." Normally he'd be able to sync his data to the AWACS so they could see what he was seeing, but nothing was normal right now.

"Good copy, Saber Four. We're trying for … uh, we're managing multiple inbound. You are clear to intercept. Repeat, you are cleared to intercept."

Precious seconds had just been wasted. The Chinese missiles had just covered nearly 5 miles during the brief exchange.

Nun cued up his six AIM-260 missiles. The challenge for Nun was "probability of kill," or PK. He had more targets than missiles. Nun wanted to wait until the Chinese missiles were within 50 miles away for the best PK … ideally even closer … before he could fire.

The radio began filling with calls from the other Saber pilots on CAP over Hawaii, from his position in the west to Big Island in the east. Nun did a quick count as they reported incoming missiles from every damn direction … 20 … 46 … 70 … my God … *80!*

They had four F-22s on CAP, everything they had airborne when the slaughterbots hit Hickam. Nothing else had been able to get off the ground.

He worked his radar, locking up as many of the incoming missiles as he could.

Four F-22s, six missiles apiece. They could take down maybe 20 of the Chinese missiles before they got into close range and could use AIM-9Xs. Each Raptor had two short-range AIM-9Xs, but they needed an infrared lock to be effective, so Nun would have to get lucky—and *close.*

Even if he did, there would still be 50 Chinese missiles for ground defenses to deal with.

Yeah, and what ground defenses, Annunzio? What the hell does US Army have on Kaua'i?

THE ANSWER to Annunzio 'Nun' D'Angelli's question was US Army Lieutenant Alessa Baruzzi.

And if he'd known that, Nun should have felt a whole lot more confident.

Unlike the Chinese armed forces, the US Army had been almost continuously defending global peace, one way or another, since 1941. Such was the price of Pax Americana, or so the experts said. It meant the American people had carried an enormous cost, but it also meant their armed forces had unparalleled combat experience.

Embodied in Alessa Baruzzi. She'd been a sergeant, a Tactical Control Assistant (TCA) in the US Army 5th Battalion, 7th Air Defense Artillery Regiment at Incirlik, Turkey, when Syrian forces, backed by Russian irregulars, had attacked the NATO base.

With chemical weapons.

She'd received a battlefield commission after her High-Energy Liquid Laser Air Defense System, or HELLADS, singlehandedly took down 12 Russian Ovod and six Krypton missiles, with her running the engagement after the death of their battery commander.

When the Syrian war moved, she was redeployed to Beersheba in Israel. To rest up, they said. Except Iran and Syria had other ideas. War came to Beersheba and Alessa Baruzzi again.

When cruise missiles were launched at Israel by a rogue Iranian frigate in the eastern Mediterranean, no one knew if they contained nuclear or conventional warheads.

Baruzzi and her crew picked up the Iranian missiles while they were still 60 miles out. A US Navy vessel accounted for two of them. Two headed for downtown Tel Aviv. Despite only having five seconds to detect and react to the incoming Iranian missiles, Baruzzi's crew was ready, and without worrying about protocols, Baruzzi synced data with an Israeli HELLADS battery and handed engagement authority to the Israeli's laser's automated "lock and fire" control system. From a spit on the coast outside Tel Aviv, beams of high-intensity laser energy locked onto the incoming Iranian Yakhont missiles and burned through their outer casings, frying their guidance systems and sending them plunging into the sea a mile short of Tel Aviv Harbor.

She got an Israeli Defense Forces Service Ribbon for that one. Class A.

After two tours during the Syrian war, Baruzzi had enjoyed the peace, quiet and comforting routine of service at Lihue on Kaua'i Island. The 7th Air Defense Artillery Regiment was about the only military presence on the east side of the island, tasked with protecting the small international airport and deep-water cruise ship berth.

A duty so routine and uneventful it could almost have been prescribed as a cure for post-traumatic stress. Until today.

They'd been on high alert since the first report of an attack on Pearl. But that was on O'ahu. Baruzzi's battery was arranged on a hillside overlooking the Lihue International Airport on the south side of the harbor on a range called Unulau. She'd been briefed to be watchful for the Chinese autonomous bots specifically targeting air defense installations, like her MML—Multi-Mission Launcher— battery.

But they had seen none on Kaua'i yet.

Let them come, is what Baruzzi thought. The US Army had learned from conflicts like Syria, Ukraine, the South China Sea and Second Korean War—your air defenses had to be mobile. The typical Patriot Missile Battery with its fixed control station, power generator unit and high-frequency antenna mast was a target just waiting to be hit. Her first HELLADS battery comprised truck-mounted laser and high-powered microwave units, but her radar and control truck were tethered to an immobile power unit.

The MML battery was less technologically impressive—it used missiles, not lasers—but it was a whole lot more mobile.

Baruzzi had learned the hard way to put a high price on mobility.

Her six vehicles were screened by defilade positions carved into the hillside overlooking Lihue from the south side of its harbor. The control center was inside a High Mobility Tactical Hawkei vehicle towing their primary Sentinel radar. Her four six-missile MML "pods" were also mounted on Hawkei vehicles, networked and linked by jamming-hardened comms.

Ready as she was, Baruzzi got taken by surprise by the panicked call from the AWACS controller east of O'ahu. She had her radar scanning more carefully east, in the direction of the slaughterbot assault. She'd ordered a low-level scan, trying to pick up the bots or their motherships skimming in over the sea. She had her pods hidden behind the lip of the hilltop that framed her position about one mile south of the Hilo main runway. Hiding them in case of slaughterbot assault, she planned to have her Hawkeis pop up over the ridge and counterattack east.

If she got the chance.

But the location also put her in the ideal position to intercept the cruise missiles the AWACS warned were approaching Lihue from the north.

"Buckle up, people! Arrays to 15 degrees. Scan zero to 5,000 feet above sea level. Call out your targets. This is the real deal," she said in a level voice.

Her sensor operator was a corporal called Kernow, from Alabama. His slow drawl belied the fleetness of his fingers across the multiple keyboards he had to master. "Radar in track-while-scan mode, tracking eight vampires," he told her.

Her TCA, the guy sitting in the seat she had been sitting in at Incirlik, was a sergeant called Kennedy, a New Yorker like her. "Pushing targets," he said. "Pods One through Four reporting ready."

Baruzzi watched the vampires—incoming missiles—track for three seconds, visually estimating where they'd be headed if they didn't deviate. The Chinese missiles were staggered, line echelon, about a half mile behind each other. Maybe the way they'd been launched, maybe the way they were designed to strike. "First wave will be SEAD," she decided. Suppression of Enemy Air Defense, using high speed anti-radar missiles. "They'll try to take out our air defenses first. That's us, people."

"How we playing it, ma'am?" Kernow asked.

"Let the first wave get within high-probability kill range. Clear of the airport and residential areas."

"Risky," Kennedy said. "If we don't hit them farther out, and they aren't coming for us, they'll hit the airport."

"They're coming here first. They know we're here, waiting for them. They have to kill us first," Baruzzi assured him. "We'll take the *second* wave farther out."

But that little voice in her head said, *What if you're wrong?*

NUN D'ANGELLI got a lock tone from his missiles, and his thumb tensed over his missile trigger.

But he waited.

He'd pushed his Raptor into super cruise, Mach 1.1, closing on the Chinese missiles as quickly as he could with the fuel he had left. He needed a buffer in case he had to maneuver to get a shot at the Chinese missiles with his short-range weapons.

Forty miles. High-percentage chance of a kill.

Game time.

His missiles had the vampires boxed, and he just had to send them. His thumb jabbed down on the button on his flight stick, the weapons bay doors flipped open, and one by one, his missiles were kicked into his slipstream, then shot away ahead of him at four times the speed of sound.

Their closing speed relative to the Chinese missiles, also traveling at Mach 4, was Mach 8. The margin for error as they maneuvered was measurable in picoseconds.

BARUZZI MADE a hell of a good call. The first Chinese cruise missiles approaching Kaua'i were headed for mapped air defense positions around two targets—the Pacific Missile Range Facility, and the port and airport of Lihue.

Lihue Airport was primarily civilian, but with the amount of military traffic moving through Hawaii to the Taiwan theater, every airstrip in the islands was seeing some military traffic. Up-to-the-minute signals intelligence told the Chinese missiles where her radar truck was at the time they launched, and the sensor suites in the noses of the first wave of East Wind High Speed Anti-Radar Missiles were designed to home on US air defense radar signals for their terminal run in.

The MML system was made to survive that. Each Hawkei launch vehicle had its own low-powered radar for terminal missile guidance, so if one vehicle got taken out, including Baruzzi's own, another could take over.

"First wave, six targets locked and boxed. Altitude 1,000, range 50," her sensor operator Kernow called in a flat monotone that belied the tension inside the command vehicle. "Second wave, eight targets locked. Altitude 1,000, range 60."

Fourteen targets. They had 24 interceptor missiles. One minute to impact.

"Pods up to firing positions," Baruzzi told her TCA, Kennedy.

"Pods moving into position," Kennedy said. From four sites across the ridge of the small volcano crater, her Hawkei vehicles rolled out of defilade and aimed their launcher boxes at the horizon.

"Set missile seekers to minimum engagement range," she said. "Radars up."

"Seekers to minimum engagement range," Kennedy confirmed.

"Pods One to Four radars up and sharing target data," Kernow advised.

There was nothing more they could do but wait for the first wave of Chinese missiles to come. She checked her tac screen and saw an F-22 join the party, firing interceptors at the incoming missiles.

Get some, Raptor guy!

Thirty seconds to wait. Maybe 30 seconds to live.

Damn, it went *slow*.

Nun D'Angelli hauled his plane around on a dime as the Chinese missiles crossed 10,000 feet underneath him.

Six missiles away, *four* kills. Tone on his AIM-9s, jabbing his finger on the trigger again. Not going for the first wave anymore, too fast. His only chance was the approaching second wave of missiles, seconds away.

Missiles off.

Kill.

Miss.

He leveled out and drew breath for the first time in three frantic minutes. Five kills.

Too few.

God help you, Army.

ALESSA BARUZZI had long ago called in every favor a reasonable God could be asked for. She knew that. She hoped maybe Kernow and Kennedy were owed a few, or prayed to different gods.

The first wave of Chinese missiles closed within 500 yards of her position, screaming right over the top of Lihue Airport. From the pods at the back of her Hawkei vehicles, interceptors blasted out to meet them.

As soon as they launched, each vehicle killed its radar and reversed into defilade again.

The attack dropped one of the two remaining first-wave missiles. But the second, slightly farther out, shrugged it off, homed on one of Baruzzi's launch vehicles and detonated right on top of it.

The blast shook their command vehicle, 200 yards distant and half-hidden behind the crater ridge.

"Radars up again. Pod status!" she yelled.

"One, Three and Four still online," Kennedy said. "Second wave inbound Lihue. Seven targets locked and ..."

"Come on, come on, come on," Kernow muttered under his breath, but still audible.

"Locked and *boxed!*" Kennedy announced.

Kernow jabbed a finger on a large button in front of him. "Pods One, Three and Four firing."

From their remaining launch vehicles, interceptors speared into the sky. One failed to lock onto its jinking target, and the Chinese missile hit Air National Guard Temporary Hangar

105, detonating stored fuel and oil, killing everyone inside and damaging two C-130s parked outside.

The other six missiles were hit, either disintegrating mid-air or getting knocked off-course. The debris of Four fell into the sea, short of the airport. One went high. One spiraled into the air before spearing into the ground, without exploding, outside the Vidinha Stadium baseball field. The last tumbled end over end as it crossed the airfield perimeter, where it flew over the roof of the Fifth District Court and slammed into the Kaua'i Police Department behind it. Two police officers and three staff died in the explosion; another 20 were wounded.

Baruzzi sat back in her chair and blew air from her cheeks. "Wide area scan," she ordered Kennedy.

"Clear air," he replied a minute later.

No one was cheering. There were no high fives, no slapping of backs.

They'd had leakers. Felt the blasts as the missiles detonated somewhere in the city opposite. Out there, people had died.

They'd been given 294 seconds to react. Together with their F-22 friend, they'd taken out 12 of the 14 missiles aimed at their sector.

An incredible kill ratio. But nothing less than perfect was good enough for Lieutenant Alessa Baruzzi.

And because she'd been there before, Baruzzi knew only too well they'd have to do better; this was just the beginning.

CAPTAIN LEI YU'S FC-31 Gyrfalcon had been at "ready 10" status for nearly 30 minutes. "*Fujian* Control, what is the delay? I can see the adversary aircraft have left their refueling point."

China's premier naval stealth fighter, the Gyrfalcon, had only begun operating from *Fujian* again in the last few days. *Fujian*'s conversion to an all-drone mothership fielding only CH-7 Chongming drones had proven very effective, allowing it to deploy with an extra 10 fighter aircraft in its crowded hangar deck. But with the losses *Fujian* had suffered in the air, and at sea, hangar deck space was no longer an issue. China had been flying its more capable Gyrfalcon fighters off the carrier *Shandong* and putting them on *Fujian* for operations to intercept US cargo, AWACS and fighter reinforcement aircraft trying to resupply Hawaii from the US mainland.

The combination of a Wing Loong signals and electronic surveillance drone, the Gyrfalcon, and *Fujian*'s CH-7 Chongmings flying as uncrewed wingmen, had proven highly effective. *Shandong*'s motto was "Loyalty, Perseverance, Readiness, Victory!" and its air wing comprised four squadrons, each taking its name from a word in the motto. Lei Yu's Victory Squadron had claimed the very first meat kill of the Chinese assault on Hawaii, destroying an F-22 500 miles west of the islands to ensure their fleet's strength and exact location remained a secret.

Since operating off *Fujian*, Lei's four pilots and their drone wingmen had claimed nearly a dozen American fourth-generation fighter kills: older F-15s that were not even aware a Gyrfalcon was stalking them. Lei and his pilots had speculated a lot about why the Americans were trying to reinforce Hawaii with their older Eagle fighters instead of their newer F-35 stealth fighters. Their theory was that the Americans had already lost so many stealth fighters in the war over Taiwan that they had very few left in their inventory to send to Hawaii.

The F-22s were also a surprise. He'd expected to meet F-35s, not decades-old Raptors. Another sign of how desperate the main enemy was.

China, on the other hand, was finally showing its true might. *Shandong* had brought 36 Gyrfalcons to the battle for Hawaii, *Liaoning* 24, while *Fujian* still had 20 Chongmings, and it had repaired its landing deck and both of its EMALS catapults so that it was running at near normal launch and recovery capacity. The only thing slowing it was that it was still operating with a single aircraft elevator, which gave hangar operations and planning just that extra degree of difficulty ...

Liu looked across the deck to his right and saw a Chongming being pushed across the deck and hooked up to the other catapult.

"Problem getting your final aircraft up from the hangar deck, Victory Leader," *Fujian*'s primary flight controller said. "It will be on the catapult in five."

There were already three drones circling *Fujian*, waiting for him and his final wingman to launch. On his tactical screen, the data from the Wing Loong to their northwest was about to degrade. It had to stay out of radar range of the American fighters as they were refueling, but refueling operations forced the Americans to use their radios to coordinate with the tanker, and the Wing Loong could track them by their emissions.

While they were circling around their tanker, they were visible. But Lei could see they were dropping off the plot as they left the refueling pattern and began their transit to Hawaii. The lead elements would already be on their way!

191

"*Fujian*, I am going to go with the three Chongmings I have. Number four can catch us up when it launches. Victory Leader requesting launch clearance," he said.

"Uh … Victory Leader, you are clear to launch. Happy hunting."

IN HER FLIGHT POD two decks down, Lieutenant Maylin 'Mushroom' Sun, flight leader, Ao Yin Chongming Fighter Squadron, cursed the impatient Gyrfalcon pilot.

She had just heard his conversation with the flight controller, and the three Chongmings he was about to depart with were hers. She had lost time waiting for their single aircraft elevator to lift her plane to the flight deck, so it was Mushroom's plane still being locked into the catapult. In reality, *Shandong*'s squadron leader had no authority to carve her planes out of her flight and depart with them, even though he outranked her. But rank was rank, and she would have to keep her grumbling to herself.

Colonel Wang, *Fujian*'s air wing leader, would have insisted the *Shandong*'s captain request her permission to depart with her aircraft, if he had been in pri-fly. But he wasn't. He was still acting captain of *Fujian*, and no doubt busy elsewhere, doing whatever aircraft carrier commanders do. A major who was a genius at logistics, but not a fighter pilot's pilot, had been delegated command of the air wing. He knew to the bolt and rivet what spare parts and how much fuel and ordnance *Fujian* had in its stores, but he still relied on Wang for tactical guidance as to how to use his aircraft.

Shandong's Gyrfalcon pilots had arrived on *Fujian* like they had already personally led the invasion of Hawaii. Their handful of kills paled in comparison with the achievements,

192

and the losses, of the *Fujian*'s pilots, but you wouldn't know it from their demeanor. The reason was two-fold. The first was that their captain, Lei, was an arrogant, entitled a-hole. A fighter pilot turned movie star turned fighter pilot again, he went everywhere as though there were a camera crew following him because, often, there was. He was the PLA Navy Air Force's own pin-up boy, and the several million followers of his social media accounts demanded a daily diet of status updates and images of his exploits.

The second reason was something Mushroom hadn't previously had to deal with on the all-drone *Fujian*: the irrefutable status divide that existed between drone pilots and crewed aircraft pilots. Mushroom begrudgingly acknowledged that every time a Gyrfalcon pilot took their plane up, there was a chance they would not make it back alive—and that her situation was entirely different since even if she lost her plane, she would just log out of her pod and into another plane as soon as one became available. She and her pilots didn't have the same "skin in the game;" that was the theory. Except they did. There was a plaque in *Fujian*'s pilot's mess that contained the names of more than a dozen pilots and double that number of sailors and flight crew who had given their lives as a result of the multiple attacks *Fujian* had survived.

Shandong had gotten through the war so far with nothing more than a scare. Attacked in the early days of the war by Taiwanese fighters, she had beaten off the attack but was then withdrawn to Hainan, where she'd skulked until the American satellite networks were crippled and she could sally forth with her escorts to join the amphibious assault force.

In Mushroom's opinion, Lei Yu and the pilots of *Shandong* had nothing to be arrogant about.

But she parked her resentment as, with a virtual look around her plane, she saw a plane captain signal that she was ready to launch. The mission package she was supposed to join was already 60 miles northwest and drawing farther away by the second.

She squirmed in her wheelchair, getting comfortable ahead of what was going to be a long flight, probably followed by an intense fight. "Ao Yin Flight Leader, requesting launch clearance," she said.

AS MUSHROOM'S FIGHTER rocketed off *Fujian*'s newly repaired deck, Bunny was headed south in super-cruise mode, at Mach 1.5 and 40,000 feet, headed for her patrol sector.

Flatline and Agony were following behind her at a more fuel-efficient Mach 0.85.

With no GPS to rely on, she checked her mission timer and inertial nav screen. She was just entering the arc of sky where Touchdown said most of the Chinese interceptions had taken place. Her helmet heads-up display was set to give her an alert if it managed to lock onto one of the new US military comms satellites Space Force was supposedly launching, but so far it had stayed stubbornly dead. She had optical infrared sensors that could detect any aircraft within 30 miles in clear skies like today's, but the lack of distance situational awareness was *killing* her.

She had five minutes to her Combat Air Patrol initial point.

"Student Two, you take east, Student Three west. Student Leader will take center."

"Two copies."

"Three, good copy."

She watched the two Raptors break left and right and slide away. With such a big sector to cover, Bunny had proposed, and the other two pilots agreed, that she'd act like a flame to moths. Rather than hiding, she'd make herself visible and try to pull a Chinese patrol to her by using her radar. The two Raptors would do the hunting, sniffing the sky invisibly with passive ELINT receivers and optical infrared sensors. If things got kinetic, she would back them with the Widow's firepower.

The idea was that if they were engaged with the Aggressor pilots, *Fujian*'s fighters weren't hunting the larger group of Widows to their north.

Time to weave the web, O'Hare, she told herself. Setting her radar to wide-angle long-range scan mode, she pulled her plane into a slow 360-degree turn, checking the sky around her. *Anyone out there?*

The Rearguard: Taipei

JENSEN HAD been given a small, anonymous delivery van—into which he loaded Squirt—a Taiwan Air Force translator who insisted Jensen just call him Mike," and a rendezvous point at a parking garage inside Taipei.

The captain was, luckily, wrong. With Mike by his side, getting into Taipei was quicker and easier than Jensen had been briefed to expect. Yes, the main city intersections, if they weren't completely deserted because of the presence of slaughterbots, were blockaded with makeshift militia forces armed with whatever weapons they'd been able to scrape together. Some were under the command of military or police officers, others by criminals, some by simple vigilantes. Most had some military training from conscription service and were doing their best to keep their city from descending into anarchy. But not all.

Jensen's credentials got him cooperation from the military and police officers, and his battle-scarred visage and M18 pistol got him cooperation from the criminals and vigilantes. "Mike" proved an unexpected asset at one roadblock at a ring road just outside the center of Taiwan and about 2 miles from their rendezvous.

They'd been crawling forward in a small line of vehicles and had just reached the front.

A thug with a red bandana, chewing on a toothpick, tapped on Jensen's window with a pistol and motioned to him to wind down the window. Two others with looted assault rifles stood behind him, weapons held in the crook of their arms, trying to look hard. Jensen obliged by rolling down his window, and the thug leaned in. "You want to pass, you pay the toll," he said. "You got food, medicine, jewelry, hand it over."

Jensen sighed. "What I've got for you, son, is an M18 pistol aimed right at your balls and a 9 mm coppertop that will go right through my driver's door and turn you into a soprano before you can blink." He turned to look over his shoulder at the man in the back of the van. "Tell him, Mike."

It was a routine they'd been forced to use three or four times already, and usually Mike just translated, the man at the door looked inside to see that Jensen wasn't bluffing, and they were waved on their way. Most of the criminal low-lifes they ran into were smart enough to think it through and concluded they hadn't survived H5N1c and rampaging slaughterbots just to die at a roadblock for a few protein bars or a box of headache tablets.

But this thug was one of the stupid ones. He looked inside the vehicle to see Jensen's pistol pointed at his groin, then grinned as the stepped back and pointed to his comrades with their assault rifles. In English he said, "Shoot me, you die too. Easier just to give me what you have in back there," he said, having seen the crate Squirt was packed in.

Jensen was preparing to shoot the guy's balls off and then gun the little van through the roadblock when Mike leaned over and began talking again in Taiwanese. The thug took a second look at him.

And the hell if it didn't seem like the two of them knew each other.

A few more words were exchanged, then the thug gave Mike some kind of gang handshake, took a step back, and waved them through.

"What just happened there?" Jensen asked him.

Mike was a lanky guy in his early 30s, with jet black hair in a ponytail and round, wire-rimmed spectacles. His spectacles had slipped down his nose while he'd talked, so he pushed them up again. "While you were speaking, I realized I knew him," Mike said. "We went to tech college together."

Jensen grunted. "He didn't look to me like the higher education type."

"Well, when I say we 'went to college,' I mean I went to college, and he sold drugs to students," Mike said, deadpan.

"What did you say to him?"

Mike looked out his window, not at Jensen. "I told him you were a crazy American deserter who had kidnapped me, stolen my van, and you were high on crack so you probably *would* start shooting at everyone any minute," Mike said, with a shrug. "Same as I told all the others."

"I thought you were translating what I asked you to translate," Jensen said.

"What you asked me to translate would have got us killed three roadblocks back," Mike told him. "My version is better."

Jensen couldn't fault his logic and was almost sad to say farewell to Mike when he dropped him at an intersection in the city center before he reached his destination.

"You going to be OK?" Jensen asked the translator.

"Sure. I have family in Taipei. Except, I haven't heard from them in a couple weeks ..." He shrugged. "I took this job for the free ride. Not many people headed *into* Taipei right now."

MASON JACKSON hadn't asked for a gunnery sergeant. He wanted a robotics specialist and an LS3, and usually that meant a private or a corporal at best. Marine Gunnery sergeants, in Jackson's experience, were a P.I.T.A.

You had to be a special kind of evil to make gunnery sergeant. A gunnery sergeant outranked a bread-and-butter sergeant like himself, and a US Marine gunnery sergeant wasn't likely to take orders from a foreign lieutenant like Chang, either. Especially a foreign *air force* lieutenant.

But Gunnery Sergeant James Jensen surprised Jackson from the moment his van drove up onto the fourth floor of Jackson's parking garage. He climbed out of the van, stretched and yawned, then ambled over to where Jackson, Chang, Xu and Fi were getting bedded down for the night. They had rigged up some juice for the slaughterbot so that it could recharge while they slept, and stripped some bench seats from an abandoned bus to lay their bedrolls on.

Jensen looked down on the four of them from an imposing six-foot-three vantage point. *Built like a brick outhouse, too,* Jackson thought. *Of course he is.*

'Sergeant Jackson?" he asked.

Jackson stood, not showing any deference. "Mason Jackson, Gunnery Sergeant," he said. He nodded at the others. "This is Lieutenant Chang, our ROC Taiwan pilot; Corporal Xu, ROC Thunder Force, and the young lady there is Fi, our slaughterbot whisperer."

Jensen had been looking at the dormant slaughterbot beside the trike as he walked up. He didn't even ask about it.

"You can call me Gunny, Jackson," Jensen said. "I brought your LS3," he said. "Just tell me where you want us."

Tell me where you want us? Well, hell yeah. It was his operation. The man had the smarts to realize that. At that moment Jackson saw he was dealing with a no BS combat

199

veteran and quietly thanked the gods who had assigned
Gunny James Jensen to his operation.

"Well that's ... more than I hoped for, Gunny," Jackson
admitted. "I'll fill you in on the mission and then you can bed
down in your van. We move out of here at 0400."

Jensen settled in to discuss the coming patrol with Jackson.
Together with the pilot, Jensen and Squirt were going to be
on point for the small squad, pathfinding the way to the
objective so that Jackson and Xu could set up their shot.
Jensen on the ground near the target to deliver the coup de
grace.

After they'd moved through the briefing and discussed
scenarios, Jensen jerked his head toward the girl, who'd fallen
asleep on a bus bench with Xu's field jacket draped over her.
"What's her deal?"

Xu spoke with something close to emotion in his voice.
"Her family is dead. We found her playing in the streets with
a slaughterbot she'd tamed. She's some kind of hacking
prodigy. She got the monster running so Lieutenant Chang
can fly it. She says she's got the gun control system working
too, but we haven't been able to test that yet."

"We should cut her loose before go time," Jensen said.

"She's alright," Xu said. "Smart kid."

"Can't boot the bot without her," Jackson said. "And I've
built a new plan around that hunk of metal, which I was
about to get to, if you want to hear it."

Jackson's original plan was for himself and Chang to
attack the front of the compound and drive their target out
the rear into an ambush. But the slaughterbot offered an
option that put fewer bodies in harm's way yet achieved the
same purpose. Jensen was quiet, heard him out before asking
a couple of questions.

"Sounds like you thought it through. I need to sleep," Jensen announced when they were done. "I got a feeling tomorrow will come too soon."

JENSEN DIDN'T want the girl around. But not for the reason Mason Jackson was probably thinking.

There was a reason James Jensen was still a Marine—a reason that had seen him deploy to Syria, then Okinawa, and now the Pacific. He hadn't planned it that way. After making gunnery sergeant, he'd been ready to get out. He'd put a little money away, had a wife and two girls he wanted to spend more time with, who didn't seem to mind the sight of him too much, and a buddy back in Indiana who could get him a job as a crew boss on a team installing wind turbines. He'd even had the job interview and made it through that and the company's damn psych test, which was worse than the interview itself.

He'd been two weeks from his pre-separation counseling session when he got word that his wife and kids had been walking a trail to Manoa Falls on O'ahu when a rockslide had killed them, and two other hikers. After burying his family, he walked into the pre-separation interview still in a daze, and came out having re-upped instead of getting out. He'd just lost his wife and kids; he couldn't stand the thought of saying goodbye to the only other family he had left in this world, the Corps. There were times—especially under fire—he felt he'd been too hasty.

But James Jensen was pretty damn sure if he hadn't re-upped, he'd probably have shot himself by now. So every day he spent above the ground was a win, even if he had to spend it at war.

His oldest daughter would have been the same age as that kid sleeping over by the wall. Except she wasn't. She'd never got any older than 10. *Not your fault*, everyone told him. *You can't keep beating yourself up about it*. Except he knew it was. If he'd been with them that day ... who knows? They might all still be alive.

The girl turned in her sleep, face toward him. Jensen looked away.

Jensen had been wounded in combat. More than once. Any of those injuries hurt less than looking at that damned girl.

JENSEN PUT his bedroll in a part of the parking garage away from the others. Sleep came quickly.

He was lying on his back with his hands folded across his chest when he heard a voice.

"I know English pretty good, you know."

He opened his eyes to see the girl standing beside him, looking down at him.

"Uh-huh?"

"I heard you tell the American sergeant to send me away," she said.

"Yep."

"But Corporal Xu stuck up for me. The American sergeant too."

Jensen put his hands behind his head and sighed. "No, they said we need you. It's not the same."

"You do need me," the girl insisted.

"Maybe," Jensen allowed. "For now. But as soon as we're done here, you need to go somewhere safe."

She said something angry in Mandarin, then paused, spoke slowly in English. "Safe? There is nowhere safe."

Jensen's voice hardened. "You can't stay with us. We're soldiers. We go where the fighting is, and that's no place for a teenage girl." She looked like she wanted to argue the point, so Jensen closed his eyes and rolled onto his side, facing away from her. "Get to sleep."

She stood there a moment longer, then he heard her walk away.

She was right. Nowhere on Taiwan was truly safe anymore. But she was also wrong; almost anywhere in a war was safer than being near Gunnery Sergeant James Jensen.

MASON JACKSON had three pieces of intelligence. He had a place, and he had a time, and he had a route. The place: where Premier Ko was going to be for an important meeting. The time: in about 40 minutes. The route: where Ko's security detail would try to effect his evacuation when the shooting started.

Which, to Jackson's mind, implied there was a guy inside the security detail providing the intel, but that wasn't Jackson's concern. As long as it was solid.

Jackson's plan for getting through the security surrounding the premier was to not even try. And contrary to Xu and Chang's expectations, which he hadn't discouraged, Xu wasn't going to be shooting the Taiwanese politician.

Not directly, anyway.

Jackson had been up at dawn, checking the intel he'd been given, scouting the premier's meeting location—a walled luxury mansion in the Da'an district, with a bombproof

203

basement. And the VIP's escape route through a rear gateway in a waiting armored vehicle.

Jackson had built multiple attack vectors into his plan already, and the girl's slaughterbot was a bonus. But he had his doubts about the gunnery sergeant's LS3.

When he got back to the garage, he made coffee and took a cup to Jensen.

"If you don't mind me asking, how does a gunnery sergeant end up in charge of a dog?" he asked. While he'd been gone, Jensen had unpacked and assembled the LS3 and it sat beside him on its haunches, powered off but still a menacing presence.

Jensen shifted his weight. "You want to know who you're working with? That's fair. I'll give you the short version. When I re-upped the first time, I was sent to Quantico—US Marine Corps Warfighting Lab—and ended up in Robotics, testing the LS3 prototype. Took it to Syria for combat certification. Got attached to 3rd Battalion, Lava Dogs, still with the Lab, testing new equipment. Deployed to Okinawa, nice billet if you forget the small civil war that erupted while we were there. Got pulled out of there, dropped on an island in the South China Sea about a month ago to evict the Chinese tenants. Just getting comfortable, when they loaded us on a plane and landed us at Taichung, where there was nobody left alive knew how to command the LS3s, so I got the job." He drew a breath. "Full circle, you could say. And now, for my sins, I'm here, with an LS3 again."

"Is it supposed to have oil dripping from its knee joint?" Jackson asked.

"Hydraulic fluid. He just had major surgery, Sergeant, but he's fit for the fight," Jensen said with a wink and patted the dog's "head." "Old Squirt just needs a little top-up at the start of every day, like most folks need their coffee."

Jackson looked dubious, but stood and looked around. "Hey, where's the girl?"

"HER BACKPACK and her laptop are gone, so she's *gone* gone," Xu said.

"For the best," Jensen said. "I don't know what you guys were thinking, bringing her here."

Jackson didn't like it though. "I remade the plan around that bot. Without the girl, there is no slaughterbot."

"Then go back to Plan A," Jensen shrugged. "Never fall in love with the plan, Sergeant."

Jackson looked like he'd already thought about that. "That bot is a tank. What you just said is the same as telling a tank crew, 'Oh, your tank broke down? No problem, we'll just go back to the plan where we attack the enemy strongpoint with rifles and bayonets instead.'"

The awkward silence that followed that was broken by Xu. "She's a teenager," he said. "She'll be looking for somewhere with internet where she can get breakfast. I'll go look for her."

Jensen sighed. "I'll come with you."

"Find her quick," Jackson said. "The clock is ticking."

"FIND HER quick, he says," Xu grumbled. He'd brought an assault rifle with him, not his Barrett, and stood down at the street-level entrance to the parking garage with Jensen, looking up and down the street.

"I'm a 15-year-old in Taipei; I'm angry, tired and hungry. Where do I go?" Jensen prompted.

Xu nodded west. "Dongmen metro station. Trains aren't running, but there's a chance of finding something open, maybe a street vendor selling congee."

They started walking. They were alone on the street except for two dogs sniffing hopefully at a pile of garbage. Jensen seriously doubted there would be any street vendors out at dawn hawking their wares in the ruined city. "What's congee?" Jensen asked.

Xu looked at him sideways. "Seriously? You been here how long? That's like me asking an American 'What's pancakes?'"

They rounded a corner. "Hey, I got off a C-130, been living underground for a month attacked daily by slaughterbots, and then I came here," Jensen told him. "So forgive me, Corporal, if I haven't picked up the finer points of the local ..."

"There she is," Xu said, stopping and pointing.

Fi was about 100 yards up on the other side of the street, looking in the smashed window of a supermarket. As they watched, she stepped over the broken glass and went through the window.

Jensen started walking quickly, but Xu grabbed his elbow. "Easy, Gunny, we don't want to scare her into running."

They'd only gone about 5 yards when three men detached themselves from a doorway farther down. Xu grabbed Jensen and pulled him into an arcade entrance. The three men looked up and down the street, then walked straight across to the supermarket and looked inside.

Then they stepped through the broken window and went in too.

"*Now* we move quick," Xu told Jensen, pulling his rifle off his shoulder and breaking into a jog. Jensen did the same.

They reached the supermarket, looked around the edge of the broken window. Jensen saw a dark ground floor, shelves emptied, boxes and cartons on the ground. The place had been thoroughly looted. At the back, escalators led up to the second floor. There was no sign of Fi, or the men.

"This floor was a pharmacy," Xu whispered. "Groceries upstairs. She would have gone up there."

They picked their way through to the back of the store. Jensen could hear voices now. Someone laughing.

It wasn't a friendly laugh.

Xu listened. "Guy just said this is their store, and she's a looter. Said they don't like looters."

Jensen didn't need to hear more.

He moved up the escalator in a crouch. Reached the top and looked around a corner.

The three guys had Fi bailed up in a corner. One took a step toward her and she swung her backpack at him. The guy stepped back and laughed. They didn't appear to be armed.

"Hey!" Jensen barked, stepping forward, rifle at port arms, visible but not threatening.

Xu, behind him, said something in Taiwanese. The guy who had been laughing put his hands up and stepped forward, blocking their line of sight to the two behind. Not good. Jensen went down on a knee and aimed his rifle. "Don't move."

Fi's scream was cut short. Using his buddy for cover, one of the other guys had pulled a knife and was holding Fi around the throat. He yelled at Xu.

"He said they're taking the girl and leaving," Xu said.

207

The guy in front with his hands in the air was smiling. Jensen decided he was the little gang's leader. "Tell the guy with the knife if he so much as blinks, I'll shoot the guy with his hands in the air first. Then, I'll shoot him."

Xu translated. The guy in front stopped smiling. He shouted angrily at Xu.

While he was yelling, Jensen closed one eye, aimed at the guy with the knife.

And fired.

The bullet struck him in the shoulder and spun him around. The knife clattered to the floor. Jensen shifted his aim to the guy with his hands in the air, who was moving one hand down toward the small of his back. *"Don't."*

He did.

He grabbed at a pistol in his belt, started to move. Xu and Jensen both fired at the same time. One bullet hit the guy in the ribs; the other punched his head sideways.

The third guy was crouching down with his hands flapping in the air.

Fi ran over, burying her head in Xu's shoulder as he lowered his rifle.

Jensen kept his gun aimed at the third man, though he was showing no sign of moving, just waving his hands over his head in surrender and muttering something. "Take her outside," Jensen said. He stepped forward carefully, picking up the pistol the gunman had dropped and checking him for a pulse. He was dead. The guy with the knife had crawled back against a wall and was glaring at Jensen with pure hate in his eyes.

He could live with that.

Jensen kicked the knife away across the floor, tucked the pistol into his belt and backed toward the escalators.

When they got outside, Xu had Fi under his arm. "That way," Jensen said, nodding in the opposite direction from the parking garage. "In case we're followed."

They walked two blocks, went left, walked another two blocks. They passed a few people coming out of their apartments, but no one paid much attention to them, and there was no sign anyone was following.

"Alright," Jensen said, stopping up. "Let's get back. Corporal Xu can fix us some congee."

"YOU TOLD me to go, so I went," the girl said.

Jensen nodded. Xu and Jackson had gone to prepare for the day's action. Chang was with the bot, checking its charge level.

"I know," Jensen said. "I was an asshole."

"Yes, you were an asshole," the girl agreed.

She wasn't a shaking, sobbing mess. Jensen had to give her that. It made him realize she'd probably already been through a lot. And maybe a lot worse.

Xu had made them some tea, and bowls of the thick rice porridge, congee, sprinkled with some kind of savory salt. Jensen handed his to the girl when he saw she was finished with hers. The salt tasted like fish—not his kind of breakfast. "We'll take you with us to the port," Jensen told her. "They'll put us in quarantine for a few days, until they're sure we don't have the virus. But you'll be safer there." He saw something in her eyes. Not gratitude. Relief, maybe.

Chang came back. "Power is at 50 percent. More than enough for what we need."

"Once I boot it up, while you are on your patrol or whatever you call it, where should I go?" Fi asked. She looked around at the big, empty parking garage. "I can't stay here."

"Safest is if she stays with you," Jensen said, looking up at Chang. "Out of the line of fire. Agree, Lieutenant?"

Chang looked at him. "She's coming with?"

"We leave no one behind," Jensen said, giving her a wink.

Fi grimaced. "*Now* you say it, asshole."

JACKSON WAS WALKING the neighborhood again with Xu. He'd already picked out two or three potential hides with a good line of fire to the target, but the choice had to be Xu's. Xu picked a second-floor office window in a deserted building with the windows already blown out. It would give him a nice clean shot at the target.

On the same walk, they planted the improvised explosive devices—two modified 60 mm depleted-uranium-tipped armor-piercing mortar shells—that would kick off the attack, if all went to plan. He'd planned to use one shell at the front of the compound, to multiply the shock of their attack, but the slaughterbot allowed both to be used elsewhere. Another reason he wanted the girl and her bot.

Their intel said Ko was always encircled by radio frequency jamming to eliminate the threat from radio-controlled bombs and FPV drones, so Jackson's IEDs had a single physical trigger. The jamming also meant Chang would need to keep the bot at least 500 yards back from the target compound, so they didn't lose their control link.

At 0800 Jackson went through the plan one last time with his motley hit squad.

At 0830 they left the parking garage and took up their assigned positions.

Ko was meeting with a group of cabinet politicians from his own Kuomintang political party who would be critical of getting public support for his emergency decree. He had made no secret of the fact he wanted cabinet unity around the invitation to China to provide emergency epidemic assistance to Taiwan, which he would sign later that day. The source inside his team said he planned to look each of the meeting participants in the eye and get their pledge of support in person.

Jackson and Xu made their way to the abandoned office building, the Barrett rifle that Xu had inherited from his dead partner broken down so that it could be carried in small backpacks slung over their shoulders that would attract no attention, either from nosy civilians or, if they were unlucky, a trigger-happy slaughterbot.

They reached their building without incident, climbed internal stairs to the second floor, and Xu assembled his rifle, then set it up on a desk a good 2 yards back from the window behind some collapsed ceiling tiles that hung from overhead.

"We're good to go," Xu reported. He looked through his scope. "Range is about 510 yards."

"Unit One in position," Jackson said over his tactical radio.

JAMES JENSEN was less than a mile away, down at ground level, with Squirt. The frequency jammers that Ko's security detail used wouldn't affect his ability to control the dog, since it was specifically designed to work with and around the jammers of allied security and military forces.

211

He waited at the rear of a boarded-up restaurant, Squirt positioned out of sight, just inside the doorway. The street outside was more alley than thoroughfare, just wide enough to permit a vehicle. But Jensen noticed it was clear of the usual obstructions like burned-out cars, piles of garbage or upended dumpsters.

Suspiciously so.

One or two people passed the shop, scurrying back and forth to scrounge food or water.

"Unit Two in position," Jensen said.

Operation Midnight: Enigma

HOW TO DISABLE the enemy's deadliest submarine without sinking it?

That's what *Agincourt* would have to do if they were to *recover* the Chinese equivalent of the Enigma Code Machine. If it was destroyed in the central Pacific, it would sink to depths no recovery vehicle could reach.

Courtenay and the NSA agent, Williams, had been cagey about how they thought it would be possible. Brunelli and McDonald had thrown around their own ideas in private. A stern shot, destroying the enemy's propulsion or rudder without breaching the hull, was all they could come up with. High risk, since it would leave the *Taifun* still able to launch torpedoes. Of course, they could also ram the enemy submarine. *Agincourt* was a good deal heavier than *Taifun*. Another crazy possibility

It had been an hour since they escaped the Chinese Piranha attack. What followed the escape was a long, tense period in the *Agincourt*'s crowded control room, where the tension rose with every mile they got closer to the Chinese fleet's inner cordon, but nothing actually happened.

Until it did.

"Contact! Bearing zero two five degrees, mechanical, subsurface …"

"Kill propulsion, ahead slow, maintain course and depth," Courtenay ordered immediately. "Rig for ultra-quiet." The orders were repeated throughout the control room and the sound of the *Agincourt*'s pump-jet propulsion system, which was so quiet McDonald and Brunelli only noticed it by its sudden absence, died away.

213

"Cavitation?" Courtenay asked his sonarman in a low whisper.

"Reactor noise," the man said. "CNNC Type Zero Seven. It's a match with the *AE1* data."

"Could be *Taifun*, or another *Type 095*," McDonald said. From what Williams had told him, both boats used the same compact China National Nuclear Corporation reactors. "One of the Chinese fleet pickets."

Courtenay nodded. "Range estimate?"

"AI is saying 6 miles. It feels closer," the man said.

Feels? Brunelli was thinking. She had come from a platform where they were taught not to question their AI, since it ran most of the systems aboard the ship and ran them well. They were certainly not encouraged to second-guess it. Should she say so? Six miles or more, Courtenay might be inclined to turn to bring his torpedoes to bear. Less, and he could risk the turn, or the flooding of his tubes, giving *Agincourt* away.

McDonald beat her to it. "You run the same sensor suite as *AE1*," he said. "If it says 6 miles, it's most likely 6 miles."

Courtenay was twirling the toothpick in the corner of his mouth.

"Take the shot, Captain," McDonald urged.

"We need to be sure," Courtenay said. "Is it *Taifun*? I need a full acoustic match."

"Then you might die wondering," McDonald said simply.

"We'd have to close at least 500 yards, sir," Courtenay's sonar officer insisted. "Maybe more."

Courtenay pulled the toothpick from his mouth. "Helm, turn to starboard, easy. Weapons, arm special weapon."

"Arm special weapon," Singh repeated, consulting a screen.

214

Brunelli shot a look at McDonald, mouthing a silent sentence. *Special weapon?*

IN THE BOW of the *Agincourt*, a very unusual weapon was loaded into a torpedo tube and the tube filled with seawater. It was a weapon that was not in the armory of either the American or Australian navies, and which, until he started looking for solutions to the problem that was *Taifun*, Carl Williams didn't know existed either. But when he learned about it, he knew he had to have it.

It took several agonizing minutes to arm. Finally *Agincourt's* torpedo door eased open, inches at a time, its design creating minimum turbulence as the *Agincourt* slid through the water.

"Sonar?" Courtenay asked.

"Intermittent reactor noise on the intercept bearing," the sonarman said. "No change to classification, no propulsion noises, no acoustic signature matches."

McDonald knew the question from the British captain was unnecessary. His sonarman would speak up as soon as he had new information. It was a sign of nerves on Courtenay's part that he'd asked.

He also knew he'd be exactly the same.

Minutes ticked past. Every second brought them closer to their enemy, and to discovery. If this was *Taifun*, the most advanced submarine in the Chinese navy, every minute also brought them a minute closer to death.

It became too much for McDonald. Words clipped, tone forced, McDonald spoke into the thick silence. "You have a bearing to target; you are approaching minimum range for your Spearfish, Captain. Take. The. Shot."

"Propulsion noise!" the sonarman said. "Confirmed bearing and range on screen. Nine ninety yards. Target is picking up speed."

"Identification, Mr. Halloway," Courtenay said tightly.

"Analyzing …" the man said, sweat running down his temple. He wiped it away, running a finger across his screen. "*Type 095-23*. It's not the *Taifun!*" he said. "Not our boat."

McDonald spun around. "Helm, engines slow, easy on the turn, make your heading 180 degrees. Depth to 600. Weapons, close torpedo doors."

McDonald couldn't believe it. They had the enemy submarine dead in their sights on passive sensors. They probably weren't even aware they were being followed. No indications there was another submarine nearby. It was an almost certain kill, and Courtenay was aborting the attack!

He gripped the back of the chair in front of him as the big British submarine turned away from the oblivious Chinese boat and began increasing its separation. Twenty long minutes later, Courtenay handed over command.

"Mr. Singh, you have the conn," Courtenay said to his XO. "When you are certain we are clear, please send up a comms buoy and report the position of the enemy submarine."

"Sir."

"Well done, everyone," Courtenay said. "Coffee, I think." He crooked a finger at McDonald and Brunelli. "Join me in the wardroom. I'd like your thoughts."

No, you wouldn't, McDonald thought.

"YOU'RE WONDERING why I didn't take that shot," Courtenay said to McDonald and Brunelli when they'd filled their mugs with steaming black coffee and sat themselves at a table in *Agincourt*'s empty officer's wardroom.

"No," McDonald said. "To be honest, I was wondering what I'd be charged with if I relieved a foreign captain of command of his own vessel."

Courtenay didn't look surprised. "While it would be amusing to see you try, I must come completely clean with both of you about Operation Midnight, I can see that now."

"There's *more* you haven't told us?" Brunelli asked. "Apart from the fact we are hunting a superintelligent underwater killer robot with a code machine onboard and you won't tell us how you're getting positioning data on it?"

"Well, yes, a little. A lot. But in my defense, I was not told you were coming aboard until we weighed anchor, and I have had no instruction on how much intelligence to share with you. I erred on the side of less, but I can see I need to …"

"Do us the courtesy of telling us everything," McDonald growled.

"Or confine you to quarters," he said. "Which is an option I retain. What I'm going to tell you can't be shared with others in your navy without the permission of my navy."

"I can't commit to that," McDonald said.

"Then we are at an impasse," Courtenay said. "That is the condition of my bringing you into the circle of need to know."

"Where do I sign?" Brunelli asked without waiting for McDonald.

"Your word is enough, Lieutenant," Courtenay said then turned to McDonald. "Captain?"

"Alright. Yes, under protest."

Courtenay took a sip of his coffee, as though deciding where to start. "I didn't take the shot at that enemy submarine because we have only one special weapon, and we cannot waste it on the wrong target."

McDonald frowned. "In my navy, 'special weapon' means nuclear. Are you saying you're authorized to use a nuclear weapon?"

"How can you be sure you won't *sink* it?" Brunelli asked. "Any nuclear-tipped torpedo is going to create hull-crushing shockwaves, and no EMP pulse is going to travel through the water far enough to disable a submarine's systems if you detonate the warhead at a safe distance ..."

"That's where our American friend Mr. Williams comes in," Courtenay said. "The 'special weapon' is an electronic warfare torpedo. We call it ELFIN—ELF Interception and Neutralization. It closes on its target and takes over the Chinese ELF communication system to send orders to Chinese uncrewed submarines ..."

"You're going to hack a Chinese sub in real time?" Brunelli said, drumming her fingers on the table. "And what is the Chinese submarine doing while this is happening?"

"Trying to kill us, we assume," Courtenay said.

"Only until we take control," a voice from the doorway said. It was Williams, leaning in the doorframe, holding a laptop. "Sorry, I wanted a cup of java. Couldn't help overhearing."

"We take control?" Brunelli said. "Simple as that ..."

"No, not simple," Williams said. "Insanely difficult. But we have an attack vector that might work. That's what Operation Midnight is really about. If it doesn't work ..."

"You better follow up with a Spearfish torpedo," McDonald said. "Because *Taifun* won't play nice while you play spook. Maybe you can get your Enigma Machine from her wreck, if it doesn't end up 30,000 feet down."

"That would work," Williams allowed. "Except that *Taifun* is the Enigma Machine. The whole submarine." He pointed to his temple. "Imagine it like your head. You pull the brain, the Enigma Machine, out of your head, the body dies. But the brain dies too."

COURTENAY AND MCDONALD left for the control room, but Brunelli hung back and waited for Williams to get his coffee. He sat awkwardly, no space on the small table for both his mug and his laptop, so he ended up putting the laptop the floor.

"You do this kind of thing often?" she asked. "Hijacking enemy submarines at sea?"

"No, not really," he admitted. "It's a British capability. First time in a submarine for me, first time trying to hijack one."

"What I was worried about," Brunelli nodded, looking meaningfully at his laptop. "Because when the torpedoes are flying is not the time for you to say, 'Damn, I really thought this would work.'"

"Oh, don't worry, it will work in the first few seconds or it won't work at all," he said. "And besides, it won't be me doing the actual hacking. It happens at quantum speeds—so I have help."

"If it happens at quantum speeds, what kind of help can you get out here?" Brunelli asked.

Williams took a long sip of coffee and put it on the floor, opening his laptop and pointing the camera at Brunelli. A small glowing circle in the middle of the laptop screen started pulsing.

"HOLMES, say hello to Lieutenant Brunelli," Williams said.

Hello, Lieutenant, a voice from the laptop said, the circling pulsing in time with the words. *I was sorry to read about your encounter with* Taifun. *But I see AE1 will be repaired within three months.*

"You have an NSA AI in that laptop?" Brunelli asked.

"Not as such, no," Williams said. "HOLMES copied himself into the *Agincourt*'s mainframe before we left port. The laptop is just how he gets around."

I like being able to see the faces and hear the voices of the people I'm interacting with, the AI said. *It makes communication more effective. For example, you seem worried.*

"You do," Williams said. "What are you worried about?"

"Not worried," Brunelli told him. "This is my resting skeptic face. We're going to be firing an EW torpedo at the deadliest boat in the Chinese navy, and it will be firing homing high-explosive torpedoes at us. You see why I might want some more detail around that? Like, does this hack shut *Taifun* down, or scramble its brain, or just overload its system like in a denial-of-service attack? Or what?"

"More like 'or what,'" Williams said. "The hack that delivered us the blueprints and source code for *Taifun* also delivered us a code sequence that will 'reset' the AI and allow us to give it new orders."

"That sounds too easy," Brunelli said, crossing her arms. "Why would its creators give it that kind of vulnerability?"

"Because a hundred things can go wrong with a billion-dollar warship 3,000 nautical miles from base," Williams said. "So you need a way to reset it to 'factory defaults,' if you like, and start problem solving. If it accepts the reset code we found, we can get into its diagnostic subsystem and make the changes that will give us control." He pointed at the laptop. "I say 'we,' but I mean HOLMES."

"*If* it accepts the code. Why wouldn't it?"

I can answer that, HOLMES said. *The source code that was obtained was for an earlier version of the* Taifun *AI, nearly a year old now. The reset code could have changed since that version. Or its operation may have changed. I won't know until I deploy the ELF exploit.*

Brunelli clearly didn't look reassured by the answer. Williams hurriedly followed on. "Uh, we also found a self-destruct sequence in the code," he said. "If *Taifun* thinks it is in danger of being compromised, either physically or in a cyberattack, it might just blow itself up before it puts a torpedo in *Agincourt.*"

"Oh, well that makes me so much happier," Brunelli said. "Except for the '*might*' part."

The Battle of Hawaii: Fujian

AS BRUNELLI weighed the odds of ending as fish food, the pilots of *Fujian* were approaching the fishing grounds east of Hawaii where they'd scored a big haul the day before.

And they got a bite again.

"Radar contact, bearing zero two five degrees. Radar type: US P-99 Black Widow," Lei said to the drone pilots trailing in his wake. His radar warning receiver had flashed for a full second before going blank again—just enough for his combat AI to register the enemy radar energy and classify it. Not enough to get a range from the signal strength though.

Lei was flying at the point of a triangle, the less stealthy drones about 5 miles behind him. He'd perfected the tactic, working with *Fujian*'s less-capable CH-7s, of using his superior stealth and avionics to detect the American aircraft, then vector the drones on them, like a hunting master setting his hounds onto unwitting chickens.

But the Widow was no chicken, ripe for plucking. A sixth-generation American fighter, even though it was nearly twice the size of his Gyrfalcon, it had half the radar cross section. And it could carry *14* missiles internally to his four.

What a prize it would make!

China's media-approved pilots, like Lei, weren't allowed to make social media posts containing any sensitive information—for example, regarding their location, personal kill tally or the aircraft types they had destroyed. Censors made sure of that. But they'd developed a kind of visual code, which canny followers had picked up on. Pilots with personal kills to their names sewed a single tiny yellow star above the flag on their flight suits.

Lei had no stars on his flight suit yet, which irritated him to no end. He had not agreed to re-enlist just to be navy's poster boy. He wanted to play a genuine part in shaping his country's destiny. He wanted his children, if he ever married, to hear with pride what he'd done during the great war against imperialism. A fellow flight leader in a Gyrfalcon had directed *Fujian*'s drones onto at least a half dozen American F-15s the day before and let *Fujian*'s fighters take the risk of engaging, and the kills.

Not his style.

"Victory flight, maintain heading. I will investigate the contact."

NOTHING. Well, not exactly nothing. Bunny saw Flatline and Agony's planes where she expected them to be. But that was all. Satisfied no one was going to jump her in the next few busy minutes, Bunny put her plane back on a heading toward *Fujian* and killed her radar, setting up her own ELINT and optical infrared scanning profile to supplement her radar. She dropped a waypoint onto her nav screen at 50,000 feet.

"Widow, you have the stick. Take us to the waypoint."

Widow has the stick, her AI replied.

It banked right and put her plane into a gentle climb, heading for 50,000 feet as she worked her sensor suite. Another thing she had mapped in her quick circle in the sky was the atmospheric conditions around her Widow. She'd found a dense band of cold air up at 50,000 feet that would act like a thermocline in the deep ocean, reflecting some of the radar energy of anyone trying to look through it. *Win the height, win the fight.* Well, not always. Her own radar would have a harder time seeing aircraft below the dense band of air.

223

But if she could surf above it down the heading to the approximate position of *Fujian* ... In the game she was about to play, advantages were measured in fractions of an inch.

And above that denser air belt, there was a better chance she could get a connection with a geostationary milsat, if there was one available.

She keyed her radio. "Student Two, Student Three, Student Leader headed up to 50,000."

Neither Raptor replied. If it wasn't critical, they'd stay emissions dark.

MUSHROOM SAW the *Shandong* pilot break from her flight of three drones and start moving north, toward the contact he'd reported. On the one hand, it made sense, since his Gyrfalcon had the best chance of finding the American aircraft without being detected himself. On the other hand, it could be exactly what the Americans wanted, pulling their aircraft away with a tantalizing decoy while another force slipped in behind it.

She said nothing.

They were making directly for the hunting ground that had delivered them a bounty the day before—the no-man's land in the Pacific sky American fighters had to cross if they were going to make the 2,300-mile journey from their west coast to Hawaii with only one refueling stop.

Burning precious fuel, she had closed with her flight, and as she came within visual range, she opened a channel to them and the *Shandong* mission lead. "Victory Leader, Ao Yin Flight Lead, in contact with my aircraft and proceeding to mission patrol sector."

"Nice of you to join us, Lieutenant," Lei said acerbically.

"I'll join when I've dealt with this contact."

"Good copy, Captain. Ao Yin flight out."

Dealt with the contact? If it really is a Black Widow, then you'll be dealing with your ejection seat, you conceited fool …

Mushroom had chased a Black Widow across half the Eastern Pacific during the blockade of Taiwan. And it had bested them, not least because a Black Widow rarely hunted alone; it usually traveled in the company of armed drones or loitering munitions. Hopefully, with the US battlenet compromised, some of that force multiplication would be denied. Still, she had no doubt that in the hands of a good pilot, even a single Widow was a formidable foe.

Like the Gyrfalcon could be, if its pilot would use it that way. And not go off chasing individual glory.

BUNNY LET the autopilot take her nearly 30 miles southwest, on the heading Crystal had told her was their best guess as to where *Fujian* might be operating. She didn't want to close on the ship itself—hers was an air-to-air mission—but if *Fujian* was there, its aircraft would be fanning out from that direction, looking for prey.

She'd picked up no radar or radio energy. The belt of cold air that was protecting her was also blinding her passive sensors. "Widow, pilot has the stick."

Confirming, pilot has the stick.

She dropped her nose and began a gentle descent for 38,000 feet. As she dropped beneath the cold air, she boosted her radar and began a lazy fishtailing motion, bathing a wide arc of the sky ahead of her in energy.

A tune Meany would hum to himself when he didn't think anyone was listening came to her, and she hummed it too.

Who will have the fishy
On their little dishy
Who will have the fishy when the boat comes in?
Dance to your daddy, sing to your mammy
Who will have the fishy when the boat comes in?

THE CHIME in Lei's ears told him his radar warning receiver had picked up the target again.

There!

Twenty degrees off his nose, and constant this time. In no time, his combat AI had both a signal ID and range estimate. *P-99 Black Widow, 40,000 feet, 20 to 30 miles.*

He brought up his PL-15 missiles, set two to autonomous search mode. He could launch right now, but the large circle in the targeting viewfinder of his helmet told him the probability of a kill was low.

The dozy enemy hadn't locked onto him yet. He could close further. The PK circle was shrinking by the second. If he could deal with this Black Widow, he would make the rest of the day's missions infinitely easier, he was sure. And that little yellow star would be his.

Ah, what a prize!

KAREN 'BUNNY' O'HARE wasn't feeling at all dozy. Sprung from the medical equivalent of jail that morning, she was back in the cockpit of her beloved Widow again. She was feeling *electric*.

226

Not least because she had a target right off her nose, coming straight at her from 20 miles away. She'd even seen it alter course toward her, telling her it knew where she was, probably steering on her radar signal.

Which told her it wasn't a Chongming. They had good passive sensors but not that good. So it was probably an FC-31 Gyrfalcon. In one of the most damaging cyberattacks of the 2020s, China had managed to steal a huge amount of data on the F-35's avionics and stealth technologies. The first generation of FC-31 had taken flight without the benefit of the stolen secrets, but the second generation had. They had passive and active radar sensors comparable with the F-35, and instead of the stealth "coatings" of earlier models, the second generation of Gyrfalcon had a radar-absorbing lattice "baked" into its skin, like her Black Widow.

So if she could see him, she had to assume her enemy could see her. And judging by his aggressive approach, he was feeling confident.

Time to shake him up.

"Student flight, target on my 12 o'clock, 24 miles. Probable Gyrfalcon. Squirting data to you. Deploying MALD in Panther mode; please intercept the target."

"Two, copy."

"Three, engaging."

She cued up a MALD decoy and launched it 45 degrees off the bearing to her attacker, with a 20-second initiation delay. Then she killed her radar, rolled her plane onto its back, pulled her throttle back to 10 percent and put her Widow into a screaming vertical dive, straight at the sea.

LEI HAD a bearing to the American. He had closed sufficiently to give himself a 60 percent chance of a kill. Only 12 miles from the enemy aircraft now. His thumb hovered over the missile release.

And the enemy radar disappeared!

He wasted precious seconds in indecision, deciding whether to fire his missiles anyway, hoping they would guide themselves to their target with their own radar. But he had only four missiles. He couldn't risk it.

His training finally kicked in. *The enemy you can't see can kill you.* He lit his radar and flicked his plane onto a wingtip and began a spiraling turn, losing altitude, scanning the sky around him desperately.

A new radar threat! His RWR chimed and a new icon appeared on-screen, from a different bearing. F-35 Panther! A new attacker!

Lei urgently opened a channel to the Chongming flight. "Ao Yin Leader, Victory Leader, I am engaged with multiple adversaries. Request immediate assistance my position." He was trying desperately to get a radar lock on the F-35, but though his RWR could see it, his radar couldn't.

Then the Panther's radar signal disappeared too.

He had gone from hunter to prey in the blink of an eye. Now he was blindly barreling through the sky, with two enemies closing on him from different vectors.

Mushroom looked at the data Lei's Gyrfalcon was pushing to her and decided she couldn't ignore it. It looked like he had been flanked by a Panther while he was pursuing the P-99 Widow. Now both had disappeared.

He was probably a dead man flying, but she had to help him.

"Ao Yin pilots, make heading zero three zero. We are buster for Victory Leader. Radars in search and track; arm missiles. If you find a target, launch *immediately*."

Even as she lit her plane's afterburner and felt the pod simulate the acceleration by tightening her harness straps, the sixth sense she had developed over multiple engagements tingled.

Something was wrong. The Widow was a damned missile truck. Why hadn't it immediately fired on Lei Yu?

BUNNY HADN'T fired on Lei Yu because she didn't want to get into a dogfight with a Gyrfalcon. She had friends who were much, much better suited to that. She was down on the deck, skimming the water at flying fish height, headed east—away from the Chinese stealth fighter at 90 degrees.

She lifted her nose gently and decided to check the sky down that bearing now.

Oh, shit.

"Flatline, I'm seeing four fast movers on your tail; not sure if they're in pursuit."

"Nothing on RWR," Flatline said. "No emissions. I see nothing, Bunny." He sounded a little uneasy. But only a few days earlier he'd been pulled out of the ocean by a US warship. Bunny knew from firsthand experience ejecting from your plane was not a confidence builder.

"Breaking to pursue. I have your six, Flatline," Agony said. "What's our play, Student Leader?"

Bunny thought hard, looking at her radar screen. The Gyrfalcon wasn't showing; it had been decoyed away to her south by the MALD. Ahead of her and closing fast was Flatline. Behind him, four more Chinese fighters. Chongmings. Ahead of them, somewhere, a sky full of P-99 Widows that did *not* want to get into a furball.

"Keep prosecuting the Gyrfalcon, Student Two," Bunny said. "We'll take the four new contacts. Box them up, Student Three. Shoot on my call."

"Student Three copies."

Bunny checked her altitude, then flipped her radar into targeting mode and locked up the four Chinese aircraft about 12 miles ahead of her. She brought up her missile menu and allocated an AIM-260 to each. Behind them, she knew Agony would do the same.

"Fox three by four," she said into her radio as her missiles dropped out of her payload bay, fell a couple hundred feet and then ignited their engines, spearing away ahead of her as they rose from the sea to the sky.

MEANY AND BUNNY'S missions were the same but different.

He, Touchdown and Flowmax were also flying Combat Air Patrol—but over O'ahu, not over the sea. And the AWACS to their east, call sign College, had just reported vampires approaching from multiple vectors. It was close enough that it could push the tactical data to the Aggressor pilots over Hawaii.

"SEAD attack," Touchdown guessed. "Sub-launched. Trying to knock out ground radar and batteries?"

"For sure," Meany agreed. Suppression of enemy air defenses was always the first move in the chess game of air warfare. "Pucker up, Teacher flight." He switched to the

AWACS frequency. "College, Teacher Leader, you got targets for us? We got missiles."

"Negative, Teacher. Hold station. Air National Guard and ground defenses are taking this one."

Meany grunted. It looked to him like a *lot* of vampires.

Meany's networked Black Widow was up at 55,000 feet as the data hub. While Meany worked the data flow, his plane flew itself in lazy ellipses, directly above the combat taking place at Pearl Harbor below. Meany could also see smoke rising from several other points across the island, the slaughterbot attack not just limited to the Port.

Then a chime sounded in his ears, his battlenet link flickered to life on a tactical screen and the *Constellation* class frigate the Combat Command-capable USS *Lafayette* announced its arrival off the southern coast of Big Island.

"Hello, Navy," Meany said with typical understatement.

"Oh yeah, baby, that's better than sex," Flowmax said, the same chime happening in the cockpit of his Raptor.

"Not sure I'd got that far, Flowmax," Touchdown said. "But it is like seeing in color again after a week of black and white."

Lafayette was the last of Harry Connaught's "ship area network" vessels to reach position, and was already relaying high-speed communications and data from the four other ships and their FireScout helos strung out between California and Hawaii. What the network lacked in bandwidth—it could never fully plug the gap in cable and satellite capacity—it made up for in speed and security, offering high-speed, fully encrypted channels for all branches of the US military to maintain contact with their commands in Hawaii.

For protection from the Chinese submarines INDOPACOM assumed were patrolling offshore Hawaii,

231

Lafayette had deployed with two uncrewed SeaHunter anti-submarine drones, which circled it restlessly, scanning the sea below.

On another screen, Meany had data he suspected was being updated by old school radio and then patched through to him, of friendly vessels, and the estimated positions of Chinese and Russian ships northwest of Kaua'i. Meany didn't have to zoom that map out very far for the enemy fleet to look frighteningly close to Hawaii.

And while he was watching the Air National Guard Raptors and ground defenses deal with the suppression of enemy air defenses, or SEAD, attack, Meany was already thinking ahead to what might come next. Which had to be why the AWACS was holding them back.

At their pre-flight briefing, Meany had been told to stay alert for warnings of cruise or ballistic missile attacks. Flying near the stratosphere, the AIM-260 missiles of Aggressor's Widow and F-22s could be called on in extremis, using targeting data provided by USS *Lafayette*. Four years earlier, a P-99 Black Widow teamed with an Aegis destroyer had successfully intercepted a ballistic missile entering the atmosphere, with an AIM-260 missile. But four other tests had failed.

Lafayette and whatever ground-based defenses remained would do the heavy lifting if the Chinese attack on Hawaii went ballistic. But if that happened …

Touchdown broke into his thoughts. "What is College waiting for, boss?" she asked. "People are dying down there, and we've got missiles burning holes in our pockets."

She was right. Despite the best efforts of Raptors and air defenses, the first of the Chinese missiles were hitting home.

232

Then an alert sounded in Meany's helmet. His tactical screen automatically zoomed out as it filled with tiny icons. Hundreds of tiny icons.

Here it comes, Meany thought. After SEAD, the main strike. A thick wave of Chinese cruise missiles moving in from northwest of Kaua'i.

The Sino-Russian fleet had finally announced its arrival.

He scanned the screen, looking for the origin of the new data. Pacific Missile Range Facility, Barking Sands. So the PMRF radar had survived the SEAD attack.

It would not survive this one, Meany could see that immediately. The missile icons on his screen—small dots with trailing tails showing their direction of travel—each had a number beside them showing they'd been grouped. They stretched from the center of his screen to the top, and more were still entering. A single number at the bottom right of the screen beside a missile icon told him how many missiles PMRF was currently tracking.

Three hundred ninety-four.

His blood went cold. No. That was simply impossible. But the minute he thought it, he knew it was more than possible. Forty-plus warships in the Sino-Russian fleet? Nearly a dozen types capable of launching land attack missiles. Meany was no naval warfare expert, but one detail had stuck in his head after several briefings—a single Chinese *Type 055 Super Renhai* cruiser could ripple-fire eight missiles a minute, and its full load of 112 missiles could be launched in the space of 14 minutes.

This was just the first wave.

The Chinese missiles were all closing in on Hawaii from the northwest, but they were still closely grouped, fanning out left and right only to pass around the Kawaikini peak in the middle of Kaua'i Island.

Bound for O'ahu, he guessed, and the 30,000 military personnel and 1 million citizens already buckling under the combined weight of the slaughterbot and SEAD attacks.

The dour Welshman in Meany was hard to stir, but his heart was pounding now. He stretched his back, easing his exoskeleton into a more comfortable position, and rolled his shoulders like a wrestler preparing for a bout. "College from Teacher Leader. Talk to me, College."

IN ALL of its planning for war against the USA, China calculated that it might be anywhere from two to ten years behind its adversary in hardware quality. So it had to make up for that in *quantity* and apply the advantage of numbers where it would hurt most.

Meany was right that the Chinese had a follow-up attack planned. China had spent decades on the problem of how to deal with the US bastion of Hawaii, and the conclusion it had reached was exactly the same as the conclusion it reached about Taiwan.

A conventional combined-arms operation culminating in an amphibious invasion, against an overwhelmingly powerful adversary, would be suicidal.

And unnecessary.

China had watched and analyzed the conflict between Ukraine and Russia with microscopic intensity. Its conclusion was that strikes targeting infrastructure with simple high explosive damaged *morale*, but were quickly repaired. The clearing of a heavily mined area, however, was a task that took months, sometimes *years*, and cost many more lives. And until it was done, that area was essentially unusable by an enemy—their personnel and vehicles could not move through it. Applied to a civilian area, the cost to local armed forces was enormous since it required huge urban areas to be evacuated, and urban environments were harder to clear mines from.

Add to that the lessons learned from studying the US Marines "island-hopping" strategy, and their early successes against Chinese bases in the South China Sea …

Inside the 300-plus CJ-10 and CJ-100 cruise missiles converging on Hawaii were over 300,000 proximity mines, each carrying one kilo of explosive.

China's high-explosive area-denial munitions—antipersonnel, anti-vehicle and anti-shipping mines depending on their targets—were not just aimed at Pearl Harbor, Hickam Airfield and the main US bases of Fort Shafter, Marine Corps Base Hawaii and Schofield Barracks. They were also aimed at the densely populated areas of Pearl City, Kailua, Kaneohe, Waikiki and Ewa Beach.

But, interestingly, *not* the Honolulu downtown area around the 'Iolani Palace.

TWO TOURIST GUIDES stood at the entrance to the palace, museum staff behind them on the tiled terrace, the emergency warning siren wailing from a tower fixed to a rear wall. As Freeth and his people approached, one of the tourist guides—the bigger of the two—walked down the stairs, palms up like he was Moses trying to hold back the flood.

In their preparations for today, they had taken a tour of the palace. They'd found no security whatsoever, just a half dozen tourist guides handing out VR goggles for self-guided tours. With a war raging around him, the poor guy in front of them was trying to "de-escalate." Duke was walking beside Freeth, other bodyguards flanking, and he knew what to do. Freeth kept walking, stepping around the poor man, flapping his hands, whatever he was saying almost inaudible over the 120-decibel wail of the siren, the explosions over by Pearl Harbor and the chanting of his supporters.

What do we want?
Free Hawaii!
When do we get it?
Today!

Duke and four men surrounded the guide, almost gently holding him and pushing him back behind them into the mob, where a couple of protesters put their arms around his shoulders with brotherly assertiveness.

Freeth walked up the steps onto the tan and gray tiles of the terrace and turned, looking over the heads of his supporters, down the palm-lined avenue at the furiously burning Capitol building. A single fire truck had responded to the fire, but its crew weren't even rolling out their hoses. It was a five-engine fire, at least, but the Capitol stood alone, surrounded by grassy parkland; the fire wasn't going to spread. The solitary engine was parked up beside the more valuable building, the State Archives, ready to protect it from ember attack if needed.

The few staff of the palace moved aside to make way for Duke and Freeth's bodyguard. They were given little choice. Freeth turned to Duke and said quickly in a near whisper, "Get to the basement; secure the royal jewels. Lock the doors to the chamberlain's offices. I don't want to hear about any looting." Duke nodded and disappeared into conversation with a couple of his trusted lieutenants.

Freeth held out his hands to quiet the mob, letting the feathered cape spread like wings.

"People of Hawaii," he began. "This palace belongs to you. The final seat of the last independent government of Hawaii, it was used as a prison for Hawaii's colonist queen, Lili'uokalani—a fitting end to a shameful period in which the House of Kamehameha aided and abetted in the subjugation of our people." He drew a deep breath and roared. "That era ends today!"

The crowd roared with him.

He waved them to silence again, motioning Duke to draw near. "This is my deputy, Duke Apana. With your help, Duke will direct the peaceful occupation of the palace, and for this, we need your help. Our oppressors are otherwise occupied right now, but they will soon reorganize and attempt to force us from our seat of government." He held his fists high. "This time, we will not let them!"

Apana handed him a scroll of paper they'd prepared for today. Freeth unrolled it and looked up, flourishing it like a banner. "We have two simple demands of our occupiers. Firstly, that besides acknowledging the illegal annexation of these islands, they agree to dissolve the illegal occupation administration and hand back control of Hawaii to its original inhabitants. Secondly, that to enable this to happen, they support free and fair elections for a new government, among all true citizens of Hawaii, Kanaka Maoli, who can trace their heritage to one of the great Houses."

He let the applause die out naturally, and nodded to Duke, who took the scroll and rolled it up. "So first, I need volunteers for a peace patrol, to secure the grounds. Then I need volunteers to set up a voter registration office inside. People on other islands can register online via our website, or

237

locals can turn up here to register." People began raising their hands and Duke looked around him at the terrace, still crowded with dumbstruck palace employees. "Alright, so, if you good people can move aside, then maybe peace patrol on the left, voter registration on the right."

Freeth left Apana to organize the occupation and turned. Behind him, the Palace Grand Staircase led up to the second floor and the rooms that had been used by the colonists as both prisons and parliamentary chambers.

There was a desk up there that was his. And he had a broadcast to the people of Hawaii to make.

SERGEANT PAN TIEN, 5th Amphibious Combined Arms Brigade, was not a student of history. What he knew of the Hawaiian independence movement he'd learned in his mission briefing and since forgotten most of.

Pan was a student of violence, and its application as a means to an end.

In this case, the end was the nurturing of the nascent uprising that they found happening at Honolulu's 'Iolani Palace.

Pan and his convoy of SUVs had arrived in downtown Honolulu to find the city blanketed by smoke from fires burning at Pearl Harbor-Hickam, a northwesterly breeze carrying the smoke across the international airport and down the coast toward Diamond Head. A particularly dark plume of smoke from the fiercely burning Capitol building made their objective easy to find.

"These people know how to start a revolution," Pi said approvingly as they cruised slowly past the burning building, a firefighter waving at them to keep moving. An Army truck packed with troops passed them, headed away from Pearl Harbor, the soldiers gawking at the burning building, but it didn't stop. Pi leaned out his window looking up and down the wide four-lane boulevard that ran past the building. Traffic was crawling, people trying to flee the city center. Pi looked down at a map, then pointed. "Left up ahead, and then left into the palace. Where are the police?"

"Running from slaughterbots, or toward them," Pan guessed. "Evacuating civilians. Guarding the rich districts. It's a small city, Pi. How many cops can there be?"

THERE WAS ONE COP watching the Capitol burn. And officer Tammy Ballard also wondered where the hell her compatriots were. Having caught up to the looter convoy, she was three cars back, on her radio to the dispatcher, trying to find some backup.

"I have no one for you, Ballard," the dispatcher said.

"Sergeant, I got about 20 armed looters in a convoy riding past the Capitol building, which, by the way, is *on fire* …"

"Fire Department is on the scene," the dispatcher said.

Tammy looked over and saw the lone fire truck, the firefighters directing traffic, not trying to put the fire out. Even over the wailing of civil emergency sirens she heard something collapse inside the Capitol building and a shower of sparks rose into the air. *That building is gone,* she decided. She couldn't blame the fire brigade for hanging back.

"Ballard, best I can suggest is you follow those guys, get some plate numbers, get their faces on video for a prosecution later if you can do it without putting yourself at risk. Or if you don't want to do that, I got a hundred other callouts I can give you."

Tammy ground her teeth. "These guys shot a police officer, Sergeant. I'll stay on them." She put her radio back in its cradle. Then she got out her cell and tried to call her husband.

Busy tone. She tried to reach her oldest girl next. Busy tone. It didn't even go to voice, which told her the network was down or log jammed. She hammered her steering wheel in frustration.

The green pickup truck with the road workers in back was turning left now, and she moved into the right lane, hiding her patrol car behind a slow-moving bus. As she drew level with the street they'd turned off, she drove her car up on the sidewalk and watched. They had been moving toward the waterfront, but if they were headed for the big shopping district at Ala Moana, where the best looting would be, there were quicker routes than …

She jumped as someone banged on her passenger window. A worried citizen, standing there, indicating she should roll her window down. She kept her eyes on the green pickup but hit the button to roll down the window.

"I saw them, Officer," the man said. "The ones who set fire to the Capitol."

"OK, sir," she said, only glancing at him. "Can you call 3311 and report it to them?"

"I'm reporting it to you," the man said, annoyed. "There were hundreds of them. They marched around to the 'Iolani Palace. They're still there."

She looked at the palace through the smoke. He wasn't exaggerating; there were hundreds of people milling around there.

"You can still catch them," the man insisted.

Oh, right, yeah. I'll just take them to the station a few at a time for the next week, shall I? Tammy thought. She spoke without looking at him, trying to keep the green pickup in view. "I'll do what I can, sir. But I'd appreciate it if you call 3311 and report what you saw, OK?"

"No signal," the man said, flourishing his cell phone at her. "I'd have to go back to my office and I ..."

She didn't wait to hear anymore. The convoy of SUVs slowed and turned again.

Into the palace exit.

Well, that's an illegal turn right there, Tammy thought wryly. Add that to the list. She jumped out of her vehicle and, grabbing the shotgun from the jump seat, moved around to her trunk and picked up some shells, jacking them into the magazine. She filled her pockets with a bunch more, watching through smoke, fences and trees as the six SUVs disappeared into the palace grounds.

Not looters then. Unless they were art collectors going for the palace antiques, which she doubted.

Then she was running through the crawling traffic, across the grass, down the side of the burning building. Past a firefighter trying to wave her down, toward the palace boundary fence with its concrete columns and high spiked iron railings. Too high to climb.

Gate, farther down.

She stopped at the gate, looking around one of the stone columns, only head high. Enormous banyan trees on the lawns to the left, roots like the fences of a stockade. Big crowd outside the front steps of the palace, people inside. Groups of what looked like staff; a couple of guys who could be security mingling with the crowd.

She saw the lead SUV nose through the crowd, stopping right outside the main steps. The passengers started climbing out. The highway workers she'd seen in the back of the pickup and …

Cops. In Honolulu PD uniforms.

The sound of the civil emergency alarm changed, taking on a higher tone, pulsing faster, interrupted by a voice.

This is a civil emergency broadcast. Danger imminent. Seek immediate shelter underground. Repeat, seek immediate shelter underground.

Underground? The only place within reach—not on fire—was the palace. There were cars parked just inside the gate, and she crouched, running to the nearest one. Shoved her shotgun underneath it. The door had a state emblem and a seal saying "Department of Accounting and General Services Central Motor Pool." Looking inside, she saw a duffel bag, some clothes—someone's dirty laundry maybe.

Pulling the pistol from her belt, she held it by the muzzle and hammered the butt into the car window. The window smashed into a thousand small cubes. Reaching inside, she rummaged through the duffel bag, and found a dark green Rainbow Warriors fan shirt.

Not her favorite team, but it would do.

Radio? It would be too obvious under a T-shirt. She peeled it off and threw it under the car, feeling strangely naked.

She took her uniform shirt off and pulled the football shirt on over her black trousers. It was a couple sizes too large and smelled of stale sweat, but it covered her pistol and utility belt.

Then she ran for the crowd, to the basement entrance beside the palace steps, trying to get inside and into cover like everyone else.

HR ROSENSTERN, Chief of Staff to US President Carmen Carliotti, had been living in a basement for a couple days now, and he didn't like it.

Not even a basement with some head-high windows giving you a view outside. A bunker. Hundreds of feet under Greenland snow and ice.

So this was the last resort escape for Washington's elite in case of a biological or nuclear attack? HR thought. *What a fitting end it would be.*

The fact he was one of those elite didn't escape him. Absent hour-by-hour interactions with Carliotti, he'd kept himself busy managing communication about the pandemic response, and more than that, of course …

"Uh … Detroit and Montpelier," the Homeland Security Secretary, Janet Belkin—a detestably passive person who he had argued Carliotti shouldn't appoint—was just finishing an update for the NSC ExCom of the major centers of activity for the new civil rights group, Defenders of Liberty, which was the main agitator against pandemic restrictions. "That's the demonstrations we know about so far."

The continuity facility under Pituffik Space Base on Greenland had the same basic structure of every continuity facility, showing the usual lack of imagination of government engineers. HR had been given a personal tour of Pituffik by the base CO, an Air Force colonel, when they arrived, including a subzero walkaround of outdoor maintenance facilities, usually only accessed in summer. Inside a large maintenance shed, HR was surprised to see a half dozen ride-on mowers. They were still in the shrink wrap they'd been shipped in.

"You got a golf course or parklands here on Greenland I didn't notice when we landed?" HR asked.

The colonel had shrugged. "You know Air Force Material Command," he said. "They don't do details. When we reopened Thule Base as Pituffik, they asked 'how many square miles,' put that in their computer and then shipped the standard equipment they ship for a base of 10 square miles." He led HR past the mowers to a row of snow-clearing vehicles. "Took three months to convince them we needed these instead." He grimaced. "My predecessor told me he had an actual conversation with a pencil neck at Wright Patterson who said to me, 'It's called *Greenland*, not *Snowland*. You sure you need snow clearing equipment?'"

Like other continuity facilities, apart from the living quarters and mess, it mimicked the basic structure of the West Wing basement: a half dozen meeting rooms; video conferencing facilities; a large Situation Room; café and a small kitchen; dedicated rooms for Army, Navy, Space, Air Force, Marines, Secret Service and Homeland Security; toilets, showers and a sick bay; and of course … a swimming pool.

Because what better way to shake off your ennui about the apocalypse than a few brisk laps?

HR wasn't a swimmer. When Belkin stopped in her briefing to draw breath, he raised a hand.

"Madam Secretary, sorry. Montpelier is Vermont, correct?"

"Last time I checked, HR," Belkin said with a condescending smile.

"Population about *10,000*," HR continued. "So why is a demonstration in Vermont even on your radar? Whether it's this 'Defenders of Liberty' Group or not?"

Belkin sighed and looked over her shoulder at her Deputy Secretary, who had also been dragged onto a transport and buried under the ice on Greenland with his boss. The man rose. "Vermont is the most troublesome state when it comes to sovereignty, Mr. Rosenstern," he said. "Its Congress has partnered with Quebec, over the border, which recently began formal proceedings to secede from Canada. There was a bombing of a Post Office in Montpelier in 2032 …"

"A … *Post Office*," HR raised his eyebrows. "In Montpelier."

"Uh, yes, sir, a Post Office. No injuries but there have been death threats to state and federal politicians opposed to an independent Vermont. The Vermont Congress this year passed a motion of secession that was …"

HR waved at him to sit down. "Madam Secretary, Vermont is about a half million people in total population. You don't need to waste your resources, or our time, with updates on civil unrest in *Vermont*."

Belkin glared at him, but the glare slid off him like oil off the skin of an eel.

There is no clinical diagnosis for a sociopath. It's a word often thrown around but rarely understood by the person using it. A polite way to say "psychopath," perhaps, which *is* a clinical diagnosis and shares many of the same behaviors.

HR didn't have a diagnosis, but he was, in every sense of the word, a sociopath. Since the age of about eight, he'd begun to display behavior characterized by a disregard for the rights and feelings of others, a lack of empathy, manipulative tendencies and a tendency toward deceitfulness or impulsivity.

HR Rosenstern regarded concern for other people's feelings as an incomprehensible waste of time and energy. So he saw the annoyance and frustration in Belkin's eyes, but it moved him not one beat of his heart. Because HR Rosenstern knew something Janet Belkin did not.

Vermont was much more than the smallest state in the United States of America, having overtaken (undertaken?) Wyoming for that title in 2035 due to higher population growth in its Western competitor. It was also much more than a pain-in-the-ass pro-secession state.

Montpelier, Vermont, was the home base of The Principal, and HR knew the less attention was focused on it right now, the better.

"Can I suggest we move to the next item on our agenda?" HR said smoothly. "Travel restrictions and policing of internal borders ..."

The Rearguard: Garage

LIEUTENANT JACK CHANG, Fi and "Fluffy" were in reserve, holding back by the parking garage until called forward by Jackson. He was listening to the civil radio and landline network for slaughterbot sightings. The updates still came with disturbing regularity.

Beitou district. Missile bot. Moving west past Beitou MRT.

Shilin district. Cannon bot. Defense force is engaging with a bee swarm.

Neihu district. Cannon bot. Just attacked a patrol at the intersection of Kangning and Xingyun. Moving east down Kangning now.

Chang was only worried about those headed in their direction.

Da'an district. Cannon bot. Engaged by Army patrol on Jinhua west, but undamaged. Moving east toward Qingtian.

East toward Qingtian Street? Chang consulted his map. Damn.

"We're up," he told the girl. "Boot the bot."

She plugged here laptop into a port and started tapping keys. "I double-checked my weapons system hack. It looks solid. You should have control of the gun too. Crosshair in the VR glasses, move it with button A and the right thumb stick, button C on the controller to shoot," Fi said.

Chang watched the slaughterbot display in his VR set go through its startup routine and then saw the targeting reticle she was talking about, a green glowing cross. It took a little practice, but he soon had the hang of transitioning from flight control to weapons control. He couldn't do both, but that was a problem for another day.

"I put an ammunition counter in the lower right of the whatyoucallit …"

"Heads-up display—HUD."

"Right, HUD. I set it to fire two shots," Fi said. "There's a routine in there for selecting single, double and then bursts of different lengths, but I didn't have time to mess with it."

"If it shoots at all, it's a bonus," Chang told her, the closest thing to praise he'd given her.

They were only one mile from the target residence and just outside the perimeter they'd been told Ko's security detail had established around him. If a slaughterbot moved within that perimeter, shit would start happening fast, which was why he'd wasted no time waiting for the order to move the bot out. They'd identified a position over a low building about 500 yards east that gave their bot a clear shot at the compound without getting too close.

Chang got on the radio. "Unit One, Unit Three. We've got a hostile slaughterbot moving in from the west. I am moving up ..."

Jackson swung to train his binos west. He couldn't see the incoming bot; it must've been keeping low.

"How far from the perimeter is it?" he asked Chang.

"We could use the extra pressure ..." Xu said. "Move our bot in from the east *after* the Chinese bot approaches from the west."

"What I was just thinking," Jackson agreed.

"Uh, about five minutes from the perimeter if it doesn't get distracted," Chang said. "I've got it on VR vision. It's headed right down Jinhua Street toward the compound."

"Security detail won't let it close. They have to react," Xu said.

Jackson nodded. "Lieutenant, start moving up. Watch for jamming. Wait for a reaction to the hostile bot from the compound, then begin your attack."

"Moving up."

"Gunny, your status?"

"LS3 in position and awaiting target," Jensen reported.

Xu looked back over his shoulder and nodded in response to Jackson's questioning look.

"Alright, people, we're just waiting for the rabbit to run."

Jackson *hated* waiting.

THE LEAD AGENT on the security detail for Premier Ko En-Le was a dour, square-faced man with a buzzcut who his agents called "Mandu" because of his predilection for putting away about a dozen big Mandu pork dumplings at the end of every shift.

And at the exact moment Jackson gave his order, he was in fact looking forward to the end of what had been a harrowing shift, and which wouldn't be finished until the moment he got Premier Ko's "special guest" safely back to tiny Zhuwei Harbor and aboard the submarine waiting there.

In many ways it had been a simpler mission than most meetings between the premier and other VIPs, since instead of six or seven principals, there were only two. And their guest had brought his own protection with him. That didn't make him less nervous though.

Because really, Mandu shouldn't even have been lead agent. The guy who held that title—who had faithfully and expertly executed it for the last three years—had been taken by H5N1c. And his deputy too. Mandu was the longest-serving agent on the detail, regularly overlooked for

249

promotion and not anyone's first choice for lead. But that was the reality of Taiwan right now—the luxury of choosing the best person for the toughest jobs was over. These days, the best person was the one who was still standing.

Their security team used to be a hundred strong. Mandu was lucky if he could pull together 20 fit men or women now. Their guest's four bodyguards—Navy SEALs, by the look of them—were independent of Mandu's team and not much interested in anything but protecting their own principal.

When his western perimeter watch officer reported an incoming slaughterbot, Mandu reacted with relative calm. He'd anticipated a Chinese bot attack and had Stinger missile teams at four points of the compass around the premier's house. He'd tried to get killer bee teams, but the Army wasn't interested in sharing the few they had.

"Stinger Team Two, deal with the bot on Jinhua Street as soon as you have visual," he ordered, trying to sound bored.

The premier was sitting at a mahogany table, his sleeve rolled up as their guest, dressed in a military uniform but with a stethoscope slung around his neck, pushed a syringe into his arm. He winced, and he looked up. "A problem, agent?" he asked.

The man hasn't even bothered to learn my name yet, Mandu thought. He smiled in what he hoped was a reassuring way. "No, Premier. Slaughterbot two blocks out. Our defenses are ready. It will be dealt with."

The Taiwanese premier turned to his guest. "Is one jab sufficient?"

"Just one is needed," Ko's guest said equably. "Then another in three months." He was a portly man, in his 50s, with slicked-back black hair held in place with a heavy application of gel. Mandu could only imagine the difficulty with which he had to be maneuvered in and out of a submarine hatch.

"And you have enough doses for all my ministers?"

"And their families." The man nodded. "You are certain your president and vice president will not be able to rally your opponents?"

Ko looked smug. "From house arrest? They are completely isolated. And will stay that way until they are brought out and tried for treason."

Mandu might have been shocked by what he was hearing, or if not shocked, just a little disconcerted at least. But he was not a man interested in politics nor the scruples of the principals he was ordered to protect. He was a man who did the job he was ordered to do, without troubling himself about the whys or wherefores … which was probably why he had successfully avoided responsibility for so long. Until today.

"Bot is inside the perimeter. Stinger Team Two engaging," a voice in his earpiece said.

Mandu nodded to himself. *Yes, those dumplings were going to taste good tonight.*

"Team Three, slaughterbot on Jinhua Street!" A new voice broke in over the radio.

Mandu frowned. "Yes, we know that, agent. Maintain a watch for …"

"No, a second bot. *Above* a building in the east. It is …" Mandu heard the unmistakable sound of cannon fire over the radio, then nothing but static. A second later, cannon fire hammered the front wall of their compound.

The compound had a bombproof basement, but what if the slaughterbots had missiles and brought the roof down on them?

Two bots? His former boss would have had a contingency plan ready for this situation, would have rehearsed his agents in it and would have responded by putting it into play immediately to secure the premises and keep the premier's business on track.

Mandu was not that man. He panicked.

He turned to the other agents in the room and twirled a finger in the air. "All teams, we're moving out. Take the principals to the limo. We're going to Safe House Two." He took two steps and put a hand on Premier Ko's elbow, trying to exude calm professionalism, annoyed his voice was a pitch higher than normal. "Uh, we have to go, Premier. The perimeter has been breached from two directions. We have a safe route out."

He was prepared to lift the man out of his chair if he was too slow, but Ko stood immediately, looking alarmed. He turned to his guest. "This is our new normal, I am afraid. We can continue our discussion when we get to a safer place."

"Safer than your own private residence?" the physician said, sounding annoyed. "I was told we were meeting here because the *coast* was not safe." His private security detail had moved up alongside him, and looked just as annoyed.

"Thanks to your government, nowhere is completely safe on Taiwan, Doctor," Ko said.

The man's agent in charge, lithe and lethal looking, put a hand on Mandu's shoulder. "We will travel with the shipment."

Mandu shrugged the hand off. "It has already been loaded in the premier's armored vehicle. The doctor can travel with us. You can follow in a civilian car."

The man wasn't having it. He gave Mandu a cold stare. "No, we will be in that vehicle."

There wasn't time to argue. "Alright, *one* of you—there is no space for more. The other three will have to follow."

As the two principals were bundled out of the room, Mandu looked around, grabbed up the folios with schedules they had been reviewing and followed them, thinking five steps ahead, like he'd been taught.

Into the limo. South on Alley 29 to Jinshan, then east into Forest Park; safe house entrance from the underground parking garage.

"North watch team, redeploy to Forest Park," Mandu said, hurrying after the principals. "South watch, clear the egress route."

Mandu smiled. *Smooth work, buddy. Maybe you are cut out for this job after all.*

"MOVEMENT in the alley," Gunny Jensen reported. "Motorbikes."

"That's the advance team," Xu said over his radio. "They'll run the route ahead of the target, check it's safe to move."

"Understood."

Jensen pulled back into cover inside the restaurant as the two motorcycles sped past, their electric engines almost silent, trash paper swirling into the air in their wake. Squirt had been crouched behind cover, but using the controller and the view in his monocle, Jensen moved him up now so that he was standing just inside the doorway—out of view of anyone driving up the alley but with an unobstructed path ahead of him.

Jensen picked up the borrowed Taiwanese T91 assault rifle Xu sourced for him, checked the magazine and racked a round into the breech. From his pocket, he pulled a single earplug. His tactical radio earpiece was noise canceling, would protect his left ear, so he squeezed the earplug into his right ear, pushing it in deep.

Things were about to get loud. What hearing he had left, he wanted to keep.

JACKSON WAS WATCHING down the alley, saw agents in suits exit the rear of the premier's residence. "Lieutenant, sitrep?"

"Security RPG team taking down the other bot ..." There was a sharp report over the radio, loud enough to make Jackson wince. "No, not down. It's moving up. They're pulling back."

Jackson was thinking hard. The slaughterbot intruder was a wild card, but one they could play to their advantage.

"Lieutenant, you have guns on the front of the compound?"

"Yes."

"Fire on the front of the residence. I want to pile on the pressure."

"Engaging."

Jackson had his eyes locked on the rear of the premier's compound. Still only a couple of agents in the alleyway. Were they opening the gates though?

"Ready, Corporal," Jackson said softly.

Xu worked the bolt on his rifle. "Believe it, Sergeant."

CHANG HOVERED the slaughterbot, aimed the cannon down over the rooftops in front of him at the front of the compound and squeezed the button on his controller. He wasn't optimistic; the girl's latest hacks were still untested.

254

But the view from the slaughterbot jerked as the cannon fired two rounds, which slammed into the wall beside the gate and sent the shooters there scurrying for cover.

The slaughterbot to their west added its fire to theirs, aiming at the same position, like it was taking its cue from him.

Chang heard a whoop beside him. "Yeah, I told you!" Fi was watching the feed in 2D on her laptop. "Take that, assholes!"

Chang wanted to shoot a glare at her but had to stay on task, instead letting his irritation show in his tone. "This isn't a video game, girl. This is war. People are dying. Keep your trap shut."

"THIS IS JINHUA STREET GATE," a voice said in Mandu's ear. "We're taking fire from both west and east now."

Mandu frowned. He'd been right. Twin bots attacking. Two could quickly become four. They had to get out.

He looked around the rear courtyard. The principals, loaded into the armored limo. Their guest's security lead standing in the open doorway, his other three bodyguards standing uncertainly around the car, snub-nosed silenced automatic weapons in their hands.

Fat lot of good those will do you against a slaughterbot, Mandu thought.

Two of his agents on their motorbikes, ready to escort the limo, one at rear. The one in front signaled the egress route was clear. He could *hear* the buzz of a slaughterbot from the other side of the compound.

He moved to the limo, opened the rear door and climbed in. Their visitor's bodyguard climbed in behind him and squeezed onto the seat opposite, between the two principals.

"Move out," Mandu told the driver.

"Sir, we haven't heard from the advance team yet," the driver said.

"Move *out*, I said," Mandu said tightly.

CORPORAL XU had his scope centered on the gap in the wall that was the rear exit from the premier's compound. He'd had more than enough time to ready his shot, and when he saw the armored vehicle nose carefully out into the alley, he pulled his sights away from the car, and down the alley ...

Range: 510 yards to the tiny square of tin sticking out of the dirt just short of the shop in which Gunnery Sergeant James Jensen was crouched, with his hands over his ears.

Four inches by four inches. That was the target Xu had to hit from a range of just over 500 yards to send a trigger pulse to the buried IEDs.

Too easy. It wasn't even moving.

"ADVANCE TEAM ONE," the radio in Mandu's ear said. He'd just settled himself back in his seat, buckling on his belt. "We're picking up some signal energy on a military frequency ahead of you."

"It's probably ours," Mandu told them dismissively. "Some army unit ..."

"No, sir," the man said, sounding worried. "Not ours. It's a US Marine frequency. We haven't been advised of ay US military activity in this sector ..."

Americans. They were cowboys. Doing as they pleased, coordinating with no one. Nothing unusual there. But these days there were rogue units, vigilantes with stolen military radios, you name it.

Damn it.

He leaned forward, talking over Premier Ko's shoulder. "Slow down," he said to the driver and then turned his attention to the radio and the team he had clearing their route. "Advance One, try to get a fix on those signals and investigate."

"Advance One doubling back," the agent on the radio confirmed.

"THEY'RE OUT," Xu said softly. "Lead motorcycle has gone past Unit Two. But the limo is slowing."

"I see it," Jackson said. "Come on, buddy, just another few yards."

They wanted the nose of the vehicle just past the small square of metal sitting at the side of the alley.

Squarely over the IEDs buried two inches under the gravel.

"YOU WANT ME TO STOP?" the driver asked Mandu. He touched a foot to his brakes.

"What is the holdup?" Premier Ko asked irritably.

"Nothing, Premier," Mandu replied, sounding more certain than he felt. "No," he told the driver. "Keep rolling. But slow."

"We must keep moving," the doctor's bodyguard said. The doctor himself was ashen faced, pressed back into his seat.

Mandu couldn't help but enjoy the irony of the man's situation. "Those are your slaughterbots out there. We will move when my team says the route is clear," Mandu said, letting his irritation at the man show in his tone.

The threat, if that was what it was, was ahead of them somewhere. No need to rush toward it, right?

XU FIRED.

He saw dust behind his tin target, thought for a horrible moment he'd missed.

Then the ground underneath the limo *erupted*.

JAMES JENSEN didn't hear the crunch of the approaching tires on the gravel outside the shop doorway. He didn't hear the sonic whip-crack of Corporal Xu's shot either.

But he heard, and *felt*, the jarring thud of the 80 lbs. of high explosive in the 60 mm armor-piercing shells detonating right underneath the premier's limo.

Gravel sprayed the rear exit of the shop like shrapnel, shattering a window and sending chips of wood flying off the doorframe. Jensen waited for the sound of flying gravel to abate, then looked up and down the alley.

Right. One agent on a fallen bike. Down, not moving.

Jensen swiveled left. Car, down on its front axle, tires shredded, motor and batteries smoking, windshield glass intact, maybe smoke inside the vehicle too?

Beyond the limo, rear escort, bike down, one man rolling from side to side, bloodied, clutching his helmet. Blast or shrapnel had flayed his shirt. Jensen put two rounds into him, not waiting to see the result.

He fixed his LS3 control monocle on the rear passenger door of the armored limo, painted a cross on the door and triggered Squirt.

The LS3 had come a long way in its development since Jensen had field-tested it in Syria, years earlier. It was used not just by militaries but also by police SWAT teams to do the dangerous work of breaking down doors and breaching into buildings.

Or vehicles.

Squirt jogged out of the shop doorway, over to the vehicle door that Jensen had marked. At the end of the robot arm that was its "neck," it had a sonic drill designed to penetrate the premier's armored limo in its weakest spot ... the five-inch-thick glass passenger windows.

It extended its jointed arm and slammed a suction cup against the window of the limo to create contact, and then the drill started humming.

Jensen shrank back into the doorway of the shop, checking to see the four bodyguards were still down. He saw a couple of heads appear at the rear gate and sent a few rounds downrange to force the agents there to pull back.

Come on, buddy, we don't have all day, he thought as the hum grew in pitch to a whine, and then a scream that penetrated even his mil-spec earplugs. He cupped his hands over his ears.

The IEDs that immobilized the armored limo weren't expected to finish Ko. The underside of the limo was also armor plated, and built to withstand the shock of a 155 mm artillery shell—a favorite of roadside bomb-makers around the world. But all Jackson wanted to do was stop the limo in its tracks and stun its occupants, which the 60 mm shells did.

As the scream of the sonic drill peaked and then went silent as it exceeded the range of human hearing, Jensen

259

heard the glass passenger window crack, and then shatter, dissolving into thick cubes. He ordered Squirt to withdraw.

"Frag out," Jensen announced over the radio, rolling out into the street as he pulled a grenade from a pouch and crouched under the now open car window. A shot from inside the car went over his head and he ducked. More shots struck the surrounding ground—agents from inside the premier's compound joining the firefight.

"Ah, Lieutenant? Could use some fire support here," Jensen said to the slaughterbot pilot.

"Moving across," the man said. "Will have guns on in one mike."

Get it done, JJ, Jensen urged himself, rising to a crouch.

INSIDE THE PREMIER'S limo, Mandu's ears were still ringing from the combined effect of the twin blasts that had lifted the front of the 5-ton limousine up and slammed it down again on shredded tire rims, then the screaming whine of what must have been an acoustic weapon of some sort by their window.

"Get moving!" Mandu yelled at their driver, who was groggily shaking his head, having taken the brunt of the explosion beneath his feet. Even jammed across the alley with shredded tires like it was, the limo should be able to push forward.

He checked the premier, sitting opposite, shaking his head to clear it, trying to unbuckle, and the doctor seated beside him, head lolling on his shoulders as he struggled to sit up straight. The bodyguard between them, the man built like a Navy SEAL—who probably was a Navy SEAL—had taken the brunt of the blast right beneath his feet. He was bent double, holding his legs, both ankles or tibias fractured probably.

But alive. For now.

"Drive!" Mandu yelled again, trying to shout louder than the screaming noise from outside the vehicle.

Then the window shattered, the glass cubes tumbled into the limo, and Mandu pulled his service pistol, firing blindly through the open window.

He could still hear screaming, then realized it was coming from him.

JENSEN TOSSED his grenade over his head. He'd set the timer to the bare minimum two seconds, relying on the limo's armor to protect him from the blast as he ran back to the shop doorway.

He reached the door right behind Squirt, rifle fire biting at his heels from agents down the alley.

Then he heard the muted *crump* of his grenade exploding inside the vehicle.

MANDU SAW the small object fly through the window. Didn't see where it landed; somewhere over his shoulder.

Grenade.

The premier saw it too and rose to his feet, throwing himself across the doctor and grabbing at the frame of the open window, trying to get out.

The other bodyguard scrabbled on the floor for the grenade. *Fool.* There was no time. Mandu did what he was trained to do. It wasn't bravery as much as ingrained reflex.

He threw himself forward, trying to put himself between the principals and the explosion.

Lieutenant Chang saw the world in his VR glasses through the targeting camera mounted above the slaughterbot's cannon.

It was 500 yards back from the compound, and he flew it higher to give himself better vision as he swung around to line up with the rear alley.

Car, down on its front axle, engine and battery compartment smoking, smoke pouring out of a broken window too, jammed diagonally across the alley.

Two motorcycle riders down.

Shooters, rear of the compound, firing on Jensen's position from the gates of the residence.

He sent a rapid series of twin 20 mm shells downrange.

"NICE WORK, TEAM," Jackson said over the tactical radio. They'd taken out the target vehicle, and the premier's security detail was tied down inside the compound by Fi's slaughterbot. The away team the premier's detail had sent on ahead of them would think twice about coming back with two hostile slaughterbots roaming the streets. They had a small window in which they could all disengage. But first …

"We need confirmation on that kill," Jackson said, almost to himself.

"No movement around the vehicle, but I can't see inside," Xu told him. "Too much smoke."

Jackson nodded. "Gunny, I need you to check inside the vehicle and confirm the kill. Lieutenant Chang, can you provide covering fire?"

"Affirmative," Chang said. "Ah ... *wait*. That other slaughterbot is moving to the rear of the compound."

The Battle of Hawaii: CAP

LOITERING OVER O'ahu with Touchdown and Flowmax, Meany didn't have to wait long for new tasking. "Teacher Flight, College. Proceed to sector echo three zero and support *Lafayette* with targeting data on vampires inbound Kaua'i," the AWACS controller ordered.

Meany repeated the order back. "Uh, College, assume we coordinate targets with *Lafayette* and support with our own missiles?"

"Negative, Aggressor," the controller said. "ELINT report from PMRF Kaua'i indicates there may be fast movers among the Chinese contacts. You will reserve your missiles to engage any Chinese aircraft trying to push in behind the Chinese barrage. *Lafayette* and ground defenses will engage the cruise missiles."

Meany opened his mouth to argue, then shut it again. There wasn't time. He keyed his radio.

"You heard the man, Teacher Two, Teacher Three. Turn to two eight zero degrees and radiate. Keep data sync with me, and I'll relay targets to *Lafayette*. Watch out for Chinese aircraft and don't ask for permission to engage if you pick any up."

"Good copy, Teacher Leader," Touchdown said. She brought her plane around and coordinated an intercept route with Flowmax. In seconds, their radars had also locked onto the incoming Chinese missiles, providing *Lafayette* with extra data points for its targeting calculations as it began ripple-firing interceptors at the vampires.

The reason Meany wanted to argue his orders was the sheer mass of incoming cruise missiles. Meany knew a frigate like *Lafayette* had only about 40 long-range surface-to-air missile tubes and 20 short-range. He didn't know how many ground batteries had survived the first Chinese anti-radar missile attack, but from his vantage point on high, he could see the US defenders were going to need all the help they could get, and his two Raptors, working with his Widow, could add 30 interceptors to the mix if they were allowed.

That thought was quickly overtaken by events.

"Uh, Teacher Leader, we have two Shenyang J-15 radar signatures, bearing two seven three, heading niner zero, look like they're down low, rounding Kawaikini peak on Kaua'i Island," Touchdown said urgently. "I'd say they put some strike aircraft in the middle of that missile package. Intercepting."

"Roger, Teacher Two. Hold back, Teacher Three, there may be . . ."

"Two more J-15s, bearing two six niner," Flowmax said. "South of Kawaikini, heading niner zero. Intercepting."

The J-15 wasn't a stealth aircraft —it was an older carrier borne type—but it could still carry a formidable air-to-ground ordnance load. Meany had the Chinese aircraft on his own tactical screen and boxed them too. They were already in range of his AIM-260 missiles. "Teacher Lead is available to support," he told Touchdown.

"Fox three," Touchdown called, releasing two missiles at the targets fast approaching O'ahu.

"Fox three," Flowmax said a second later.

Meany held his breath. Missiles were also lancing out from the PMRF, from ground batteries across Hawaii, and from *Lafayette* behind and below him. Looking down through his fuselage with his DAS cameras, he could see a latticework of missile contrails crisscrossing the sky—some American, most Chinese.

265

"Four aircraft kills," Touchdown said with satisfaction. "Chinese missiles crossing below us now," she said, sounding less happy.

"Lafayette from Teacher Leader, you want to set us loose on those missiles *now, Lafayette."*

TOUCHDOWN AND FLOWMAX had not shot down four Chinese J-15s.

They had shot down four Chinese GJ-100 Sharp Sword drones—cheap flying wing decoys designed to mimic the radar and electronic signature of a J-15 fighter. Among the 300-plus missiles launched at Hawaii were dozens of the Sharp Sword drones, and they were doing exactly what they were intended to do, attracting the attention of US fighters and soaking up their missiles.

ONE HUNDRED twenty miles south, Mushroom's sixth sense went from a tingle to an ice-cold certainty. The Gyrfalcon pilot had flown them right into an ambush.

"Ao Yin pilots, evade!" she called.

Ahead of her, a fighter radar had locked onto her. Behind her, another radar locked her up, causing her RWR to warble frantically. Her intuition saved her. Half-expecting the enemy to show themselves sooner rather than later, she already had her PL-15 missiles in home-on-radar mode and snapped a shot off immediately before she locked her eyes on the steering cue in her helmet visor and sent her Chongming corkscrewing toward the sea at a right angle to both the missile in front and the missile behind her. She pumped radar and infrared decoys into her wake.

266

IT SHOULD have been a slaughter, and it nearly was. The four Chinese fighters were caught in a vice, with no easy option. In seconds, three were atomized.

One however, reacted instantly—almost before Bunny had even fired—and got a missile away in Bunny's direction before powering toward the sea.

Now *Bunny* was defensive.

She was already down on the deck, the Chinese missile only 10 seconds out, her options limited. But it had been fired so quickly, her attacker couldn't possibly have gotten a radar lock on her. *Infrared, or emissions guided.* She hauled her plane into a desperate turn, holding her thumb down on her infrared flare decoy release even as she tapped the key to shut her radar down.

Out of the corner of her eye she saw a flash, then felt a jarring thump in her back as something exploded behind her. She leveled out, then turned in the opposite direction, head over her shoulder, seeing a spout of seawater rising high into the air.

Too close, O'Hare, she thought.

She didn't want to light her radar up again, but she had a picture in her mind of where the surviving Chinese fighter was and angled her plane away from it so it wouldn't pick up her hot exhaust but she could put some distance between them again.

"Student Three, there's one still alive," she said into her radio mic.

"Got a new problem, Student Leader," he told her. "Your Gyrfalcon friend is back. I'm locked."

"Chill, Student Three. He's mine," Flatline said. "Fox three."

LEI YU HEARD Mushroom's desperate call to her pilots to "Evade!" and realized he'd been suckered. He could see the formation of Chongmings split apart like a starburst firework, then pulled his plane around and focused his radar down the bearing to the drones.

Whatever had fired on them was not registering on his radar. More American stealth fighters—but real this time. Then he got a return. Up high.

F-22.

He smiled. Easy meat. Long-range shot, but he wasn't going to fool around this time. He sent two missiles downrange immediately in semi-autonomous mode. Invisible to the aircraft he had fired at, they would take their guidance from his Gyrfalcon until just before impact.

He was so focused on the icons and tracks in his helmet visor that his hands jerked on his throttle and stick when the missile warning started screaming in his ears.

Followed by a disembodied AI voice. "Dominator has the stick."

What the …?

The missiles he'd fired lost their lock. A big red X and a smaller white one painted themselves across his helmet vision, blanking out everything else. The designers of the Gyrfalcon AI had learned that if an aircraft in Lei's situation was to have a chance of surviving, the pilot had to be taken out of the equation.

The Empire Dominator AI yawed the plane and pulled its nose around until the small white cross was centered in the red one. The maneuver gave it the best possible chance of surviving the next few seconds. As it was flying the plane, the AI also handled jamming and missile decoys, sending radar energy down the bearing to the missile and firing two active jammers on parachutes into his wake, at the same time as it sprayed chaff and flares either side of him.

"MISSED, DAMMIT," Flatline said. "I've lost lock. He's gone ninja."

"Pull back to me, both of you," Bunny said. The missiles the Gyrfalcon had fired at Agony both went wide, neither going anywhere near him. Bunny was still down low but had increased her separation from the last contact she was engaged with to 30 miles. She was coming around again to look for it, and draw both it and the Gyrfalcon to her while she did. With every twist and turn they forced on the Chinese fighters, the P-99 Black Widows of the 173rd and the 354th moved closer to Hawaii, undetected. "I'll play a little electronic tag with these guys, see if I can fix them here a little longer."

"Roger, pulling out," Flatline said.

"Agony copies."

Bunny cued up her last MALD, set a one-minute initiation timer, and fired it down a bearing that would put it at the complete opposite side of the compass to the Widow convoy behind her. The Chinese fighters were not emitting any energy. But neither was she, so they were all blind to each other. She needed to wake them up again.

Game's not over yet, China, she muttered to herself.

MUSHROOM HAD recovered her plane down at flying-fish height and was climbing out again. One minute ago, the sky had been full of aircraft and missiles. Now it felt like she was alone.

But not quite.

"Ao Yin from Victory, looks like being late to the party saved your hide, Lieutenant," Lei said. Mushroom checked her tactical view and saw he had reappeared about 5 miles off her port wing. "Check fuel," he ordered.

A good idea. It had been a long flight to catch up with her pilots, and she had done it at speed. "Uh, 53 percent," she said. She was running a calculation on how much longer she could remain in the hunt when her RWR pinged again.

"New contact, bearing one seven nine, F-22 radar type!" she said. "In search mode. Your orders?"

"We can't afford any more losses today, and you will soon be at bingo fuel. We'll have to call it a day," he said. But he didn't sound disappointed or annoyed; he sounded ... shaken. "I will return to *Fujian*. Watch my six on the way back."

The order rankled. It shouldn't have, but it did. He was saying to her: *You are safe in your pod. It's my ass on the line out here. You'd better make sure nothing happens to me.*

RADIO EMISSIONS.

The brief spikes of distant energy were all Bunny needed. She had a bearing to the Chinese fighter or fighters, and she still had a belly full of AIM-260 missiles. She had no idea whether the Chinese fighters were still hunting for her, or fleeing from her, but it didn't matter. She just had to keep them busy for the time it took the last Widow in the convoy behind her to get past them.

She put her AIM-260s in autonomous seeker mode and gave each of them a heading with a half degree of radial separation. They would fly down the bearing to the Chinese fighters with their onboard radars scanning the sky ahead of them, looking for anything that didn't have an allied Identify Friend or Foe beacon on it.

She rippled them off manually, putting a couple of beats between each launch. "Fox three by *six*," she said with satisfaction as the last one lanced away into the sky. Then she turned her plane northwest, toward Hawaii.

"MISSILE-TARGETING RADARS!" Mushroom said. "Six o'clock. I count ... six missiles!" It was the Widow; she *knew* it was. Nothing else had that kind of firepower. Nothing else could have engaged and stayed engaged for so long against so many Chinese fighters. It had help, of course ... not all of the F-22 and F-35 signatures out there had been decoys. But this last deadly volley. It could *only* be a Widow.

"Going low," Lei said. "You know what to do, Lieutenant."

Yes, she knew what to do. He was ordering her to sacrifice herself.

She brought her plane around. The enemy missiles had been launched at nearly 60 miles' range, their targeting radars lit, looking for prey. She had to be that prey. Shoving her throttle through the gate, she put her plane behind Lei Yu and on an intercept course for the missile farthest to her right. It was too small for her to kill with one of her remaining missiles, but that wasn't her plan.

At 30 miles out, she pumped a huge cloud of radar reflective foil into her wake, then swung left, rocketing

271

through Mach 1.2 as she aimed her plane ahead of the last missile in the line, pumping more foil into the sky as she went.

One by one, the American missiles took the bait, first swinging toward the big clouds of foil and then seeing something they liked much, much better.

Mushroom's Chongming, flying straight and level, broadside on to them.

Two of them were suckered by the foil and exploded harmlessly behind her. Four weren't. Curving in on her from east and west, despite being launched in series, the lateral distances they had to travel meant they reached her almost simultaneously, and one by one, they struck her plane, then the wreckage of it.

Her Chongming soaked up the entire attack as Lei scurried away down low. They had lost four drones to the Americans in this engagement, and claimed no kills. But their hero pilot had survived to fight another day.

A fitting victory for Victory Squadron.

"Ao Yin Leader is down," Mushroom said inside her pod, lifting her hands away from stick and throttle. The air inside her pod, like the taste in her mouth, was sour.

"I'M WINCHESTER," Meany announced. After they dealt with the Chinese fighter incursion, he'd fired his last interceptor at the incoming Chinese cruise missile onslaught.

Together with *Lafayette* and ground defenses on Hawaii, its air defenders had taken out nearly a hundred missiles, but 200-plus had reached their targets. Though not in the pattern or with the effect Meany had expected. He'd predicted most would be aimed at O'ahu with its multiple military installations and personnel, and around 200 were.

272

But at least *20* made it through the islands' defenses to strike the Pacific Missile Range Facility. Its radar was off the air, and it had gone radio silent. Meany dreaded to think how many casualties there might be.

Another 20 missiles curved around Kaua'i's Kawaikini peak and hit targets in and around Lihue City's airfield and cruise ship port. A lone MML battery had survived the initial SEAD attack and accounted for dozens of incoming cruise missiles, but it could only do so much.

Lihue was burning.

"Fox three. That was my last," Touchdown added.

"Winchester here too," Flowmax said.

Meany had seen the Chinese missiles course-correct on reaching O'ahu and fan out to attack targets across the entire island. Others skimmed the sea either side of the island, then struck targets on Big Island.

Among them, Hilo Airport.

As he was cruising back over O'ahu, angry plumes of black smoke rising from multiple strikes across the island, Meany tried to raise Hilo Tower.

Instead, he was hailed by an Air National Guard Raptor driver. "Teacher, you're 68 Aggressor, right?" he asked.

"Affirmative," Meany replied. "Is that you, Nun?"

Meany had met Captain Annunzio 'Nun' D'Angelli of the Guard's 199th Squadron over a game of pool at the USO at Hilo and recognized the voice.

"Roger. Look, I was talking to Hilo Tower when they went off air. Took a direct hit. Then I got an Army pilot on VHF said his helo just took damage at Hilo, landing on a cluster mine."

"Cluster mine?" Meany asked.

273

"Proximity mine," Nun confirmed. "The helo pilot said the whole airport is littered with them. I got onto the tower at Marine Corp Base Hawaii. MCBH is out, just like Hilo. Hickam is still no-go. I got told to put down at Bellows instead."

"*Bellows?*" Meany asked, surprised. "I didn't realize that was still an active airfield." Meany's knowledge of US military facilities on Hawaii wasn't exhaustive, but he was pretty sure the World War II–era landing field at Bellows was more nature reserve than airfield.

"It's not," Nun said. "Not officially. It got resurfaced 10 years ago with highway bitumen. Marines use it to train their pilots to land on rough landing strips. Probably why China didn't target it ... yet."

Meany pulled up his Hawaii airport database and paged through to Bellows. It was listed "for emergencies only." No tower, no radar, no refueling facilities. Four runways, the longest 1,700 yards long. Long enough to land a Raptor, but touch and go for his bigger Widow.

"Wait, the P-99s coming in from Oregon and Alaska, where are they putting down?"

"Bellows," Nun said. "*Everyone* is putting down at Bellows. It's the only damn option."

WITH HER REQUEST to be flown into a war zone, President Carmen Carliotti had caused the head of her security detail to sweat bullets.

He didn't care that she told him Abraham Lincoln did it, visiting Fort Stevens during the Civil War. Or about the other names she threw at him, like Roosevelt, LBJ, Nixon, two Bushes, Biden or Cruise.

Secret Service Special Agent in Charge Greg Kitchen only cared about one Carmen Carliotti, and her determination to "stand with the people of Hawaii in their darkest hour," as the press release announcing her detour had put it. So he tried directing the pilot to fly into Hilo on Big Island. When Carliotti found out, she said firmly she wanted to fly into Honolulu and meet with the Commander of INDOPACOM, Admiral Harry Connaught, face to face.

"Ma'am, O'ahu is under attack. All airports are closed," he told Carliotti. They were sitting in the conference room midships on the USAF Bombardier 9500 that was functioning as Air Force One, an hour out of Hawaii, after a 12-hour flight from Greenland during which no one got any sleep.

Nerves were fraying.

"Not to me," Carliotti insisted. "China doesn't dictate at which US airports I can land this airplane."

Kitchen had asked the Chair of the Joint Chiefs, General Earl Maxwell, to join them, because he needed someone else with more stripes on his side on this one.

"General?" he said, inviting Maxwell to step in.

"Greg is right, Madam President," Maxwell said. "I can't guarantee you or anyone else aboard that plane would survive long enough to deplane if you try to put down at Honolulu right now. Air Force has closed the airspace. Defenses there are ..." The USAF Colonel, Taylor Charles, entered the small space and crouched beside Maxwell, whispering. Maxwell turned his head. "Excuse me, ma'am."

"Apologies, ma'am," Charles said when the sidebar was finished. He left quickly.

Carliotti looked irritated. "What is happening, General?"

"Ma'am, we've just received a report that China has launched a large-scale cruise missile attack on multiple targets across the Hawaiian Islands. Uh …" Maxwell looked down at a screen. "Military facilities on Kaua'i, O'ahu, Maui, Big Island … airports, ports have all been hit. There have been significant casualties. Air defenses were overwhelmed. This bird can't refuel midair, so we're just checking if we have the fuel to return to the US mainland …"

"*Not* happening, General," Carliotti maintained. "We can put down at a different airport than Hickam Field if we have to, but we will put down."

"Ma'am." Maxwell looked pained. "Maybe once the situation stabilizes …"

Carliotti snapped. "General, consider this an order from your Commander in Chief. Your pilot will put us down on O'ahu. I don't care if it is at an airport, highway or damn basketball court. Organize with Secret Service whatever security you need to organize, but the moment I get down, I want to visit with the doctors and nurses who are treating our casualties. Then you and I will meet with Admiral Connaught and his INDOPACOM staff officers so I can hear firsthand what the situation is across his command, and what he needs."

"Madam President, that puts at risk your life and the lives of everyone aboard this aircraft," Maxwell said bluntly.

Carliotti met the remark with a cold stare. "Then we have that in common with every single civilian and person in uniform on Hawaii, General."

Maxwell caved, merely nodding meekly. "I'll speak with the pilot, ma'am."

"You are welcome to join any or all of my meetings, of course," Carliotti said, throwing him a bone. "Now you had better get back to what you were doing."

When Maxwell was gone, Carliotti skewered Kitchen with a glare. "Do not pull that kind of move again, Greg."

"Madam President, your safety is my priority," Kitchen argued. "That means that sometimes I will tell you things you don't want to hear."

"Tell me, by all means, but do not try a full-court press against me with any member of my staff, least of all the Chairman of the Joint Chiefs. Is that understood? General Maxwell has more important things to worry about than where I land my plane."

I seriously doubt that, Kitchen thought. "Heard and understood, ma'am," Kitchen told her.

Carliotti nodded, looking down at a list of calls she still had to make. She looked up again. "Anything else we need to discuss?"

Kitchen had a tablet PC in front of him. "Uh, since we are going to O'ahu, just your transport. There was no time to fly in Cadillac One, and we don't have a vehicle pre-positioned. We can put you in back of an armored military vehicle …"

"A tank? No. Makes me look scared."

He nodded like he expected the response. "Or our people on O'ahu have sourced a suitable armored limo, but it's privately owned, so the media could raise favoritism questions if they find out."

Carliotti sighed. "Owned by who?"

"Vali Corporation."

She nodded. Vali was a tech company. Its owner had gotten rich on the back of a video sharing app called Nik Nak—stepping into the market to fill a gap when a similar

Chinese-owned app was banned—before he turned his wealth toward the hardware side of the industry, specifically quantum computing cores.

Carliotti knew the company well because Vali was a big donor, and she'd signed off the legislation that had allowed it to complete an acquisition of USA's largest semiconductor manufacturer, making Vali the second largest chip manufacturer on the planet, behind Taiwan's TSMC. Carliotti had become personally involved because she'd been pressured by Vali's competitors to veto the acquisition on security grounds, since it gave Vali a virtual monopoly on the production of quantum computing chips approved for national defense use. She'd let the deal go through because Vali was not just a big donor; it was US owned, with the majority share owned by an individual she'd met and regarded as both patriotic and level headed—unlike most of the tech entrepreneurs she met. A billionaire called Miles Davis.

Yes, his real name. And yes, he was a jazz fan, like Carliotti. For a billionaire, his reputation was relatively benign.

"On the scandal scale, it won't register with anyone except Vali's competitors. I'll let HR know. He can prepare damage control in case it's needed."

"Yes ma'am. I'll get the limo rolling as soon as I find out where we're landing."

As he left, Carliotti looked at her to-do list. Top of the list was HR Rosenstern, who must be feeling like she'd dumped him on Greenland in a fit of pique.

It suited her for him to think that.

If her plans were unfolding smoothly, she would have replaced HR as her Chief of Staff by now. Had planned to do so in the immediate aftermath of the Raven Rock bombing, but she'd needed him to manage the Manukyan situation.

He'd done that. He'd served her well, but if possible, a little too enthusiastically. More than once he exercised initiative in a way that created risks for Carliotti. So far, those risks hadn't been realized, but events were too finely balanced now to have a joker in her deck.

How to cut him loose and not lose his loyalty, that would require considerable finesse. Where could she move him that would seem like a step up from Chief of Staff? A cabinet role? Ambassador somewhere? Anything less risked slighting him, and a former Chief of Staff with a grudge she definitely didn't need.

The evacuation to the Greenland secure facility had presented her with the opportunity to sideline him that she needed and she'd seized it, feigning irritation and trying to appear like she was acting on impulse ordering him to deplane.

On Greenland, he would be contained. He was an animal who fed off the energy of the Beltway the way Godzilla fed off nuclear radiation. Stuck in a bunker on Greenland, he would be neutered, without blaming her for his emasculation.

She played with ideas for where to move him. Head of the Presidential Pandemic Task Force? No, it would have to be more than a task force. Director of a newly created agency— say "Department of Pandemic Security"? A continuation of the work he'd already done for her, but more focused. She'd include him in the National Security Council ExCom group, but just setting up the department, with all the turf fights it would entail with Health and Homeland Security, would take every ounce of his prodigious ambition.

She could sell him on that.

Looking out the window next to her seat, she saw with satisfaction a sleek, bat-winged deltoid fighter aircraft slide

279

into formation off their left wing, replacing the F-35 that had been there. Another joined further out, and she assumed more were on the starboard side of the aircraft.

Someone was taking her arrival seriously at least.

THE FIGHTERS forming up alongside Air Force One were from the USAF 173rd Wing. Four Black Widows, each carrying 14 air-to-air missiles. Both ahead and trailing behind Air Force One were the four fighters' "loyal wingmen" Valkyrie drones, sweeping the skies around the president's formation for threats.

An hour ahead of them, their compatriots and their drone wingmen were in a conga line landing pattern over MCBH, waiting for their turn to land on one of the airstrips at Bellows. Among the chaos that was O'ahu at that moment, the staff of Reg Samuels were frantically organizing to get prodigious quantities of aviation fuel and ordnance transported from storage at Hickam and MCBH to the makeshift base at Bellows.

On the ground at Ford Island, 'Niko' Akiu was trying not to die ... again.

"Don't move!" he yelled at the girl, Presley.

"Make up your mind," she said churlishly. Not long ago he'd berated her for being too slow. They'd been running through trees along Wasp Boulevard, headed for where Presley's teacher had last seen her students, into the housing area at the northwest corner of the island.

Where he'd seen a group of civilians, teenagers among them, mown down by a slaughterbot, but he didn't tell Presley that.

280

Then something streaked overhead and exploded on top of the tsunami warning center. Hanging in the air in its wake were hundreds of small objects dangling from parachutes.

Cluster bombs! Niko's training screamed at him. *Cover, find cover.*

He'd grabbed the girl and shoved her toward a parked pickup, the only cover within reach. "Get under!" he'd yelled, scrambling in beside her, underneath the chassis, trying to put the front wheel between himself and the line of parachutes falling to earth about 20 yards away. He shoved her with his foot and pointed. "Those are *bombs*. Get behind the back wheel!"

He watched the parachutes fall with dread fascination, knowing he should pull his fool head in, but unable to look away.

The first of the small bomblets hit the grass beside the road opposite. He covered his head with arms.

Nothing happened.

No explosion.

He looked out again. Other bombs were hitting the grass now too. Maybe it was too soft? Or they were on a delay?

Farther down, a bomb came down squarely onto the road. He could hear the metallic thud as it hit.

Nothing.

The bomblets stayed inert, but the surrounding sky was filled with the supersonic boom of more missiles, most of them flying over the island to strike the main port area, the airfield and the city to the southeast. The sky was filled with hundreds of small drifting bomblets and the sound of the missiles themselves detonating, but nothing exploded near them.

Finally, the barrage stopped.

The slaughterbot assault wasn't over though. As the sound of the missiles died away, Niko heard gunfire from up by the bridge to the main island and the ripping sound of a Chinese autocannon.

The girl was restless. "Forget this," she said, and started crawling out from under the truck.

That was when he yelled at her, "Don't move!"

And she'd sighed at him and rolled her eyes, getting up on her elbows, halfway out from under the truck. "We can't *stay* here. I have to find my friends."

A small dog ran out of one of the nearby houses and stopped by the side of the road, then sat on its haunches, shaking.

"Oh, poor thing," Presley said. She clapped her hands and whistled. "Here, boy!"

It stood, looked back at the house, then looked at Presley and Niko again.

"Come on, boy!"

It ran in a circle, stopped and then started running toward them. It barked excitedly.

As it got to the road, there was a loud report like the slam of a rock on an iron sheet from in front of the dog. Niko ducked. When he looked up again, the dog was gone, leaving just a lump of flesh and fur on the road and a cloud of white smoke, drifting in the breeze.

"What ... what happened?" Presley asked.

"*Mines*," Niko breathed. "They're mines."

From across the island, he heard a couple more similar reports. Hard. Sharp. A small white cloud rising behind a house across the road.

"What does that mean?"

"It means if you go near one, like that dog did, you're dead."

"Near? How near?"

Niko tried to picture the dog running. The explosion. How close did it get to the mine? A meter or two? Say five. Niko knew nothing about Chinese air-dropped anti-personnel mines. How were they triggered? Vibration? Or sound? The dog was barking. Ah hell, it could be either. The things could have a small camera in them for all he knew.

He looked around. "Did you see any come down behind us?"

"I don't know," the girl said. "I was looking across the road, not behind."

Niko was pretty sure he'd looked behind him and had only seen parachutes in front. They were only about 50 yards from the shoreline again. Any mines that had fallen in the water wouldn't work, would they? They should have exploded because of the waves on the shore, right?

How sure are you, Niko? Sure enough to bet your life on it?

"We should stay here," he decided. "Navy or police will have to come sooner or later."

The girl fixed him with a baleful glare. "You are the worst firefighter I ever met in my entire life. Aren't you supposed to run into burning buildings to save people? All you ever want to do is save *yourself.*"

That stung. Because maybe she was right. He'd been sitting in the brig when the slaughterbots hit because he'd been too lazy to get his ass back from leave on time. Or was it just he'd had enough? That he didn't really *want* to be a darned firefighter?

283

Niko Akiu might have been the worst firefighter on Ford Island. But he was also still a teenage boy, and this girl lying there, staring him down, was more than he could take.

"Alright, dammit," he swore. "You want to die, Charger? Sure, fine, let's go kill ourselves." He got to one knee. "Don't forget your first aid kit."

"Wait, that's *them*!" Presley said, pointing across the road to where a small group of girls, maybe three or four, was coming around the side of a house 30 yards away. They were a ways off, but their blue polo shirts were unmistakable. "Hey! Over here!"

They looked over and waved, then started walking toward Niko and Presley.

"No!" he shouted at them. "Stay there!"

They stopped, uncertain.

"We'll come to you!" Niko yelled. "Don't move! There are *mines* everywhere." He looked around, taking Presley's arm. This was crazy.

He had thrown his rifle under the truck as he climbed under it, and he reached back to pull it out. He put the heavy rifle on semi auto.

"What are you doing?" Presley asked.

"Making a path, I hope," Niko said. "Get behind me." He cupped his hand around his mouth and yelled at the other students. "I am going to shoot the ground. Just stay there!" He lifted the rifle to his shoulder and pointed it at the ground just in front of him, then squeezed the trigger, putting two rounds into the dirt just ahead of them. Then two more, farther out. Then 10 yards out, another two ...

Crack!

A mine exploded. He flinched, Presley crouching, holding onto his legs.

"Walk right behind me," Niko said, trying to walk where he'd fired, toward the black smudge and white cloud where the mine had exploded. Lightning couldn't strike twice, right?

Yeah, right.

They reached the site of the explosion, a small black crater in the road. They were only about 20 yards from the other girls now. They were clinging to each other, terrified, looking at him like he was mad, but too scared by the explosion to run.

Good. "I'm going to clear a path again," he yelled at them. "Just stay *exactly* where you are."

Two shots. Aim forward. Two more. Two more.

Presley in a small voice. "No explosions. I think the way is clear, isn't it?"

He looked up. They had to hope. "Stay a couple yards behind."

"OK."

Niko Akin, you are insane, he was thinking. But they walked slowly over to the group without seeing or setting off any more mines, and the girls all collapsed into one another's arms, hugging and sobbing.

He looked around. They had to find somewhere where the mines couldn't have landed. He looked at the house they were standing beside.

"Hey, did you girls come out of this house?"

"No, it was locked," one of the girls said. "We tried a couple of houses, trying to hide from the robots. No one is home. They're all locked."

Not to me, Niko decided.

"We're going inside this one," he said. He pointed to a back porch, steps going up to a small rear door. "Follow me straight from here to that door, alright? Single file, right behind me."

They held hands, Presley nodding.

Niko led them to the back door. Lifting the rifle, he slammed the butt into the lock. It gave first time, the door not much more than plywood. He kicked it open and called out. "Anyone here?"

No answer. Just his luck there was a terrified house owner hiding inside with a shotgun, waiting to shoot at anything that moved.

"Federal Fire Service!" he called. "Anyone here?"

Nothing. He repeated himself. The house was silent.

He waved to the four girls. "Alright, inside."

Niko was standing at the back door, holding the doorframe. Presley was the last one in, and she paused in the doorway. "Hey, I'm sorry for what I said back there. You're not ..."

From a group of trees farther up the road, Niko heard a now familiar ripping sound. He just had time to register the first 20 mm slugs tearing into the wall by the corner of the house and start chewing their way toward him.

His stupid mine-clearing strategy had attracted a slaughterbot.

"*Inside!*" He shoved Presley, felt something slam him sideways, and fell inside the house.

CARMEN CARLIOTTI was used to a fanfare greeting her as she deplaned from Air Force One, but not like the one that greeted her at the Bellows Marine Training Facility.

Sirens, howling in the distance.

286

She was rushed from the top of the steps down into a waiting armored limousine before she even had time to register what was going on. Kitchen bundled her into the car and sat opposite, pulling the door shut behind them, banging on the driver's partition.

"Drive!"

"Is this airfield under attack too?" Carliotti asked.

"One of a few that isn't," Kitchen said, hand cupped over his earpiece, listening to his radio. "Big strikes on Kaua'i, O'ahu and Big Island. We're getting you to a training bunker inside the old air base."

Carliotti had been warned she was flying into a war zone, and it came home to her now, looking out the limo window at the hurrying military personnel and listening to the alarms. But she still had a job to do.

She looked around the inside of the vehicle. The Vali Corporation company logo was stenciled on a drinks cabinet mounted against the driver partition. The initials of the company name were superimposed on a stylized motherboard like small transistors.

It shouldn't have surprised her, maybe, that the armored limo she was riding in belonged to Miles Davis and Vali Corporation. She knew he had a holiday house, or two, on the islands. As the car sped across the tarmac toward a set of low buildings, she remembered a recent conversation at a fundraiser hosted by Davis.

He had a Vermont lumberjack's physique, not the sallow complexion of a tech dweeb, with shoulders twice as wide as hers, not leaving a lot of room at their table for others to get close to them. Which suited them both. The event had been about a year earlier. He'd leaned in and lowered his voice.

"Madam President, can I get your read on an international question? Not asking you to discuss anything sensitive, of course," he'd said.

"If I can," she'd replied, carefully.

"I have a big team of open- and not-so-open-source intelligence analysts and AIs tracking everything from trade and government spending to consumer trends, making sure I don't miss any big signals that could affect the semiconductor business ..."

"I'd hope so," Carliotti told him with a smile. "Anything less would make me worry about Vali's long-term prospects."

"Thank you, ma'am," he'd said, tipping a finger to his forehead in a mock salute. "But see, my people are telling me China is finally serious about going to war over Taiwan, if we force the issue. The sand has been running through that hourglass for decades now, but it seems it's finally running out."

Carliotti considered her answer. At that time, she'd been building her private "coalition of the willing"—those who shared her views about the need to deal with the existential threat of Chinese Communism once and for all. She'd decided to test Vali.

"I see. Let me ask you a question then, Miles," she'd replied. "Where does Vali stand on the question of Taiwan?"

He'd given it thought—that much was clear. "China gets control of Taiwan, it gets control of 60 percent of global semiconductor production. It would be a national security catastrophe without peer, Madam President." He drummed his fingers on the table thoughtfully. "Ain't a plane or tank or guided artillery shell in our arsenal doesn't rely on Taiwanese chips."

"And those made by Vali Corporation," she pointed out.

"Well, another time we can discuss how the US government could benefit from putting a little more business our way, sure, ma'am, but it might surprise you, that's not my biggest worry right now. As a patriotic American, I'm more worried about what it all means for my shareholders, employees and their friends and families."

She was a little surprised. "If the supply of chips from Taiwan was interrupted, even temporarily, your companies would have a virtual global monopoly on a critical resource. Some people would see a development like that as a lucrative business opportunity."

He gave her a sad smile. "World War III is not a business opportunity, ma'am."

"But what if, Miles, the means to *avoid* a world war is to confront Communist China in a limited conflict over Taiwan and put the Chinese dragon back in its box, once and for all?"

"Then I would ask what a 'limited conflict' looks like," he'd replied. She was pretty sure, by the end of their conversation, he'd come around to her way of thinking. His financial support for her second presidential campaign signaled he had, and he clearly was still in her corner, if he'd agreed to lend her his personal ride.

She remembered the conversation with chagrin. How naive she had been to think China would be so easily cowed.

"I know what you're thinking. It's not the Beast," Kitchen said, mistaking her glance around the vehicle. "But Vali's security chief here on Hawaii assured me it'll take a hit from a Hongjian missile and keep rolling, ma'am. Best thing short of an Abrams tank."

"Does this tank have a phone?" Carliotti asked. She couldn't see one, and she'd been told to leave hers on the aircraft in case China used it to track her location.

289

Kitchen looked around too, then tapped on the drivers' partition. "Phone?"

The driver tapped a control on his dash and a panel slid aside in the door next to her elbow, revealing a handset.

"It won't be mil-spec encryption," Kitchen warned, reaching over her, picking it up and looking at it. "But you have a satellite signal, which is probably the main thing."

"Can you get HR on a line for me, Greg?" she asked.

Kitchen nodded, calling a number and asking to be routed through to the Greenland Continuity Facility.

They approached some gates, Marines either side, and drove through.

"What is this place?"

"Marine training facility," Kitchen said, looking out as he waited to be connected, pointing at buildings. "Boot camp, mock forward operating base and urban warfare zone. That tower is for firefighting practice, those are the helipads, and uh … there's a golf course. Nine-hole, looks like." He put the handset to his ear and then handed it to her. "Mr. Rosenstern."

"HR, you there?" she asked, hearing only static on the line.

"Yes, Madam President," Rosenstern said. "In the frozen flesh."

"Well, be glad no one is firing missiles at you is all I can say, HR," she said. "I should have listened to people who told me this was a dumb idea. We just landed in the middle of an air raid."

"Told you so seems inadequate right now, ma'am," HR said.

"Yes, well, I'm here," she said. "But I'd like an update on the situation stateside. Do I need to make a quick address from here, or can I get some business done first?"

290

"I had a call in to Secret Service asking you to contact me as soon as you landed anyway, ma'am. Washington media got word of the evacuation flights, tried contacting key administration figures and went straight to answering service, so they put two and two together. We've got headlines there like 'Washington elite evacuates,' 'Government flees,' 'President AWOL,' and worse of course on the social media sites."

"I need to speak to the nation," Carliotti decided. She put the handset against her chest. "Comms facilities?"

"I'll set it up, ma'am," he said, having heard her side of the conversation.

"I've sketched out a three-minute to-camera piece," HR said. "Pandemic threat, people need to follow government advice, administration is doing that too and has moved to a secure facility—not saying where, Greenland would freak people out—from where it's business as usual. 'Stay calm and carry on' kind of thing. I'll send it through."

"Except I'm not at a secure facility, HR," Carliotti said. "I'm on Hawaii."

"People outside the bubble don't need to know that," he insisted. "You stay non-specific, have the video taken against a generic background, you could be at Cheyenne Mountain, Mount Weather, even Raven Rock ..."

Carliotti breathed slowly in and out. "We are putting the country into pandemic lockdown, and Hawaii is under attack by China and Russia. What is going to give the American people more confidence right now, HR? Their president telling them the government is hiding under a mountain somewhere but everything will be fine, or their president showing she is on Hawaii with our troops and everything will be fine?"

291

He was silent a moment. "Is there a third option, like a variation on one of those two?"

"No third option," she said. "Send me what you prepared. I'll make it work."

"Alright, ma'am. Uh, there's something else," he said.

She tensed. "This isn't a completely secure line, HR."

"No, you'll see it in media reports soon enough. The executive orders regarding the pandemic lockdown and Chinese citizens ..."

Before departing Washington, Carliotti had signed a number of orders. The first put the National Guard on the streets of every US capital city to support local police forces to enforce lockdown regulations. The second was to deport all Chinese citizens and place dual American-Chinese citizens under digital house arrest. The order went further, ordering all federal agencies to suspend the employment of Chinese citizens or dual citizens for the duration of war with China. The third dramatically restricted cross border travel.

"Which one?" she wondered.

"All," he replied. "There are a lot of prominent Chinese Americans—businesspeople, actors, musicians, politicians, academics—screaming about being interned."

"And most have a right to scream. But the alternative is thousands of Chinese collaborators in government and business answering the Communist Party call. We stand firm."

"On the Chinese citizens, I agree. But we could give the dual citizens the option to surrender their Chinese citizenship or leave the country. Make it look like we sympathize, but drag the approvals out, keep them out of circulation during the conflict."

She thought about it. "Alright. Make it look like it was always going to be part of the plan."

"Understood. Now, the National Guard deployment ..."

"That's not negotiable, HR. I'm not going to be the president who condemned half the US population to death because we didn't take this virus seriously. It's a damn bioweapon! Is it the state governors? Make them understand the consequences, get them on board."

"Most of them are already," HR said. "They've had the Army bioweapon briefings, seen the classified US military video footage from Taiwan. We've been offering them and their families space in continuity of government facilities in their states. It's not the state administrations ..."

"What then?"

"A civil resistance group calling itself 'The Defenders of Liberty' is taking out media advertisements, announcing rallies across the country, warning they'll resist any pandemic restrictions," he said, sounding genuinely worried. "Their message is simple: there is no bird flu, it's all a deep-state lie and you are the devil incarnate, who just wants to take away their rights."

See how that plays when people start dying by the hundreds of thousands, Carliotti thought. She did a mental speed search. "Defenders of Liberty? Like Paul Revere's 'Sons of Liberty'? Why haven't I ever heard of them?" she asked.

"A week ago, no one did," HR said. "Homeland Security is totally blank. But they're a serious threat, and they've been preparing this for some time, to be up and running so quickly. FBI is working up a profile now but says they'll be tough to penetrate. They're doing their recruiting online, working in small cells and coordinating their protests on encrypted apps.

Their cell leaders all use the pseudonym 'Sam Adams.' Like the founding father. He was apparently one of ..."

Carliotti frowned. "The Civil War Sons of Liberty. I know. Am I paranoid for seeing China's hand in this too? Sounds more like a state-sponsored terrorist group than a genuine civil rights movement."

"Exactly what FBI is saying, but these guys haven't done anything illegal yet. We need Homeland Security to get some multi-agency focus on it before they do."

"I agree," Carliotti said. "You need anything from me? You want me to speak with Janet?" Janet Belkin, the Homeland Security Secretary, had been evacuated to Greenland along with the rest of her administration, and she should be amenable, but she couldn't be ordered into action by HR against her will.

"Not yet. You have a presser to organize, ma'am."

They approached some brick administration buildings and the driver headed for an underground parking garage entrance. It was dark and her eyes took a moment to adjust, but she just had time to see scaffolding, a low aircraft silhouette and then bright lights as they began driving down a ramp into an underground parking garage.

The limo was swinging around to park in an underground lot comprising mostly light tactical vehicles. A reception committee of officers, more junior and hastily arranged than she was accustomed to, in Air Force, Space Force, Army, Marine and Navy uniforms stood waiting for her to get out of the car.

"Alright, I have a lot of people to meet before then," she said. "Thanks for keeping the ball rolling over there, HR."

"What I'm here for, ma'am," he said.

She cut the call and unbuckled. Kitchen was already out of the limo and opening the door. As she stepped out, she heard what sounded like a jet fighter right outside the building, flying low over the airfield.

She looked up. "Ours or theirs?"

Kitchen held the door for her and cocked an ear. "No explosion. So I want to say ours."

THE AIRCRAFT President Carliotti had heard blasting over her head belonged to one Karen 'Bunny' O'Hare. A Marine Joint Tactical Air Controller on a VHF radio had guided her and the other Aggressor pilots in. She was directed to a parking slot beside the runway she'd landed on by a Marine Corps Aviation airman waving red batons. As she slid from the hatch beneath her Widow, she looked around in stunned disbelief.

The chaos she'd seen from the air as she landed was nothing compared to the sight and sound of being right in the middle of it.

The four "runways" at Bellows, she could see now, were more like rural highways. They even had traffic lines painted down the middle of them, marking four lanes. Scrub ran down both sides of the runways, with a grassed area on either side on which aircraft were being parked in haphazard rows. Both runways on each of the chopstick-shaped configurations were being used.

Twin-engined Widows were circling, landing and taxiing. The sound was deafening as she pulled her helmet off. A constant stream of vehicle traffic was rolling down an access road to buildings at the western end of one of the runways, led by a British-made Aardvark mine-clearing flail. She saw fuel trucks, a HELLADs battery setting up on one side of the field, MML battery on another. She saw at least two Stryker anti-air vehicles, radars spinning. Backed up in traffic, more trucks were pulling trailers loaded down with ordnance, ground crew riding on top of the missiles like kids on a hayride.

Someone walked up beside her, pulling off their helmet. Touchdown. She said nothing at first, just stood with O'Hare, watching the scene. "China drops a single cluster bomb on this field right now, they take out the whole of Hawaii's air defense," O'Hare said.

Touchdown tucked a strand of hair behind her ear. "Meany said half of these kites are flying out to Dillingham Airfield as soon as they're refueled and rearmed."

"Dillingham, why do I know that name?" Bunny asked.

"Probably because it was named in a briefing sometime as the place Chinese amphibious forces are most likely to come ashore?" Touchdown guessed. "I'm guessing that's maybe why it was spared so far."

"Why didn't we fly more planes up there already?" Bunny asked. "Why cram everyone in here?"

Touchdown shrugged. "Because Dillingham is just a small general aviation field—fine for basing, but no logistics chain. Bellows is right between US Marine Corp Base Hawaii and AFB Hickam—plenty of fuel and ordnance stored nearby."

Not for the first time, Bunny realized she should think twice before asking obvious questions.

They stood watching the spectacle until Meany, Flowmax, Flatline and Agony joined them. Meany was on his telephone and clomping around impatiently as he talked. He finished his call and pocketed the phone.

"That was Crystal. Everyone at Hilo from the 68th is alright. The airfield took about 10 direct hits from cruise missiles, but the main problem is proximity-fused cluster mines, like Nun said. China laid thousands of them across the airfield, across the whole damn island. Casualties are already in the dozens at Hilo alone. The whole airport is in lockdown, everyone staying in place until they work out how to demine it." He pointed at the Aardvark. "Those things are few and far between."

"Those things are nightmares," Agony said. "Russians dropped them on Incirlik the start of the Syrian war. China uses the same design. Bastards are the size and shape of a baseball, made of HE, ball bearings or tungsten penetrators, and plastic. They detach from their chutes before they hit the ground, then drop and roll before they activate. Anything comes within 2 yards, they explode. We didn't have enough mine-clearing equipment either."

"What did you do, then?" Flowmax asked.

Agony winced. "You have to blow them up, one by one. Would you believe we had ground crew out there in bomb suits, throwing handfuls of gravel in front of themselves? They'll be hiding in long grass, under vehicles, stuck in the gutters of buildings, under swings and merry-go-rounds."

Bunny shuddered. "If they can detect movement, they must need a power source. They'll deactivate after a while, right?"

"Not completely. Power runs out, they are still motion triggered. Disturb them, they explode."

"Not our immediate problem, people," Meany told them. He had to raise his voice to be heard over the roar of jet engines. "Higher-ups are worried a Chinese satellite will spot us here and drop a strike. The plan is to fuel up, load up and get airborne as soon as we can."

"Don't tell me," Bunny sighed. "They're sending us against *Fujian* again."

Meany shook his head. "You'll wish they were. Every available airframe is going to be thrown into an attack on the Chinese fleet northwest of Kaua'i," he said. "And 68th Aggressor's Raptors are tip of the spear."

"Way we like it," Flowmax said, without conviction. He turned to Bunny. "Right?"

She slapped the mountain man's back. "Right, Flowmax. Oo-rah."

"You said Raptors," Touchdown noticed. "What about our Widows?"

"They're being loaded with hypersonics—Waveriders," Meany told her. "Widows will be in the first wave too. Our targets are still being decided, but if they're giving us Waveriders, then it's an anti-ship mission."

Touchdown couldn't help herself. "We'll sweep the road for you, O'Hare. Try not to miss this time."

Bunny looked at her feet. "I didn't miss," she mumbled. "That damn carrier is a zombie."

No one could hear her. A Black Widow on final approach came in long on the short "runway" and lit its tail, blasting back into the sky with a deafening roar.

"You think he heard about the next mission and changed his mind?" Flatline asked.

COLONEL ALICIA 'The Hammer' Rodriguez, 615th Combat Operations Squadron, Space Launch Delta 45, was trying to change someone's mind. And since it meant she

298

would have to go around her CO to do it, it might cost her a long, hard-fought career.

But she knew no one could question her motivation.

Rodriguez had family serving on Hawaii—a cousin in the US Army headquarters at Fort Shafter. And because she was tapped into the data from the small but growing number of satellites the US had managed to get back into orbit, she knew better than most what was happening on the islands. From the bot attacks to the waves of cruise missile strikes.

Rodriguez knew Space Force was only using a fraction of the potential her Skylon platform offered, so she'd put an idea to her CO, Commander of Delta 45, Brigadier General Chris Panhagen. And he'd killed it dead. "You are talking about taking a concept straight from Operational Test and Development to combat deployment," he said. "That system is not ready."

"It's ready," Rodriguez insisted. "Skylon has already shown what it can do. It's time to let it off the leash."

"Nice words, Colonel, but your squadron's next mission is intelligence, surveillance and reconnaissance—that is all. I'd rather hear ideas for how you can shorten time to launch than expand your mission envelope. Clear?"

Message received, understood and not accepted.

A chance conversation with her counterpart in USAF 419th Flight Test Squadron, Colonel Nick Holt, had only increased her frustration. They had long planned a test of Skylon's optical infrared tracking capabilities to see whether the space plane could detect a B1-B in flight. He was calling to warn her he might need to cancel the test.

"I've got a call with INDOPACOM in about an hour that I expect will see us deploying to support operations in the Hawaii theater," he told her.

"*Combat* operations?" she asked. The 419th was a test squadron, and more than that, the B1-B hadn't been used in a combat role since Syria, nearly eight years earlier.

"The availability of strategic bomber assets is pretty tight. I've been asked by General Samuels how the 419th can change that. He's apparently a skeptic."

A rush of blood overtook Rodriguez. "Can I join that call?" she'd asked. When she explained why, he reluctantly agreed. His reluctance was not because she'd be gatecrashing his call but because, as he put it, "he didn't like to see a friend crash and burn."

Rodriguez waited impatiently on the call as Holt made his pitch, convincing Samuels that upgrades to his Bones meant they could network with the rest of the USAF strike package in the same way a B-2 or B-21 could. "We can pull targets in real time from AWACS, from Navy, satellite or other aircraft, and my Bones can carry double the payload of a B-2, three times the payload of a B-21 …"

Samuels was sold. Then Holt told Samuels he had Rodriguez on the line. Rodriguez had only met Samuels once, when they were both in the adjudication panel for a war-game run by INDOPACOM Joint Operations Command.

"Colonel, whatever this is, make it quick," Samuels said, looking distracted.

"General, what if I told you I have a platform on the runway at Vandenberg, being prepped for launch, which could take out a large part of that Sino-Russian fleet if someone had the balls to make the call?" she said.

He frowned. "The president has ruled out any use of nuclear weapons, Colonel."

"Give me two minutes, General," Rodriguez said. She took five, to explain what kind of mission she was talking about. She finished with, "I need to advise you, General Panhagen does not support this option because the system is not battlefield tested."

Samuels tapped a pen on the table in front of him, looking off-camera as he considered. "I've been ordered by the Commander INDOPACOM to identify and requisition all available assets for the defense of Hawaii, including Space Force, so you can tell Panhagen *I* approached *you*. If he doesn't like it, he can call Admiral Connaught."

Rodriguez wasn't smiling when she got off the call. Skylon D4 'Mako' really was on the runway, being prepped for takeoff. But it was nowhere near ready for this mission. She'd have to deal with a hundred moving pieces to deliver what she'd just promised Samuels.

"SHOULDN'T THIS be one of those missions where they ask for volunteers? Because I know how my feet would vote," Lieutenant Robert E. 'Uncle' Lee, 18th Flight Test Squadron, had muttered.

He hadn't had a good week. Two days sobering up their CO and covering for him for everything from reporting the damage to their AC-130X, 'Outlaw,' to writing up the combat report from their last mission—an ISR patrol around the flank of the Sino-Russian fleet that turned into a combat drop with palletized weapons, that turned into a fiasco that nearly sent Outlaw to a watery grave.

But it was a photo recon analysis that indicated their improvised attack may have damaged a Russian *Gorshkov* class frigate—knocking out its radar at least—that had roused Outlaw's pilot, Rory O'Donoghue, from his drunken stupor.

301

He'd gripped Uncle's arm like it was a lifeline thrown to a drowning man. "You mean it? You aren't lying to me? We actually hit one of the bastards?"

"Not just hit it, boss," Uncle said gently. "Took it off the air. A British Skylon took photos of the fleet that showed a *Gorshkov* with a mess of twisted metal where its superstructure was. And our friends on the USS *Canberra* took out an *Udaloy* destroyer and a Chinese XLUUV." He gripped the hand holding his arm. "Old Outlaw gave 'em hell, Rory, and we've only just started."

O'Donoghue had been hallucinating, talking about a little boy who was watching him in the dark ... That talk stopped when he learned their last mission hadn't been the failure he thought it was. Uncle wasn't a blind optimist. He knew that little boy was still lurking in a dark corner of O'Donoghue's mind somewhere. But they could work with that.

As long as the boy stayed hidden while they were flying.

But now Uncle almost wished his CO was still lying on a cot, sweating bourbon, and not standing there in a ready room at Pago Pago, telling them Outlaw was being sent out like a sacrificial lamb to the slaughter.

The rest of the crew were either dumbstruck or too loyal to express their doubts. But where Bob Lee came from, loyal meant speaking your mind, damn the consequences.

"Funny enough, they didn't give me the option of refusing," Rory said. "Look, the situation is we have a Sino-Russian invasion fleet northwest Kaua'i, and one chance to hit it before it lands troops on Hawaii. But *Fujian* is a threat in the south Hawaii can't ignore, so that's the reason this airfield looks like an F-35 yard sale."

They'd arrived at American Samoa's Pago Pago Airport to find it teeming with Australian RAAF F-35 fighters, aerial refueling tankers and Globemaster heavy transport aircraft. Uncle had counted at least 36 of the stealth fighters—two full squadrons.

"Look, we got the easy role in this package. All of Australia's Maritime ISR assets are in the Taiwan theater or patrolling the Australian coast for submarines. Without other eyes in the sky, our job is just to pinpoint the Chinese pickets and their carrier. The RAAF will take on *Fujian*."

When Chinese drones started attacking Hawaii, US diplomats had reached out to their Australian cousins for support, and as it had done in Korea, Vietnam, Iraq, Afghanistan, Türkiye and Syria, Australia had picked up the phone.

And they'd arrived on American Samoa with four palletized air-launched drones for Outlaw. Which, Uncle had to admit, tipped the scales a little in their favor.

He'd still grumbled about the mission. But now they were flying it, and they were well past the B&MCP—Bitch and Moan Cutoff Point.

IF UNCLE BOB E. LEE had been a fly on the wall in the mission briefing for the pilots of *Fujian* at that same moment, he might have gone into battle with a lighter heart. And more than a modicum of surprise.

Because Lieutenant Maylin 'Mushroom' Sun, flight leader, Ao Yin Fighter Squadron, PLA Navy carrier *Fujian*, was more than a little surprised.

She was not privy to the Chinese battle plan for Hawaii, of course. Not all of it, anyway.

But the small part of it that had just been shared with her and the pilots of *Fujian* did *not* involve troops landing on

O'ahu to take Pearl Harbor and engage the nearly 30,000-strong American military force there.

Which was what everyone aboard had expected when they heard about the size of the fleet assembled for the attack on Hawaii. And the briefing had certainly started as expected.

"Your target is Pearl Harbor." Colonel Wang Wei, acting commander of the *Fujian*, had kicked off the briefing in person. "Literally," he added. "Your mission will be challenging, but if successful, you will make the American harbor unusable to our enemies for months, perhaps for years." He stepped from the lectern at the front of the ready room. "Major Tan."

The PLA Navy intel officer, Major Tan Yuanyuan, was loved by the pilots of *Fujian* for her blunt "sugar-free," non-propaganda style of briefing. She told the pilots what they needed to know, nothing more, and never less. Multiple engagements had proven she held nothing back from them—if there were surprises, they were a surprise to Major Tan too. And there were few of those.

Tan's style wasn't always appreciated by the cadre of Communist Party political officers standing at the back of the ready room looking on, and Mushroom had seen her taken aside after one particularly honest briefing and lectured about "the fragility of morale."

"My job is not to preserve pilot morale," Mushroom had heard her reply, her fine-boned face impassive. "My job is to ensure they succeed in their missions. If they do that, morale will look after itself."

The Major stepped onto the lectern.

"The mission objective is long-term area denial," she said, bringing up a graphic of the area around Pearl Harbor and the sea to the south. "Tianyi autonomous drones are already

304

engaged with enemy ground forces. You will be flying at nap of the earth, making your ingress from the south, following a heavy anti-radar and ground-attack cruise missile barrage that should seriously degrade enemy surface-to-air anti-aircraft capabilities. However, you can expect some standing defensive air patrols to be operating over the target." She brought up a satellite image showing multiple aircraft parked alongside a runway and in concrete aircraft shelters. "This satellite image is only hours old. It shows the only significant remaining force of enemy aircraft, at Hilo airfield on Hawaii's Big Island." Tan made what passed for her as an attempt at humor. "You can count them on two hands. I will wait."

A flight of Gyrfalcon pilots from PLAN *Shandong* had made the *Fujian* their new home, and their 'Victory' Squadron CO, Captain Lei Yu, had apparently decided to try to befriend Mushroom after their first rather inauspicious mission together. He had positioned himself beside her, telling one of his pilots to move so that he could sit. Mushroom reflected he had mistaken her expression of sympathy for his poor showing as a gesture of goodwill. In fact, she intended it as a starting point for giving him some advice, but he hadn't been interested in listening.

"P-99 Widows," he said dismissively, leaning over to whisper to her conspiratorially. "Like an AWACS with its own missiles. Easy meat, right?"

It was like their last mission—in which an American aircraft she was pretty sure had been a Widow had sent him running back to *Fujian* with his tail between his legs—didn't exist for him.

"We chased a single Widow across the Pacific from Palau to Taiwan," Mushroom told him. "It destroyed five Chongming fighters, and we never caught it."

"Chongmings," he nodded. "No offense. But your little drones are not Gyrfalcons."

"Quiet up the back," Tan snapped, glaring at Mushroom. "Plan of attack: *Shandong*'s Gyrfalcons will precede the *Fujian* aircraft and secure temporary air superiority."

The Gyrfalcon pilots, led by Lei, gave a throaty cheer and earned another glare from Tan. "*Fujian*'s Chongmings will drop mines in the harbor entrance and here, along the east and west side of this island, Ford Island," she continued.

Mushroom raised her hand. "Standoff or gravity?"

"Questions in your squadron briefings," Tan said curtly. "But the answer is gravity. Each Chongming will carry four Chen-12 sinking mines. You will need to overfly the target to deliver them."

Mushroom nodded. It made sense. China's CJ-100 supersonic cruise missile could be launched at standoff range and spread small cluster munitions over a target, but to really shut down the harbor, the 500-kilogram Chen-12 heavy naval mines would be needed. Designed to be air dropped, they were made almost entirely of nonmetal components—except for their computer guidance systems. As soon as they hit the water, they filled ballast tanks and sank to the bottom of a sea lane or harbor and waited, almost undetectable.

The acoustic signatures of enemy ships and submarines were stored in their onboard memories, and once sunk, they simply sat and listened. When they got a match on their database that was within range, they floated up from the seabed and into the path of their target, detonating with the force of a heavy torpedo as the target passed.

They could lie dormant on the seabed for up to two *years.*

"Therefore, this will be a one-way trip for *Fujian*'s Chongmings," Tan said. A small murmur went up from the

Chongming pilots, but only a small one. It was not a true kamikaze flight; no one's life would be on the line. But a strike like this would demand the commitment of nearly every operational aircraft *Fujian* could muster. *That would leave almost no aircraft for carrier defense.* *Fujian* would be almost entirely reliant on her destroyer escorts for protection.

Which meant *Fujian*'s pilots, in their carbon fiber pods down in the bowels of the carrier, would be very much at risk if the enemy counterattacked.

"Pilots, move to your squadron-level briefings," Tan instructed.

"This is going to be one to remember, eh?" Lei said, clapping Mushroom on the shoulder.

Mushroom had given him a wan smile. *Only for those left alive.*

The Rearguard: Jinhua Street

THERE WAS NOTHING underwhelming about the firepower the Marine Sergeant Jackson had brought into play in Taipei. The premier's limo was down on its front axle and smoking. From east and west, the ripping-paper noise of slaughterbot fire chewed the air.

Confirm the kill?

Jensen stuck his head out into the alley again. If Squirt had a camera on his robot neck, he could send the LS3 out to the vehicle, but they'd only deployed with the sonic drill module.

Jensen saw shadows near the compound gates, like someone there was preparing to re-engage maybe. At the same time, he heard the whir of slaughterbot rotors as the hostile slaughterbot came into the western end of the lane. Someone inside the compound tried to engage it, attracting only a withering burst of fire.

"Lieutenant," Jensen told Chang. "Can you tag the other slaughterbot?"

"Will do. Covering on your mark."

"Good copy. On three. One, two, *three* ..."

Their tame slaughterbot opened up, sending measured two-round bursts at the hostile bot that hammered it 2 yards backward. It steadied, aimed its gun toward the bot attacking it, but *didn't fire.* Some kind of protocol preventing blue-on-blue attacks? Whatever the reason, it trained its gun on the compound, loosing off a short burst, even as Chang opened up on it again.

Jensen took the chance he'd been given and ran from the shop door at a crouch, pulling in a lungful of acrid smoke that sent his chest into a spasm. But he reached the vehicle and the shattered window.

The grenade blast had triggered the heavy passenger door lock mechanism, and it hung partially open. The interior of the limo was filled with smoke from burning upholstery, and he pulled open the door fully, sticking his head inside as far as he could. He saw shapes through the swirling smoke—bodies, or parts of them. The smoke cleared for a moment and he recognized Ko from the photographs Jackson had shared. A bodyguard was lying across him, but only covered him from the waist down. The body of another man lay on the floor, more a collection of body parts than a corpse. The back of Ko's skull was missing. A fourth body, in green uniform, had been blown partially backward into the limo's luggage compartment, the seat behind him collapsed, or just shredded.

Jensen pulled a miniature camera from a pocket and took video of the occupants inside the limo. He retched, pulling back to get some clear air. "Target is … Target is down."

Then he saw a silver gleam from inside the exposed luggage compartment. A metal document case maybe? He put the camera away and reached past the bloodied body of the man in uniform and tugged at it. It wasn't light, and he could see a lock under the handle. It looked like some sort of secure case.

"Four KIA inside the vehicle," Jensen said as he worked the case free. "There's some kind of locked briefcase here, heavy. I'm trying to free it."

The slaughterbot cannon rattled again, and this time someone tried to return fire from the compound. Unless they had a rocket launcher, they wouldn't dent the bot, but if they turned their aim on Jensen again …

"Forget the case," Jackson said over Jensen's radio. "Pull out."

309

Jensen grimaced, pulling harder. The hole in the rear seat wasn't large enough with the body blocking it. Pushing aside his revulsion, he pulled the uniformed body onto the floor of the limo. The hole into the luggage compartment was big enough now. "I can get it out. Might be valuable."

With a last heave, he pulled the case free and landed on his ass in the alley, with the case on top of him.

Damn, it was heavy.

More rifle fire from down the alley, heavy rounds slamming into the rear of the limo. Jensen tapped his helmet and signaled Squirt.

On me.

Corporal Xu saw movement on the roof of the premier's compound and swung his scope in that direction. Someone was emerging from a hatch in the roof that led out to a flat roof area.

And they were carrying a rocket launcher.

"RPG team, rooftop right," Xu said. "I can take him out, but those men are Taiwan government, Sergeant. Technically our own. I'm not comfortable …"

"Shoot to wound, then," Jackson told him. "Or aim for his body armor."

"At this range, with this caliber, any hit is going to be fatal," Xu said grimly. "They're most likely hunting slaughterbots. Not *our* people."

"Dammit," Jackson cursed. "Jensen, talk to me. RPG team on the roof. They're probably going for one of the slaughterbots, but you're also in the firing line."

JENSEN PUT SQUIRT beside the open door, then manhandled the metal case onto Squirt's back, strapping it down with the LS3's cargo belts. When he had the case settled, he tapped his helmet again, putting the LS3 into "trail" mode so that it would follow behind him.

"I have the case. Pulling out."

His radio crackled as Jackson acknowledged. "Good copy. Lieutenant Chang, new target. Can you put a few rounds into the roof of the residence, near that RPG gunner? Corporal Xu can cover the LS3 team's egress."

"Roger that. *Near* the target, not into?"

"Just keep his head down," Jackson said. "We've done what we came here to do. As soon as Gunny Jensen is clear, you can pull your bot back too."

THE RPG GUNNER and spotter weren't moving onto the roof to engage Jensen and his LS3. Nor either of the two slaughterbots.

Mandu's advance team had triangulated the worrying tactical radio signals ahead of the premier's convoy, and traced them to a building on the premier's egress route. That had allowed agents inside the compound, using thermal imaging equipment, to locate the exact floor and room in the abandoned office building where the signals were coming from, and the two individuals inside it.

It hadn't taken an AI to tell them the attack on their compound was being coordinated from the overwatch position.

As Chang squeezed his trigger to send a few warning rounds into the roof, the RPG gunner on the roof of the compound aimed his Kestrel high-explosive fragmentation

311

missile launcher at the building about 500 yards away, and
fired.

The Battle of Hawaii: Vandenberg

HAMMER RODRIGUEZ had made it her personal mission in life, as commander of Space Launch Delta 45's 615th Combat Operations Squadron, to ensure she could deliver on the motto of the 615th, a variation on the Space Force motto of "Semper Supra"—*Always Above*. The motto of the 615th was "Semper Supra, Parata Ad Pugnam," *Always Above, Ready for Battle*.

Skylon D4 'Tiger' had already seen battle. It was back at Patrick Space Force Base in Florida, being worked over so that it could be deployed again if needed. That left them with D4 'Mako,' which had been prepped and was waiting on the runway at Vandenberg AFB for a recon mission when Rodriguez had called to rewrite the tasking order.

Despite the value of rotating her crews to give more officers combat experience, Rodriguez had decided to go with her combat-seasoned crew for the next mission: Colonel Dan 'Tug' Boatt, lead pilot, and Captain Sally Hall, co-pilot. She had a feeling this war would be long enough for all of her Skylon crews to be blooded eventually.

Rodriguez had flown to Vandenberg to brief Boatt and Hall on the mission herself. Big picture, at least. They would work out the details with her staff and the other officers of the 615th.

They were seated around a table in the big hangar at Vandenberg where the needle-nosed, midnight black space plane stood ready. Even standing still, it looked fast. And deadly.

In its assault on Tiangong Space Station, it had already proven to be.

"You will be conducting *armed* reconnaissance for our attack on the Sino-Russian fleet currently about 220 nautical miles northwest of Kaua'i Island, Hawaii," Rodriguez told them. "We are moving a communications bird into geostationary orbit over the enemy fleet to supply GPS and communication support, but we have limited available photoreconnaissance assets, so you will supplement what we do have to provide our attacking forces with updated position data on the enemy fleet every time you pass over."

"Which, at 17,000 miles an hour, is only every 90 minutes, Colonel," Boatt pointed out. "That's a long time between passes when the missiles start flying."

"Like I said, you'll be supplementing whatever else we can put overhead," Rodriguez told him. "We're launching everything we had in our inventory, as fast as we can, but we're only talking in the dozens of satellites, and China destroyed hundreds. We won't have anywhere near real-time saturation coverage, but your data won't be the only intel our strike force is getting ..."

"You said 'armed reconnaissance,' Colonel," Hall interrupted. "We've been briefed on the weapon being loaded on Mako. Does your comment mean the decision to use it hasn't been made yet?"

"That decision will be made based on the outcome of a strike on the enemy fleet with conventional weapons," she said. "How confident are you of successfully deploying the weapon?"

Boatt and Hall exchanged a glance. "We've had three test deployments, Colonel, the last two successful. We had two more missions planned to finalize this test sequence, but they were focused on the warhead's terminal guidance systems, not weapon deployment."

314

Hall had nodded. "Give us the order, we'll kick it into space and put it on target, ma'am."

Sally Hall remembered that conversation now, as Mako swung around for its first pass over Hawaii and the Pacific Ocean northwest of Kaua'i.

She'd been a pilot on the British RAF Skylon program: the first astronaut in anyone's Space Force to log 100 hours in a Skylon. She'd joined the US program because she was more of a test pilot by mentality than squadron pilot. She enjoyed pushing the envelope in ways that hadn't been proven yet, and Boatt had promised her she'd be able to do that with the 615th.

Reflecting back on the assault on Tiangong and the months of preparation that had allowed them to execute it flawlessly, she had to acknowledge he hadn't lied.

And now they were pushing the envelope again.

"Kaua'i on the horizon," Boatt said. "Optics up."

"Cameras rolling; data sync with satellite LX9 is solid," she confirmed. Space Force had been able to get a new satellite into geostationary orbit over the Pacific northwest of Hawaii. The LX was the latest in the Advanced Extremely High Frequency satellite series, and had enough bandwidth to handle traffic from 200 platforms simultaneously. The package that the US had assembled to attack the Sino-Russian strike force would test it, but shouldn't overload its data management capabilities.

Mako was locked onto it, ready to squirt its AI-filtered and classified optical data to the LX satellite, which would beam it at the speed of light back down to earth for further analysis by Air Force and Navy analysts on the ground on Hawaii. Who would assign targets to the cloud of aircraft forming up over Kaua'i for the strike.

By the time Mako came around the earth to the Pacific again, that strike would have gone in, and Mako would be making a battle damage assessment.

And more, if needed.

Hall hoped it *wouldn't* be needed. She had no qualms of conscience about the legitimacy of the weapon in Mako's payload bay. It wasn't a treaty breaker. But Sally Hall was a girl whose parents raised her with a strong streak of humanity. She'd done her job in the attack on Tiangong, but hadn't reveled in the loss of life, even if the officers aboard the Chinese space station had probably been responsible for, or at least enabled, the loss of thousands of innocent lives.

Yes, they were the lives of a rampaging enemy. Killing them could save the lives of hundreds, maybe thousands, maybe *tens of thousands* of Americans.

Sally Hall wasn't a particularly religious woman, but she'd grown up in a Protestant family that regularly went to church. A phrase from her childhood came back to her at that moment. *"Father, if you are willing, take this cup from me; let not my will, but yours, be done."*

NIKO PUSHED himself back inside the house, shoving the door that had been blown out of its frame off him.

He was inside a laundry that led into the kitchen, where the girls had run. All except Presley, who helped him up. Or tried to. When he tried to stand, his foot screamed in pain and, looking down, he saw a bloody mess where his boot should be. He tried putting some weight on it, and swore.

Another rip of cannon fire and the small window above their heads exploded. Shells punched through and hit the kitchen wall. Screaming from the others in the kitchen.

"Can't you *shoot* it?" Presley asked. "It's going to kill us. These walls are like cardboard."

"If I ..." Propping himself on his good leg, he looked around for his rifle. "Oh, shit." The XM250 lay on the ground at the bottom of the small back porch. Only 2 yards from the door, but it might as well be a hundred. The shoulder strap lay against the bottom step though. Maybe he could reach ...

Ignoring his pain, he got down on his belly and crawled toward the shattered doorframe. As soon as he got close, cannon shells tore into the doorway, whipping over his head and exploding into and through the laundry wall, into the pantry beside it. A cloud of flour and plaster dust filled the air. Niko pulled back.

"I'll get it," Presley said.

"No!"

She jumped over him, hopped down the two steps like a gymnast on a bar, grabbed the rifle and turned ...

Sound of tearing paper. She was punched forward into the back wall of the house. Niko looked away. When he looked back, he could hear the drone edging closer, but he couldn't see the girl.

"Charger?!" he yelled. "Talk to me!"

Nothing. He dropped his head onto the floor and swore. He heard a noise behind him, turned and saw a dark-haired girl on her hands and knees, staring out the door with wide eyes. "Is she ..."

He clicked his fingers at her. "You, what's your name?"

"Uh, Lindsay."

"Lindsay. I need you to go to the front door. Check there is nothing outside and open and slam the door, loud as you can. Couple of times." He was hoping a slamming door might

317

sound like a gunshot to a slaughterbot. It was all he could think of to get it away from the back of the house.

"I don't ..." More cannon shells punched through the back wall, exploding against the kitchen wall again.

"Lindsay, I want to see if Presley is OK. Do it, alright? Loud as you can. Got that?" He raised his voice. "The rest of you stay *down*, on the floor."

She nodded, and crawled away.

"Presley, hang on out there. I'm coming, alright?" He got onto his hands and knees too. He'd have to drag his injured foot behind him, but he could get outside, if that damned bot ...

SLAM.

The front door. Whir of rotors outside, still close.

SLAM.

The whirring rose in pitch as the slaughterbot pulled away to investigate the sound. He heard it round the side of the house.

He focused on the steps, the gun ... the blood.

Now, Niko. Go.

His legs wouldn't move. The blood. A trail of blood, from the doorway, where he'd been standing. His blood, or hers?

Move, dammit. Rotors around the front of the house now.

He crawled like a demented toddler, down the stairs, vision jerking, missing a step, nearly tumbling, rifle strap by his hand. He grabbed it, looked left where Presley had been thrown by the force of the cannon fire.

Looked away.

Don't vomit. Don't you vomit.

He half-crawled, half-rolled up the steps and through the door again, dragging the rifle behind him. Lay on the floor inside the laundry, panting.

The girl, Lindsay, had crawled back in the kitchen doorway. "Presley?"

"She ..." *She's what? Don't say it.* "She's hiding, I think. Maybe under the house." He checked the rifle, charged the handle, looked for a semi-auto setting. There wasn't one. *Thing is a machine gun, idiot,* he told himself. *Full auto or nothing.*

Fire from the front of the house now. Front windows exploding, glass and window frame flying around the sitting room. Not reaching the kitchen though.

"Get down," he told Lindsay. "Flat on the floor." He crawled into the kitchen. "All of you. Stay flat."

The firing stopped. A piece of window frame fell outside with a clatter. Niko crawled into the sitting room, two knees, one hand, the other shoving the rifle ahead of him to try to push the broken glass out of the way as much as he could, which meant not completely. No time to think about that.

He reached the wall. At least the front of the house was brick. The slaughterbot cannon fire had punched out the windows, exploded on the interior walls, but hadn't penetrated the brick. Another short burst from outside. He curled into a ball. Rotors whirring as the drone moved side to side. Trying to see inside or flush them out? It was like a damned cat, waiting for a rat in a bush to make a run for safety.

The thought made him angry.

He lifted himself onto one knee using the rifle as a crutch. Blood on his trouser knees from the glass. He was level with the smashed window now. Bad foot behind him—he'd have to edge out on one knee and fire. It would see him for sure.

How did you kill a slaughterbot? They'd talked about that at the station, watching videos from Taiwan. Aim for the body, some guys said. Biggest target. Smash the electronics or

319

battery. Go for the rotors, other guys said. Bot can't fly without rotors. Big gun slung underneath—you bring it down, doesn't matter it isn't dead; it can't shoot you.

Niko looked at his XM250. Full auto? He wouldn't be "aiming" at anything. He'd be blasting away and hoping for the best.

Wait it out, Niko, a voice told him. *It will go away.*

And kill someone else.

Not your problem.

Except it was. Another short burst splintered the front door, sent it dancing back into the sitting room like it was possessed before it hit a fireplace. Girls in the kitchen, screaming.

When the cannon fire stopped, and before he could think anymore, he rose a little higher, put the barrel of the rifle on the busted windowsill and scanned. Left. Nothing. Right ...

Slaughterbot. Five yards up, 20 yards out.

He aimed, squeezed the trigger, gun chattering, slamming back into his shoulder, shots going low, then high. *Lower.* The cannon barrel under the slaughterbots, which had been facing away, swung around toward him now, *firing* ...

His bullets chewing into the body of the bot, sparks flying. It staggered backward. He kept the trigger down. Cannon shells exploding against the front of the house to his right. The noise of his own gun loud in his ear.

Sound like a ricochet in a Western movie. He saw something fly off the bot. One side dipped. It started slipping through the air, getting lower, gun still firing. He dropped, lying on the ground under the window. Cannon fire through the doorway, through the window, exploding on the wall behind.

A thud. Mechanical whine.

He listened, the stink of cordite filling the small sitting room. Nothing. No rotors. Just sobbing, from the kitchen.

"Everyone alright back there?" he yelled.

Low voices, then the girl, Lindsay, calling back, "We're alright. Did you get it?"

Question of the day. He edged back under the broken window, pushing himself with the butt of the rifle, muzzle still hot. Listened again. No rotors.

Up on one knee, eyes just above the windowsill. The slaughterbot was lying at a tilt on the ground about 10 yards out, gun half-buried in the grass of the front yard, rotors not moving. He grinned and turned toward the kitchen. "I got it!"

Then it exploded.

RORY'S AC-130X 'Outlaw' had been given the call sign 'Hound-dog'. He liked it since, just like a hound-dog, they'd been sent out ahead of the Australian fighters to map the positions of *Fujian*'s pickets, and the carrier itself—if they could get close enough without getting Outlaw's fat ass shot out of the sky.

It didn't have an electronic warfare suite of its own, but for that, it had four palletized Ghost Bat loyal wingmen, courtesy of the RAAF. Similar to the LongShot UAV in nearly every respect, the only problem was that he didn't have pilots rated to fly it, and there were no other US personnel on American Samoa who were qualified, so he'd taken two Australians aboard.

At the mission briefing, they introduced themselves as Chip and Dale, and didn't understand why the Americans smiled at that, or why Outlaw's crew gave them the call signs "Chipmunk One" and "Chipmunk Two."

Outlaw was at 30,000 feet, 200 nautical miles south of *Fujian*'s estimated position. Not out of range of low frequency radar if one of the air warfare destroyers was looking their way in the few minutes they were at that altitude, but hopefully not within sight of *Fujian*'s standing combat air patrols.

Uncle was up front, flying, while Rory was in the combat information center—the glorified name for the cubicle crammed with personnel just behind the cockpit.

"Second pallet away," Uncle announced, lowering Outlaw's nose. "Taking us down to 10,000."

"Hounds Three and Four deploying wings. Wings deployed; good telemetry," RAAF Flying Officer Dale Farquar reported. He was in command of Ghost Bats Hound Three and Hound Four. Chip was in command of the already-launched Hound One and Hound Two.

"Walk me through the game plan again," Rory said, standing between their chairs in the CIC and watching their displays over his shoulder.

"Hound Four is our command aircraft," Dale said. "He stays within radio range of our plane. We send commands to him, he relays them to Hounds One through Three. If we stay at 10,000 feet, that gives us a command reach of around 250 miles, give or take. Any further than that, we need to move Outlaw closer, or send our birds in autonomous."

Rory nodded. He had no desire to put Outlaw or its crew in harm's way again if he didn't need to. They'd been lucky to return from their last mission. But they still needed to get their job done.

"And you keep your machines low, passive sensors only," Rory confirmed. "One in the east, one in the west, one up the middle."

"We won't go active unless you say so, or we're engaged," Chip confirmed. "But if we are, I recommend we shirt-front 'em."

"Shirt-front?" Rory asked.

"Go balls out," Chip explained. "Hit them with everything we've got instead of trying to sneak away. Best chance of survival."

"Ghost Bats are designed to be expendable," Rory reminded him.

The man smiled. "Not mine, Captain. Haven't lost one yet. My bats always come home to roost."

You haven't been up against Fujian, Rory thought. But he didn't say it aloud.

MUSHROOM'S AO YIN SQUADRON had drawn the short straw for the coming attack on Pearl Harbor. As far as she saw it anyway.

Carrier defense duty.

She approached *Fujian*'s commander and air wing CO, Wang Wei, immediately after her squadron mission briefing, finding him in the CIC under the carrier's flight deck since its superstructure had still not been repaired. She rolled her wheelchair up behind him and waited for him to notice her.

"Colonel, I wish to …"

"Protest? Complain? Question?" Wang said with a sigh. "Which is it this time, Lieutenant Sun?"

"Suggest, Colonel," she said. "I *suggest* Ao Yin's pilots, as the most combat-experienced in the wing, would be better used in the attack on Pearl Harbor than on carrier defense."

Wang crossed his arms across his chest. "Why do you think I put Ao Yin on carrier defense, Sun?"

"I can see no reason," she maintained. "If the mission is to penetrate American air defenses and mine the harbor, my pilots are ..."

"The best air-to-air pilots in the Wing," Wang finished her sentence. "And as I have committed all but *six* of our aircraft to the attack on Pearl Harbor, I need the best fighter pilots in the Wing defending *Fujian* until more aircraft are flown in from *Shandong* tonight."

"Colonel, it will take good pilots to even reach Pearl Harbor. Its ground defenses will not all have been destroyed. Its air defenses may have been reinforced."

"Good air-to-ground pilots have been dispatched to attack Pearl Harbor. My best air-to-air pilots will defend *Fujian*." Wang turned his back. "You are dismissed, Lieutenant."

Six aircraft. That fact had also pained her. *Fujian*'s once mighty strike group had been reduced to just two air warfare destroyers—*Dalian* and *Haikou* and the unarmed fleet tender *Taihu*. A single *Type 093* submarine, *Hull 415*, had joined them after running the gauntlet of the American Coalition over a long voyage from the South China Sea, but it would only really be useful to counter any naval attack—its chances of picking up an enemy submarine on its own were infinitesimal.

The *Type 055* destroyer *Dalian* had proven itself a valiant defender through multiple engagements. One hundred of its 112 vertical-launch missile cells were loaded with anti-aircraft missiles, just 12 with anti-ship missiles—a calculated risk Wang had taken before departing Port Aeon on Kiribati. *Haikou* was an older *Type 052*, its sensor suite less capable, and its much smaller 64-cell missile magazine carried only 60 air-to-air missiles.

Wang therefore had *Dalian* out ahead of him, watching the sky around the carrier with its focus on attacks coming from

Hawaii in the north or the US mainland in the northeast. He knew American strategic bomber assets were stretched thin, but he couldn't rule out a blizzard of missiles being launched at *Fujian* by land-based US bombers.

He had the older *Haikou* trailing, watching their southern flank.

In her pod, watching the skies around *Fujian* through the lenses of her aircraft's DAS cameras at 30,000 feet, Mushroom decided there was no quarter from which an attack could not come. They were a long way from Australia now, and they'd been assured Wake and Midway islands were out of commission, but *Fujian* was alone in hostile seas.

With just six aircraft, Mushroom's strategy was to keep a reserve of two aircraft—including her own—orbiting over the carrier, and have two patrolling northeast and northwest while the other two patrolled southeast and southwest.

Her flight had been given the call sign *Quehuoque*, after a mythical fire-breathing bird. A motivational name. She guessed the intelligence officer, Major Tan, might have been trying to appease their political cadre. A contact appeared on her tactical screen, flashed to her by *Haikou*. "*Fujian*, Firebird Leader. I am seeing a high-flying heavy to our south, bearing one niner zero, altitude 30, range 250 miles. Please confirm." The slow aircraft, probably a transport of some kind, was showing a civilian transponder code and was headed away from them, moving southeast and descending.

What her enemies had taught her so far was that meant nothing.

"Confirmed, Firebird. You are to stay on patrol. *Fujian* out."

Maintain station? Her instincts told her that would be A Bad Idea, but she didn't argue the order. It still gave

Mushroom a little latitude as flight commander. "Firebird Leader to Firebird Three," she said. "Break off and fly down the bearing to that heavy. Be alert for small fast movers ahead and on your flanks. At the first sign of enemy radar or jamming, don't try to ride it out; put your fighter in autonomous-attack mode and send it at the signal."

"Firebird Three copies; breaking south," her pilot said.

Fool me once, shame on you, Mushroom muttered to herself in a singsong voice. *Fool me twice, shame on me.*

"HOUNDS TRIANGULATING a new contact, designate S-3," Dale said. "Bearing three five eight, range from Outlaw three niner four, *Luyang* destroyer air warfare radar type."

Rory tapped the back of the Australian's chair. That made three solid contacts. The *Luyang* class, probably *Haikou*. Air traffic control and satellite signals from a ship about 10 nautical miles ahead of it—likely the *Fujian*. And radio signals from a third ship. No radar. Maybe the tender, *Taihu*.

There had been a fourth ship in the strike group that had anchored at Port Aeon though. The deadliest of the four—for Australian fighters at least. *Dalian*.

"Can you work wide, try to stay out of range but move around the *Luyang* to get a look north of *Fujian*?" Rory asked. "We're missing a Panther killer—the *Dalian*."

"Can't have that," Chip said. "I'll send Hound Two around the right flank, but we'll need to move Hound Four closer to keep a signal lock. Which means ..."

"Got you," Rory said, tapping his throat mic. "Uncle, we need to scooch a little further north. Can you bring us around and take us up another 5,000?"

326

"How much of a scooch?" Bob Lee asked.

Rory conferred with the Australian pilot. "We're thinking 30 miles."

"That's not a scooch," Uncle grumbled, but Rory felt the plane bank into a sliding turn. "Getting hip to hip with your lady on the sofa, that's a scooch. Thirty miles is a shimmy."

"*Shimmy* north, then," Rory said patiently. "Thirty miles."

Mushroom saw the heavy to their south alter course toward them and start gently climbing. It was still nearly 250 miles away, but she didn't like it. One little bit.

"Firebird Three, Firebird Leader. Arm missiles: you may have enemy aircraft off your ten o'clock. Be alert. Scan high and low."

"Firebird Three copies. No contacts."

Was she getting target fixation? It was possible the lumbering transport was deliberately making itself visible, trying to draw their attention away from an attack from another quarter: Hawaii, for example.

No, they're there. I know they are, she decided. *This isn't a feint.*

"Firebird Leader is breaking south. Four, stay on station over *Fujian*," she told her wingman. She pushed her throttle forward, accelerating from 400 to 500 and then 600 knots in the space of a few seconds. "*Fujian*, that heavy has altered course toward us. Firebird Leader investigating." She armed her missiles.

"Acknowledged, Firebird Leader."

It wasn't that she didn't trust the pilot she'd sent south to investigate. But she trusted her own skills with the Chongming's radar more.

327

She took a bearing to the unknown aircraft and then began searching right and left of it. Right high, right low, left high, left low. Nothing.

"Firebird Three, still no contacts."

Frustrated, she rolled her wrist, yawing her plane further left. Maybe they weren't looking out wide enough. Same procedure. Radar high right, low right, low left …

Contact.

"Firebird Leader has a fast mover bearing two six four degrees, altitude 2,000, range 100 miles. Engaging." The contact was comfortably inside her PL-15's missile range, and she locked the target up quickly. "Fox three," she said, sending a missile downrange.

"TARGETING RADAR, missile launch," Dale said. Hound Three was his, and it had gone from spy to prey in the blink of an eye. "Coming around. Three is jamming. Send Two away low," he said to Chip.

"Why not push your other bird forward while the Chinese are occupied?" Rory asked Dale.

"That's risky," the Australian said. Rory was about to make it an order, but the Australian surprised him. "I like it. Move Two up the middle, now."

"FIREBIRD THREE, search your two o'clock," Mushroom ordered. Where there was one enemy sneaking in low, there would be more. "Enemy is trying to jam. Moving to auto-attack mode." She hit a couple of switches. "Dominator, you have the stick; prosecute the designated contact."

Her AI responded. *Dominator has the stick. Automated attack authorized. Confirm.*

Mushroom didn't hesitate. "Confirm."

Her helmet display began flashing to show she had surrendered control of her Chongming, and her stick went slack in her hand. She could still watch the aircraft executing its mission on her tactical screen, still see through its fuselage-mounted cameras. For now.

Target locked. Fox three, the AI said. Then the camera vision started glitching. Snow.

Mushroom leaned back in her seat, flexing her fingers in front of her. She was out of the fight.

But her plane wasn't.

THE AUSTRALIAN Ghost Bats were unarmed surveillance aircraft. But unarmed didn't mean defenseless. Under attack, the Ghost Bat automatically switched its electronic warfare systems from snooping to attacking and started jamming enemy aircraft radar.

At the range they were being painted from—over 100 miles—jamming was difficult, and it couldn't stop the aircraft from firing on it. First one missile, then another.

Hound Three had no altitude to play with as it was already down at 2,000 feet, so it started zigzagging through the sky, trying to force the enemy missile to burn precious fuel by constantly adjusting course. When the first missile got within 30 miles, the Ghost Bat launched an active decoy down the bearing to the missile—a small rocket-powered miniature missile with a big radar cross section and no infrared shielding.

329

It closed on the incoming Chinese missile at a combined speed of Mach 5, and convinced it that its target had changed course and was coming right for it. The Chinese missile homed on the decoy and blew it out of the sky.

The Ghost Bat put itself into a flat skid, going flank on to the second Chinese missile and firing its second and last active decoy, still focusing jamming energy on the attacking Chongming with its radar dish at the limit of its gimbals.

The Chinese missile kept coming straight for it.

"GOT YOU," Chip said. "New contact, bearing zero zero four, range four forty. *Renhai* class air defense radar ..."

"That's our friend *Dalian*," Rory said, clapping a hand on Chip's shoulder. He turned to his comms officer. "Send those positions to the Australians, include the ship types. Mark the message 'confidence high.'"

"Done, boss," the woman said a moment later.

Rory did a little air punch, on the inside. He had a feeling his luck was changing. He looked out of the corner of his eye to the dark shadows deeper down the aircraft, as though daring something to show itself.

"Bugger. Hound Three is down," Dale said. "Orders?"

"Bring them home, gentlemen," Rory said. "Our work here is done."

AS SOON AS the American drone was destroyed, the jamming stopped, and Mushroom got command of her aircraft back.

"*Fujian*, Firebird Leader. Target down. Request permission to pursue the enemy heavy launching these drones," Mushroom said.

She heard Wang's voice reply. "Lieutenant, you can send one plane; bring the rest back to CAP position."

Yes. Mushroom keyed her mic. "Firebird Three, return to carrier CAP. I will pursue the enemy heavy."

The man sounded ashamed. "I am sorry, Lieutenant," he said. "I was too slow to pick up ..."

"Don't apologize," Mushroom said. "You will do better next time." She checked the aircraft circling around the strike group. "Firebird Two, you are flight lead. Maintain CAP. Firebird Leader going dark."

"Firebird Two is lead, maintaining CAP."

Mushroom put her nose down, heading for the sea. She set her emissions profile to "dark," shutting down her radio and radar. She laid in an intercept course for the big transport.

There may be more recon drones out there, but Mushroom ignored that thought. She was going for the mothership.

And its crew. Without really thinking about it, her thoughts went to her lost comrade, Asien 'Shredder' Chen. It seemed like years since she had last seen his cheeky smile, heard the teasing lilt in his voice. She'd had too few opportunities to pay the enemy back for taking her best friend from her.

It was time.

AS MUSHROOM headed south from *Fujian*, Captain Lei Yu's six Gyrfalcons were heading north.

Fujian's CO, Colonel Wang Wei, had gone on deck to watch the last aircraft launch. He felt enormous pride at the

331

sight of China's most powerful naval fighter aircraft rocketing past *Fujian*'s ruined superstructure and climbing into the air: something he would not have thought possible just a few days earlier.

As a senior officer, Wang had been given more insight into the Chinese battle plan than Mushroom had been granted. Yes, this attack should deny the use of Pearl Harbor to the US Navy for weeks, maybe months. But China had no intention of invading O'ahu. It had in fact stolen an idea, never executed, from a draft Japanese invasion plan for Hawaii, created in 1940.

Hawaii had been a US bastion even then, and the Japanese general command had ambitions for a wider war across the Pacific that meant they could not devote the resources needed to eject the Americans from Hawaii in the same way they had ejected the British from Singapore or the Chinese from Taiwan. The Japanese, like the Chinese, had also realized that the challenges of supplying an occupying army on Hawaii for an extended period would be insurmountable.

But take and hold the island of *Kaua'i* for several months? That they could do.

Though neither the Russian marines aboard their *Ivan Gren* class landing ships nor the Chinese marines aboard their *Yushen* helicopter docks knew it, China planned to land an amphibious force on Kaua'i, but it did not plan to reinforce or resupply it. The invading force would take the island quickly and then dig in. Six thousand troops or more would be landed, and only 1,000 shell-shocked Americans were expected to oppose them.

Among the systems that would be landed with the invading troops were a higher-than-usual number of hyper-long-range artillery barrels capable of firing rocket-assisted

155 mm shells nearly 120 miles—developed to allow China to bombard Taipei from mainland China—more than the distance from Kaua'i to O'ahu. A lower-than-usual proportion of armored vehicles was supplemented by a higher-than-normal number of mobile and fixed anti-air systems. And finally, the Chinese landing helicopter docks carried almost no vehicle fuel; instead the weight had been dedicated to loading dozens of containerized YJ-18 Eagle Strike mobile land attack missile systems with the range to hit with precision any target on Kaua'i or O'ahu.

Every spare inch of storage space on the Sino-Russian hovercraft was loaded with 155 mm shells, anti-aircraft, anti-ship and land attack missiles. In concert with cyberwarfare, political subversion, and submarine-launched and long-range aerial attacks, Kaua'i was to be turned into a "porcupine"—a Chinese base that would take months, and untold lives, for the Americans to take back.

It was a play right out of the US Marines' own playbook.

When the full scale of China's ambition had been revealed to him, along with the scale of the sacrifice it would entail— none of the 6,000 men being landed on Kaua'i were expected to come home alive—he felt emotion well in his chest.

Pride, yes, at the scale of China's ambition and *Fujian*'s role in achieving it. But also horror at the coming human cost, on both sides.

CAPTAIN LEI YU of Victory Squadron was surprised that they had penetrated to within 60 miles of the Hawaiian Islands without being met by the USAF.

Or perhaps he shouldn't have been. According to their briefing, the Americans had been down to a handful of fighters after the slaughterbot and cruise missile strikes. All but their smallest general aviation airfields had been knocked out—maybe not permanently, but for the duration of their present mission, certainly.

Lei Yu was indeed the arrogant gung-ho fighter pilot robot Mushroom took him for. As he closed on Hawaii, he felt nothing but nationalistic fervor at the thought his People's Communist Party had finally decided to take its rightful place in history as the dominant power in the Pacific. And hubris because it was wholly appropriate that his 'Victory' Squadron was leading the attack on Hawaii and was first to see the Americans on radar.

Or to be more accurate, the American. Singular.

"Contact, bearing zero zero niner, altitude 30, range 55," Lei said. "Radar emissions. Single fast mover. Victory One and Two will engage."

Single fast mover? Were the Americans down to their last aircraft?

Lei armed a single PL-15 and sent it downrange in "home on emissions" mode. His lone enemy wouldn't see it coming until it was too late.

NATIONAL GUARD F-22 pilot Captain Annunzio 'Nun' D'Angelli sure felt like he was the last pilot aloft over Hawaii.

Of course, he wasn't. Nun had just seen nearly 50 USAF Black Widows and F-22s lighting out for the skies northwest of Kaua'i. He knew another 20 F-35 Panthers were converging on the Sino-Russian fleet after taking off from the decks of *Fallujah*. And, he'd been told, 16 venerable B1-B

'Bones' flying from California were also part of the strike package.

He hoped there were other assets he didn't know about. It still seemed a pretty small package to be throwing at the biggest amphibious landing force the US had ever faced.

Nun wasn't alone over O'ahu. Not entirely. He was leading a flight comprising the last three combat-capable National Guard F-22s. Nun and three other pilots against the world. That made a kind of twisted sense to Nun. His great grandfather was a former naval aviator who flew the TBF Avenger and SBD Dauntless during the Battle of Midway, the A-1 Skyraider, and F9F Panthers in Korea.

From an early age, Nun knew he wanted to go fast and do big things.

He rode horses competitively while in high school and college and got a job in finance to support himself as a professional equestrian competitor. Then he fell, broke a leg and missed the Hawaii championships. While he was recovering, his thoughts turned to his other dream. Flying.

At 25, he was assigned to Raptors. At 30, he got his first command.

At 32, he was flying CAP over his home islands, watching them burn.

Lei Yu only saw one fighter over O'ahu because Nun D'Angelli planned it that way. He was up at 30,000 in his no-longer-so-stealthy F-22, but his three wingmen were down low, lapping the tuna-like dorsal fin of the Lē'ahi ranges at near treetop height, waiting to be unleashed at an enemy.

His pilots were as hungry for payback as Nun was, and they were about to get it.

"Fanfare flight, Fanfare Leader. I got a ghost at one nine one degrees," Nun said. "Nothing solid, just a whisper on

RWR." He banked his aircraft south and started searching on radar, switching to the air controller frequency. "Hickam, Fanfare Leader, possible bogey at one nine one degrees. What do you see?"

"Sky is clear on that bearing as far as we can see, Fanfare," the Hickam air controller told him. Their only AWACS had been moved west with the rest of the attack package, and it didn't surprise him that Hawaiian ground-based air defenses couldn't see what he could see. Kaena Point long-range radar had been knocked out by slaughterbots, and cruise missiles had taken out most of the fixed air defense radar sites across O'ahu. Only shorter-range mobile units were still operating.

A single Navy *Constellation* class frigate, the *Lafayette*, was also scanning the skies around Hawaii, but was 50 nautical miles east, off Big Island. *Still, it should be able to see an enemy approaching O'ahu, unless …*

He modified his radar signal to scan low, right down to sea level, filtering out the sea clutter.

Contact.

Contacts, plural. "Four fast movers south Honolulu, altitude 1,000, range five zero. Fanfare pilots, fan out and engage. Hickam, you have incoming."

As he worked to box the contacts and assign weapons, Nun cursed. Fighters flying off *Fujian*—they had to be. That carrier should have been dead, 10 times over. Would have been if they had a single satellite tracking it. Instead, it was hanging around like the proverbial thorn in their side. Did its commander *know* they had just sent every other available aircraft west, or was the timing of this attack just dumb luck?

"Fanfare Leader engaging," he said. "*Fox three by four.*"

Then a missile warning screamed in his ears, he bunted his plane into a blood-vessel-bursting tip-over as it sprayed decoys into its slipstream, and the next several minutes became a kaleidoscope of adrenaline-fueled mayhem.

Calls from his wingmen as they engaged.

Pushing his aircraft to its limits to regain height and speed.

Trying to get a lock on the Chinese fighter that attacked him. Failing. Dodging another missile, searching down the bearing it closed from, finding his attacker.

Finding him *close*.

Tracer fire screaming past his canopy as they closed on each other, head-to-head.

Then began a dance that could only end with one of them dead.

THE LEAD ELEMENT of the anti-ship strike package headed northwest from Kaua'i Island was 68th AGRS. Meany had been told they'd earned the dubious honor of being "tip of the spear" because of their high kill to loss ratio.

It wasn't an honor they'd asked for, and so Meany made a strong case for letting his team create their own plan of attack, based on the time on target they were given and the estimated position of the Sino-Russian fleet.

They were promised updated target information once airborne, but Meany wasn't betting the farm on that.

They'd used Crystal's paper map to do their mission planning.

"The mission is suppression of enemy air defenses, SEAD. We have to take out the air warfare pickets on their southern flank without getting our own asses shot out of the sky by either their missile cruisers or fighter defenses. Make life easier for the second wave. Ideas?"

"Play it straight," Flowmax said. "Send in the Valkyries in growler mode to spot targets and jam naval radars, Raptors behind them, ready to ambush whatever aircraft they have overhead. You and O'Hare come in behind us once the sky in that sector is clear and drop the hammer on a couple of anti-air destroyers."

"I like the simplicity." Meany nodded. He'd been thinking much the same thing. "Alternatives?"

"Same basic plan, but we pull a bait-and-switch," Touchdown suggested. "Raptors come in from the southwest at 30,000, supported by Valkyries to draw the heat. We pull the Chinese fighters to us. While they're busy, you come in low from the south."

"Good idea," Meany agreed. "Crystal, run fuel calculations for both scenarios. O'Hare, why so quiet?"

Bunny looked up from the map. Both of the plans suggested so far sounded to her like a great way to fight the fight China would be expecting. "You told me I need to be more constructive in these sessions," she said. "So my silence is me being constructive."

"Constructive means if you have a better idea, you put it on the table," Touchdown said testily, and pointed at the map. "Literally."

"Alright. Wing is using us to test China's defenses for the main attack; they don't expect us to succeed. It's just a dumb way to die, which is why they gave it to Aggressor Inc."

"Constructive, Lieutenant." Meany sighed.

"Sorry. But if I'm going to die, I want to take the enemy with me. The best way to suppress China's air defenses isn't to knock out a couple of picket destroyers. We need to try for a decapitation strike that will take *half* of China's fighters off the board."

338

"We've got six aircraft, O'Hare. How do you propose we destroy 40 Chinese fighters?" Touchdown asked.

"We need to change the mission from SEAD to something else," Bunny insisted. "Put 600-gallon drop tanks on our F-22s, flank the Chinese fleet and hit their fighter CAPs from behind, in the west, out of nowhere. You, Meany, Flatline, Flowmax and Agony go up with 38 AIM-260s between you, start swatting their fighters from over the horizon while I take all four Valkyries, both of the Waveriders, and go after *Liaoning*."

"Just change the mission," Touchdown said, shaking her head, "so you can make a Hail Mary kamikaze run at a carrier?"

Bunny shot Touchdown a defiant look. "Week one of this war, I was able to penetrate *Fujian*'s cordon, put a missile in her hide and get away clean, *without* anyone riding shotgun. So we know the Widow can defeat Chinese naval radar. If you fly it right."

Meany coughed like he was about to choke. "Give you both Waveriders, *and* the four Valkyries?"

Flatline whistled. "It's ballsy. We think they've been using *Liaoning* to leapfrog fighters from the Russian Kuriles to their other carriers, *Shandong* and *Fujian,* so its strike group could be trailing the main fleet, not sailing side by side with *Shandong.* We knock out *Liaoning* early in the fight, we take out 36 Gyrfalcons, plus we cripple China's airframe supply line."

Crystal looked at his watch. "Space Force has promised an update on the Chinese fleet's position 30 minutes before time on target," he said. "We could re-evaluate on the fly, move to the other plan if *Liaoning* looks too well defended."

Bunny could see Meany was actually thinking it through. "Even if we tied up their CAP cover, you'd have to sneak past at least one *Renhai* cruiser and a couple of *Luyang* destroyers, maybe a Russian *Gorshkov* corvette too. More firepower than *Fujian* had protecting it when you hit it, for sure. If anyone puts their neck on the line like that, it should be me," Meany said.

Bunny looked at him skeptically. "You'd have to manage four Valkyries on EW and anti-ship duty at the same time as you thread the needle between the Chinese pickets *and* set up your attack on a Chinese carrier. No offense, boss, but there's only one Widow pilot here with a hope in hell of doing that."

"She's right, Captain," Flowmax said, looking sheepish and not meeting Meany's eyes. "No offense."

"Offense taken," Meany said. "I'm not agreeing with O'Hare." He looked around the group. "But let's just say I'm willing to go up the line and ask to revisit the mission objective if we have a good case. Let's chew it over some more, see if we can make O'Hare's plan work."

"I volunteer to play devil's advocate," Touchdown said immediately.

"Did nobody see what I did there?" Crystal asked, disappointed. "*Re-evaluate on the fly?* My humor is wasted on this audience."

TOUCHDOWN FOUND a dozen problems with O'Hare's plan but then helped find workarounds to most of them herself. Meany took the plan up the line, arguing that if it worked, they could deal an early blow that could take two Chinese squadrons and a carrier out of the equation. He'd also pointed out that if it didn't work, it would only cost six aircraft, but he didn't share that detail with his pilots.

While Meany was negotiating, Flowmax and O'Hare were catching up over a cup of day-old, rewarmed-in-a-microwave coffee.

"So where's my tattoo?" he asked her.

"What?"

"You get a tattoo for everyone you care about who dies, and you thought I was dead, so where's my tattoo? I want to see what you got."

"I … Hey, I was fighting slaughterbots on Taiwan," she said, feeling a little awkward. "Not a lot of tattoo parlors open on Taiwan these days."

"Come on, I bet you put it somewhere intimate. That's why you won't show me." He winked.

"Gross, Flowmax. I should report you."

"Or … you could just show me," he said, not giving up.

"Let it go, big guy. You said it yourself, I get tattoos for people I care about." She stood and picked up his empty coffee cup.

He actually looked hurt. "You care about me."

"Nope," she said. "Unless you owe me money. I can't remember, do you owe me money?"

"No."

"Because there would be interest, for all that time you were a POW and didn't pay me back. I care about interest."

"No."

"Then what can I say? No tattoo. Deal with it."

She walked off.

"Yeah, you care," he called after her. "And you got my tattoo somewhere, I know it."

The change in mission scope was approved, but their time on target remained the same. 68th Aggressor was still going in first. Which meant once their planes were fueled and loaded, they had no time to waste.

Meany was already in his plane and taxiing as Bunny ran to hers. Entry to her Widow was via a hatch under the nose, already hanging open. She'd done her walk around earlier, high-fived a crew chief and clambered up into the cockpit. The first thing she did was plug in her helmet, which booted it to life and gave her a voice link to her combat AI. "Lieutenant Bunny O'Hare," she said.

Pilot recognized; ready for input, the AI responded.

"Auto startup routine: scramble," she said as she pulled her seat harnesses over her shoulders and strapped herself in. OK, it wasn't technically a scramble, but hey, she was in a hurry.

Scramble routine initiating. Please check the cockpit and aircraft are clear of foreign objects and obstructions.

Bunny looked to see none of the ground crew had left anything in her cockpit, then scanned around the plane, her DAS cameras following her head as she checked the space around her plane. The voice in her helmet started running through the accelerated takeoff checklist.

Power on, power to normal.

Throttle to idle. Check ground crew are clear of aircraft.

Bunny looked behind her. "Tail clear."

Engine one start.

Engine two start.

Engine operations nominal.

Avionics startup. Confirm HMD visible.

"Helmet Mounted Display up," Bunny confirmed, checking the instrument readings flashing along the bottom of the viewscreen in her helmet display.

Comms power on. Confirm status with ground crew.

"Chief Delray, Bunny. Good to go?"

"Cables and pins pulled; you are clear to depart, pilot," the crew chief said over the radio. "Happy hunting."

Establish communication with ground traffic control as required.

"Ground traffic control"? That was a good one. Ground traffic control was a couple of Marine Joint Terminal Air Controllers in a portable surf life-saving tower towed up from Lanikai Beach.

But as first pilot out, that was Meany's job. She heard him on the radio. "Bellows Tower, this is 68 Aggressor two-plane with four Loyal Wingmen requesting permission for immediate takeoff."

"68 Aggressor, Bellows Tower. Runway 3/21, cleared for takeoff. Wind is 080 at 10 knots. You are cleared for immediate departure."

Bunny keyed her interplane channel. "Right behind you, boss."

"Good copy. Bring it, O'Hare."

Bunny switched back to the AI command channel. "Widow, get us to the runway."

Widow has the stick for taxi. Confirm.

"Confirmed, Widow has the stick for taxi."

Taxiing to takeoff point runway 3/21 Bellows AFB. Confirm that all warning lights and caution messages are cleared.

Her plane jerked forward as the AI ground autopilot took over and began taxiing while Bunny flipped through engine and avionics screens on her flat panel interface and double-checked everything was in order. Then she turned her attention to her four Valkyrie loyal wingman drones, setting them up to take off and follow her out.

Fuel: full tanks.

Weapons: Waverider hypersonic anti-ship missile. Short-range Peregrine missiles, two. That was it. Under the wings of each Valkyrie, two Peregrines for eight total.

Meany's proposal that O'Hare be given both of their Waverider hypersonic anti-ship missiles had been refused. Air Force had precious few of the $6 million hypersonic missiles and was not happy putting both eggs in one basket. It had no opinion on how Meany should distribute his four Valkyrie wingmen, but both Widows would be used for the attack on *Liaoning*.

If they were given its bloody position.

Her Widow reached the end of the runway, and she made one last check around her plane. Touchdown and the other Raptor pilots were taxiing out behind her, planes laden with twin 600 lb. fuel tanks. "Widow, pilot has the aircraft," she said, putting hands on throttle and stick.

Pilot has the aircraft, the AI confirmed.

Bunny tested her stick, checked her nosewheel was centered, then eased her throttle forward, relishing the buzz she always got as the big fighter's acceleration slammed her back in her seat.

She looked sideways as her plane rotated and began lifting into the air, and saw a long, sleek limousine flying US flags appear from between two lines of trucks and stop beside the runway. Strange sight in the middle of a war, but she knew exactly who was in it—because, of course, everyone had heard the rumor.

And there she was, stepping out of the vehicle. POTUS, come to wave them off.

Bunny snapped the president a salute as her plane rocketed past her.

That girl has cojones, she thought.

344

CARMEN CARLIOTTI smiled. The Black Widow that had just taken off had a narrow slit for a cockpit window, but she was pretty sure she'd seen its pilot sending her a Hawaiian "shaka" gesture.

No problem with morale there, Carliotti thought.

She'd spent the morning at MCBH visiting with doctors and nurses treating casualties who had been evacuated from Pearl Harbor-Hickam. After that, she'd chaired a meeting of the Joint Chiefs focused on getting INDOPACCOM Commander Harry Connaught and his senior officers what he needed to do the job of dismantling the Sino-Russian fleet. Connaught and his operations commander, Samuels, attended in person, the other Joint Chiefs via video link from bases across the globe.

With the losses China inflicted on heavy aircraft on the ground at Kadena in Japan, Clark Base in the Philippines, Guam, and Midway and Wake islands, stealth missile trucks were hard to find. The conclusion was that they had the assets to take out *either* the three Chinese carriers *or* a large number of their landing ships, but not both.

"The reality is we don't know how many mission-capable B-21s and B-2s we have right now in the Taiwan theater," the head of Air Force had told the meeting. "Estimate is maybe six."

Carliotti had winced. Each B-2 cost upwards of $2 billion. Having learned that lesson, each B-21 Raider came in at "only" $1 billion apiece. Nevertheless, while USAF had asked for a fleet of 100 B-21s, a Congressional budget review in the 2030s had cut that to 50, then 30—just enough to replace the existing B-2 fleet as it was phased out. Two days of Chinese attacks and now they could field only *six* aircraft? Not for the first time, Carliotti had cursed the lack of foresight of her predecessors.

The USAF General continued. "We already emptied CENTCOM and EUCOM to support Taiwan operations. The 293rd in Missouri was in the process of converting to Raiders, but their B-2s are still parked up at Whiteman. I've asked how long before we can work them up again and throw them at the problem, but they won't be ready in the next 12 to 24 hours."

Troops were no issue. Finding enough airlift capacity outside the Taiwan theater was, not to mention the challenge of where to land the aircraft.

"How long to clear the mines China has planted all over our airfields?" Carliotti had asked.

The awkward silence told her more than she wanted to know. It was US Army General Reg Samuels who took the question. "Ma'am, it took the Halo Trust over 20 years to clear a minefield in Afghanistan that covered an area of just 1.2 square miles. And that was mostly in noncombat conditions," Samuels said. "We are looking at hundreds of thousands of mines over hundreds of square miles, from cities and beaches to military bases. We're going to have to decide, do we prioritize urban areas or military? No matter what we do or how fast we do it, hospitals *will* be overwhelmed with casualties, and that's even before the virus hits.

The head of Air Force spoke up. "It will be quicker to build new air strips, or expand smaller ones like Dillingham that China didn't hit." He looked grim. "And we have to make sure they can't continue doing it."

346

The news delivered by Admiral Connaught from other theaters was mixed. On the plus side, the Marine campaign in the South China Sea had displaced Chinese troops from two more installations, on Gaven and Johnson South reefs, and repelled Chinese special operations forces attacks on Calderon and Subi reefs.

Chinese forces had withdrawn from Midway and Wake islands after destroying infrastructure and mining both the surface and surrounding seas. They had been particularly thorough regarding the runways on both islands. Not satisfied to blow holes in them with demolition charges, they dug channels to the sea and submerged them before mining the remaining land surface. But the islands were no longer under Chinese control, and the US military and civilian survivors on the islands had been rescued.

Clark Base in the Philippines and Kadena on Okinawa in Japan had been hit hard, again with area denial munitions, but China and Russia had held back from wider attacks on Philippine and Japanese military bases. Japan was nervous about Russia reinforcing a disputed island in the Kuril chain just 30 miles from Hokkaido in northern Japan, But US analysts saw this as more political than military in nature. The message from Russia was clear: stay out of this fight unless you want to face a new front in a wider war.

The situation on Guam was critical. Chinese airborne troops had captured the international airport and dug in. An effort by China to reinforce them by air had been repulsed, so they were isolated, but showing no signs of capitulation. The island had been subjected to similar sea-launched cruise missile attacks to those used against Hawaii, with airports and ports mined. The main military facilities of Andersen Air Base and Marine Camp Blaz had been effectively shut down.

More than one officer around the table was regretting the decision of their forebears in the 2020s to dramatically cut spending on US Army Short-Range Anti-Air Defenses, and their own decisions not to speed up the theater-wide deployment of Stryker-based M-SHORADS and Hawkei-based MML systems.

"China's Pacific War strategy is becoming clear," Connaught said. "They show no intent to permanently occupy US possessions across the Pacific, rather to deny their use to our militaries. We can eject them, reinforce air and anti-ship defenses, but unless we destroy every one of China and Russia's fleets of 90-plus cruise-missile-armed submarines and their strategic bomber forces, they will retain the capacity to overwhelm air defenses and deploy area denial munitions against our facilities. There will be short- to medium-term interruptions to our operations each time."

"This is not just a military strategy; it's an economic one," Carliotti said. "They want to make the price of maintaining our presence in the Pacific untenable." She gestured with frustration. "They shut one of our bases down, we bury the bodies, demine and build it up again, they shut it down again. And as the Admiral says, this won't stop unless they are defeated gentlemen."

Carliotti had asked the Homeland Security Secretary, Janet Belkin, to dial in on video link and give the Joint Chiefs an update on the security situation at home, with a focus on how it might affect the military campaign. "Well, Madam President, firstly, we now have 3,200 active cases of H5N1c on mainland USA and around 1,000 deaths, mostly among service personnel recently returned from Taiwan and their close contacts. There are currently 35 active cases on Hawaii. Those numbers will increase exponentially. We expect the number of infected on mainland USA to be 100,000 by the end of this week and the number of deaths ..." Belkin paused. "The number of deaths will follow infections up. Mortality on Taiwan is around 50 percent, probably because of population density. So far on mainland USA it has been lower, around 30 percent, but that can change."

The anger around the table was palpable. "This bioweapon is a nuclear attack in slow motion," the Marine Corps chief said. "Dear God, 50 percent mortality? We have to respond to it as we would to a nuclear attack, while we are still able!"

Emotions boiled over, and several more members of the Joint Chiefs weighed in. Carliotti let the anger flow. She didn't disagree with the sentiment, just the conclusion. Any nuclear attack on China would only result in Russia, North Korea and Iran joining the inevitable Chinese nuclear response.

"Ladies and gentlemen," she said at last. "You still lead the largest, strongest, most capable military on the planet. You are supported by the armed forces of Japan, South Korea, the Philippines, Australia, New Zealand, Canada and the UK. We are invoking NATO Article 5 and will soon join the full strength of NATO to our cause. No one is more furious than me at the pestilence China has unleashed on the world. The Chinese bioweapon is moving in slow motion, but it *is* moving, which means there is an urgency to this war. We must defeat China now, here, on these islands, and then push their armies back behind their borders before this bioweapon lays our forces low. I need you to put the idea of nuclear weapons out of your minds, and dedicate yourselves to achieving this objective with all the other means at your disposal." She paused, letting that sentence sink in. "You are not the horsemen of the apocalypse. Your task is to ensure

349

the future of our great nation, not just the destruction of our enemy."

She could sense she didn't have the entire room with her yet. Committing suicide was so much easier for some than dealing with the thought of a long and painful struggle. "Madam Secretary, please continue," Carliotti said.

"Yes, Madam President. Uh, the pandemic travel restrictions are causing problems for military personnel answering the call up," she said carefully. "Different states and police forces are interpreting them differently, even though we have said military personnel are exempt. So we have tens of thousands of personnel—guards, reservists and regulars—being stopped from traveling across state borders. Civil protest movements are also gathering momentum. We're in negotiation with several state governors, and DoD is organizing dedicated transport for military personnel, but that will take time. I can't ..."

Before she could continue, Carliotti interrupted. "Madam Secretary, I toyed with the idea of creating a Department for Pandemic Security with HR Rosenstern as Secretary. I thought it might make sense to move certain Transport Security, FBI and Secret Service responsibilities to the new department." Everyone saw shock in Belkin's face. The idea would mean the emasculation of her Homeland Security Department, and the beginning of an unholy turf war. "In the circumstances I have decided against this. But it is your responsibility to ensure pandemic regulations are enforced, including exemptions for military personnel on active duty or being recalled to active duty. State versus federal politics *cannot* be allowed to interfere. I have put the National Guard on the streets of every city to enforce civil order and you will work with Army to see they support pandemic enforcement as needed, including at state borders. Is that clear?"

"I, uh ... yes, Madam President."

Carliotti also looked at the head of Army. "General?"

"Yes, Madam President."

"Now, Madam Secretary, you said protest movements are gathering momentum. What is the latest on this 'Defenders of Liberty' protest group?"

"Uh, there ..." Belkin looked at a sheet of paper by her elbow. "There are rallies planned in several major cities this weekend. We'll be able to judge the level of support for the group from the turnout. FBI is ..."

"No. There will be no rallies, Madam Secretary," Carliotti said. "Gatherings of over 100 people are banned under Pandemic Executive Orders. Anyone who joins these protests, or anything like them, will be arrested and quarantined for health reasons."

"Madam President, you could be talking thousands, even hundreds of thousands of people. We don't have the quarantine facilities for that number of ..."

"Then build them, pronto. That is a matter for the Pandemic Response Executive later. Please be ready for that meeting with a clear idea of what quarantine facilities we will build and where. Which leads me to a question of civil order closer to where we sit now, Admiral Connaught."

Connaught was caught reading messages on his tablet. "Ma'am?"

"Who the hell is Jonah Freeth, and what the hell is the Hawaiian Freedom Alliance?"

"I don't ..." Connaught looked across at Samuels, who was operationally responsible for the defense of Hawaii. He wasn't, however, responsible for internal affairs. "General Samuels?"

"Ma'am, I think it is a peaceful political movement that lobbies for Hawaiian independence, but with respect, I think that is a question for the governor, FBI or Hawaii PD," Samuels replied.

"It would be, except before I walked into this meeting I spoke with the governor. He said your 'peaceful political movement' has just burned down the Hawaii State Capitol building. He has asked me to direct the National Guard on Hawaii to support his officers in arresting the insurrectionists. Since you are Joint Commander Hawaii, I am passing the request to you."

"Madam President, those troops are needed for—" Connaught interrupted.

"The defense of Hawaii, I realize that, Admiral. General Samuels, have your people prepare a response for the governor ... There must be something you can do."

Samuels looked annoyed, and shot a glance at Connaught, but nodded. "Ma'am."

Carliotti looked around the table and at the faces assembled on the big screen on the wall. They showed a mixture of engagement, frustration and anger, which were emotions Carliotti could work with, but also disinterest and distraction, which she couldn't.

It was *come to Jesus* time.

"Ladies and gentlemen, China has been preparing for this war for decades. Our ally Taiwan's preemptive attack on their invasion force may have disrupted their timetable, but their preparations are now becoming more evident with every passing hour: the attack on me and the cabinet at Raven Rock; the slaughterbot and bioweapon attacks on Taiwan; the

352

coordinated attack on our Space and undersea communications links; the simultaneous land, sea and air attacks on our bases across the Pacific; and at home, inside our own borders, a constant stream of cyberattacks on infrastructure and economic targets plus, now, civil uprisings led by so-called 'civil rights' organizations that weren't regarded as a threat or didn't even *exist* just a few weeks ago." Carliotti let the steel in her heart flood into her voice. "This is what Total War looks like, people. And we, the people in this meeting, who are responsible for the defense of our nation, are ready for it *because we have been preparing too.* This moment, here on Hawaii, today, is where the excuses stop, and we start to bring the war to China."

REALITY RARELY accommodates the fine speeches of politicians.

Even as Carmen Carliotti delivered what was supposed to be a rallying cry to the Joint Chiefs, Captain Annunzio D'Angelli was outnumbered and engaged in a deadly knife fight with Lei Yu and the Gyrfalcons of PLAN *Fujian inside* the Hawaiian Air Defense Identification Zone.

Behind and below the swirling dogfight, the Chongming pilots of the *Fujian* Air Wing started their terminal attack run with Pearl Harbor air defenses a fraction of their usual strength.

On Hawaii itself, officer Tammy Ballard was down in the basement of 'Iolani Palace as, two floors up, Jonah Freeth prepared to broadcast his "Declaration of Independence," flanked by Sergeant Pan Tien and soldiers of the People's Liberation Army of China, in Honolulu PD uniforms. At different points across O'ahu, special operations troops from

353

Pan Tien's 1st Battalion, 5th Amphibious Combined Arms Recon Brigade, prepared to launch a campaign of sabotage and guerilla warfare as soon as the broadcast went out.

On Taiwan, two US Marines, a verbose Taiwanese sniper, a pilot without an airplane and a 15-year-old hacker were trying to prevent the capitulation of the Taiwanese government.

Less than 215 nautical miles off the coast of battered Kaua'i Island, from the decks of three PLAN *Yushen* class helicopter landing docks and four Russian *Ivan Gren* class ships, dozens of helicopters carrying special operations troops were lifting into the air for the one hour run into Kaua'i, under the cover of a heavy fighter escort from *Shandong*. Below deck on the *Yushen* and *Ivan Gren* class ships, 15,000 Chinese and Russian marines went about the business of preparing for an amphibious assault across the long sandy beaches fronting the still-burning PMRF base on the west coast of Kaua'i.

They were just hours from H-Hour for the landing, and not particularly worried, since they'd been assured that there would be few, if any, American combatants left alive on Kaua'i to oppose them.

But perhaps sometimes, just occasionally, a politician like Carmen Carliotti could bend reality to their will, if only through a bloody-minded belief in the righteousness of their cause. Of course, it also helped to have the firepower of the US Armed Forces backing that cause.

Even if that firepower, in terms of numbers, might look a little underwhelming.

Operation Midnight: Máo-niú / Yak

CAPTAIN ALLEN 'Tidewater' Courtenay didn't deserve the nickname his crew gave him. Not really.

Sure, he was prone to changing his mind, a little like a tide going in and out. Like he had about the Australian "observers" that had been put aboard his vessel against his wishes. He'd been fully expecting to have to assign an officer to babysit them and make sure they in no way or by any means interfered with the good operation of his vessel.

But he'd changed his mind on that. They presented their opinions freely, but with respect for the fact the ultimate decision was his. He'd still rather they were someone else's problem, but he had decided to tolerate them.

Courtenay didn't change his mind about the important things, in the important moments. You didn't give command of His Majesty's most potent attack submarine to someone fickle, someone lacking backbone and conviction.

No, you gave it to Allen Courtenay because he was ... what was the word his former CO had used?

Resolute.

In the moments that mattered. Like now.

"Your concerns are noted, Lieutenant Brunelli, Captain McDonald," he said. "Nonetheless, we shall proceed. We have one target and one only."

Brunelli and McDonald shared a glance that Courtenay interpreted to mean, *Are we going to push this?* and was happy to see they decided against doing so.

COURTENAY, McDonald and Brunelli had no idea what was happening above the surface of the Pacific 600 feet overhead.

All they knew was that were inside the Sino-Russian fleet submarine pickets, having passed through its outer screen of anti-air, anti-submarine ships. And still no *Taifun*.

But they were in an otherwise "target-rich environment."

They had one *Yushen* landing craft—in all likelihood, judging by the acoustic signature, the 40,000-ton PLAN *Anhui*—about 6 miles off their starboard bow. But pinging its sonar like it wanted to be heard, just 3 miles away, was a *Type 093* hunter-killer submarine.

Courtenay had just decided *Agincourt* was going to try to evade the *Type 093*, as it had done the *Type 095* earlier. McDonald had pointed out that the last position they had for *Taifun* showed it headed directly underneath the Sino-Russian fleet. On the other side of the *Type 093* submarine. If they turned away, they not only risked losing it; they risked being detected by any one of dozens of ships sailing directly above them.

"The Lieutenant is not saying you should attack that troopship, Captain," McDonald continued. "As much as I dearly wish we could. But I agree you should take the shot at that *Type 093*. There is so much noise in the water here, we can make the kill and push further in after *Taifun*. We don't, and we might as well give up the chase."

An awkward silence followed, into which the XO, Singh, stepped. "Captain," he said softly. "For what it's worth, I'd take the shot and trust our ability to escape too."

To his credit, Courtenay paused. He bit his lip. "Sonar, threat environment?"

"*Nanyang* corvette at 2,800 yards, moving away. The *Anhui* has slowed to 10 knots but has not changed its heading. No other threats on the board, Captain, apart from that *Type 093* at 2 miles, and it's ringing like a damn bell. It will get a return off us any minute unless we change course and depth, sir."

Singh spoke again. "The American *Virginia* class boats would have engaged by now. It could explain why the troopship is slowing and that *Type 093* is shouting into the water. They're spooked and they're looking for submarines, Captain ..."

Courtenay slapped the back of the chair he was standing behind, causing several personnel to flinch. "Very well. Weapons, load Spearfish, tubes one to four. The target is the *Type 093*. Prepare for stealth launch. You know the drill, people. Show our guests how it's done."

McDonald watched intently. Before taking command of *AE1*, he'd been at the receiving end of a simulated attack by *Astute* submarines more than once, and one of those had completely blindsided him. He was about to see how that had been possible.

Once again, the *Agincourt*'s crew flooded the torpedo tubes and opened the outer doors as they brought its bow to bear on the target.

"Target bearing zero zero four, range 2 miles and steady, speed 15 knots, depth 200," the sonarman said.

"Confirm your shot, Mr. Singh."

"Weapons report ready. Target data uploaded. I have a solution," the XO said.

"Tubes one and two, shoot," Courtenay ordered. "Helm, begin your turn."

As his order was relayed through the boat by Singh, a small, almost silent pump jet in the rear of each torpedo kicked it out of its torpedo tube and then cut out. With neutral buoyancy, the two torpedoes slid slowly through the water on momentum alone, away from *Agincourt* as it started a gentle diving turn. Gossamer-thin cables connected the torpedoes to the submarine.

"Weapons, separation to torpedoes?" Courtenay asked after a couple of minutes.

"One sixty yards," his weapons officer replied.

"Sonar, target update."

"Target now bearing zero zero niner, speed and heading constant, range estimated 7 miles. Still pinging."

No change, Brunelli thought, then realized she'd been holding a breath. She let it out. *It hasn't heard us.*

"Separation to torpedoes?" Courtenay asked again.

"Torpedoes one eight nine yards."

"Low pulse at 200."

"Low pulse at 200, aye."

The stealth torpedo launch was not one Brunelli had seen done before. But she and McDonald had speculated about it, having been at the receiving end of something like it in exercises against the British boats. She found it more than a little disconcerting that despite all the hours she and McDonald had spent in *Astute* class submarines, they'd never been allowed to see this particular tactic until today.

It seemed once again the Royal Navy liked to play its best cards close to its chest.

"Torpedoes 200."

"Low pulse initiated," the weapons officer announced.

Brunelli turned her attention to a flat screen in front of *Agincourt*'s XO, Singh. It showed their boat, and the target, trailing a line that showed both where it had been and where the AI predicted it was headed. It also showed the two torpedoes, now falling behind the *Agincourt* as it glided away from the scene of the launch. The torpedoes were gently accelerating now, putting more distance between themselves and the British submarine, though they were still tethered to it. They were following what looked to her eyeball judgement like an intercept course, but at the speed they were traveling, they had no chance of catching the Chinese submarine.

"Losing contact," the sonar officer said.

"Range to torpedoes?" Courtenay asked.

"Torpedoes four ninety yards."

"Full pulse at separation 500," Courtenay said. "Helm, hold your turn; planes 45 degrees down, engines full stop."

The orders were repeated in loud whispers. It was as though the whole boat was holding its breath now.

"Torpedoes 500."

"*Full pulse, terminal sonar homing, cut the cable!*"

"Torpedoes full pulse, sensors terminal sonar homing, cutting cable."

And with that, the two torpedoes on the screen in front of *Agincourt*'s XO began speeding toward their target. In the space of seconds, they went from 10 knots to 80 and began overhauling the Chinese submarine.

But Brunelli wasn't watching the torpedoes track—they would still have several minutes to run—she was watching to see if any other Chinese submarines, or worse, incoming torpedoes, appeared on the screen.

It stayed clear.

"Torpedoes running; no reaction from target," the sonar officer said. "Impact in four minutes."

"They have to hear them soon," Singh said.

"They're coming from astern," Courtenay pointed out. "In her baffles."

"Cavitation!" the sonar officer said, voice jumping to near normal, loud in the unnaturally quiet space. "Target is accelerating. Decoys in the water; she's running and turning." He looked up. "Torpedoes fired!"

"Toward or away?" Courtenay asked. Without sonar, only the strength and pattern of the sound coming through the water to their passive sensors could tell them if the Chinese torpedoes were coming toward them or going wide.

"*Away*," the man said. "They're pinging, but it's fading."

Brunelli and McDonald shared a glance. The British stealth launch had suckered the Chinese into counterpunching down the bearing of its attack, where the *Agincourt* had been when it launched its torpedoes, not where it was now.

"Come on, boys," Courtenay said, urging his torpedoes on. "No point staying quiet now."

As though they heard him, the sonar officer spoke again. "Torpedoes are pinging, active homing."

The Spearfish used a combination of sonar and acoustic processors to track its target and sort decoy noise from the noise made by a submarine maneuvering. But the UK Spearfish had one more trick up its sleeve. Ahead of its 300-kilogram PBX explosive warhead was a magnetic anomaly detection sensor or MAD. One of the last bits of data uploaded to the torpedo before its guidance wire was cut was the MAD profiles of the Chinese *Type 093* and *Type 095* submarines.

The acoustic sensors in the two Spearfish torpedoes considered steering toward the noisemaking decoys the Chinese boat had launched into its wake as it crash-dived, but their MAD sensors overrode them and kept them on an intercept course, turning tightly to stay with their target as their sonar fine-tuned their trajectories to aim them at the submarine's midsection.

"IMPACT!" the sonar officer said. Seconds passed slowly. "Uh, cavitation stopped. I'd say she's either dead in the water or … ballast blowing! She's trying to get to the surface." There followed a terrible minute of silence in the command center. "No. I'm hearing mechanicals. Hull collapse. She's going down."

For the next few minutes, the control room was quiet, each officer left alone with their thoughts, but it was a pretty safe bet a lot of them shared the same thought.

There but for the grace of God go I.

They got no further time for reflection.

"New contacts! I …" Courtenay's sonarman frowned. "Surface. Multiple. *Dozens*. Bearing due west, range … estimate 4 miles … closure rate high … type …"

"Come on, man," Courtenay said.

"Running signature analysis again," he said. The tightly packed control room was suddenly stuffy. Courtenay felt sweat rolling down his temple.

"Can't say, sir," the sonarman admitted. "No database match. Sounds to me like patrol boat size and speed, maybe pump-jet propulsion …"

"Helm ahead slow. Take us down to 700 feet," Courtenay snapped.

His orders rang through the boat and *Agincourt* began nosing down, seeking the safety of the deep.

"You're thinking swarming surface drones?" McDonald asked him. "Anti-submarine?"

Courtenay nodded. "We just accounted for one of their sub pickets. It might have been in the act of reporting in or another vessel could have heard our torpedoes. I'd be looking for us if I was their commander ..."

The sonar officer shook his head, holding his earphones tight against his ears. "Doesn't sound like small drones," he said. He looked up from his screen. "Hovercraft!"

"Hovercraft?" Courtenay asked. "We're 110 nautical miles from the Hawaiian Islands. Did US Space Force report hovercraft in the enemy fleet?"

His XO replied. "No sir."

"I was looking for a ship signature," the sonar officer said, rapidly tapping keys on his console. "Chinese or Russian. I didn't ... here! I have a match. *Yak* class hovercraft! But China only has a few of those, and Russia retired all theirs. I've got at least 20 discrete signatures, maybe more. There's a *lot* of noise ..."

Courtenay turned to his comms officer. "Code a message to Pearl and fire a comms buoy. Message reads: *Agincourt* at position ..." He read off their coordinates. "Multiple small unidentified enemy surface craft detected on heading for ..." He clicked his fingers. "Projected heading?"

The sonar officer leaned over to another screen. "Uh, coming ... That's ... Kaua'i Island."

"Heading for Kaua'i Island," Courtenay said. "*Agincourt* attack aborted, will seek targets of opportunity when able."

"They're overhead," the sonar officer said, pointed upward, though only he could hear them.

"Already?" Brunelli asked. All eyes reflexively looked upward. "What the hell are they?"

362

"Captain, I've just picked up a *Renhai* cruiser to starboard, moving away from us. It's turning, moving through zero two zero degrees. Looks like it is reversing course."

"Log it and include it in the burst transmission," Courtenay ordered, then slapped the sonarman's back. "Good work. Now find me the bloody *Taifun*."

The Battle of Hawaii: Northwest Kaua'i

HALF AN OCEAN away from Taipei, the pilots of 68th Aggressor were 120 miles south of the enemy fleet, sliding around its flanks and also reporting back what they could see and hear.

The pilots of the P-99 Widows, with their particularly sensitive electronic warfare suites, were busiest. As Space Force had promised, after they got about 120 miles out of O'ahu, the Aggressor aircraft were able to lock onto an overhead US military satellite.

"Thank you, Space Force," Meany said to himself as he dictated and then cued up a quick text burst transmission, marking the time, their position and most importantly their observations. Bunny was flying off his wingtip, and they'd been communicating target observations to each other via their laser optical comms link. They were flying at wavetop height and in "ninja mode," emissions dark, but Meany's text report required just a few watts of energy and a millisecond of time to squirt up to the orbiting satellite and down to USS *Lafayette*.

- 68 Aggressor Wolverine flight approaching waypoint three. Signal analysis follows:
- Heavy aircraft radio traffic bearing zero eight four degrees from waypoint, consistent with multiple aircraft moving at 400 knots toward Kaua'i. Speed and flight profile indicate possibly helos inbound Kaua'i.
- Further signals, bearing zero nine five degrees from waypoint, speed 600 knots, also toward Kaua'i. Speed consistent with fighter escort of helos.
- Heavy naval radio and radar emissions north of waypoint. Radio and radar types identified so far by

class: *Renhai, Luyang, Gorshkov, Yushen, Ivan Gren* and *Shang.*

After the text message, they sent an estimate their decision support systems had made for the bearing and range, based on signal strength, for each of the ships discretely identified. But both officers knew that data was so imprecise it wasn't worth a damn, beyond confirming the enemy ships were still headed for Hawaii.

That last had been a surprise. The *Shang* class submarine would likely have been on the surface and broadcasting for Meany and Bunny to have picked up its transmission.

"If they are running subs on the surface, they are too bloody confident," Bunny had remarked.

"I look forward to us denting that confidence, Lieutenant," Meany replied.

The next part of their long flight around the southern flank of the enemy fleet was uneventful, allowing them to make two more signals interception reports before they reached their "ingress" waypoint. Worryingly, despite the heavy concentration of Chinese aircraft they'd picked up headed for Kaua'i, there was still a pattern of signals around the fleet indicating a heavy fighter screen around the Chinese carriers. Touchdown and her three wingmen had been busy mapping every contact they picked up on their passive sensors.

Touchdown, Flatline, Flowmax and Agony in their Raptors were 12 miles ahead of Meany and Bunny, circling the ingress waypoint, waiting for the order to begin creating mayhem at the rear of the Chinese fleet.

Bunny's plane was locked onto Meany's wing with laser formation keeping and communication active.

"Space Force got a satellite overhead, but they couldn't launch one with a bloody camera on it?" Bunny complained.

Meany smiled as her voice broke into the silence. He could hear her chewing on something. "Be grateful we even have satcoms at all. What are you *eating*, O'Hare?"

"What? Oh, 'Ling Mooey' something. Plum candy, I think. A Marine at Bellows gave it to me."

A chime sounded in Meany's helmet, and text started flashing across his comms screen.

Go time.

He flipped his comms system from laser to burst encrypted VHF. "Wolverine pilots, we have the carrier's position. It is further west than we expected. Pushing position to you. Wolverine One and Two changing course and beginning attack run. Touchdown, bring the chaos."

"Wolverine Three, bringing it, boss."

"Four copies, turning in hot."

"Five copies."

"Six turning in hot."

"Good luck and Godspeed, Bunny," Meany said, lighting the tail on his Widow and pointing it straight at the Chinese carrier's position.

"You too, boss. Going ninja," Bunny replied, killing her comms.

PLAN LIAONING was China's first, and so oldest, aircraft carrier.

It had started life as the Soviet carrier *Varyag*, and was abandoned in a Ukrainian shipping yard after the collapse of the Soviet Union before being sold to a Chinese shell company on Macau. It surprised no one when the People's

Liberation Army Navy was revealed as the real buyer in 1998, but it was 2008 before work began restoring what was essentially a rusting hulk. The herculean task of turning *Varyag* into *Liaoning* took four more years and cost the equivalent in workforce and resources of 10 *Luyang* class destroyers.

Liaoning was commissioned in 2012, but by then China was already planning its sister ship, *Shandong*, based on the same design. The *Shandong* launched in 2017, and *Liaoning* transitioned from carrier operations to a testbed for new aircraft and naval technologies.

That change in status meant that far from becoming rapidly obsolete, *Liaoning* remained a potent power platform, a testing ground for the latest in Chinese air and naval weapons systems.

PLA Navy Northern Fleet Commander Admiral Li Bing had taken a personal interest in the fate of *Liaoning*, since he had been its CO when *Liaoning* was sent to confront the Philippines and USA off <u>Pagasa Island</u> in the Philippine Sea in 2035. That had been Li's first armed encounter with US forces, and it had not ended in China's favor. His pilots showed their inexperience, throwing their lives away with zealous stupidity. China's J-16 carrier aircraft, still China's dominant naval air platform at the time, had proven wholly inadequate against America's fifth-generation stealth fighters while its navy proved vulnerable to its missile-carrying bombers.

So many pilots were lost in that brief conflict, it set back plans to build up China's air force by several years.

At 68, Li might have been older, but he was also wiser now than he had been in 2035. He had accelerated the replacement of the J-16 with the Gyrfalcon on *Liaoning* and

Shandong. After testing the Chongming drone on *Liaoning,* he approved the decision to deploy their newest carrier, *Fujian,* as a "drone carrier," able to project power across the oceans without risking the lives of pilots, China's most precious resource.

Li Bing didn't have his flag on *Fujian.* He had it on the venerable *Liaoning.* Perhaps he was sentimental. Certainly some of his officers thought so. He had moved into his old captain's quarters aboard the carrier, allowing only modest modifications to turn it into an admiral's stateroom. What was that if not sentiment?

A signal, he hoped. A signal of both frugality and confidence. He could have stayed in China for the start of the Pacific campaign, shuttling between Northern Fleet Headquarters at Qingdao and Beijing. Instead, he had moved his flag to a frontline carrier, at a time when some were beginning to question whether China's aircraft carriers even had a place in a modern navy against a foe armed with hypersonic missiles: fine for flying the Chinese flag and showing its growing power in African and Middle Eastern ports but not so useful for waging war.

Li might be sentimental, but he wasn't a romantic. Deep down, he agreed with the critics. The lessons of the first weeks of this war couldn't be ignored. The aircraft carriers of both sides had proven so vulnerable they were pulled back to safe harbors under the cover of shore-based missile batteries.

But for the heroic efforts of its air wing commander and crew, their former fleet flagship *Fujian* should already be lying at the bottom of the Pacific.

But under the right conditions, under conditions in which the enemy was blind and deaf, in an environment in which it could not spy with satellites, aim missiles with GPS, communicate with its drones and aircraft across the huge distances of the Pacific … under these conditions, the value of the aircraft carrier was still *indisputable*.

And Li had managed to get his fleet so close to the American bastion of Hawaii that his troops were, literally, able to reach out and touch it. Just hours ago, he had given the fleet the equivalent of the Japanese naval order to strike Pearl Harbor. The Japanese code phrase had been "Climb Mount Niitaka." Li Bing's code phrase had been rather more colorful: "*Tiger Roar.*"

A knock on his stateroom door disturbed his small, uncharacteristic moment of hubris. He'd retired to take a small rest before the next phase in the operation.

His aide stepped into the room and bowed. "Admiral, you asked to be interrupted if there were any unanticipated developments."

Li raised himself to his feet. "Yes, Captain?"

"Sir, American aircraft have just engaged our fighter screen from a position 120 miles west of *Liaoning*."

Li nodded, not alarmed. The attack had to come; it was a credit to China's strategy it had not come sooner. "Strength?"

"As yet unknown," the man admitted. "And …"

"Go on, man."

"Submarine *Type 095-33*, just missed its last radio check-in."

It has begun, as we knew it would. "Convey the order to all vessels: Dragon Chant."

"Dragon Chant, yes, Admiral."

Tiger Roar, Dragon Chant—two sides of the same coin. The attack on Hawaii—*Tiger Roar*—would inevitably provoke a violent response from the Americans. *Dragon Chant*—enemy engaged. "All vessels to move to heightened alert and be prepared for enemy action." His officers, and the men and women of the PLA Navy Northern Fleet, had trained for this, for *every* eventuality, from a conventional counterattack to chemical or even nuclear.

But to train was one thing.

As he had learned in the Philippine Sea, to execute under fire was another.

OFFICER TAMMY BALLARD had been under fire before. Northern Syria—that had been the first time. Fire base called COP Meyer outside the Kurdish-held town of Kobani. Deployed with Hawaii National Guard 29th Infantry Brigade Combat Team on her only combat tour. Hunkered down inside the COP under daily mortar fire, patrolling the streets of Kobani with their Kurdish PKK allies, under fire from Russian-trained Syrian snipers. Happy to see the back of the place the day they flew out.

Then FoodLife Ala Moana—two ice addicts with AR-15s, pissed there was no cash on the premises, started shooting the place up for the giggles. First officers on the scene, she and Tony didn't even make it out of their patrol car before it took about a hundred bullets. It turned into a siege and negotiators talked the guys down. Guys? Kids. One of them was 15.

And, of course, today. But both the other situations, she had context. On patrol in Kobani, you were in the middle of a war; you knew who the good and bad guys were. FoodLife siege, same—bad guys shooting out, good guys shooting in. Not complicated.

This cluster? There were people in black Hawaiian Freedom Alliance T-shirts, most of them Kanaka, Indigenous

Hawaiian. Call it, like, 200 or so. 'Iolani Palace employees, or management, fussing around trying to make sure no one stole or broke anything. A tourist guide, just standing by the big front doors, looking stressed. And people off the street who ran into the palace when the sirens started screaming, looking for shelter.

Like her.

They were all corralled into the small coat hall and kitchen area at the entrance to the basement. Freedom Alliance members blocked the doors leading into the rooms that held the more precious antiques and the royal jewels, taking their duties as guardians of history seriously. Down in the basement, she ended up next to one of the black shirts, a Kanaka woman in her 40s. "Hey, can I ask you a question? What is with the shirts?" she asked innocently. "You guys on a tour or something?"

The woman laughed. "On a mission, not a tour. Taking Hawaii back for Hawaiians, sister." She was about to give Ballard a flyer, but everybody ducked when something big, like a missile or a bomb, landed not far away.

"Hell of a day to start a revolution," Ballard said as they stood up again.

"Or maybe the best day," the woman said with a smile.

Ballard took the flyer. Unlike most protest flyers, it didn't have a ton of text written on it. Just a couple paragraphs:

In 1993, the US Congress passed a resolution stating that it: "acknowledges that the overthrow of the Kingdom of Hawaii occurred with the active participation of agents and citizens of the United States and further acknowledges that the 'Native Hawaiian people' never directly relinquished to the United States their claims to their inherent sovereignty as a people over their national lands, either through the Kingdom of Hawaii or through a plebiscite or referendum."

The Hawaii Freedom Alliance is a coalition of organizations dedicated to restoring the independence of the Kingdom of Hawaii through a national referendum.

It all sounded very reasonable. Except the same people had apparently torched the Capitol building and taken over the 'Iolani Palace. And …

"So what is their deal?" Ballard asked about the Honolulu PD uniforms standing at the entrance to the basement, talking with an organizer. The cops had come down last, and some left immediately, heading upstairs again, even though the emergency sirens were still wailing.

"I guess they support the cause," the woman said. "You're welcome to as well."

"Do I get a T-shirt?" Ballard quipped, only joking.

"Sure. You a medium?" the woman asked.

The question took Ballard by surprise, but she thought quickly. "Uh, give me a large."

The woman turned behind her to another woman in a black shirt, holding a box.

"Hey, Malia, give me a large T-shirt?" She turned back and held it out to Ballard. "Twenty bucks."

Ballard fished in her pocket for her money clip. Like everyone else, she never used cash anymore except if she ran across someone sleeping rough, doing it tough. She would sometimes slip them a few bucks while Tony wasn't looking. Way she was brought up.

She handed over a double sawbuck and took the T-shirt. Looking around the basement she spotted a ladies' bathroom and squeezed through the crowd, stood in line a while, then went into a cubicle. Swapped her football shirt for the

Freedom Alliance shirt. It came halfway down her butt, covering her pistol and belt.

She came out of the bathroom right behind one of the "cops." He was talking to another cop in a low voice. Chinese or Korean? Ballard was no language expert. That wasn't unusual; plenty of ethnic Chinese guys in the Honolulu PD, born and raised in Hawaii.

What *was* unusual: they both had non-standard-issue pistols on their hips. She didn't recognize the make. OK, not totally unusual either; plenty of cops had personalized weapons they preferred. But both with the same identical make?

That made her look closer. Their badges were wrong. Honolulu PD badges had been changed about a year earlier. Every badge now had your station number on it. Just a simple numeral, under "POLICE," at the bottom. Also, they didn't have standard issue Honolulu PD radios; they had earpieces with wires leading down into their shirts. Tactical radios.

These guys didn't have a station ID on their badges. Well, sure, sometimes she didn't have a clean shirt with the new badge, and she took one of her old ones, but two guys, both having a bad laundry day? Traveling in convoy that just shot up her roadblock? Talking Chinese during a Chinese attack on Pearl Harbor?

Ballard's internal alarm was ringing louder than the sirens outside.

Which suddenly went quiet. Or not quiet, just back to the voice announcement: *This is a civil emergency announcement. All citizens are asked to return to their homes …*

People began pushing out of the basement again. Ballard followed the flow, upstairs to the ground floor of the palace, past a camera crew organizing their gear. More particularly, she followed the two cops. They were headed upstairs. A couple of Freedom Alliance people on the stairs were stopping civilians going up to the second floor—mostly palace staff who wanted to get their stuff and bug out—but they were letting Alliance members past. They let the "police" go past too.

Ballard trusted her T-shirt to get her past the gatekeepers, just gave them a nod and followed the two cops up.

They went up, looked around, then went right. Ballard saw why. Room second on the right, museum sign on the door said "Governor's Office." Inside were about six more Alliance members, and two more "police," talking with a man in a traditional feathered cape and pareo.

She recognized the face. Where from? Then she remembered. A protest a few weeks ago she was assigned to for traffic management.

Jonah Freeth.

"Help you, ma'am?" A big Kanaka dude was suddenly standing in front of her.

"Oh, uh …" Ballard looked around. "The camera guys downstairs sent me up here to check for power outlets?"

Weak, Tammy. Weak.

"Power outlets."

"Yeah, some sound guy, I think. Power for his sound gear? I'm just supposed to see how many, or does he need to bring, like, a power board."

The guy nodded, slowly, like he wasn't sure. "Duke, over here," Freeth said, motioning him over.

"Be quick," he said, and left her.

Oh, yeah, I'll be quick.

She went to a desk in the middle of the room, found a pad of paper and a ceremonial pen, which probably wouldn't write, but she didn't really need it to.

"Leave that," an Alliance organizer with a clipboard said. "No souveniring."

"No, I just … I need a pen," Tammy said, holding up the paper.

The woman sighed, and handed her one from her pocket.

OK, looking for power outlets, she reminded herself. She turned to the wall nearest her, squatting down. Drew a map of the room, marked the windows and doors with crosses. She worked her way around, behind Freeth. No one was paying any attention to her anymore.

The cops were all Chinese. Talking English now though.

"… downstairs at both doors," one cop was saying. "So 10 downstairs, dressed as construction workers. And we will have six up here. Police, like us." Both Freeth and the Chinese cops looked at the door, and Ballard followed their eyes. Two more cops walking in, each carrying two assault rifles, one in each fist. They leaned them against a wall and went out again.

"We don't want anyone getting hurt," Freeth said, eyeing the rifles. "Threats are one thing, but …"

"How do you say, 'Better safe than sorry'?" the Chinese officer said amicably. "Our job here is to keep you safe."

Safe? From who? Ballard realized they were talking about her. Or officers like her.

Then one of the Chinese cops ran in, blurted something in Chinese to the man talking with Freeth and ran out again.

"The police are here," the man told Freeth, and walked into the next room, to the windows facing the front of the palace.

Damn right, they are, Ballard thought. *Closer than you think, buddy.* But at least someone at dispatch had taken her call seriously. She felt her hopes rising a little, but her tension too. If that was possible.

The guy called Duke raised two hands in the air. "Alright, everyone, clear the room." He turned to the clipboard lady. "You too, please." She started debating with him.

While his back was turned, Ballard looked around for somewhere to hide. A screen she could get behind. Desk or bureau. Wall column. Nothing. Big plush red curtains—could she hide behind those?

Don't be stupid.

The clipboard lady lost her argument, and Tammy followed her out. There was tiny corridor she hadn't noticed, like a walk-in closet that let out to the grand stairway lobby. Small door on her right, unlocked. She stepped inside, expecting a bathroom.

From the light of the doorway, she saw a small windowless room. Tiny desk with just enough space for an antique typewriter and telephone. *Secretary's room*, she guessed. Voices outside. She ran around behind the desk, got out of sight. Held her breath.

The door opened, the light came on, then went off again. The door closed.

Chinese voice shouting something as it moved off.

OK, Ballard, now what?

SERGEANT PAN TIEN closed the door to the small room he'd just checked, shouted "clear!" and looked for a lock on the door. It didn't have one. No matter. He checked the next room, a bathroom, lockable from the inside, not the outside.

A urinal, a marble bidet and a toilet cubicle. He looked inside the cubicle.

Empty.

Leaving the now empty office, he walked back into the front sitting room as Pi ran in. "Top floor is clear except for these two," he gestured at Freeth and Duke. "You want us to clear out the bottom floor too?" he said in Chinese.

Pan thought about it. They'd agreed to leave some details to be decided depending on the tactical environment. You couldn't plan everything based on 3D models.

"No, let people stay inside. We might need hostages," Pan said.

Freeth was standing at the window. "There are four police cars. They're talking with each other, deciding what to do, I think. One guy is on a radio."

Pan checked the scene outside the window. People milling around—some Alliance people, some just civilians or maybe palace staff still hanging around, or passersby left over from the raid alert or just come to see what was happening. The police didn't seem in a rush to do anything; they were probably waiting for orders about what to do.

"Alright." Pan nodded. He turned to Duke. "You, go downstairs and go out to the police. Ask them to send an officer up here to talk."

"They'll probably send more than one," Duke warned. "They won't like sending in a man alone."

"Tell them only one, just to talk. You don't want them to inflame the situation."

He shrugged. "Alright. I'll try. And if they say no, they want to talk outside?"

377

"Then you tell them that is not happening and you come back here," Pan told him. "Tell them we don't want any trouble."

"What is the plan?" Freeth asked, looking worried. "I don't want any of my people getting hurt."

"We're here to make sure that doesn't happen," Pan assured him. "We will talk to the police. Tell them we support your cause, and are here to defend you. We will tell them to stay outside. When they see police officers here with you, they will have to reevaluate; that will take time. You make your broadcast, appeal for the public to come to the palace to defend you and defend their nation."

"Yes, yes, alright." Freeth nodded, biting his lip, then getting a little fire in his belly. "They'll come. The police are already outnumbered. Soon we will be thousands, tens of thousands."

Pan clapped him on the shoulder. "Good. And when you are King again, you will remember who stood with you."

"Of course, of course," Freeth said, looking out the window again.

FIVE MINUTES later, a little to Pan's surprise, Duke reappeared, a sweaty police sergeant in tow. He had the roly-poly, friendly face of exactly the kind of person you'd send in to defuse a situation. And he came in smiling, getting ready to hold out a hand and start greeting people.

Until he saw Pan and Pi, standing beside Freeth.

"What the hell is going on here?" the sergeant said.

Pan pulled his pistol in a smooth movement and pointed it at the sergeant's face. "Get his gun," he said to Pi. "Bind him."

378

"What are you doing?!" Freeth asked. "I thought you were going to negotiate, buy us time."

Pi had his own pistol out and carefully disarmed the police sergeant, then plasticuffed him with his hands behind his back as his face reddened in anger.

"This is a very bad idea," the sergeant warned.

Pan motioned with his pistol. "Sit." In the center of the room was a curious sofa, designed so that four people could sit on it, but with their backs to each other, facing out.

"Your name?" Pan asked him.

"Screw you."

Pan smiled, nodding at Pi. Pi clubbed the man across the temple with his pistol.

Pan leaned forward. "Your name is on your chest, Sergeant Cuccino. C. Cuccino." He stood. "You just got hit for no reason. So let us try that again. Your first name?"

"*Sergeant.*" The man spat blood at the ground.

Pan liked that. He looked soft, but he talked hard.

The man called Duke took a step between Pan and Freeth. "What exactly are we doing here?" he asked in a cold, level voice. "You heard Mr. Freeth. No one gets hurt unless *necessary.*"

Pan looked at him properly for the first time. He was clearly Freeth's "master at arms." Pan had seen him delegating jobs to the crowd of black-shirted Alliance members. Everyone he talked to deferred to him.

And he wasn't panicking at the sight of the bound police officer and the pistols in Pan and Pi's hands. His face gave nothing away. He looked more like some kind of street gang leader than a lieutenant in a peaceful protest movement.

Pan sighed. The time for play-acting was over. *Speed and violence.* He raised his pistol and shot the man in the forehead.

379

IN THE SECRETARY'S cubicle, Ballard heard the shot just a few yards away and rolled to her knees, pistol out. She'd heard voices talking, then the shot.

Now, nothing.

Slowly, carefully, she tipped the desk over so it faced the door, and got behind it on her knees. It was made of heavy varnished teak at least, not painted plywood. Might stop a shotgun round. Probably wouldn't stop a 9 mm pistol round. *Definitely* wouldn't stop a round from the assault rifles she'd seen the Chinese cops carrying.

No, don't stay here. They're in the other room. Move!

She wasn't sure where that voice came from, but it made sense. Jumping up, she went to the small door, listened, and heard a voice in the other room. Freeth, angry.

She opened the narrow wooden door and looked out into the grand staircase foyer. Noise from downstairs—they probably didn't even hear the shot. No one running up. Should she go down?

No, room across the hall. She ran on the balls of her feet, pistol extended, into the room opposite. Big, empty. In the center in a glass case, a vast quilt. She knew the story. Queen Lili'uokalani, the quilt she made while she was a prisoner in the palace. The display case not high enough to use for cover.

Next room, completely empty, bare floors. *Damn!*

Toward the back of the palace now, through the next doors. Bedroom, four-poster on the left, big head-high teak bureau on the right in the corner.

Perfect.

She got behind the bureau, flattened herself against the wall.

She couldn't see shit.

Not good enough. Mirror on a floor stand, up against one wall. She ran over to it, angled it so she could use it to see out the door she had just come in but stay out of the reflection until she needed to.

Better.

She tried to remember what the Chinese cop had said. Ten men downstairs, four upstairs? No, six upstairs. They must all be in that front room.

Well, maybe five, Ballard, if someone has just been shot. Maybe if you wait long enough, they'll all shoot each other.

Yeah, right.

"CONTROL YOURSELF," Pan said to Freeth. He put a finger to the tactical radio in his ear. "Liberator One to Team A. Three and Four, join us upstairs; bring the cases. Five and Six, take the stairs. No one comes up. Minimum necessary violence if they insist. Liberator Team B, set incendiaries."

"B Leader, affirmative. What about all the people here?"

"Tell them to leave. If any of them give you trouble, lock them in the basement."

"Understood. We have police outside, looking impatient. Your orders if they approach?"

"If they come at you hot, you are free to engage," Pan said. "If they come at you cold, let them come in, disarm them and lock them in the basement with any others."

"Yes, Sergeant."

Pan turned back to Freeth. He was staring with dread horror at the pool of blood spreading across the dark wood floor under Duke's head.

"Mr. Freeth," Pan said. "You have a broadcast to make."

381

Freeth looked up blankly. "We can't ... The equipment ..." Pan could see shock setting in. "You ..."

Pan's men came into the room carrying two large metal cases and dropped them on the desk. Freeth jumped at the noise. They opened the first, taking out a PC, a small camera on a stand and a satellite telephone. "We have the equipment you need to make your broadcast to the world, not just to your website, Mr. Freeth." He pointed at the chair behind the large desk. "Please, sit." From his shirt pocket he pulled a piece of paper, large words printed on it. "And your script. Please get ready."

The police sergeant had been silent through the shooting. He was still silent now, just watching carefully. Not just a defiant man, also a smart one, Pan decided.

"Now, Sergeant Cuccino," Pan said. He walked over and lifted the radio handset from the man's left shoulder. "You will tell your colleagues downstairs that everything here is under control, but they should remain outside. Say whatever you need to convince them that trying to come inside will just make the situation worse." In case he needed persuading, Pan waved his pistol in front of the man's face.

The sergeant looked like he wanted to spit in Pan's face, but he just nodded. Sweat was running down his brow, and Pan took a kerchief from his pocket and wiped it gently. "Under control, stay outside, yes?"

"I got it," Cuccino said.

Pan put the pistol against his temple. "Alright, go." He pushed the "talk" button on the radio.

Cuccino leaned his head left, putting his mouth near the radio. "This is Cuccino. Code Blue! Officer down!" he said loudly.

Pan's finger jerked on the trigger, the report muffled by how close the muzzle was to the man's head. He slumped forward, onto his knees, then onto the floor.

Pan checked his uniform for blood, stepping away from the body. Funny, he almost felt like saluting him. A dead man, but a brave one.

"This is … You are *insane*," Freeth said in a choking voice. "For God's sake …"

"No, not for God's sake," Pan told him. "For liberty, Mr. Freeth."

BALLARD HEARD the second shot. Muffled, but definitely another shot.

People are being killed, Tammy! Move!

She checked her weapon, then edged to a place where she could use the mirror to see out the doors. Door leading to the front of the palace, through the big empty room … Still empty. Door out to the grand stairway lobby. Someone going down the stairs. She pulled back, panting.

Six shooters upstairs, maybe five now, 10 down.

This was only going to end one way: Ballard dead and her kids motherless.

That thought nearly broke her.

Just stay here, a new voice said. *They might not search here. You want to see your kids again, right?*

Then she heard more gunfire, downstairs this time. Glass shattering. People screaming.

Shit shit shit.

She stepped out from behind the bureau and padded over to the door, out to the grand stairway.

The Rearguard: Overwatch

MASON JACKSON had his binos trained on the alleyway, watching Jensen and his dog pull back to the rear door of the shop. They weren't moving quickly because of the heavy load the LS3 was carrying.

Jackson flinched as Xu fired again from right beside him. "Movement at the gate again," he said.

Come on, move move move, Jackson urged Jensen.

A shadow in the corner of the binos' field of vision caught his eye. He lifted the lenses away from his face, looking at the compound roof. A blur. White smoke. *Coming right at them.*

"RPG!" he yelled.

But that was all there was time for. The missile flew through the empty frame of the window through which they'd been shooting, and struck the desk on which Corporal Xu rested his rifle bipod.

JENSEN REACHED the doorway to the shop, heard the unmistakable *whoosh* of a shoulder-fired missile being launched and looked over his shoulder in time to see the missile streak toward Jackson and Xu's overwatch position.

Hit low, Jensen urged the missile.

It didn't. The front of the building blew out in a shower of glass and masonry, fire and smoke following behind it.

Jensen didn't need to see more. He moved into the shop, Squirt and his cargo following. When he reached the front, he checked the street outside. An old lady scurrying for cover into a doorway; no one else. The shooting from around the premier's compound had cleared the street. From the shop, he headed for a small lane opposite.

"Jackson, Xu, report," Jensen said over the radio. He didn't expect a reply, and he didn't get one. "Lieutenant Chang, our sniper position was hit."

"I saw," the Taiwanese officer replied. "Are you clear?"

"Pulling back now. I'll meet you at the staging point. Stay off the radio. That was more than a lucky shot; I think they're tracking our signals."

"Understood. Chang out."

A left, then right into another lane. A group of youths ransacking a dumpster, stepping back to let him and his strange companion pass. Right, into a shattered building.

Stand, he ordered the LS3.

He waited. Listened. No pursuit.

He checked the case was still held securely on the LS3's back. *Follow*, he told Squirt, heading toward the parking garage that was their base.

Jensen was examining the case he'd taken from the limo when Chang and Fi reached the rooftop. He looked up as they ran up the ramp from the floor below.

"Where's our bot?" Jensen asked. He'd heard the buzz of its rotors, but it wasn't with them.

"I left it one floor down, away from prying eyes," Chang said, pointing at the sky. "We took the other bot down and pulled out. No sign of Jackson or Xu?"

Jensen gave him a look that said all he needed to know. He couldn't meet the girl's eyes.

Chang crouched beside the case. "Smaller than I expected," he said. "I hope it was worth nearly dying for."

"Worth Jackson and Xu dying for, you mean?" Jensen asked him.

"Not what I said," Chang said.

"Is Corporal Xu dead?" Fi asked.

Jensen stayed crouched. "We don't know. Right now, we need to have a look inside this case. It has a digital lock. Can you open it?"

"Maybe," Fi said, looking over Jensen's shoulder. "There's a USB port beside it." She reached into her backpack for her laptop and some cables. "I can try."

Jensen stood up and stepped back, letting her get to work. He handed Chang his camera. "Got video of everyone inside the vehicle. So no one has to take my word about the kill." He showed it to Chang on the camera's small screen.

"That's him alright." Chang winced. Then put his finger on the screen. "Wait. Go back." He squinted at the small image. "That guy is wearing a PLA Army Medical Corps uniform," he said. "Captain rank."

"PLA Army? Chinese? They're already here?"

"This one was," Chang said. He looked over at Fi. "You sure we want to even open that case?"

Jensen frowned. "Not as sure as I was five minutes ago."

"Too late," the girl said. There was a beep, and the lid of the case clicked open. Without even asking, she flipped it up.

Inside, packed in Styrofoam, were hundreds of ampoules with rubber tops. In a compartment on the side were disposable syringes and needles.

Chang grabbed the girl's shoulder. "Move away. That could be weaponized virus."

"Or the cure for it," Jensen decided. Ignoring Chang's warning, he reached for an ampoule and pulled it out. It held a pale-yellow liquid. There was writing on the glass, and he showed it to Chang. "What's it say?"

Chang squinted. "Uh, *Serum 4.2. Store below 25 degrees Celsius.*" He read it again, lips moving. "Yeah, that's all. Could be anything."

Jensen shook his head. "Nah. This is something. A PLA Army physician in a meeting with the Taiwanese premier as he's about to issue a decree inviting China to send emergency medical aid to Taiwan? This is definitely something."

"Important enough they took it with them when they ran," Fi said. "I volunteer to inject one of you. No?"

Jensen put the ampoule back and closed the case again. "We have to get back to port and report in. We take it with us. Someone with more stripes can decide what to do with it."

"But what about Corporal Xu?" Fi asked. "And the sergeant? You said we don't leave anyone behind."

Looking into her eyes, Jensen felt the sharp knife of grief once again. He reached out and pulled her a little closer, rising onto one knee so that they were face to face. "We don't. We'll go look for them now. But we need to keep moving in case the people back at that compound start searching for us."

They doubled back to look for Jackson and Xu before they left the area, with Fi's slaughterbot riding shotgun behind them.

"I'll go up with Squirt," Jensen said at the entrance to the building. "Wait here."

He sent the dog up the stairs ahead of him, landing by landing, in case there was anyone waiting. But the building was empty. The smell of smoke led him to the room where Xu and Jackson had made their sniper nest. The smell of charred flesh led him to the bodies.

He laid them side by side and went through their pockets, took off their tags and pulled a builder's tarpaulin over them. There was no time for more ceremony than that.

He stood, taking one last look down at the scene of the firefight. There were some civilians gathered around the still-smoldering vehicle. He couldn't see any of Ko's men in the streets, and the dead or wounded in the alleyway had been carried off. The premier's former compound 500 yards east was deserted now too, civilians going in and out, some carrying furniture and other loot from the building. It looked like the premier's protection had melted away.

When Jensen came out of the building alone, the girl looked in his face and turned away, biting a knuckle. "Alright, let's move. When we get closer to the port, I'll let US forces know we're coming in." Jensen looked over his shoulder at Squirt and the slaughterbot. "And I'll warn them we're bringing friends."

Should he have forgotten about the case? Would Jackson and Xu still be alive if he'd just pulled out when ordered, instead of wasting precious minutes more? Those minutes might have proven lethal to Jackson and Xu.

No way to know. He had to own what he did.

They'd executed their mission, achieved the objective. Premier Ko was dead, and his emergency decree with him. Jensen was willing to bet that if they were alive elsewhere on the island, another operation was underway to liberate Taiwan's president and vice president.

And what was in that case might be useful to someone, somewhere.

The Battle of Hawaii: Pago Pago

"PANTHERS OVERHEAD," the RAAF pilot, Dale, told Rory. He was back in the command module with the Ghost Bat pilots while Outlaw was skimming across the water, on course for American Samoa now, job done. "Get some, boys and girls!" the drone pilot said to the sky above them. He gave his fellow drone pilot, Chip, a high five.

"Where are your Ghost Bats?" Rory asked.

"In trailing formation," the man replied. "Fuel will be tight, but we'll get them all back on the ground. Well, all but one."

"Sorry to break your perfect recovery record," Rory told him.

"Died in a good cause, Captain," Dale said.

"Send one back down the bearing to *Fujian*. I'd like to know our six is clear."

He didn't like that, Rory could see in his face. But he didn't argue. "I'll send Hound Four," he said to Chip. "He's still got fuel. Snake him, high and low frequency search."

"I've got Two and Four," the other drone pilot replied. "Let me know if you need me to break them out of trail."

A STRONG RADAR signal suddenly appeared off Mushroom's nose. She had gone dark, was flying down at nap of the earth, without radar, using targeting data from *Dalian* to guide her toward the enemy heavy. She knew the heavy, or the wingmen it had with it, had jamming capability. She wanted to get within optimal optical infrared missile range, 12 miles, to give herself the best chance of bringing it down. An optical lock was nearly impossible to spoof.

The new radar didn't have a lock yet. She could risk moving closer, but …

No, she'd have to take the shot.

She lit up her radar. The enemy heavy appeared exactly where she expected it to be and, closer, a smaller fast mover. Drone wingman, heading right for her. She locked both targets, armed her missiles …

Then her world *fractured*.

Six new targets suddenly appeared right above her. The target ID flashed across her HUD, chilling her blood.

F-35 Panthers! One hundred eighty miles south of *Fujian!*

Her finger jabbed down on her missile trigger twice as she keyed her radio. "*Fujian*, Firebird Leader, multiple fast movers inbound *Fujian* from my position. Repeat, multiple fast—"

Radar lock. Missile warning! She'd been spotted.

She hauled her plane around at what would have been neck-breaking speed had she actually been inside the cockpit to face the missile spearing down on her from on high, a snapshot from one of the Panthers overhead.

She saw the missile contrail. Instinctively twisted her flight stick to skid her plane away from the interception point.

Miss!

Looking over her shoulder, she saw a spout of water rise from the sea where the Panther's missile had hit. Her attacker was a boxed dot on her HUD, growing larger, and she tried to bring her nose around for an off-boresight shot.

The Panther fired again.

"MISSILES INBOUND," Chip said with forced calm. "Two. Outlaw is the target."

"Jam them," Rory ordered.

"Hound One already jamming," Chip confirmed.

"Bringing Hounds Two and Four to bear."

Rory touched his throat mic. "Uncle, get ready on the stick."

"I heard, boss," Uncle Lee said from the cockpit. "Decoys armed. How long I got?" He would be seeing the incoming missile's radar on his warning screen, but only its bearing and signal strength.

Rory looked at the data from Hound One on the screen in front of Chip. "Thirty-two seconds to first missile."

"Hound One is out of play. First missile blew right by it," Chip said. "Two jamming."

"Four jamming," Dale called. "Come on, boys."

"Impact in 20," Rory said

"Four out of position. Missile has passed, still closing," Dale said. "Dammit. Ten seconds to impact."

"Firing decoys," Uncle said. "Maneuvering."

They had no altitude to play with. Rory heard the *thump thump thump* of decoys flying out of their dispensers, grabbed a handhold in the command module as Uncle put the enormous plane into a flat, skidding turn.

Then it happened. The world around Rory seemed to fall away. His vision narrowed to a long, dark tunnel. He swung around in confusion.

Behind him.

The boy.

Grinning. Pointing at him.

No, not pointing, crooking a finger. Calling to him.

391

THE PANTHER pilot closed on Mushroom's Chongming behind his missile.

Which would have been a fatal mistake if Mushroom didn't know hers was one of only six fighters left defending *Fujian*.

Any other day, she would have taken the point-blank missile shot she had at the Panther and let her Chongming die, certain in the knowledge she'd taken her enemy with her.

But she couldn't afford to throw her plane's life away. Hauling her stick over, she threw her fighter into a snap roll, then pulled hard back on the stick to reverse her direction, sending the enemy missile wide again.

Now they were both down at sea level, the Panther on her tail, trying to get a gun solution on her twisting, turning Chongming.

A line of cannon fire chewed into the water beside her plane, and she jerked it away. She could look over her shoulder and see the Panther with disturbing clarity, none of the airframe restricting her rear camera view.

20/20 vision of her killer.

The Panther suddenly slowed, trying to get separation for a missile shot, but she saw his control surfaces flare and read the move even as he was making it. Shoving her throttle through the gate, she hauled back on her stick, flipping up and looping right over the top of the Panther, holding at the top of the loop a dangerous second before hauling the nose down behind the Panther.

The enemy pilot wasn't tricked. Seeing her reverse on him, he'd crossed his stick and rudder and spun his own plane on its vertical axis, trying to keep his nose on her.

But the Panther was a jack of all trades, expert in none. It was a stealthy killer, able to strike air and ground targets from vast distances, stay invisible and escape untouched. But it was no dogfighter. Not like a Raptor. Not like Mushroom's Chongming.

Her missile lock tone hummed in her ears.

Who shoots first wins.

She fired, banking away, firing chaff and flares into her wake, saw the enemy's plane explode in a blinding flash, flew through the fireball and out the other side.

No time to celebrate being alive. She frantically checked her tactical screen. The rest of the Panther flight had ignored her, leaving their comrade to deal with her drone. They were already 60 miles away, and 60 miles closer to *Fujian*.

She lit her fighter's tail and tried to close the gap to them. "*Fujian*, Firebird Leader, I repeat, you have enemy fast movers inbound from my bearing …"

SHOUTING. Rory heard shouting. Was flung off his feet, crashing into a bulkhead. He curled into a ball, eyes shut, waiting to die.

Blackness.

The boy. Standing there, laughing. Clapping.

Dead. Rory must be dead after all. This was hell. He'd joined the boy in hell.

"You alright, Captain?"

Someone shaking him. He opened his eyes. Chip kneeling beside him.

"I …"

Gone. The boy was gone.

Rory tried to sit up. "I … I must have hit my head." He felt his scalp, checking for bleeding.

"I reckon you did," Chip said. "You were out cold for a while there." He helped Rory to a sitting position. "Mate, your pilot up front there is a *maniac*. I never saw a fat-arsed bird like this do the things he just made it do."

Rory let out a painful laugh. "Maniac he is," he agreed, touching his throat mic. "Uncle, how we doing?"

"Peachy," Bob Lee said. "Hope you didn't spill your martinis back there?"

"I'll bring you one," Rory told him. He looked out a window. Unless he was wrong, they were heading *north*, not south. "Uh, what's your heading there, Uncle?"

"O'ahu, boss," Uncle said. "Just got orders via USS *Lafayette*. We're to put down at Bellows Field and be prepared to evacuate wounded or, quote, 'whatever other duties may present.' I've plotted a dogleg that will take us nowhere near *Fujian,* though I doubt she's still worried about us with our Australian friends about to pay her a visit."

Rory let the Australian drone pilot pull him to his feet. "What's the status on that Chinese fighter?"

"Bugged out. Our six is clear," Dale said. "Your pilot dodged the first missile. Hound Two jammed the second."

Rory's legs nearly went from under him.

"You probably want to sit down, Captain," the Australian said, looking worried.

"I'll go forward," Rory told him. "Good job. I need you to …"

"Keep a drone watching out behind us," Chip nodded. "I already sent Hound Four. I guess he's not coming home either. But at least *we* are."

"Teaming air power, baby, that's how you do it," Dale said as Chip sat beside him again. "Nine Squadron!"

"*See but never seen!*" his fellow pilot chanted.

In tandem they chorused, "GHOST BATS!"

Rory shook his head. He was getting too old for this shit.

YOU'RE GETTING TOO OLD *for this*, *boyo*, Captain Anaximenes Papastopolous, CO of the 68th Aggressors, nearly said out loud.

He was down at 50 feet above sea level, threading the needle between a *Renhai* cruiser and an *Udaloy* destroyer. Both had their radars in search mode, fingers of radiation sliding across the skin of his Widow with unsettling regularity.

Two countries trying to kill you—you should be flattered, Meany.

O'Hare somewhere to starboard, doing the same, aiming for a gap between the *Udaloy* and a *Gorshkov* corvette.

They had every ship in the Sino-Russian fleet pegged on their tactical map, the data from Space Force triangulated by ELINT from the orbiting satellite and their Widows' own passive sensors.

Ahead of him about 50 kilometers, said all that intel, was the *Liaoning*. Pickets arranged around it like the diamonds on a 10 of diamonds playing card, four pickets in staggered formation to port, four to starboard, *Liaoning* and its fleet tender in the middle. Air defense radars overlapping. Only the Widow's stealth tech keeping him alive right now.

Above and behind him now, Touchdown and their Raptors trading missiles with *Liaoning*'s fighter screen.

He'd tuned that furball out, both on his screen and in his head. He didn't have the bandwidth to worry both about Touchdown's team and his own mission.

He had no wingmen to manage; he'd given all four to O'Hare. Like she said, she was the better Valkyrie pilot.

Trying to manage the drones as well as his own machine would just overload him.

Udaloy passing to starboard now. One less to worry about.

But dead ahead of him, a *Luyang*. Sixty-odd long-range vertical launch cells, one nine-cell short-range missile turret, and a 50-kilowatt laser for close defense.

But none with your name on them, Meany, he thought grimly. *There isn't room.*

He leaned forward, brought up his weapons menu and armed his hypersonic missile.

Get past the Luyang, release your Waverider, get the hell out again. Like stealing griddle cakes from your mam's baking tray.

KAREN 'BUNNY' O'HARE wasn't thinking about her mother's cooking. She couldn't remember her mother anyway, even if she'd been minded to.

She'd been raised by her grandfather, and that man couldn't boil an egg.

Bunny wasn't thinking at all. She was in the *zone*.

Bunny was the organic brain of a four-limbed flying organism. Ahead of her, skimming the waves about 5 kilometers out on her port and starboard quarters, were two Valkyries, Paul and Ringo. Not their official IDs, but she was radio silent, so she could call them what she liked.

Tucked in behind her, hiding in her radar-reflecting shadow, were two more limbs, George and John. Her body and brain was her Widow, and she was plugged into it like it was an extension of her nervous system.

Terrain-following radar emitted energy, so she was flying manually, like Meany, 50 feet over the water, rolling waves sometimes so close they felt like they were trying to suck her down. But the flying—yaw, throttles, pitch—was like her heartbeat, something just happening, not something she thought about.

Renhai, to port. She was more worried about overhead radar, a Chinese AWACS or Wing Loong, bathing the strike group in low-frequency stealth-revealing energy. An infrared-sensing satellite, passing over in the wrong place at the wrong time.

Admiral Gorshkov ahead. The ship a busted-ass Russia poured the last of its ship-building expertise and money into, so they would have at least one modern stealth warship in their fleet. Russia called it a frigate; NATO dismissively called it a corvette.

But it could sting. Thirty-two anti-ship and 32 air-to-air missiles. Axehead long-range hypersonic surface-to-air missiles. She wasn't worried about those; she was already inside their minimum engagement range. She was more worried about its Verba optical infrared short-range missiles. What they could see, they could usually kill.

She had to get around the *Gorshkov* next. Behind that was a less intimidating *Luhu*, probably built last century, more likely here to serve as a missile sponge than to intercept modern stealth aircraft or missiles.

First, the *Gorshkov*. If she was lucky, it might be the one USS *Canberra* hit, sent to the rear of the fleet to protect the less valuable *Liaoning* with whatever weapons it still had functioning. She could see only a Monolit radar active on the *Gorshkov*: a long—range, over-the-horizon system, probably tied to its Axehead missile launcher.

She aligned her flight path around the *Gorshkov* to reduce her radar cross section even more. Maybe *Canberra* knocked out its short-range radars?

She was due some luck.

Lady luck was not Bunny's friend at that moment. The *Gorshkov* class corvette, *Admiral Gromov*, was not the one hit earlier by USS *Canberra*. That was the *Admiral Gorshkov* itself, and his captain (since Russians referred to their ships in the masculine gender) had requested that Admiral Li Bing allow him to return to port, his superstructure, with its vital radars and antennae, a tangled mess that couldn't be repaired at sea.

As Li Bing's alert command—*Dragon Chant*—was relayed across the fleet, the *Gromov*'s captain ordered his air defense officer to supplement their long-range Monolit radar with the short-range Poliment phased array system, specially optimized for picking up low-flying stealth missiles and aircraft.

Its operator powered the system on. It took several minutes for its CPUs to come online and establish a link to the ship's Rif-m swarming missile defense system, but its radar started emitting energy immediately.

RIF-M SYSTEM.

The *Gromov*'s captain had either been saving a little surprise for her or had just woken from post prandial nap. Whatever the reason, the threat environment had just gotten uglier.

Bunny had 64 Valkyrie tactical algorithms pre-programmed into the Widow's AI, which could be initiated with a combination of the buttons on her flight stick. With twitch-speed reflexes as soon as she saw the Rif-m radar light up, she hit a three-key combination that sent Paul and Ringo soaring into the air, blasting jamming energy down the bearing to the *Gromov*.

At the same time, the payload bay doors opened along their center lines, and a super swarm of hundreds of LOCUST drones dropped out of each aircraft.

The *Renhai* cruiser to port already had its short-range air defense radar up. It didn't see Bunny, but it saw the two Valkyries pop up. It immediately sent four missiles at the big drones.

The *Gromov*'s operator saw his system come online, only to have alerts start screaming immediately in his ears.

"Contacts! Two. Bearing one seven zero, low, range 50, speed 400, breaking north and south ..." he called out. Then saw a message on his screen. They had a data link to the Chinese battlenet, the interoperability of Russian and Chinese ships something their technicians had ironed out several years earlier. He relaxed. "Cruiser *Wuxi* intercepting."

But something else started blinking, demanding his attention. "Swarming drones incoming! Same bearing. Sending data to Verba battery."

The *Gromov* was a *Project 22350 S-type*, its 130 mm naval gun mount replaced with a 32-cell Verba missile turret, to counter the emerging threat from swarming attacks. While the earlier *Gorshkov* vessels could only track 12 targets at once and fire 24 missiles, *Gromov* could track 200 and shoot 32 missiles, with a two-minute auto-reload time.

A readout on the air defense officer's command display did the math for him. The enemy swarms were 40 kilometers out, traveling at 200 kilometers an hour. Twelve minutes until they were on top of *Gromov*—enough for six Verba volleys, or 192 missiles. Many would miss. *Gromov*'s last line of defense was an outdated six-barrel autocannon. It didn't have the Chinese vessel's laser defenses.

He registered *Wuxi*'s missiles knocking down the enemy aircraft that launched the drone swarms. Without hesitating, he hit a button on his console to request further assistance from *Wuxi* to intercept the swarms.

His counterpart on the Chinese ship flashed a message back.

Wuxi engaging.

BY PULLING the *Wuxi*'s attention to her drones, along with the attention of half the strike force, no doubt, Bunny had created clear air for Meany.

He eased around the *Luyang* destroyer undetected at a range of about 10 kilometers.

Low-powered air traffic control radar, dead ahead, 40 clicks. Liaoning. He fed the final coordinates into the Waverider.

He had to pop up to 1,000 feet to launch the missile and eased his stick back a fraction to begin a gentle climb.

But then his luck ran out too.

Aircraft radar. Gyrfalcon. Lock. Missile fired!

The enemy fighter was coming down on him at a steep angle and its missile even steeper. He hauled back on his stick, bunted flat, released the Waverider, and then threw his Widow onto a wingtip, hauling it around toward the incoming missile as he bled both speed and height, forcing the Chinese missile to sharpen its dive.

It was a maneuver that guaranteed nearly every ship in the Sino-Russian fleet had just picked him up on radar, but the only one that would give him a chance of dodging the incoming missile.

Meters above the water, he pulled his nose level, fired active decoys into his wake and began praying.

AS PAUL AND RINGO disappeared from her tactical screen, Bunny registered a tone from the overhead satellite indicating that Meany had launched on the *Liaoning*. She checked her range to the carrier. His would be similar.

Forty kilometers. Thirty-six seconds for Meany's missile to run.

She had the obsolescent *Luhu* destroyer directly ahead of her now. No sign anyone had a radar lock on her.

Fastest way through is a straight line, O'Hare. She aimed her Widow directly at the *Luhu* destroyer at Mach 1.1.

Fingers flitted over her flight stick, tapping buttons. George broke out from inside her radar shadow and pulled nearly vertically into the air. The biggest threat to O'Hare right now wasn't the destroyer in front of her; it was the Chinese air defense screen high above her.

And she needed a fix on where it was.

George engaged its radar, scouring the cone of sky just in front and right overhead of Bunny.

Bingo. Chinese four-plane. Gyrfalcons—*and a KJ-600 AWACS!* That was a target too valuable and dangerous to ignore. She tapped another key combination, sending John out from behind her and directly at the AWACS. She ordered George to engage the Gyrfalcons. Each drone only had two air-to-air missiles, but she only needed to keep the Gyrfalcons busy, not try to knock them all down.

Both drones launched their missiles at the Chinese aircraft before they were detected, then dived for the sea.

George was hit by a missile from the *Luhu*. She saw the contrail, arcing up into the sky from right ahead of her.

Sorry, baby.

As the Chinese destroyer loomed in front of her, huge and getting bigger, she twitched her flight stick to lift herself over it and then dropped back down the other side.

She hoped she'd just burst more than a few eardrums.

John was still alive, trying to stay with her, but she was moving too fast now. She sent it at the *Luhu* behind her, ordering it to deploy its payload of LOCUSTs and then make a kamikaze run at the warship.

She didn't watch to see what happened. Her full attention was on the sea ahead of her, looking for a radar or radio signal that could only be the *Liaoning*.

Her sensors stayed stubbornly silent.

ADMIRAL LI BING was on the bridge of *Liaoning* when Meany launched his hypersonic missile. One of *Liaoning*'s *Renhai* escorts picked up the missile in its supersonic boost phase … and misclassified it.

"Vampire, bearing one seven five relative, speed Mach 1.4, AI classification … LRASM," *Liaoning*'s air defense officer reported.

Standing in front of his admiral, *Liaoning*'s captain reacted calmly. "XO, shut down all emissions and prepare to maneuver."

The order blanked all air defense, air traffic and fire control radars and radio broadcasts, but would make *Liaoning* instantly invisible to what *Liaoning*'s captain assumed was a radar-homing missile.

It was the right response. Li Bing tried not to look relieved, in case anyone was watching him for a reaction. The enemy had launched some small swarms, and a single cruise missile. His pilots were engaged with several enemy Raptors and a Widow, and a couple of drone wingmen. It was a probing attack only, easily beaten off.

"*Wuxi* and *Zunyi* intercepting vampire. Confidence high, Captain," *Liaoning*'s XO reported. "*Admiral Gromov* reports minor damage. Several swarming drone strikes, none critical."

"Vampire has … Vampire now Mach 4, Mach 4.2," the air defense officer reported, his voice an octave higher. "Classification: hypersonic!"

"Helm, flank speed; make your heading 355 degrees relative. XO, signal the fleet: *Liaoning* maneuvering."

The XO repeated the orders. "*Gromov* engaging enemy missile."

The knot in Li Bing's stomach returned. There was no chance of outmaneuvering a hypersonic missile. His captain had just ordered his helmsman to meet the missile with his stern, if it got through.

LIAONING'S CAPTAIN had guessed right. Meany's missile was launched in "home on emissions" mode. As *Liaoning* went dark, it lost its bearing to the carrier and was about to switch to optical infrared targeting.

But then the target reappeared, radiating brightly. A clean, clear, strong radio signal. The missile made its final course correction.

Except it wasn't *Liaoning* that reappeared. It was the 24,000-ton fleet tender *Luomahu*, traveling 5 kilometers behind *Liaoning* and loaded with volatile aviation fuel for *Liaoning*'s Gyrfalcon fighters.

With *Liaoning* signaling it was maneuvering, the captain of *Luomahu* had his comms officer broadcast a warning to the entire fleet that he was maneuvering too, and they should remember to keep a five-kilometer separation from his vessel, in case of …

Well, in case of what was about to happen.

"LUHU REPORTS multiple swarming drone strikes," the XO said. "And one cruise missile. *Luhu* unavailable for intercept."

Li Bing cursed, silently, and held his breath, hands clenched tightly behind his back.

"Vampire range 5 kilometers. *Wuxi* and *Zunyi* launching again. *Liaoning* lasers have optical lock."

Optical lock on a hypersonic missile with lasers? The heat of a laser weapon would be negligible compared to the heat the missile was already generating on its nose cone. Li Bing spread his feet, bracing for the coming impact.

A blindingly white light filled the bridge, and Li Bing closed his eyes, throwing a hand up over his face. Then it was like a giant hand grabbed the *Liaoning* by the fantail and lifted it into the air.

Li Bing held his breath and waited to die.

But instead, he was shoved against the bulkhead behind him as the mighty ship surfed down the wave building under its keel. Then the sound of the explosion behind reached it, like the sonic boom of an asteroid entering the atmosphere right overhead.

Their surface warfare officer recovered first. He was staring at a set of screens in front of him and sent the vision from their rear-facing camera to a flat screen on a wall at the side of the bridge, pointing. His voice was strangled, "*Luomahu*, she's …"

Gone, Li Bing thought. Where the low, squat form of the fleet replenishment vessel had been was a racing circle of white water, and in the center of it, a mushroom-shaped vapor cloud.

"Helm ahead standard—hold her steady," *Liaoning*'s captain said. "Radar and communications, resume operations. XO, damage reports from all sections."

His XO turned to his radio handset, then hesitated. "Damage reports from *Liaoning* only, or across the fleet?"

The captain frowned. "Contact ships within 10 kilometers of the explosion. But first, give me full reports from every section on *Liaoning*." He turned to Li Bing. "Admiral, I recommend *Luhu* be detached and allocated to the rescue operation."

Li Bing studied the expanding cloud on the screen. "There is no point, Captain," Li Bing said, softly enough only the captain and XO could hear. "No one could have survived that blast. We can send our prayers for their souls, but we cannot afford to weaken our defenses or delay our approach to our objective."

Liaoning's captain's lips tightened, but he faced forward again. "Air Combat, situation report!"

IT WASN'T THE FIRST TIME Bunny O'Hare had been up against the Chinese carrier. But the other time was during a period of political tension that spilled into a limited kinetic conflict. Rules of engagement were strict. The velvet gloves were well and truly on.

Not today.

A flash of bright light ahead of her forced both her helmet vision and her cockpit glass to polarize to protect her eyesight. Seconds later, her machine rode a series of shockwaves, and she saw a fat, dome-shaped cloud spread across the horizon. Meany's missile hitting home!

And there you are, old friend. Bunny smiled as a hotspot of energy appeared on her RWR, smack bang where *Liaoning* should be. She glanced quickly at the mission timer. Maybe the radio energy she was seeing was *Liaoning* frantically sending a mayday?

Except … The new signals were coming from a bearing slightly to the right of the mushroom cloud, and a range just beyond it.

Think later. Act. Now.

Her leapfrog over the Chinese destroyer, the last of its westward inner missile pickets, put her just 15 kilometers behind the signals from *Liaoning*. The way it had winked in and out of electronic existence told her it was trying to defend itself against radar-homing missiles. She leaned forward, set her Waverider to fly on bearing and use optical targeting only.

It would barely have time to go hypersonic, but it would aim for the last known position of *Liaoning* at wavetop level, then pop up and look for the carrier with its high-resolution optics, making a visual match before beginning its terminal attack.

Assuming there was a carrier left to attack.

Bunny held a breath, double-checked her threat environment, saw 'John' was still in the fight and tangled with the Gyrfalcon CAP overhead, then slid her thumb over the Waverider missile release. There was nothing more she could do.

She eased back on her stick, taking the Widow up to 1,000 feet. Her thumb twitched on the trigger, her payload doors flipped open, and the Waverider dropped into her slipstream, steadied and then ignited its first-stage booster. In seconds it would go supersonic and then ignite its second-stage scramjet, going hypersonic.

Bunny eased her machine into a gentle bank and turned to a heading that would enable her to avoid the *Luhu* and *Gorshkov*. The range at which she'd taken the shot gave *Liaoning* and its escorts under 15 seconds to react.

MEANY'S BLACK WIDOW was not gently banking. He was throwing it from one wingtip to the other as the Chinese missile closed on him. But rolling a big bird like the P-99 Black Widow was like trying to spin a top in a tub of treacle.

His eyes flicked to the missile tracking icon in his helmet heads-up display. A small circle showing his machine, a small cross with a tiny tail showing the incoming missile. He spun his head to look behind him, but couldn't see it.

It was still tracking. Seconds to impact.

Time dilated.

He was back in the cockpit of an RAF Hawk T1, completing his first jet-powered solo.

He was tumbling through the sky over Syria, punching out after his Tempest fighter ate a Russian missile.

He was lying in a hospital bed, being told he'd never walk again.

He was taking his first steps in his exoskeleton, proving the doctors wrong.

He was dancing with a girl at a bar in Cyprus who didn't care his legs were made of metal.

He was back in the cockpit of his Widow northeast of Hawaii, listening to the *THUMP THUMP THUMP* of his Air Trophy defense system firing thousands of small metal slugs into the curving path of the Chinese missile.

Missing.

And then Anaximenes 'Meany' Papastopolous's time was up. His aircraft came apart in a violent explosion, and his body tumbled, lifeless, through the air toward the sea.

The first Coalition casualty of the attack on the Sino-Russian fleet.

"ENEMY BLACK WIDOW destroyed," *Liaoning*'s air warfare officer reported with satisfaction. "Enemy offensive fighter patrol to our west is withdrawing."

"Losses?" Li Bing asked.

"Two Gyrfalcons lost in the fighter engagement, one lost engaging a drone. And …" the air warfare officer looked up, then looked away again. "We have lost the KJ-600 AWACS."

Not good. Could be worse. Will be worse. There is at least one enemy submarine inside our submarine perimeter. Li Bing could see worry in his captain's face. "The enemy may dent our paint, Captain, but he will not prevent our victory."

"No, Admiral!" the man replied.

"Damage reports coming in," *Liaoning*'s XO said. "*Wuxi* reports shockwave damage to its Dragon Eye radar system. *Zunyi* reports vibration on port propellor shaft, shutting down to …"

"Vampire! New contact. One seven zero degrees relative, altitude 200, range … *Impact in ten seconds!*" The air defense officer looked eyes-wide at Li Bing, not his captain, as though the more senior officer had the greater power to save them.

"Sound the collision alarm!" *Liaoning*'s captain ordered. There was no time for anything else. "Brace for impact!"

BUNNY O'HARE may never have, *would* never have, penetrated as deeply as she did if Meany Papastopolous had not successfully made his attack when he did, from where he did.

The destruction of *Luomahu* had not just taken out the fleet replenishment vessel, but its destruction had sent a shockwave through the air and water that damaged the air defense radar antennae of the *Renhai* class cruiser *Wuxi* and sent panic through officers aboard vessels like the close escort *Zunyi*, suddenly dealing with propulsion problems.

Five seconds out from its target, traveling at 5,000 kilometers an hour, Bunny's missile popped 2,000 feet into the air and looked ahead. There were two big ships in front of it. Only one matched the images of the *Liaoning* stored in its database.

It dropped its nose, jinked left and right to confuse defensive fire that wasn't there, and then buried itself in the deck of the *Liaoning*.

THERE IS AN INSECT in northern Australia called the fire ant. Unlike many other ants, which bite and then spit or spray acid on the wound, fire ants bite only to get a grip and then sting and inject a toxic venom. Advancing in huge numbers, they can attack and kill birds and animals.

They are a roiling tide of venomous fury, consuming flesh and bone with agonizing bites, leaving only smoldering ruin in their wake.

Such were the three squadrons of F-35 Panthers of the Royal Australian Air Force that set upon the carrier *Fujian*.

Mushroom Sun's warning from behind the advancing Panthers was received, but in the end, her acting commander, Colonel Wang Wei, could do nothing about it. He had been ordered to allocate all but the bare minimum of aircraft to the attack on Pearl Harbor, and had been left with a fighter defense screen in name only. His two remaining escort ships, *Dalian* and *Haikou*, were woefully insufficient to protect his carrier against an enemy determined to obliterate it. Only the fog of war that his Space Force had been able to draw over the eyes of his enemy had protected *Fujian* this long.

And now it was gone.

Like a rolling wave of fire ants, the Australian Panthers took out *Dalian* and *Haikou*. They chewed through the five remaining Chongming fighters circling *Fujian*. And then they launched a blizzard of venomous LRASM missiles at the Chinese carrier.

In *Fujian*'s CIC, Wang Wei looked at the panoramic tactical screen that showed his ship had only minutes to live, and gave his final orders.

"XO, get a message to the aircraft attacking Pearl Harbor. Tell them they will need to divert to *Shandong* or *Liaoning* after their attack."

His XO stood at attention, shaking but not breaking. Not yet. "Yes, Colonel. Divert to the other carriers."

"Sound the collision alarm, firefighting and emergency personnel to action stations ... What am I forgetting, XO?" he asked, sounding as though he was simply trying to remember the recipe for his grandmother's jiaozi dumplings.

"I ... Colonel?"

"Oh, yes, order the engineer on watch to kill turbine power to the shafts. There is more. Come on, man." Wang clicked his fingers. "Help me. I'm a pilot first, sailor second."

His XO was crying now, tears streaming down his face, but still he didn't break. Wang had underestimated him.

"Colonel, we can ... before ... we can centrally activate the Emergency Position Indicating Beacons and search-and-rescue transponders on all life vessels."

"Yes, that's it," Wang said. "See to it. When that is done, proceed to your emergency muster station."

Men were already running from the CIC as the XO croaked out his orders. Wang didn't blame them. This was how all ships died. In tears, blood and fear.

The collision alarm began ringing throughout the ship.

Wang Wei turned away, reached out his hand and ran it along the brass railing behind him. *You fought well, proud* Fujian, he told the ship in its last moments. *You taught the enemy to fear your name. It took the might of an entire air force to lay you low, and generations to come will know your name and speak it with reverence.*

Then the CIC shuddered as the first enemy missile struck, and the dying started.

TWO DECKS DOWN, Mushroom Sun heard the collision alarm sounding in her pod. Pulling off her helmet, she saw other pilots—most of whom were flying the attack on Pearl Harbor—bail out of their pods and start running for

411

the ladders that led up to the flight deck. Their combat AI would finish the attack if it detected a loss of pilot input, so she couldn't blame them for abandoning their aircraft.

Mushroom couldn't run. But even if she could, she wouldn't have.

She'd lived with this ship through two attacks already. She had tried to save it, so many times, and ultimately, had failed.

She was ready to die with it now.

EMILIO 'NUN' D'ANGELLI was engaged in a turkey shoot where the turkeys outnumbered the shooters.

And shot back.

The other fighters of Fanfare flight were marked on his Raptor's tactical display with an F inside a box. There had been three others before. There were only two now.

There had been six enemy icons on his threat display.

There were *16* now.

There had been many more—Chongmings, coming in low from across the sea to the south—but then USS *Lafayette* began laying into them, rippling missiles from its vertical launch magazines, joined by mobile shore batteries along the Hawaiian coast.

His pilots were engaged with their Gyrfalcon escorts, unable to unentangle themselves to engage the Chongming air assault on Pearl Harbor.

Nun grunted, rolling his Raptor onto its back and pulling it into a diving loop, trying to reverse on his opponent, a Gyrfalcon he'd traded missiles with and was now matched with in a tooth-and-nail turning fight with guns, neither fighter able to find a firing solution.

"Gyrfalcon is just a Raptor copy, they said," he grunted, following the Gyrfalcon around as it tightened the circle. "Chinese engines ... suck. Thrust ... to ... weight ... Raptor will win every time." He laughed out loud.

How's that working out, Nun?

LEI YU had been told the aerodynamic advantages of his modern Gyrfalcon would more than compensate for the combat experience of America's Raptor pilots in a guns fight. The Raptor was a 30-year-old plane, built with 50-year-old design principles and technologies.

So how come, Yu was asking himself as he hauled his Gyrfalcon around the circle again across from the American, *How come you can't get guns on this damn Raptor? How come every time you get close, he breaks high, low or sideways, and you are suddenly defensive again?*

NUN HAD HIS HEAD screwed painfully over his shoulder, trying to keep the Chinese fighter in sight.

Low yo yo, that's what his instincts were telling him right now. *Throttle back, reverse, dive, come up on him from below.* Except he'd tried that, and the Chinese pilot had countered it smoothly, nearly getting guns on him in a head-on pass that should have been impossible to achieve.

He was *good*.

Nun's F-22 was old, its avionics not a patch on those of an F-35 or P-99, but his helmet was almost identical to those used by Panther and Widow pilots, and it suddenly showed him the solution to his problem.

A little box with an 'F' inside it, 3 miles away.

413

"Fanfare Three, are you engaged?" Nun called on his radio. "Need … an assist."

Cannon tracer fire flashed by his cockpit, so close his buttocks clenched.

"Got you, Fanfare Leader. Prepare to drag and bag."

"I'll break high," Nun suggested.

"In position. Missile cued. On your mark, Nun."

Nun grabbed his throttle in his left hand, stick in his right. "Breaking!"

LEI SAW his tracer slide into the Raptor's wake. *Short. Any … second … now.*

Radar warning! Enemy behind him. The aircraft ahead of him broke out of its turn, rocketing vertically into the sky. Bad move. An easy kill. He instinctively followed it up before realizing his mistake.

Missile warning!

It was the last sound he heard.

BY THE TIME Nun and his wingman had regrouped, the Chinese drones had … disappeared.

All of them.

There were no targets on his radar, nothing being flagged to him by *Lafayette*. He listened to the radio. No one was calling targets either. Nun tipped his plane onto a wing as he flew over the harbor, and saw no new fires. Maybe a couple further inland, but nothing like he'd expect from the scale of the Chinese attack. Then he saw some wreckage in the water, short of the harbor entrance. Chinese drone, floating belly up.

"Fanfare Leader, Fanfare pilots, form on me." He changed frequency. "Fanfare Leader to Bellows Tower, what just went down?"

"Uh, Fanfare, we ... we're trying to update the ..." Nun heard voices speaking in hurried tones in the background. "Fanfare, Navy is saying the Chinese drones dropped on Pearl, naval mines maybe, then they ..." More voices, static, and the Marine JTAC returned with a new urgency in his voice. "Then they blew right over and went out to sea to the north. Fanfare, we need you to get your flight back down to refuel and rearm. Space Force reports a Chinese airborne assault under heavy escort inbound Kaua'i."

"Sorry, Bellows, did you say Kaua'i?"

"Roger that. *Kaua'i*. You are cleared straight in on runway R-21, Fanfare. Get down pronto."

FROM HER HIDING spot on the second floor, Tammy Ballard could hear a full-on firefight taking place at the front of the 'Iolani Palace. She didn't need to see it to understand what was going on.

Honolulu PD had responded to her call. They'd tried to enter the building and had been fired on. Maybe by the Chinese "police," maybe by armed Alliance members. Or maybe by both.

From the sound of the gunfire on the floor she was on, the Chinese were *definitely* part of the fight, since the second floor was, as far as she could tell, all theirs. Downstairs from inside the building, she heard a couple of pistols firing, shotguns, as well as ARs. She heard only heavy assault rifle fire on her floor. No pistols.

That's your people getting shot at out there, Ballard.

415

Ah, hell.

Pistol up, she started edging toward the grand staircase.

A man came running up the stairs, turned right, back to her. Chinese, police uniform. Carrying a handful of tactical ballistic vests over one arm, a rifle in the other. He stopped at the top of the stairs, dropped what he was holding at his feet and started ripping Velcro straps so he could put a vest on himself.

Without overthinking it, she aimed at the base of his neck and fired.

INSIDE THE ROOM with Freeth, Pan, Pi and their two specialists, Pan tried to ignore the sound of the firefight outside, the emergency sirens and now police sirens wailing as more police responded to Sergeant Cuccino's death warning.

Pan had to stay focused. So did Freeth. Pan slapped the table, leaned forward and pushed the script across it to Freeth. "Mr. Freeth, when you are ready, you will look at the camera, and you will read these words. We will do the rest."

Freeth flinched as what sounded like a stun grenade exploded downstairs. Pan clicked his fingers. "Now, Mr. Freeth."

Their mission here was nearly done. *Speed and violence.* They had to get this done and keep moving. Freeth's broadcast would be beamed via satellite to an editing team in Hong Kong. They would edit the sound, the vision, and then broadcast it to the world via every social media and streaming news service. It wouldn't matter if Freeth and his cause were dead or alive at that point. Reality was what China was about to make it appear to be.

And when the video was sent, Pan and his team would set fire to the building, break out of the palace in the ensuing mayhem and begin their campaign of guerilla warfare in the heart of the enemy bastion. They weren't relying on the people of Hawaii to rise up. Pan and the men of 1st Battalion, 5th Amphibious Combined Arms Brigade (Recon), would *be* the rebellion.

But first ...

Pan turned to his cyber specialist. "Ready?"

The man nodded. "Ready."

Pan stood, nodding at Freeth.

With trembling hands, Freeth straightened the paper in front of him and began reading.

"My name is Jonah Freeth, *Ka Moʻopuna Pono o Kalakaua*, Descendent of Kalakaua, the last true King of Hawaii. Today, with the help and support of the government of the People's Republic of China and the Russian Republic, the Hawaiian Freedom Alliance has taken the first steps in the liberation of Hawaii from colonialist oppression. We call on ..." Freeth was reading ahead and stopped, frowning, then looked up to see Pan's pistol pointed at his face. "Uh, we call on all Kanaka people, and all who support the idea of freedom, to take up arms and resist the oppressor." And maybe the next words spoke to Freeth, or maybe he was just a good actor, swept away in the emotion of the moment, because he lifted his head and looked directly at the camera on the desk, his voice suddenly strong and proud. "*Kū Kiaʻi Mauna* ... Stand as Protectors of the Mountain!"

Pan let the words ring around the room before looking at his comms specialist. The man nodded. "We're good."

417

Pan smiled at Freeth, who gave him a relieved look. Then he clubbed the Descendent of Kalakaua across the temple with his pistol. Freeth fell off his chair, unconscious. Pan touched his tactical throat mic. "Liberator Team, prepare for egress. Disengage, pop smoke, set your thermite charges and meet at the rear doors."

From the second briefcase on the desk, Pi took a thermite grenade. He looked for a good place to throw it. Pan pointed at the thick curtains and heavy leather upholstered chairs lining the wall. "But help me bring the dead cop in here first," he ordered Pi. They dragged Cuccino into the room and cut the ties around the police officer's wrists. Pan arranged the bodies so it looked like Cuccino and Duke were standing by the window. There would still be blood from the execution in the other room, but that might not survive the fire he was about to set. He cleaned his pistol of prints, and put it in Freeth's hand, taking Cuccino's sidearm instead. He threw the sidearm with Freeth's prints onto the floor beside Cuccino. Then he motioned to two of his men to lift Freeth. "I wish I could be there when they try to work this out.," Pan said to Pi. "Get the fire started and then join us at the rear door, first floor."

He followed his two men dragging Freeth out into the stairway lobby. They heard a heavy burst of fire from the rooms across the lobby and smiled.

Listen to the revolution we started, Mr. Freeth, he thought. *Are you not proud?*

BALLARD SAW the Chinese officer drop with a thud and waited for a response, but with the amount of incoming

418

and outgoing fire coming from below and around her, it seemed her shot had gone unheard.

Running to the body, she took the man's rifle, checked it and ran to the wall leading into the study where she had last seen Jonah Freeth.

The study where she'd heard those first two shots.

From across the corridor, she heard automatic weapons firing outward. More Chinese, she assumed. Should she take them first?

Hell yes, she should.

Every room on the floor joined every other. Going back and moving across, she approached the front room at the other side of the small palace from behind.

She saw Honolulu PD out front of the palace, behind squad cars, or taking cover in the thick roots of the banyan trees. Three Chinese, firing out of broken windows at the police below. Picking their targets. Not spraying, aiming. They weren't wearing vests.

She pulled back, pulling out the mag, checking and reseating it, checking the rifle again. These guys weren't house and garden insurrectionists. They were trained. Maybe vets, like her. Or, something else …

Chinese special ops?

Should she give them the chance to surrender?

Hell no, she shouldn't.

She swung out into the doorway. None of the three men saw her. With short, controlled bursts, she dropped them one after the other.

She spun back into the room, expecting a volley of fire to follow her, but heard only the guns firing downstairs and outside. She looked into the room again.

Three tangos down.

She went and checked the bodies. Dead, all of them. The smell of blood thick in her nostrils. She nearly gagged. They had the same rifles as hers, extra ammunition by their feet. She scooped up a full magazine and changed it over for the one she'd just used. Put another in her trouser pocket.

Back to the lobby. Could hear voices inside the office. One of them, Freeth.

So he was alive, for what it was worth.

Then a thud from inside the room, like a body hitting the floor.

Alright, maybe not.

She ran across the lobby, to the entrance to the room she'd been hiding in, remembering the small corridor leading inside. That was a kill zone. Wasted precious minutes trying to remember the layout, think of a way to get into the room where she'd heard Freeth.

Across the lobby. Queen's bedroom. Then governor's office. They're in there. Move.

Stuck her head out, saw movement on the stairs, pulled it back in again. Waited a beat, looked again. No one. Ran across the lobby, through the queen's bedroom, swung into the open door of the governor's office.

And saw more of the Chinese police, down the other end of the room, piling chairs up against some curtains. But closer to her …

What she saw next almost made her vomit. The big Kanaka she'd seen earlier, dead, shot in the head. Lying on the floor beside him, a Honolulu PD sergeant, his head also shot.

Executed.

You never know how you're going to react to that kind of shit. Some people buckle. Puke. Curl into a ball and want their mama to come and take them home.

Or just *run*.

Those are all perfectly reasonable human reactions. You can't judge anyone until you're there yourself, up to your neck in blood and bile.

Officer Tammy Ballard turned into a ball of cold fury.

Like the time she'd been crossing the road at a pedestrian crossing and that car sounded its horn and tried to cruise right through, expecting *her children* to jump out the way. She leaped in front of that car and had the driver out, spread-eagled across the hood with his hands cuffed behind him before he could even count to five.

What happened next was *that* Tammy Ballard.

She walked into the office, stepping around the dead bodies, trying to get closer so she couldn't miss, ready to shoot if they reacted at all.

They didn't even notice her. One pulled the pin on a grenade. *No, you don't.* She aimed first at the one in the middle with the grenade. Opened fire, moving the gun left, then right, shooting until the bolt clicked.

Then she reloaded.

The grenade exploded.

THE ANSWER to Brunelli's question lay in a major strategic challenge China faced in contemplating an invasion of Taiwan: how to cross the 100 nautical miles of open water between China and Taiwan in the face of a powerful adversary's navy and air force, and land hundreds of

421

thousands of troops on beaches bristling with physical landing barriers and anti-ship missiles.

Through the 2020s, it built a dozen big landing craft, the *Yushen* class, landing helicopter docks equivalent to the US *Wasp* class, able to carry thousands of troops and dozens of attack or troop helicopters. It created mandatory design rules for ocean-going civilian car and passenger ferries so that they could be militarized when the time came and pressed into service to ferry armored vehicles and troops across the Strait.

By the late 2020s, China was confident it had the capacity it needed to move hundreds of thousands of troops if it needed to.

But both Chinese and Western military analysts concluded these would not be enough. Capacity was not *capability*. Taiwan and its allies had not stood idly by as China built up invasion capacity. They strengthened landing beach fortifications, created defenses in depth, dug fixed anti-ship missile emplacements, pre-sighted long-range artillery and invested in mobile long-range precision missiles that could decimate any navy trying to approach Taiwanese shores.

As it had throughout its history, China found a solution to these obstacles in numbers rather than advanced technology. In the 2020s, Russia canceled production of its *Zubr*, or "*Bison*," class landing craft, the largest military hovercraft ever built—able to carry five infantry fighting vehicles and 300 troops—because it no longer had the resources or imperative to maintain construction.

China bought the Russian manufacturer's shipbuilding facility at Khabarovsk on the Chinese border and took over production of the *Bison*, renamed to *Máo-niú* or *Yak*. Western analysts noted the Chinese development of the *Yak*, and its use in limited numbers in amphibious landing exercises over the next several years. The small number deployed raised no alarms.

By 2038, Western analysts assessed China had 12 operational *Yaks*. Six had been destroyed in the early days of the Taiwan conflict when the invasion force being prepared for Kinmen and Matsu islands was hammered in a surprise Taiwanese attack. That left China with just six known *Yaks*.

In reality, in warehouses around Khabarovsk, China had stored *over 200 Yak* landing hovercraft. Its original intention was to use them in the Taiwan Strait to overwhelm Taiwanese defenses with sheer numbers, speeding 60,000 troops across the Strait at speeds up to 60 knots, driving them straight up onto the coast, over landing obstacles, bypassing the Taiwanese first line of defense.

When the decision was made to bring Taiwan to its knees by other means, a new use was found for the *Yak* class landing hovercraft, with the aid of China's new ally, Russia.

They were moved in camouflaged containers from Khabarovsk, up the Amur River and across the Okhotsk Sea to the Russian Pacific Fleet base at Korsakov. There, they were reassembled while China awaited the results of its strike on US space assets.

Under cover of joint exercises on the nearby Kuril Islands, China loaded the *Yak* hovercraft and their amphibious assault troops aboard its *Yushen* landing helicopter dock ships and *Yuzhou* heavy lift vessels. Russian vessels like its *Ivan Gren* class landing ships, though smaller, were already built to accommodate the big hovercraft, and Russia contributed four to the Hawaiian operation.

The Sino-Russian plan to deny the use of Hawaii to USA was to *invade without capturing*. Its major amphibious landing ships and aircraft carriers would come no closer to Hawaii than 100 nautical miles—the range at which the fleet's 50 *Yak* hovercraft could be launched.

It only needed 20 hovercraft to survive the landing and put troops and materiel ashore.

Russia and China planned to land a minimum of 6,000 troops on Kaua'i, and dozens of infantry fighting vehicles, mobile anti-air and anti-ship missile vehicles, hundreds of long-range artillery barrels and thousands of shoulder-launched missiles.

And it planned to land them on the near undefended beaches of the now decimated Pacific Missile Range Facility on Kaua'i.

US ARMY GENERAL Reg Samuels and Admiral Harry Connaught returned to the INDOPACOM Joint Operations Center secure facility after their meeting with the US President, Samuels to manage the defense of Hawaii, Connaught the larger war in the Pacific.

Connaught had pulled himself out of a briefing on Guam to join the group of officers following the progress of the air attack on the Sino-Russian fleet.

JOC's Air Force operations support officer, a Major, was at Connaught's elbow. "68 Aggressor reporting two strikes on *Liaoning*. RAAF reports *Fujian* and escorts *Dalian* and *Haikou* hit and sinking."

Connaught saw some fist pumps ripple around the room and had trouble suppressing his own reaction. But the carriers and their aircraft weren't their primary concern right now—he was more worried about the big troop transports they were protecting.

"Report from HMS *Agincourt* in contact with enemy fleet," the JOC Navy Lieutenant said. "Twenty-plus small vessels detected, possible hovercraft, inbound Kaua'i. *Agincourt* reports nearest enemy fleet vessels reversing course!"

Hovercraft? Connaught's eyes sought out *Agincourt* on the wall screen. "How far is *Agincourt* from Kaua'i?"

The Navy officer conferred with a colleague at a station in front of him. "One twenty nautical miles, Admiral."

"Any confirmation on *Agincourt's* report?"

"No sir."

"Can't we detach an aircraft from our strike package?"

"They're about to make their ingress from the south, sir," the JOC Major said. "We can break out a plane, but it would be at least, uh … 30 minutes before it was overhead that position. Let me look for other options."

Reg Samuels had joined Connaught, looking over his shoulder at the screen. "If the 68th hit *Liaoning* like they claim, maybe the commander of that fleet is scrubbing his attack. It would explain the escorts reversing course." The words were optimistic, but his voice said he didn't believe it himself.

"But those hovercraft, Sam," Connaught said. He turned to the JOC Lieutenant. "What amphibious hovercraft does China possess, and how fast can they move across open ocean?"

Samuels looked at a Navy lieutenant. "Uh, pulling that up for you, sirs."

Connaught moved closer to Samuels, his voice deep with concern. "Another reason that fleet might be turning back, Sam, is that it's done its job and launched its invasion force."

"Sirs, Chinese heavy landing hovercraft, *Yak* class, range 150 nautical miles, complement 300 troops, five vehicles, plus crew …" the Lieutenant relayed.

"Speed," Samuels reminded him.

"Speed 60 knots in fair seas." The man anticipated Connaught's next question. "Weather northwest Kaua'i is fair, light winds, light swell." He looked at his screen again. "But our intel assessment is China only has a half dozen *Yak* class vessels left, Admiral. Most were taken out in the first days of the war."

Connaught did the math. "One twenty miles at 60 knots in fair seas. Two hours. If that British boat's report is right, they'll hit the beaches at Kaua'i inside two hours. They might still be coming for O'ahu, but I doubt it. What force strength do we have on Kaua'i, Sam?"

Samuels didn't need to check. He knew exactly. "PMRF got hit badly. Dozens dead, hundreds wounded. Total combat-capable Army and Marines? About a battalion. Air defenses, next to nothing. Long-range fires, same."

A thousand troops, Connaught thought. Against what? Several thousand? He and Samuels were about to make the biggest gamble of the battle for Hawaii. *Fallujah* was carrying a Marine Expeditionary Unit of 2,500 troops, but it was six hours out at best.

"Are they coming for Kaua'i, or is their target O'ahu?" Connaught asked Samuels.

"That's the question," Samuels said. "The answer is, it depends. How many hovercraft are we talking about? A half dozen? Then the target is Kaua'i, but you wouldn't turn your ships around if all you launched was a half dozen hovercraft."

"We need to know how big that landing force is, and we need to know now," Connaught said. "Not 30 minutes from now."

"Permission to interrupt, sirs?" the JOC Air Force major said.

"Go ahead," Connaught told him.

"68th Aggressor is returning from its attack at the rear of the enemy fleet. They can overfly *Agincourt*'s position quicker than any plane we could detach from the strike package. Space Force will also be overhead with a Skylon in 20 minutes."

Samuels grabbed his shoulder and squeezed. "Go. Send the Aggressors the order."

Operation Midnight: Tag

"SONAR, UPDATE," *Agincourt's* Captain Courtenay demanded. They were deep inside the Sino-Russian fleet's footprint now, where they had hoped the Chinese submarine would be. Their last "sighting" was nearly an hour old.

"Lost both the *Renhai* and those small surface vessels, Captain," the man admitted, sounding deflated. "Nothing but fish noises all around."

Courtenay looked at the plot of the Chinese and Russian ships that they had identified surrounding them. McDonald had to credit the British captain for his cool head. The sight of so many enemies so close was both tempting and terrifying. Courtenay's ability to keep on mission was formidable. "Navigation, plot me a course that will put us ahead of the *Renhai* assuming it maintained course and heading."

McDonald nodded approvingly. "You're thinking *Taifun* could be coasting underneath one of their big ships, hiding in its shadow?"

"We have a Chinese *Renhai* cruiser ahead, and a Russian *Ivan Gren* helicopter dock to starboard. The *Ivan Gren* is bigger, but the *Renhai* is Chinese. If you're going to hide under someone's skirts, you'd want them to be friendly."

"I would," McDonald agreed.

"So would I," Brunelli said.

Agincourt's crew went to work.

"You know what would be nice?" McDonald asked Brunelli quietly. "If we got out in front of that *Renhai*, deployed a towed array and found *Taifun* glued to its keel like a damn sucker fish. Is that too much to ask?"

"You're asking the wrong girl, Captain," Brunelli told him. "I'd give my left tit for that chance."

IRONICALLY, as Brunelli was making an offering of the flesh to the gods of the sea for a chance to meet *Taifun* again, *Taifun* was about 3 nautical miles behind *Agincourt*, and had just picked up the sound of *Agincourt*'s pump-jet propulsion system as it accelerated to get ahead of the Chinese *Renhai* cruiser.

It would have been ahead of *Agincourt*, as that boat's commander expected, if it hadn't been delayed by its engagement with the *LA* class submarine.

Taifun turned to follow the acoustic contact—quickly classified as an *Astute* class submarine—and rose silently to ELF depth and sent a message to her base at Huangpu Wenchong.

British Astute *class submarine detected in a position to engage multiple friendly vessels.* She sent the coordinates, bearing, and an estimated range to the contact. *Acoustic ID HMS* Agincourt. Taifun *trailing. Will await orders.*

She matched the target's speed and heading, damped her reactor noise, switched to battery propulsion and followed the contact patiently. There was no indication she had been heard.

Several minutes later, the order came.

Engage and destroy enemy vessel.

She'd ejected the empty Tianyi launch magazines from ports at the bottom of her hull as soon as she was clear of the US sensor perimeter, to reduce her mass. Her torpedo tubes were empty after the previous encounter, and she'd kept them unloaded in preparation for taking aboard new Tianyi magazine modules from a fleet replenishment vessel.

She began loading torpedoes again—a process that might have gone faster with a human crew that scented a kill, but which took *Taifun* the time it took.

No more, no less.

And the time to her first Yu-9 torpedo being ready to fire was exactly 11 minutes and 16 seconds.

ONE SYSTEM that made *Agincourt* the deadliest attack submarine afloat was called HELF-D: Hydrophonic Extremely Low Frequency Detection. HELF-D was a secret His Majesty's Navy had reserved completely for itself. As quantum compression technologies advanced, the ability of the newer classes of submarines to communicate with their bases or with other ships over vast distances via ELF became a reality. But so did the possibility of using those transmissions to detect the submarine that was transmitting them.

The British had been using passive HELF-D sensors dropped across the Pacific to track the ELF signals of the newest Chinese submarines for several years. HELF-D was how they knew a *Type 095* submarine, possibly *Taifun*, was making a run for the Sino-Russian fleet.

"HELF-D contact!" *Agincourt*'s electronic warfare officer had reported as soon as *Taifun* sent its message to Huangpu Wenchong. "Bearing 180 relative!"

"What's HELF-D?" Brunelli asked, loud enough that Courtenay heard her.

"*Classified* is what, dammit," Courtenay growled. "Behind us? Weapons prepare active countermeasures."

"Countermeasures armed, Captain."

"EWO, range estimate?"

Their sonar couldn't give a precise range to a contact, and HELF-D was even less accurate. "Close, sir," the EWO said. "Damn close."

"Nothing on sonar," the sonar officer reported. "Whatever it is, it is damn quiet."

"Helm, steady as you go. Arm special weapon in tube one; arm Spearfish in tubes two to six," Courtenay ordered. "Someone fetch Mr. Williams."

Singh repeated the order and started watching the countdown to launch readiness on the monitor in front of him. The electronic warfare torpedo needed to be within 50 feet of its target, and loiter there, to be able to get a signal through the water to its target.

"Special weapon armed. Ready to launch."

"Ready for stealth launch."

"EW readied for stealth launch."

"Could it be American?" *Agincourt*'s XO, Singh, wondered out loud.

"The only boats the US Navy has in the Hawaiian OA are north and south of us," Courtenay said. "More likely a Chinese or Russian picket sub, doubling back."

McDonald heard the NSA agent before he saw him, feet thumping down the gangway before he emerged, panting, in the doorway to the control room. "Is it *Taifun*?"

"Don't know yet," Brunelli said.

He dropped his laptop on a foldout table and opened it, plugging in a cable. "Linked to the EW torpedo," he said. "HOLMES online."

"Second signal on HELF-D," the EWO said, excitement in her voice palpable. "Contact confirmed. Holding at 180 and *close*."

"I need a signature confirmation, sonar," Courtenay said.

"The boat that took out my *AE1* was as silent as Christmas night," McDonald told Courtenay. "And as aggressive as a Sydney funnel web spider," he added. "Nothing but *Taifun* could have gotten so close behind you as this mystery contact did, and it would have taken a shot at us by now if it could have. It is probably loading weapons right now, just like we are. Or waiting for orders. Whatever the reason, your attack window is closing, Captain."

"Shut up, damn you!" Courtenay said, his calm demeanor breaking at last. "Sonar?"

The sonarman was sweating again. "Nothing, Captain. Nothing but the bearing from HELF-D."

"The HELF-D pattern," Singh said. "A hit two minutes ago. A hit again now. It's consistent with a bot contacting base for orders. A human captain would have taken the shot already, sir."

Courtenay stared ahead as though he hadn't heard, then. "Unless it *can't*," he said to himself, almost in a whisper. "Unless it's a missile boat that fired all of its weapons off the coast of Hawaii."

"Then it wouldn't be stalking us," Brunelli said. "For whatever reason, the boat behind us got itself into a killing position, but isn't taking the shot."

"Then we have time," Courtenay said. "Sonar, I want *confirmation* our pursuer is *Taifun*."

The Battle of Hawaii: Bellows 'AFB'

BUNNY HAD joined up with Touchdown and the Raptor flight at 20,000 feet for the return trip to Hawaii—which was going to be touch and go for the Raptor pilots after the fuel they'd burned in their long-range engagement with the enemy's fighter patrols.

She'd been high on adrenaline at the successful strike on the Chinese carrier. Until she saw there were only two aircraft in Touchdown's flight.

Herself and Agony.

And though they loitered longer than they should have, Meany didn't rejoin either.

Flowmax gone. Meany too?

Bunny couldn't believe it. No SAR beacon from either. No aircraft locator signals.

Just gone.

It wasn't possible. Meany was indestructible, literally made of metal.

And Flowmax had just come back from the dead. You didn't survive against all odds on one mission only to die on the next.

"Did anyone see Flowmax go in?" Bunny asked over laser comms.

"No, we were emissions dark, not in visual range. What about Meany? You were closest," Touchdown reminded her. "What did *you* see?"

"A bloody great mushroom cloud, like his missile touched off the carrier's weapon stores or fuel or something," Bunny said. "Could he have gotten caught in the blast?"

"Possible," Touchdown said.

"Unlikely," Flatline added. "He shouldn't have been close enough."

"Wait one," Touchdown said. "I'm getting a message from *Lafayette*." Touchdown was flight leader now, with Meany MIA.

And if Meany is dead, she'll be CO, Bunny was thinking. It wasn't a prospect she'd even considered, and she was pretty sure Charlene 'Touchdown' Dubois hadn't either.

"Job for you, O'Hare," Touchdown said, speaking quickly. "INDOPACOM needs a camera pass over a position ahead of the enemy fleet. Record and relay. Squirt your data to *Lafayette*. Sending coordinates."

Bunny copied the message data into her nav computer and checked the screen. She saw why Touchdown gave her the mission instead of taking it herself or giving it to any of the others. The Raptors didn't have the stealth, nor the suite of cameras her Widow had, but more importantly, they didn't have the fuel.

She didn't wait. It was something to shake the numbness that was blanketing her soul. "Breaking left, moving to 60,000 and going dark." She tipped her plane into a banking turn and trimmed it to climb steadily without losing airspeed.

"Bring it, O'Hare," Touchdown said. "We'll see you at Bellows. If we're lucky, the others will be back before us."

BUNNY FELT … naked.

At the edge of the atmosphere, skimming along at 60,000 feet above the Sino-Russian fleet, her controls were sluggish, and she felt as though every ship beneath her was looking up at her.

Which it was. But looking and seeing weren't the same thing.

Ahead and 30,000 feet below, she could see waves of Chinese fighter aircraft in three plane arrowheads. Gyrfalcons, a couple of Wing Loong ISR drones trailing. Quick count, maybe 30 to 40 fighters, an entire carrier's worth. If just one of them got lucky and got a return off her …

Well, she'd probably be greeting Meany and Flowmax in hell soon afterward.

Don't think, she told herself. *Just do.*

She had her Distributed Aperture Cameras slaved to her joystick while her combat AI flew her plane, and she zoomed her belly camera, focusing on the surface of the sea.

Coming at the fleet from an oblique angle, she saw smoke at the rear of the enemy formation—the *Liaoning*, she hoped—but she was too far east to get a closeup high-definition shot. Her target area was directly ahead and underneath, and she panned the camera in wide view first, sliding across open water, then slowing as she picked up a few picket ships—destroyers or cruisers, she guessed. One of them was listing, lifeboats in the water beside it. Victim of a submarine attack, maybe? She panned onward, the camera picking up a big landing ship. It wasn't a flat top, so she guessed it was a Russian *Ivan Gren*: the Chinese landing ships were helicopter docks, like small aircraft carriers. And it appeared to be in the middle of a long, wide turn, from east to west. Bugging out because *Liaoning* was killed? Somehow, she doubted it.

Then … *What the …?*

She panned out. Dozens of tiny beetles, scuttling across the sea, roiling white foam in their wakes. She panned right out so that the analysts who got her feed could do a clean count, but by grouping in bunches of 10, using her thumb for scale, her own quick count came to *50*.

A swarming surface drone attack on Hawaii? It explained the heavy fighter cover overhead.

She zoomed the camera to give her a 5K high-resolution image of one of the beetles. No, not a drone. *Hovercraft*. Not a type she recognized. Big. Triple blowers at the back, with what looked like twin autocannon and maybe a laser mount forward. Defensive weapons, not offensive. China had built these things to survive a contested beach landing. *Wait*. She leaned forward, peering at her screen. Couldn't zoom in any closer, but was pretty sure she saw a six-barrel mortar launcher behind the bridge superstructure. She clicked a button on her flight stick and took a still image. Now that she had a satellite link, she had a few more tools at her disposal.

"Widow, upload and analyze image on screen now. Tell me what type of vessel this is."

Analyzing.

While it worked, she ran the camera across several more of the hovercraft in close-up mode, in case there were any slight differences, but to her untrained eye, they all looked like they came from the same cookie cutter.

And they looked … evil. Like flesh-eating scarabs from a mummy movie, converging on their victim.

She shuddered. Her AI returned with its answer.

Vessel type unknown. Nearest match is Russian Federation Zubr *class hovercraft. Do you want information on the* Zubr *class vessel?*

"Just tell me how fast it can move," Bunny said. "Top speed."

Depending on conditions, the Zubr *hovercraft has a top speed of 60 to 80 knots.*

Whoa. They were booking. "How soon could the first hovercraft reach Kaua'i, Hawaii?"

At current speed, the first hovercraft would reach the west coast of Kaua'i in one hour and 50 minutes.

Bunny hit her radio. She was streaming her video in real time to the satellite overhead, but she might as well tell the world what she was seeing. And thinking.

"*Lafayette*, 68 Aggressor recon flight overhead recon waypoint. I count around 50 high-speed hovercraft, possible *Zubr* class, heading southeast. They appear armed with mortar, cannon and laser weapons." She drew a deep breath. "They have about 40 Gyrfalcons riding shotgun at about 30,000 feet—I can't hang around."

"Good copy, Aggressor. We are downloading your data now."

Bunny zoomed the view out again, so she could see both the trailing edge of the Sino-Russian fleet and the quickly separating force of fighters and hovercraft. Her AI had been mapping every contact it picked up on its optics and plotted it on her tactical screen. She zoomed that out too so that it showed the ships' positions relative to Kaua'i. Then she got back on the radio. "*Lafayette*, I'm not the commander INDOPACOM, but if I was, I'd abort the attack on the Chinese fleet and hit this amphibious landing force in the flank before it gets any closer to Hawaii."

Because I know you don't have enough assets to do both, she didn't say.

BUNNY'S VISION was streaming live on the wall screen in the war room on O'ahu. And Harry Connaught had arrived at the decision point Bunny had just verbalized.

437

"Forty fighters, 50 landing craft, 15,000 assault troops, Sam," Harry said. "Chinese fleet looks to be reversing course. They can still launch cruise missiles, but they're no longer closing on Hawaii. It's nowhere near enough troops to take O'ahu. Why would you commit a fleet that big to a force so small?

"They're not trying to *take* O'ahu," Samuels decided, watching the insect-like hovercraft skim over the sea. "We were wondering why they air- and sea-mined the hell out of O'ahu, Maui and Big Island, but on Kaua'i it seemed they only used HE warheads and went mostly after our anti-ship and air defenses. They're planning to land on Kaua'i."

"Kaua'i?" Connaught asked. "If they land on Kaua'i, that's as far as they'll get. And, all respect to the good people of Kaua'i, there's virtually nothing there."

"That's the point. I think they read *our* Pacific playbook," Samuels said, thinking out loud.

"What do you mean?"

"You know what I mean. You helped write the manual, Harry. 'Distributed Maritime Operations,' 'Littoral Operations in a Contested Environment,' 'Expeditionary Advanced Base Operations,' 'Rapid Maneuver from the Sea' …" Samuels said, quoting the titles of published US INDOPACOM strategy documents. He pointed at the hovercraft on the screen, now in close-up. "China read our war plan, and they're turning it against us."

"Turn Kaua'i into an EAB." Connaught nodded. "Attack where we're weakest, dig in, support their troops by submarine with subsurface logistics and missile attacks, hold on for as long as they can, pull out when it gets too hot."

Samuels nodded. "Except this is China. They won't be pulling those troops out. They might sub-drop some food and ammunition, but they'll leave them there to fight to the last man."

"You have a decision to make, Sam," Connaught said. "The fleet or the landing force." He wasn't ducking it. He was respecting the Army general's role as Joint Operations Commander for Hawaii.

"I know," Samuels said. It wasn't the sort of decision for a committee larger than two. They stepped aside and put their heads together, then Samuels turned back to the war room. He looked up at the screen showing the position of their anti-ship air strike package. The opening wave of SEAD fighters had just left their ingress point. Offensive air patrols were already engaged with the Sino-Russian fleet's defensive fighter patrols. He raised his voice to address the USAF team at its station. "Major, if I give the order to abort your attack and redirect it to target those landing craft, can we do it?"

The USAF JOC officers had been watching the video feed on the wall screen, and had been expecting the question. "Yes sir. *Fallujah*'s fighters can keep the Chinese defensive patrols occupied and threaten their ships. We can scrub and re-task all anti-ship aircraft in the package. But we need to do it …"

"*Now*. I know." He looked at Connaught for a steer and saw only trust looking back. He turned to the Air Force major. "Alright. Do it."

He called the Marine Corps and Army JOC liaisons over. "Arm every attack helicopter we have with anti-ship weapons and fly them to PMRF. Load every available Valor and Defiant helo with troops and materiel and put them down at the airfield at Barking Sands. Update me with numbers. Let me know if anyone or anything gets in your way. We need every air mobile asset we can muster, digging in on Kaua'i, *inside the next hour*."

Connaught watched people spin into action. He put a hand on Samuels's shoulder. "Next call is mine."

"Skylon?" Samuels asked.

"Skylon." Connaught looked across the war room. "Someone get me the president."

THE PILOTS of 68th Aggressor were given no time to mourn the loss of their comrades.

No one was pouring champagne over their heads for carrying out the apparently successful attack on *Liaoning*.

As they entered the landing pattern, they were briefed that all of their planes, both Raptors and Widow, would be refueled and loaded with air-to-air missiles and thrown back into the fight against the amphibious landing force's air escort, which was doing too good a job of protecting its navy.

Bellows AFB was strangely quiet after the mayhem of their last scramble. Bunny looked for Dubois as soon as they landed, sliding out of her cockpit and then suddenly finding herself on her ass in the sand alongside the runway because her legs cramped up after so much time in the cockpit.

When she got them working again, she found Touchdown standing with Flatline and Agony. She guessed they were talking about Flowmax and Meany because the two missing pilots weren't standing there with them.

So they hadn't made it back.

She didn't want to think about it. She certainly didn't want to talk about it.

"Suggestion," she said to Dubois as she walked up to them.

"What?" Touchdown sighed. "The suggestion box is not yet open, O'Hare. We're waiting for word on Flowmax or

Meany. Grab some water, for goodness's sake, and get something to eat, before you fall on your ass again."

"I will," Bunny said. "But before you or anyone signs off on the loadout for my plane, I want you to see if you can get me a growler pod."

Touchdown appeared to think it over. A "growler" pod would give them the ability to blind enemy aircraft and jam missiles. There was a catch, which Flatline pointed out.

"Your Widow can't carry a growler pod internally," he said. "Your stealth profile will go to shit."

"I know," Bunny said. "So my next request is: have them load my plane in beast mode since my stealth profile will go to hell anyway."

"Beast mode," Touchdown repeated. "Beast mode" meant using the Widow's external wing mounts for an additional eight missile launch rails. Or six, if one mount was taken up by a growler pod. It would give Bunny's Widow a formidable load of 20 air-to-air missiles, or over 50 across the entire Aggressor flight. But it meant Bunny's plane would lose most of its stealth advantage.

"Yeah, beast mode. *Plus* the growler pod," O'Hare said.

"Alright, assuming Meany is … I'll see what I can get." Touchdown pointed a finger at her. "But *you* go get some food, and grab something for me."

FOOD.

Major General Reg Samuels was having one of those restless pauses between action, when no new intelligence was coming in and the orders he'd already given were still being executed.

He filled it by walking to a table at the back of the war room stacked with sandwiches and trying to find one without mustard on it. He found one labeled "provolone and lettuce" and bit into it.

Mustard, dammit. He poured himself a glass of juice.

He was a Louisiana native. Hot sauce, yes. Cajun seasoning, definitely. Mustard, no.

A piece of lettuce fell from the sandwich, and Samuels realized his hand was shaking. He put the sandwich down quickly and looked around, hoping nobody saw. He didn't think they had.

Adrenaline, he told himself, *that's all it is.* His mind was racing. Hard to focus. Had he thought of everything? Of course not. What had he missed?

He had every available unit that could walk, crawl, swim or fly headed for Kaua'i.

Would it be enough? It had to be. Their best estimate was China was sending between 6,000 and 10,000 troops at the small island. He had the 500 surviving personnel of PMRF digging in at Barking Sands, because that was the only place on Kaua'i a sizeable amphibious force could land. Army, Navy and Air Force from Lihue, another 500. Two thousand Army and Marines being airlifted in. Three hundred National Guardsmen. Most would arrive before Chinese troops hit the beaches.

A large number would arrive as the Chinese were already coming ashore.

They'd be outnumbered, but he had air cover overhead, and combat air support—a handful of Apaches. The Chinese wouldn't, or shouldn't, have air support at all. He had no artillery on Kaua'i, but he was flying that in too. It wouldn't

442

be there in time to oppose the landing, but if they could just hold the Chinese on their beachhead for a few hours ...

Coast Guard? The cutter at Lihue was an unarmed *Juniper* class tender. He had no idea if it was even still afloat after the cruise missile barrage. He had two *Heritage* class cutters inbound Lihue. Both sailing from Maui since those in O'ahu had either been sunk by slaughterbots or were penned by the Chinese air-dropped sea mines. They'd been underway two hours ... were still four hours out, but they could lend their 57 mm guns to the fight when they got there—or evacuate civilians if it came to that.

Kaua'i had a population of 70,000. Add another 10,000 tourists, stuck over there when the missiles started raining down and all air and sea traffic was halted. How did you evacuate 80,000 people when you needed every available ship or aircraft to fly troops *onto* an island? You didn't want your aircraft waiting on the tarmac loading civilians when they had to be cycling straight back to pick up more troops from O'ahu, that was for sure. He'd done what he could. Civilians and tourists were being evacuated from the west of the island by Kaua'i PD. Pulled back to Lihue port, where they could be lifted out by ship or plane if it came to that.

Then it hit him. What he was overlooking. *Civilians. Tourists.* Eighty thousand of them. Probably half were between 18 and 50. Forty thousand adults. If even 10 percent of them knew how to handle a gun? That was another 4,000 rifles. A citizen militia. Could he *order* civilians to take up arms? Not a chance—not even the governor could do that. Could he ask the police to find volunteers and get them to Barking Sands? Why not?

He put down his sandwich and juice, and called a police liaison officer over to him and told him what he needed. The

443

man asked a couple of questions and then went to find a landline to call Kaua'i PD.

There was a call Samuels could make too. One of the reasons Harry Connaught had picked him to lead the defense of Hawaii: *Reg Samuels knew people.* High and low. Far and wide. Haole and Kanaka Maoli. On Kaua'i, Reg Samuels knew a local community leader called Benny Matsunaga. He was a member of the Hawaiian sovereignty movement, and he was also a good guy. A Baptist minister. Straight talker.

It was a call Samuels would have to make personally. It took a couple of calls to find Matsunaga, but he got him at his church in Lihue, where people were gathering so they could be bused to the port.

"General, good to hear your voice," Matsunaga said. "Is it true what they're saying? The Chinese …"

"It is, Benny," Samuels said. "That's why I'm calling …"

"General, if this call is about that business at the Capitol, I wanted nothing to do with that. I didn't think Freeth was serious. My God. I told my people to stay here, and far as I know …"

"This isn't about the Capitol, Benny. But right now, we need every Hawaiian patriot we can get to help us fight this fight. I am hoping you can gather your people together and get them to the Lihue Police Station."

There was a moment's silence at the other end. "General, I appreciate the situation. I do. But I am a man of God. I can't ask my people to take up arms."

"Not asking them to, Benny," Samuels said. "There's a lot of ways to serve, and most of them don't involve carrying a gun. We need drivers, people who can work earthmoving equipment, nurses, doctors—hell, anyone who can carry

444

water or stretcher. And we need them at Barking Sands. Lihue PD will get them there."

Another silence at the other end of the phone. "I don't know, General …"

Samuels took a chance. "You once taught me a prophecy, Benny, you remember? I do …" Samuels said. "E iho ana o luna, E pi'i ana o lalo …"

That which is above will come down
That which is below will rise up
The islands shall unite
The walls shall stand firm

Samuels knew his pronunciation was terrible, but he hoped he'd gotten the words across. "That prophecy sounds like it was meant for a day like today, if you ask me, sir," Samuels said.

"We … I'll put out the call, General," Matsunaga said. "As many as I can. Lihue Police Station?"

"That's right. Thank you, Benny."

BUNNY FOUND a table with bottled water, fruit and protein bars and started filling her pockets. Then she heard the unmistakable nasal twang of Australian accents. Farther down the flight line, she saw the crew of a four-engined AC-130X sitting on the side of the runway, watching as ground crew busied themselves with fuel and ordnance for the big bird.

She wandered over. "Aussies?" she asked the two pilots nearest, before she saw the flags on their flight suits, so the question was redundant.

445

"Nah, Lieutenant," one man said. "We're just impersonating Australians because it impresses the ladies."

"Not this lady." Bunny smiled. She tried to place his accent. "You're a Territorian."

"Not even close," the pilot said. "West Aussie. I'm Chip; he's Dale." He pointed down the line to two other pilots. "That old guy there is Captain Rory O'Donoghue, commander of the good ship 'Outlaw.' The even older guy lying down is the most ancient Lieutenant in the USAF, but one hell of a pilot—Uncle Robert E. Lee." The two Americans looked over and gave her a tired wave.

They all looked beat. But who wasn't?

"They sending you up again too?" Bunny asked. She could see bomb armorers pushing palletized munitions up the AC-130's loading ramp.

"Not us," Chip said, pointing with his thumb at the other two pilots. "These guys. Soon as their loadmaster says he's done. You too?"

Bunny looked back at her Widow, fuel hoses, electrical cables hanging from it, ground crew bustling around it and armorers standing around waiting for someone to tell them what to load it with. "Looks like it."

"That *your* Widow, Lieutenant?" Chip asked.

"Today it is."

"But you're Australian. In a USAF uniform," Dale said. "With some pretty impressive ink underneath it."

"Amazing powers of observation, for a Sand Groper," Bunny said.

Dale nudged Chip's shoulder. "She's being cagey. There's a story there, Chip me old mate."

"Maybe we'll meet when your next sortie is over, Lieutenant," Chip said to Bunny. "You can tell us that story."

"Which one?" Bunny asked with a wink, and turned to leave, but one of the American pilots stood.

"Wait up. Walk with you, Lieutenant?"

"Uh, sure, Captain," Bunny said as he fell into step beside her.

"You're Aggressor Inc., right?" he asked. "68th AGRS."

There hadn't been time for their official USAF patches to catch up with them, so the Aggressor pilots were wearing generic flight suits. But their aircraft still had the Aggressor Inc. logo stenciled underneath their cockpits.

"Yup."

"I heard you guys put a hole in *Fujian*. A few weeks back?"

"I heard that too," Bunny told him. "But I also heard she's still out there, giving us grief."

"What I was going to tell you," he said, stopping up. "We got her today. She's history."

Bunny looked past him at the battered old AC-130. "*You* did?"

"Yeah. Well, no, not us. The package we were part of. Joint strike with your RAAF. We dropped smoke on her position. Your Panthers brought the harm."

A wave of relief flooded through Bunny's slight frame. She hadn't realized how much the continued existence of that carrier had been weighing on her, until the 70,000-ton weight of it was suddenly lifted.

"That, Captain, is the good news I needed right now," she told him.

He stood looking at her for a moment, searching her face. "You lost someone today," he decided. It wasn't a question.

Bunny nodded. "We did. Not the first. But a good one." There was something in his face too. Like a ghost, or a shadow. It came and went.

447

"Well, I'd better get back," he said. "Good hunting up there." He gave a casual salute and shuffled back toward his plane.

His huge, squat, black plane. Looking just about as tired as its pilots, patches on its wings where it had recently been repaired, paint on its props worn away through hundreds of hours of pulling the plane through rain, sandstorms and humid skies. Parked up among the sleek gray sharks of the 21st century, it was like something from prehistory.

"Good hunting to you too, Captain," Bunny said to his back.

Then she noticed something. A dozen small somethings all happening at once, that spoke to her sixth sense. People running. An ambulance, starting up, accelerating away. Fire crew, running for their vehicle. Airman, up ahead, running up to Touchdown and Flatline. And then all of them spinning around to look at the sky to the south.

What the ...?

Bunny ran, came up behind Touchdown and had to grab her to slow down.

"What is it?" she asked. "What's going on?"

Touchdown didn't look at her, kept her eyes glued on the southern horizon. "Raptor coming in on autopilot," she said. "Pilot isn't responding."

"Flowmax?" Bunny didn't dare hope.

"No transponder," she said. "But radar signature says it's a Raptor."

"Could be National Guard," Flatline said.

The aircraft came into view, bobbing and yawing as it lined up on the runway a long way out.

"No, that's a shit approach," Bunny said. "It's Flowmax."

"Could be a dead man on the stick," Flatline said glumly. "Seen it before."

Bunny felt like slugging him on the jaw.

FLOWMAX'S last-generation Raptor was still an amazing feat of engineering.

A Chinese missile had chewed off half of his port horizontal stabilizer and put him nose down for the sea. Trying and failing to get control, in desperation he'd engaged the aircraft's autopilot and, by some feat of fly-by-wire magic, it had managed to level out.

Then an engine flamed out, and Flowmax shut it down. The autopilot compensated for the lack of thrust, and kept the aircraft flying. Flowmax checked for damage to other systems and saw his comms were down too. But he was getting a GPS signal, and he laid in navigation waypoints for Bellows.

As he entered O'ahu airspace, Flowmax saw emergency vehicles lined up beside the runway. He checked the sky around was clear, no one else making an approach, and began his final into Bellows.

He lowered the gear, one hand on his ejection handle in case the drag caused the autopilot to lose control, but the wheels came down and locked.

The fact he was about to make an autopilot landing on bitumen that was more like a country road than an Air Force runway was something he was trying very, very hard not to think about.

"AWAY FROM THE RUNWAY, move back you people!" a Marine emergency responder was yelling from the window of his vehicle. "Get a hundred yards back!"

The Aggressor pilots backed away, but didn't take their eyes from the sky. Bunny saw the Raptor closing, a couple of miles out now, 500 feet in the air and sliding down the glidepath.

"Actually, that's a textbook approach," Flatline said when they'd reached a safe distance. "Autopilot landing."

"Doesn't mean he's injured," Bunny insisted. "Damn you, Flatline."

"Easy you two," Touchdown said quietly. "You believe in a higher power, you should both be praying right now."

Bunny saw Touchdown's lips moving. Praying, like she said.

The Raptor floated in slowly, that optical illusion you get when an aircraft is coming straight toward you even though it is traveling at a couple hundred knots.

Then it flared for landing.

The rear wheels hit, bumped, hopped on the uneven bitumen, and the Raptor thumped down heavily, nose wheel slamming onto the runway ...

FLOWMAX WAS LIFTED out of his cockpit by a couple of Navy corpsmen and put on a gurney even though he was protesting he was fine. Looking at his shredded tail section, the still smoking port engine and other damage to the airframe, they wouldn't believe he hadn't been injured either.

But their way from the aircraft to their ambulance was blocked by five feet eight of platinum-haired, tattooed fury.

Bunny moved aside, but then stepped in again, forcing the gurney to stop. Raising a fist above her head, she brought it down on Flowmax's midsection with all her might, forcing the wind out of him.

"Don't you ever, ever bloody do that to me again. You hear me?!" she said.

He couldn't reply, and after sending him a glare that could have peeled paint, she stormed off.

Flowmax got his wind back as the gurney was lifted into the ambulance.

He folded his hands across his chest and smiled. "Yeah, she cares," he said.

ONLY A HALF MILE away and unaware of the drama outside, Carliotti closed the connection to Admiral Connaught and leaned back in her chair. She was still in the underground bunker at Bellows Field, alone in the video conferencing room, with Kitchen on the door outside, waiting to hear where she wanted to go next. Probably fearing she was going to say "Honolulu." It was past time for her to leave Hawaii.

She reflected on the call with Connaught.

So China had one more surprise up its sleeve, and suddenly they were facing *two* threats: the ships and aircraft of the fleet, and the amphibious landing force headed for Kaua'i. Now headed in two different directions.

She'd asked Connaught if they could afford to let the Chinese ships escape, focus everything on preventing the amphibious landing. After all, they'd destroyed two of the three Chinese carriers in the day's action already.

451

"Those ships, aircraft and troops could be headed for Guam next, Madam President," Connaught had said. "Or our positions in the South China Sea. We need to do whatever we can to hit them as hard as we can, here and now."

So she'd agreed to his request. Provided him with codes she had hoped never, ever to use.

Was it a decision motivated by simple righteous anger? She'd vowed to serve the revenge for China's bioweapon attack hot. No, it was not revenge. That would still come. This was simple cause and effect. Would China realize that?

That thought was for another time. The battle was far from over. Connaught had told her their anti-ship strike was about to engage the amphibious landing force. Confidence was high.

But so was the number of enemy landing ships.

ALESSA BARUZZI didn't believe the whole "revenge was a dish best served cold" thing. She was very much a "serve it boiling hot" kind of girl.

She'd lost one Hawkei crew in their first engagement. Each launch vehicle had a crew of two: a driver and a loader. The vehicle was quickly replaced. The men in it could never be. One had a family.

She didn't lose anyone in the follow-up cruise missile strike.

Or the third.

In between waves, Kennedy had been out, painting missile silhouettes on the side of their command truck. They had 15 confirmed kills.

But Lihue hadn't escaped unhurt. They'd done a reasonable job protecting the airport, but missiles aimed at the town itself, especially the northern side of town, were often too far or too many, and several had gotten through.

Then things had gone quiet—for Baruzzi's MML battery, at least. Her radar was only really effective at picking up non-stealth targets, not high-flying stealth aircraft. But there were still some Iron Dome mobile low-frequency radar units alive on both sides of the island, and every now and then one of them would send a missile skyward after a Chinese fighter.

The reports on the radio said things on O'ahu were anything but quiet though. Slaughterbots still roamed the countryside, even though a new swarming microdrone system deployed against them appeared to be working. The last Chinese cruise missile strikes had strewn tens of thousands of proximity mines across Pearl Harbor-Hickam, Honolulu and military bases and airfields across the island.

And the US President ... They almost couldn't believe their eyes when they were told to tune into local TV for a broadcast.

"My fellow Americans," she started. "I am here today on Hawaii ..."

"The hell you are ..." Kennedy said. He hadn't voted for her. "That's some kind of fake background."

Baruzzi *had* voted for Carliotti, and the background didn't look fake to her. It looked a lot like the training range at MCBH she'd visited a half dozen times. "Quiet," Baruzzi said.

Carliotti continued:

I want to talk to you plainly about what is happening here on Hawaii and across the Pacific as we speak.

In the simplest terms, what is happening is this: We are defending the democracies of the world, and our own nation, against the unbridled aggression of a global authoritarian alliance.

453

Several weeks ago, I spoke about the threat to world peace from Communist China and I asked you: what is the best time to meet that threat, and how is the best way to meet it?

I said then, as now, the best time to meet any threat is in the beginning. That is what we were prepared to do in defending Taiwan against Chinese aggression. We were trying to avoid a world war. We hoped China would do the same. Instead it was preparing to unleash one.

China wants the Communist Chinese flag to fly from the rooftops of Beijing to the palm trees of Hawaii.

This plan of conquest is in flat contradiction to what we believe. We believe Korea belongs to the Koreans, Taiwan to the Taiwanese, Japan to the Japanese; we believe that all the nations of the Pacific should be free to work out their affairs in their own way. This has been the basis of peace in the Pacific for nearly a hundred years.

To help realize its aims, China has unleashed a pestilence upon the world that it hopes will decimate the democracy-loving populations of the globe. It will not. Our best scientists are already working on a vaccine against the Chinese virus, and the measures we are taking to restrict gatherings and non-essential travel across the nation will protect us until that vaccine is available.

It is essential for your safety, your family's safety, and for the future of our nation at this time that you respect these restrictions. Anyone who does not do so is not only committing a crime but acting to undermine our war effort as well.

China, with Russia, North Korea and Iran at its side, has unleashed its aggression, showing beyond doubt the scope of its intentions—in space, against our bases across the Pacific and against the brave people of Hawaii.

We now have one simple goal: to defeat this unholy alliance and restore peace. We are united in this endeavor with all the nations of the North Atlantic Treaty Organization, NATO, who today voted to invoke NATO Article 5 and to mobilize their armed forces in the defense of America in the Pacific. Our NATO allies are joined by our Coalition allies across the Pacific—from Japan and South Korea to the Philippines, India, New Zealand and Australia. Free nations uniting their strength to ours in an effort to return the world to peace.

You will be concerned about the threat of global nuclear war. It is right to be. I remind China and Russia's leaders that NATO has the largest nuclear arsenal on the planet and the capability to deploy it at any time. But we will not be the first to use nuclear weapons in this conflict. Let us be clear minded. There is no such thing as a limited nuclear conflict or a winnable nuclear war. That way lies Armageddon, and we will not be the ones to lead humanity there.

The struggle of the Coalition of Democratic Nations in the Pacific is a struggle for peace. Peace here on Hawaii, peace across the entire Pacific.

May God bless you, our brave armed forces and the people of Hawaii, and may God bless our United States of America

As Carliotti finished speaking, three jets crossed the sky in the background and the sound of a helo lifting off threatened to drown out her last words.

"OK, alright, maybe she *is* on Hawaii," Kennedy allowed. "Because the production values at the end there sucked."

"Give the lady *some* credit," Baruzzi said.

"The internet says the government is hiding under a mountain somewhere," Kennedy remarked. "Safe from the nukes and the virus while people back home are waiting to get nuked. I heard there's a 20-mile line at the border to Canada. People headed for Alaska."

"That's dumb," Kernow said. "That's *closer* to Russia."

"Yeah, but viruses don't like the cold," Kennedy pointed out.

"No one is nuking anyone," Baruzzi said, hoping she was right. "China could have nuked Hawaii, but it didn't. Chinese don't have a death wish any more than anyone else."

455

The radio broke in on their conversation. "Fifth Battalion Air Defense Battery, Unulau, from Lihue Tower, you read?"

Kernow answered. "Lihue Tower, 5th Battalion Unulau."

"Unulau, we have Army air cavalry and Marine air inbound Lihue Airport from the east. You're going to see a lot of traffic. Didn't want you to be surprised and shoot our own guys down."

"Well thank you kindly for the vote of confidence, Lihue Tower," Kernow replied.

Baruzzi gestured for the handset and Kernow handed it to her. "Lihue Tower, how much traffic, and why?"

"Uh, Unulau, we've been told to expect every helo on O'ahu and Big Island to be shuttling in and out to PMRF Barking Sands over the next hour."

"*Every* helo?"

"Every damn helo. As for why, you want to check with your battalion commander, and if you find out, let *us* know? We just direct traffic; no one tells us anything. Lihue Tower out."

That was a call Baruzzi wanted to take in private. "Give me a minute," she told Kernow and Kennedy. She knew the minute she stepped out of the control module Kennedy and Kernow would be on a cell phone to their buddies trying to find out what was going down. But she didn't mind. Between the three of them, they might get to the truth.

When Baruzzi returned to the truck, Kennedy opened his mouth to talk, but Baruzzi signaled with a hand gesture for him to shut it. "Lock everything down," she said. "Battery is moving out."

Kennedy sprang into action; Kernow was a little slower. "What's happening, Lieutenant?"

456

"We're moving to the west coast," she said, packing her station down. "PMRF Barking Sands."

"What ...? Who's protecting the airport?" Kernow asked.

"Not our problem, soldier," Baruzzi told him. "You should be more worried about the brigade of Chinese marines I was just told are planning to pay Kaua'i a visit."

IT WAS NEARLY an hour before Outlaw got loaded up and took off, but they were still quicker than their new friends from Aggressor Inc.

Alright, they'd had a head start.

Rory's orders were simple. Take off, proceed southwest, contact USS *Lafayette* for tasking.

Rory was on the stick, Uncle on the radio. In back they had a loadmaster and six person crew. And two pallets of munitions. Each pallet contained 60 parachute-deployed cannisters containing 20 LOCUST self-guiding drones, so each pallet could generate a swarm of 1,200 drones.

They were about to unleash two swarms, 2,400 drones, into the path of the Chinese hovercraft. Each LOCUST was armed with the equivalent of a 40 mm grenade wrapped in fragmenting depleted uranium, capable of shredding 20 mm thick rolled armor plate.

Rory didn't like to think what they would do to anyone caught out on the deck of the hovercraft they were attacking, but then, he didn't even know if hovercraft had decks. He'd never seen a '*Yak*' class landing craft in his life, even in exercises. He'd been told they were fast, low to the water, highly maneuverable and armed with close-in weapon systems—autocannon and laser—designed specifically to deal with anti-ship missiles.

They might also be armed with short-range anti-air missiles, so Outlaw was warned to just shoot and scoot. Get out in front of the incoming waves of hovercraft as soon as Air Force cleared the skies for them, drop their load and run like hell.

Luckily, they didn't need to pull up to 30,000 feet to drop the LOCUST pallets. Just 10,000.

Which was about 9,000 feet more than Rory liked.

TOUCHDOWN DUBOIS needed more time. Time to get her head into this mission. Time to understand how to approach it so that she could get the job done and keep her people alive.

Time to get her head around the fact Meany was gone.

He'd been more than her CO. At Aggressor Inc., he was her mentor, helping her understand the world of corporate warfare as well as she understood the military. Which she hadn't, coming in as an experienced pilot, blown away by her new fat salary.

What role did their majority shareholder, billionaire Aaron Aaronson, play? As one of his senior operations executives, what should she expect of him and what could he expect of her? What about the board of directors? Minority shareholders? The media? Life had been so much simpler in the Air Force, but then the mental bandwidth she'd needed had been limited to what was required to be a damn good pilot, then flight leader, then operations planner.

Every time she got lost down a corporate rabbit hole, Meany had been there to pull her out. And he just understood stuff. Stuff he'd learned along the way that only he knew, and because he did, she didn't have to.

Like what do you do when the USAF points to the clause in your contract that says it has the right to recall all the aircraft you're leasing? How do you manage the contracts of USAF and Navy Reserve pilots who are called back to active duty but still employees of Aggressor Inc.? What allowances do they lose, what do they get? Who pays what?

Aggressor Inc. was stood up as 68th AGRS, then deactivated, then re-activated as 68th AGRS again on Hawaii. Did they have a choice? Where was that paperwork? Who signed off on it? Did she? Did Aaronson? Who defended their pilots when Air Force threw them at one target after another, mission after mission, until their ears were bleeding and hands shaking. Who had their backs?

Meany.

And who did all the paperwork for the pilots they lost? Who took care of their entitlements, their bodies if they were recovered, their families?

It was Meany, always Meany.

Except now it wasn't.

She'd made the call to Aaronson to tell him about Meany as soon as Flowmax made it back and it was clear Meany wasn't going to.

He'd been shocked to silence. "Is there any chance …?" he'd asked. "No one saw him go in, correct?"

"He went down over open sea, no emergency locator transmission, no search-and-rescue beacon. There are no resources for a search, no friendly ships anywhere out there, sir," Touchdown said.

"He's MIA," Aaronson insisted, surprising Touchdown with the passion of the statement. "Not KIA, until it's confirmed."

"Yes sir."

"O'Hare made it back, Flatline was rescued, Flowmax …
twice," Aaronson pointed out. "There's always hope."

She didn't comment on that one. She just wasn't feeling it.

"Dubois—Charlene—Air Force will decide who it puts in
charge of 68th AGRS, but they'll probably ask me, if just as a
courtesy. They did when the 68th was stood up, so I expect
they'll ask again now. I'll be recommending you."

"Can we see who's still standing at the end of today, sir?"
Touchdown asked. "We're going up again in less than an
hour."

She didn't expect his reaction.

"Lesson one, Dubois," he said. "The world doesn't wait
for you to be ready for it. You are, or you aren't. I suggest
you get your head around that."

She wasn't ready. Not even close. Look at her, about to
lead her flight into combat and thinking about whether to
accept a battlefield commission with her CO not dead more
than a few hours? Who does that?

Head in the game, Dubois.

She checked her tactical display. They'd taken off from
Bellows, Raptors out front, O'Hare trailing in the Widow, and
headed due west over Maui to gain altitude before they
turned back to take on the Chinese fighters pushing in toward
Kaua'i.

The strike force that was supposed to hit the Sino-Russian
fleet from the south had swung northeast and hit the
amphibious force and its escort from the rear.

First the air-to-air elements had engaged, firing their
missiles at the Chinese Gyrfalcons from maximum range to
pull them off-task, peel them away from the hovercraft they

460

were escorting. A furious exchange of hide-and-seek followed, stealth fighter against stealth fighter, trading missiles across distances of 30 to 40 miles. The USAF force, predominantly Widows, was trying to keep separation from the nimble Chinese fighters, pulling them farther and farther away.

Their few B-2s and B-21s, with a backbone of B1-B 'Bones' from the 419th Flight Test Squadron, then went to work, each one sending dozens of LRASM anti-ship missiles in pursuit of the hovercraft. But the Long-Range Anti-Ship Missile was optimized for large warships, not the skidding, skating hovercraft that could change direction on a dime. They were low-profile, fast boats designed by China specifically to be hard to detect and able to defend themselves against anti-ship missiles fired at them from sea, air and land.

Many of the big supersonic LRASMs found and homed on Chinese targets. But many more were decoyed away with loitering radar and infrared decoys, blasted out of the sky by autocannon, or burned and blinded by laser defenses.

Ship-hunting Widows went in at sea level underneath the furball of air combat, launching a mix of both LRASM and slower, ironically better-suited, Harpoon missiles. The Harpoons had an easier time finding and following their small targets, but the hovercrafts' defenses had an easier time knocking the Harpoons down.

When the attack was done and the primary strike force disengaged, 32 Chinese *Yak* landing craft, carrying 9,600 troops, were still powering toward Kaua'i. Covered by a distressingly high number of Gyrfalcons.

"LAFAYETTE, 68TH AGGRESSOR Emerald Flight Leader: three Raptors, one Widow, loaded for air-to-air,

461

available for CAP tasking," Dubois announced as they leveled out at 20,000 feet and began a slow turn toward the conflict front from behind Maui. Flowmax had been scratched from flight duties, even though he tried to insist. So it was just herself, Flatline and Agony out front, Bunny riding shotgun 2 miles back and 10,000 feet higher.

There had been no time for mission planning or briefing; that would be given to them on the fly. Literally.

"Emerald, *Lafayette*, lead enemy surface elements still advancing under air cover, now 25 miles from Kaua'i."

Dubois checked the data being fed to her by both the satellite overhead and *Lafayette*, consolidated with the radar returns of the dozens of US fighters actively engaged. "Ah, *Lafayette*, this is Emerald. I can still see our strike force *withdrawing* and around 20 Chinese aircraft still pushing in ..."

"Emerald, the situation is the aircraft in the strike package are now Winchester, returning to O'ahu. Army and Marines are ferrying troops onto Kaua'i by chopper and fast boat. We need you to intercept those Chinese fighters and regain air superiority to allow a follow-up attack on the Chinese landing force."

"Good copy, *Lafayette*. Emerald moving to intercept. Uh, *Lafayette*, how many Chinese landing craft are still inbound?"

"Emerald, that would be ... uh, our estimate is 30 approximately."

Thirty? Touchdown's gut fell through the floor as she did the math. Twenty nautical miles, at the speed those hovercraft were doing—that meant ... 20 minutes until about 9,000 Chinese troops hit the beach.

And Aggressor Inc. was about to fly into a fight against odds of nearly five to one.

No one told you life was meant to be easy, Charlene. Usually she'd be waiting for Meany to give them tactical instructions for the coming engagement, but that would not happen. It was on her now. An image of the battlesphere formed in her mind.

"Emerald pilots, flanking attack," she said. "Emissions dark everyone. Emerald Two, left flank, 12 miles south, sea level. Emerald Three, you and I, sea level 10 miles north. Emerald Four, you are bait ..."

Emerald Four was Bunny. "Nicest thing you ever called me," she said dryly.

"Meant in the nicest way," Touchdown said. "See what you can pick up and engage at maximum range. Pull them to you; we'll ambush."

TOUCHDOWN'S ESTIMATE of the odds facing Aggressor Inc. was correct, based on the information she had. She just couldn't know China hadn't brought all its aircraft to the party yet.

Under camouflage aboard every *Yak* hovercraft, forward of its navigation radar, was a small uncrewed helo—ingloriously named the AR500CJ 'Ju,' or Jay, a play on its technical designation. It was lightweight, designed especially for use on small vessels, but could fly at speeds up to 170 kilometers an hour, or 90 knots. It also packed a punch, with each Jay armed with eight compact Hongjian Red Arrow missiles, the Chinese equivalent of the US Hellfire—the same missiles deployed to terrifying effect on China's slaughterbot drones.

As the US anti-ship strike aircraft pulled away, the crews of the remaining *Yak* hovercraft pulled the covers off their Ju helicopters, fixed their rotors into place and started their engines. In minutes, the first of 50 Jays were speeding low across the water ahead of the landing craft that launched them.

Not long after that, their pilots aboard the *Yak* hovercraft saw the golden beaches of Barking Sands come into view. Beyond them, smoke was rising from earlier cruise missile strikes on radar and air defense targets.

They also saw a lot of activity: helos landing, vehicles in long lines along the coast road leading back to Lihue Airport, columns of troops working along the beach to dig themselves in on a stretch of unprepared coast US forces had never expected they'd have to defend.

The Jays fanned out, their skids 50 feet above the sea, as their operators began picking out targets.

AS THE WAVE of attack helos approached the western coast of Kaua'i, Bunny was circling over Lihue Airport at 30,000 feet engaged in a deadly long-range game of tag with the Chinese Gyrfalcons 12 miles out and 6 miles ahead of their landing craft. She'd already emptied her wing pylons of AIM-260 missiles and jettisoned the weapon mounts.

She was having no trouble picking up the Chinese stealth fighters at what was just beyond visual range, but they weren't interested in pushing closer in because a couple of them had tried before Bunny arrived overhead and a US Army Hawkei-mounted MML unit had knocked one of them from the sky.

A hard lesson for China that the SEAD attack on PMRF earlier in the day hadn't been entirely successful.

Seeing wasn't killing though. Bunny fired six missiles and claimed only one of the nimble Gyrfalcons.

The Gyrfalcons could see Bunny too, of that there was no doubt. They'd fired several missiles at her but she'd successfully evaded them with a combination of jamming by her growler pod and deft use of active decoys.

Pretty soon they'd have no choice but to come closer though, since the landing craft they were protecting were rapidly closing on the Kaua'i coast. Bunny was painfully aware that until Aggressor dealt with the Chinese fighters, whatever follow-up attack was planned for the landing craft was being held back.

"Emerald Leader, Emerald Four. Gyrfalcons aren't playing ball. Recommend I move up and stir the hornet's nest for you."

Touchdown had just reached the same conclusion as O'Hare. "Roger that. Emerald pilots, prepare to engage," Touchdown said, breaking radio silence for the first time.

Time like this, Bunny would have loved to have a couple of Valkyries on her wing she could send in ahead of her. But they'd all been allocated to the fleet strike, and you did what you could with what you had, right?

She brought her nose around west and lit her tail, clawing for the sky. She already had intermittent lock on three Gyrfalcons, and as she climbed and pushed west, the intermittent lock became solid and she launched.

From her payload bay, three of her remaining 14 missiles were ejected and boosted ahead of her. Her growler pod was already blasting jamming energy down the bearing to their targets as she closed.

Ten miles, 35,000 feet … eight … 40,000…

More targets. She sent four more missiles downrange.

Then Touchdown sprang her trap. From north and south of the Chinese fighters, Bunny saw missiles converge. The

Chinese escorts scattered like a flock of antelope from a pride of lions.

And ... what the hell?

New contacts, 40,000 feet below her, moving in from the sea. Not landing craft ...

Helos!

"Lafayette, Emerald Four, I'm seeing multiple rotary winged aircraft on DAS, moving east toward Barking Sands. You better warn them they have incoming."

She checked the furball out ahead of her. The Raptors had attacked the escorting Gyrfalcons from down low, unseen. They'd already knocked down three and were still engaged.

She was torn, but the Chinese escort force was in disarray. Touchdown confirmed as much seconds later. *"Lafayette* from Emerald Leader, Chinese escorts are bugging out, heading west for their carrier. Emerald is pursuing. You can send that follow-up strike, *Lafayette."*

Alright. Bunny rolled her plane on its back and pointed it at the sea below, bringing her nose around to face the incoming helos, locking up the nearest four.

"Fox three!"

ALESSA BARUZZI had been stationed on Kaua'i long enough to know the shortest distance between two points on the island wasn't always a straight line. Lihue City to Barking Sands via Highway 50 south was a 50-minute drive on a good day, and this was not a good day.

The road was already choked with military traffic, crawling along at 30 miles an hour.

Her battalion commander had told her to get her Hawkei MMLs, and the Medium Tactical Vehicle that carried their reloads, to PMRF "pronto." He hadn't told her how to get there, or where to set up. There were four presighted MML positions along the coast at Barking Sands, and Baruzzi made an executive decision about which one to aim for, halfway along the highway. She radioed the driver of her lead vehicle.

"Hennessy, Kekaha Lookout turnoff is coming up on your right. I want you to turn off there and make speed through State Canyon Park to the Makaha Ridge road. I'll tell you when you're getting close."

"Yes ma'am," the driver replied. "Right at Kekaha turnoff to Makaha Ridge."

Makaha Ridge, with its sweeping views up and down the coast, was where the main radar dishes for PMRF were sited. *Had been* sited. Baruzzi knew Chinese cruise missiles had hit the site hard. But there was no quicker way for her to get to a defensive position overlooking PMRF and probably no better site for her battery.

Baruzzi had taken the "Multi" in MML literally as she loaded her vehicles for the scramble to the west coast. A Multi-Mission Launcher was designed to fire air, sea and land attack missiles of different types—from AIM-9X and AIM-120 anti-air missiles to Hellfire anti-tank and Naval Strike anti-ship missiles. With a Chinese amphibious landing force inbound, Baruzzi had loaded up with anti-air and anti-ship interceptors.

She got on the radio to PMRF as they climbed up through the national park toward Makaha Ridge to get an idea of what they would find at the site when they got there.

"What they say?" Kernow asked when she pulled her earpiece from her ear.

"Rubble, that's what," Baruzzi said, staring straight ahead. "We won't get any help to unload and set up. It was evacuated after the last Chinese strike."

What she didn't say ... most of the personnel at the radar facility had been killed, caught in unprotected buildings when the first Chinese SEAD attack hit.

THEY SAW the smoke before they even reached the gates to the Navy facility: thin, white, wispy trails leading up from destroyed golf ball domes just past the front gates. They followed the ridge road around and toward the cliffs overlooking the sea. Another enormous dome, down to the left, blackened concrete, melted metal. At the end of the road by a turnaround, a smaller dome, flattened. Buildings next to it just smoking shells.

Baruzzi set about siting her Hawkeis, directing vehicles into prepared defilades. She put her radar and command vehicle out in the open by the turning circle. Three-hundred-sixty-degree view with no occlusions, quick exit to the cover of damaged buildings if they had to scram.

Up the coast to her right, red cliffs plunging down to the dark blue sea. To her left, the long sandy beach of Barking Sands with the runway at the far end.

Usually empty. Right now, an ants' nest of activity. Helos dropping in and lifting off like aerial trains pulling in and out of a station. Lines of troops dismounting from trucks, with more trucks backed up all the way past the runway and around the headland. A traffic jam she would have been caught in if she hadn't turned off.

She found a relatively protected site inside the brick walls of a burned outbuilding for their ammo truck. Hard to hit, and the walls would contain any secondary explosions. Maybe. Best she could do.

High overhead, they saw contrails as an Air Force fighter sent its missiles toward the horizon.

"So we know where the bad guys are," Kennedy observed, hands on hips, staring at the sky.

"Let's get synced up and see what we can see," Baruzzi said.

They linked to a satellite overhead—something she had once taken for granted—and started pulling data on Chinese aircraft and ship positions from the battlenet.

None were in range. Yet. But she saw Chinese landing hovercraft on the plot, and they were closing. She called in to her Battalion HQ to advise she was in position on the headland. They'd traveled with a mix of AIM-9X and Naval Strike missiles loaded. But the Chinese landing craft were still 20 minutes out, at least. She looked at the tactical plot again and made a snap decision.

"Pods Two and Four, get back to the ammo truck. Switch out your Naval Strike missiles for 9Xs."

They were still swapping out their missiles when they were put on alert.

While we're two pods down. Of course. "Enemy helos incoming," Baruzzi said, grabbing the comms link. "9X missiles up. Targets are attack helos, southwest, low."

"Scanning. Got nothing," Kernow said, voice tight. "Just sea clutter."

Baruzzi swung out of the door of the Hawkei with binos and scanned the horizon.

Her eye was caught by the same aircraft that had sent missiles down range earlier. It was diving now, firing at the sea! She followed the missiles down, saw the flashes of warheads exploding. Focused her binos.

There! A line of tiny bobbing dots.

"Targets. One nine four degrees, altitude 200, range ... uh ... 5,500 yards."

"Got them," Kernow said. Now he knew exactly where to focus his search. "Targets locked."

"Pods One and Three humming," Kennedy said.

"Fire at will," Baruzzi said, pulling herself back inside the Hawkei and slamming the door. From left and right of them, missile after missile punched out of their launchers and nosed *down*, accelerating away toward the water.

As soon as the roar of the last missile died away, Baruzzi got on her radio. "Two and Four, get into launch position with whatever you already have loaded! One and Three, reload, reload, reload."

BUNNY SAW HER MISSILES hit home and began pulling her plane out of its dive, when off to her left she saw a fanlike spray of missiles seemingly blast out of a cliff face overlooking PMRF and scream toward *her*. She grabbed her flight stick.

No, not you, the helos below.

She pulled back on her stick, clawing for the sky again, double-checked that her Identify Friend Foe beacon was transmitting. Getting swatted from the sky by her own side's missiles wouldn't be a great way to die today. She saw the air defense missiles hit home. Eight, maybe 10 explosions. Chinese helo debris spraying the sea, throwing up foam.

Get some, Army! Bunny thought.

Throwing her plane onto a wingtip, she brought her nose around again, locked up another two helos.

"Fox three!"

BARUZZI WAS OUT of her Hawkei again, as though her burning gaze alone could hurry her Hawkei launch vehicles back into firing positions.

"Six targets locked," Kernow said from inside the vehicle. "Waiting for ready signal."

Baruzzi saw a big delta-winged fighter plane out to sea, ominously closer now, spin on a wingtip like a child's top and send a volley of missiles to the south. More explosions.

"Get some, Air Force!" she said, unable to stay quiet.

"Two of those were my targets," Kernow said, like a surly child. "Retargeting."

"Missiles up, Pods Two and Four ready for launch," Kennedy said. "Launching."

TEN THOUSAND FEET over the sea, 6 miles south of Barking Sands, Rory and Outlaw were setting up for their drop.

"If the sky ahead of us is clear, what are those?" Uncle said, pointing at the horizon.

"Not party flares," Rory said. "Look like missile contrails."

A ripple of bright explosions lit the sky over the water.

"Chinese boats got to the beach already?" Uncle speculated. "Maybe we need to rethink this run."

"*Lafayette*, this is Honeybear," Rory said, wincing at their call sign. "Beginning ingress, but we see air-to-air activity ahead."

"Honeybear, *Lafayette*. Enemy has deployed attack helos targeting our ground positions. Maintain your ingress. No change to mission orders."

"Good copy, *Lafayette*, proceeding with LOCUST drop."

"Oh hell," Uncle said. "And those helos aren't carrying air-to-air missiles? They know that?"

"Ah, come on," Rory said. "Not the first time you've had to fly through a hot target area. You have the stick. I'm going aft for the drop."

"Copilot has the stick," Uncle confirmed as Rory stood. He looked out his side window panel. "I guess I could jump from this height. Water looks warm."

THE FIRST of the Chinese Jays reached the surf offshore of Barking Sands. As Stinger missiles reached out toward them from troops dug into the sand, Hongjian missiles came the other way, kicking up huge gouts of sand up and down the six-mile-long stretch of coast.

Several helos staggered and fell to Stingers.

Others turned south, skimming at treetop height along the coast, attracted by the convoy of vehicles crawling along Highway 50.

It was the definition of a "target-rich environment," and in moments, dozens of vehicles were ablaze, troops were jumping from inside the flames and rolling on the ground, and more Stinger missiles followed the Jays out to sea to the south, dropping several.

Then the next wave swept in.

472

BUNNY HAD NO MORE safe targets. It wasn't that she couldn't pick out the fast-moving helos from the ground clutter with her radar. She could. But if she fired while they were over land, she risked her missile missing and striking the troops below.

She pulled up and began circling, looking with frustration for something to hit. She checked her fuel state and ordnance. Fuel, no problem. Missiles …

One remaining.

Just as well she had nothing to shoot at. Or did she …?

She'd completely forgotten her growler pod. She'd seen that the Chinese helos were uncrewed, just plain panels where a cockpit should be. Her growler pod was doing its job automatically, preparing to jam any enemy radar or missile signature, but it could do more than that

She pulled up the EW menu, set her pod to search for and jam drone satellite control links, then set a course for the beach and took her plane up to 10,000.

There was nothing sexy about it; she just had to get within 2 miles of the Chinese drones and let her pod do the rest. The golden sands were off her left shoulder, blue sea to the right.

Bloody big aircraft right ahead!

"Collision warning, pull up! Collision warning, pull up!" an automated voice began calling out.

Recognizing the midnight black AC-130X, she hauled back on her stick and blasted right over the top of it.

She wiped her face.

She should have seen it on her radar plot. It was right there, big boxed ID blinking at her in warning. She realized with dismay that fatigue might well be her biggest enemy right now.

"WHAT THE HELL, wake up you dozy bastard!" Uncle shouted.

A moment later, Outlaw rocked violently as a jet engine roared by, sounding like it was right on top of them. Rory had luckily been holding onto the netting of a pallet and rode the turbulence until Uncle had Outlaw flying straight and level again.

Rory touched his throat mic. "What was *that*?"

"Air Force Widow pilot asleep at the stick," Uncle muttered. "We'll probably both need to change our underwear when we get back down."

Uncle might have been angry, but he was looking out the right side of the cockpit as he flew, and what he saw a mile inland was … bloody mayhem. Ground-to-air missiles shooting into the sky, Chinese helos raining fire on US positions. That fighter pilot had a lapse of concentration? Who wouldn't?

A heads-up display bolted onto the instrument panel in a recent upgrade, along with the combat AI that did Rory's job when he wasn't in the cockpit, showed a pulsing line leading from their plane to the drop zone, where X marked the spot.

"Coming up to release point," Uncle said. "Dropping the ramp." He reached forward and pulled a lever.

Then a light began flashing on his instrument panel and his eyes locked on Outlaw's simple radar warning receiver. It showed an enemy radar locked onto their plane. Still distant, but steady.

He reached forward and changed the radio to the joint operations frequency. "This is AC-130X Honeybear to US aircraft over Barking Sands. We are being painted by enemy air-to-air radar. Need an assist."

"Honeybear, this is Emerald Four. I *thought* that was you who tried to ram me, Outlaw," a voice said.

Uncle's blood pressure started to peak. "Who tried to ram who?" Uncle asked. "You in a position to help, Emerald?"

"Got your back, Outlaw," the voice said. "Engaging your threat."

BUNNY TURNED north and saw Outlaw's stalker on her passive sensors. A Gyrfalcon had given Touchdown's Raptors the slip and made its way back to Kaua'i, looking for prey, radar pulsing. It was still 20 miles out, but that meant it was within PL-15 missile range of the lumbering AC-130X. It probably would have fired already, if it thought it had been spotted.

Or it was looking for a juicier target.

Bunny decided to make herself one. She shoved her throttles forward, lifted her nose to the sky, shut down her growler pod and lit her radio. In case the enemy pilot was blind and deaf, she also popped the Luneburg lenses along her spine that turned her radar cross section from a bumblebee to something like a commercial airliner.

She could see Touchdown, Flatline and Agony on her tactical screen, now nearly 30 miles out, in pursuit of the other Chinese fighters. In no position to help.

Seconds later, her radar warning receiver began chirping as the enemy fighter picked her up. She was blowing through 20,000 feet on her way to 30,000 and rolled to present her full profile to the Gyrfalcon. She had it on radar now. Its own radar warning system should be shouting in the pilot's ears.

It turned toward her. And fired.

Bunny returned the favor. "Fox three," she muttered as her last missile punched out of her weapons bay and turned away toward the target.

She dropped her nose, pulled in her lenses and brought her growler online again. Looking outside her plane, she saw the red cliffs of Makaha Ridge flash past as another volley of missiles from the defenders on the ridgetop shot out to sea.

Out to sea?

Her eyes flicked to her tactical display. A line of small dots had appeared about 3 miles offshore. The enemy landing craft were moving in.

Bunny checked the trajectory of the incoming Chinese missile, tightened her turn, preparing to react if the growler pod couldn't jam it.

Then she got an idea.

UNCLE PULLED Outlaw's nose up 10 degrees.

Down back, Rory slapped his loadmaster on the back.

Clamps dropped into the floor, and the first LOCUST pallet slid backward and fell off the ramp, parachute billowing out behind it. Immediately behind it, the second pallet began sliding and dropped.

"Pallets away. Get us out of here, Uncle," Rory said. The plane tipped onto a wing and started a curving turn toward the north of Kaua'i.

Guiding his safety tether down a rail, Rory duck-walked to the back of the plane, wind roaring around his ears, and watched the two pallets sway under their chutes.

Then, row by row, the oil-barrel-sized cannisters inside the pallets started falling out and splitting open. In no time, the air was thick with swirling drones, moving as a single organism, like a starling murmuration. Inside a minute they'd all formed up and started heading for the sea below.

The sight made Rory shiver.

BUNNY'S GROWLER pod blinded the PL-15 missile's seeker head and sent it wide. But her own missile also missed, the Gyrfalcon pilot deftly decoying it into a tight turn it couldn't follow.

Bunny was up at 30,000 feet and turned east, heading for the center of the island. The Gyrfalcon began closing again. It had lost interest in Outlaw, as she'd hoped, and it was trying to push closer for a kill on her Widow.

She had no more missiles. But she knew a friend who did.

She switched to the joint forces cooperation frequency. "Emerald Four USAF Black Widow to US Army Missile Battery Makaha Ridge, do you read?"

"CALL FOR YOU, BOSS," Kernow said, tapping his headset. "USAF. Putting it through."

Baruzzi didn't have time. They were in the middle of switching out their 9X missiles for anti-ship Naval Strike Missiles. The Chinese landing craft were just minutes from coming within range.

"Lieutenant Baruzzi, go ahead," she said tersely.

"Baruzzi, 68th Aggressor overhead. I'm south of your position and I'm dragging a Chinese fighter with me, can you assist?"

Baruzzi checked their radar plot. She saw the USAF fighter. She didn't see the Chinese one yet. She turned to Kennedy. "Has Pod Two pulled back yet?"

"No, it's still on the line. Three is still loading," Kennedy said.

"Keep them there," she told him. "Air Force, we can assist, but we need a bearing to your target."

"You got it, Army ... That's three five one degrees, range 20, closing."

Kernow was already swinging his radar around, tightening his beam, looking down the bearing. "*Got it*," he said. "In range."

Baruzzi turned to Kennedy. "How many shots does Pod Three have in the locker?"

He checked a display. "Three, ma'am."

"Lock and fire. Send them all. Three missiles, one-second separation."

"Launching."

BUNNY TURNED her plane north again, shrinking her profile to the enemy Gyrfalcon, tempting it further in, the Army MML battery right in front of her.

But the Chinese fighter wasn't following. Instead it turned sharply to port, appearing to search again for the departing AC-130X, now disappearing low over the island to her right. Easier meat.

Come on come on come on, she chanted to herself.

Then three missiles exploded from the bluff over the cliffs, one after the other, and climbed into the sky. Bunny knew they would be terminally optical infrared guided. There would be no warning for the Chinese pilot until he picked them up on his own radar, giving him just seconds to maneuver. He might evade one, but surely not all three.

She watched them on radar all the way to their target.

Thank you, Army.

"Outlaw, Emerald Four. US Army has dealt with your threat. Safe trip home, gentlemen."

BARUZZI WAS TOO BUSY to even register the kill. She ordered the pod that had just emptied its magazine to pull back and reload with Naval Strike Missiles. They were big missiles, weighed twice what a 9X anti-air missile weighed, and had to be lifted into the pod with a sling and crane.

She had three Hawkeis on the line, loaded and ready, with 18 missiles. Now she needed targets.

She looked at her plot, at the AC-130X exiting northeast. What the hell had he even been doing flying right over a hot landing zone in the middle of a firefight? That thought disappeared as quickly as it appeared, as the plot showed a sight that chilled her blood.

Dozens of landing craft, moving in.

"Radar to Ground Moving Target mode," Baruzzi ordered.

"Radar to GMT mode, searching," Kernow confirmed. The small enemy landing craft would be hidden in wave clutter until they were almost within visual range, but they might get targeting data over battlenet before then.

Baruzzi swung out of the open door of her command vehicle, scanning the coast to the south. An ugly column of smoke rose from the highway. Multiple vehicles had been hit. But most of the enemy helos were down—she could see only one, skimming back out to sea with tracer fire from a squad weapon following it.

On the beach and back at the airfield, she could see troops setting up defensive positions, Army shoulder to shoulder with Marines.

"2-6th Air Cav moving up," Kennedy said. Baruzzi swung her binos, saw a line of Enhanced Apache attack helos powering through swirling smoke on the highway and sprinting out to sea. On any other day, it would have been the kind of sight to raise a cheer.

But there were only six. And there were so many landing craft.

Operation Midnight: *Taifun*

DEEP BENEATH the Chinese fleet, with a Chinese submarine in their baffles, Brunelli could see McDonald had reached a breaking point. He was going to step forward—to do what, she could only imagine—but she grabbed his arm and dug her nails into his skin.

He gave her a look that made her feel like she was the problem.

"He's right," she hissed at him.

"What?"

"Courtenay. He's right," she repeated in a low voice. "We have only one shot. We waste it on the wrong target, Operation Midnight is a bust. We may never get this chance again. We have to be sure."

FIVE MINUTES 30 *to first torpedo*, *Taifun* noted. *Six minutes 15 to second torpedo.*

She was running hundreds of possible attack scenarios through her decision support system. One decision she considered was whether to fire on the target as soon as she had one torpedo ready, or wait until the second was ready too and fire two together.

The first option would give her an earlier shot, but the second option would give more certainty of success. She checked the target's speed and heading. No change. No sign it was aware of *Taifun* trailing behind it. It was making noise like it didn't care—another sign it thought it was alone.

Her programming forced her to choose certainty of a kill over speed of attack.

Five minutes 14 to torpedo launch.

She checked the distance to the target. If she closed just 100 yards, she could increase the kill probability dramatically.

Taifun nudged her speed up a couple of knots.

"PROPULSION NOISE!" the sonarman said. "Signature match. It's *Taifun*! It's her!"

Courtenay nodded. "Thank you, Sonar," Courtenay said. "Mr. Williams, are you ready with your exploit?"

"Yes, Captain."

"Very good. XO, stealth launch, special weapon, tube one," Courtenay said. "Arm Spearfish in tubes two to six."

Singh relayed the orders. A gentle burst of its pump jet kicked the EW torpedo out into the water and it turned back toward *Taifun*, loitering in the path of the Chinese submarine.

"Advise as soon as you achieve handshake with the enemy submarine, please, Mr. Williams," Courtenay said, trying to project calm again. "Helm, steady as she goes. We don't want to spook our prey. But you will prepare to make a crash turn to port at best possible turning radius to bring our bow to bear on the contact if so ordered."

"Helm, steady as she goes. Ready crash turn, best possible turning circle on your order, sir, aye!"

"Mr. Williams," Courtenay said.

Williams looked up from his laptop. "Sir?"

"How long do you need from the moment you have handshake with *Taifun* until you know whether the attack has succeeded or failed?"

Williams wiped his brow. "A minute. Maybe less. No, a minute."

"You will have 30 seconds," Courtenay said. "XO, please start a count from the time Mr. Williams tells us he has handshake. Prepare to launch tubes two and three at the 31-second mark. If we can't hijack *Taifun*, we will destroy her."

Singh checked his console. "31 seconds, aye, sir."

THE TEMPERATURE in *Agincourt*'s command center was rising palpably as hearts beat faster. Their EW torpedo was drifting behind them, but they had no idea how far behind them their pursuer actually was.

Only Williams would know, when he got an ELF signal handshake with the Chinese sub. Or got his hand slapped.

McDonald was the impatient one, but this wait was nearly more than Brunelli could take. She knew the *Astute* class boats almost as well as she knew her own—OK, she hadn't known about this 'HELF-D' system, whatever witchcraft that was, but she knew just about everything else there was to know—and she knew that turning a 7,400-ton boat at 20 knots was not something you did on a dime.

Three minutes since the launch of the EW torpedo came and went and Courtenay stayed impassively staring at his tactical screen, an Easter Island statue in human form.

"Sonar?" Courtenay asked.

"Nothing, Captain. I'd say she's right in behind us, hiding in our wake. We'll need to angle starboard or port for me to get a read on her, or go to active sonar."

"Which will tell her we are onto her," Courtenay said.

"What is it waiting for? Why doesn't it *shoot*?" Singh said, gripping the console in front of him.

"Because it can't," Brunelli said. "For whatever reason. But if it isn't *Taifun*, that is one cold-ass captain."

Brunelli saw Courtenay had bitten his lip so hard he had a line of blood running down his chin.

"Forget this for a lark. Helm, prepare to maneuver. Hard to port, tight as you can on my mark, please." Courtenay said, looking up at last. "Mr. Singh, ready on torpedo tubes two and three."

"I'll spin her like a blinking top, Captain," the helmsman replied.

"*Handshake*, I have handshake!" Williams announced. "Don't fire!"

"EW torpedo maneuvering," their weapons officer said. "It has target lock and is matching speed. Bearing 180, range 900 yards, speed 20 knots."

"Start your timer, Mr. Singh."

"Counting down from 30 seconds. Tubes two and three ready for launch," Singh confirmed. Brunelli could see *Agincourt*'s XO's hand was already hovering over the torpedo launch control. And it was shaking. Singh caught Brunelli looking, and she gave him a nod.

"You have this, Mr. Singh," Brunelli said softly. "Cool as a cucumber."

Williams had his eyes glued to his screen. Whatever he was looking at, it wasn't what he wanted to see—that was obvious in his face.

A dozen heartbeats went by. "Mr. Williams?" Courtenay asked.

"*Nothing*. We haven't been booted out, but aren't getting …"

Sigh straightened. "Thirty seconds!"

"Helm, turn to engage," Courtenay ordered.

There were no more orders issued. The control room was full of submariners who knew their lives depended on what happened in the next two minutes, and they'd spent the last six minutes rehearsing it in their minds.

McDonald braced himself. The boat heeled over like a train on rails headed down a hill on a curving track. The sound of their own sonar pulsing began ringing through the hull.

It was time to kill. Or be killed.

TAIFUN WAS MANAGING the unusual command it had just received over ELF. The code phrase given was valid but referred to a superseded routine. *Taifun* had no reason to ignore the order, but needed to retrieve an older version of its code base in order to be able to interpret it. And that, like all things, took time.

As she was working, she registered a sudden change in the target's speed and heading. She wasn't distracted. She could manage both tasks at the same time. The moment the target's speed began dropping, *Taifun* eased back her own speed. As the target began turning, she began her own turn, sharper than the one the target was executing, and started to cut across the circle to make it harder for the target to get a solution on her.

If she'd had torpedoes ready, she would already have fired. It didn't worry her that she didn't.

Taifun didn't do worry.

One minute 35 to torpedo readiness.

"WE HAVE COMMUNICATION!" Williams said, his voice high pitched. "It's interrogating us. We're in!"

"Do you have control?" Courtenay asked.

"No, but …"

"Contact on sonar. She's turning inside us," the sonar officer said. "I have a range estimate. Eight seventy yards."

"Jayzoos, that's *close*," Brunelli hissed.

"I don't have a solution!" Singh said.

"Wait for it, Mr. Singh," Courtenay said. "Don't launch until you have."

McDonald knew what Courtenay was saying. At the range the two boats were circling each other, he didn't want Singh's nerves to drive him to take the shot early.

"Helm, increase dive angle 10 degrees please. Tighten your turn," Courtenay ordered.

"Don't shoot!" Williams pleaded. "We're negotiating!"

TORPEDO ONE READY, *Taifun*'s loading system reported.

She ran her attack algorithm again. The certainty threshold shrank the moment the target began maneuvering. It was now saying she should launch. She launched her only ready torpedo in autonomous homing mode and began a crash dive, spiraling toward the safety of the Pacific Ocean floor as she fired acoustic and MAD decoys into her wake.

She was still negotiating the ELF communication request even as she dived.

"TORPEDO INCOMING; sonar homing," *Agincourt*'s sonarman said. "Jamming."

"No solution on the target," Singh said, desperation in his voice. "She's too close!"

"Incoming torpedo locked," the EWO replied. "Deploying Sea Gnats."

From ports on *Agincourt's* bow, tiny Sea Gnat submersible drones, looking almost identical to the insects they were named after, though much larger, were launched into the water and began following an intercept path to the incoming torpedo.

Just like a swarm of gnats, they stayed close together, forming a cloud of noise and metal directly between the Chinese torpedo and the diving *Agincourt*.

Taifun was no longer in control of its torpedo, or it might have seen through the ruse and the sonar energy *Agincourt* was blasting in its direction. But the Chinese Yu-9 torpedo didn't need *Taifun's* quantum core computers to help it anymore, and though it was pulled off-course, it blasted through the swarm of Sea Gnats and then curved around to look for its target again.

It found *Agincourt* right where it expected.

TAIFUN WAS PROGRAMMED to self-destruct if she detected that a successful cyberattack had penetrated her security protocols.

The ELF signal she had just received was unusual, but not threatening in the manner she had been trained to react to. It was sending a valid code, just with an outdated syntax, so *Taifun* asked the sender to rewrite the code sequence with the correct syntax.

Which HOLMES had done.

Taifun negotiated this while managing the engagement with the enemy submarine. She sent a message back to the ELF sender.

Code accepted. Immediate reset of all systems except ELF.

"RESET!" WILLIAMS EXCLAIMED. "We did it!"

The explosion as *Taifun* issued a self-destruct order to her torpedo was audible inside *Agincourt*'s hull. So close, it rocked the submarine and lights inside *Agincourt* dimmed, then cut out. Emergency lighting came on.

"Detonation!" the sonarman reported. "The enemy torpedo detonated. No impact!"

They were still turning, trying to bring their own torpedoes to bear on the Chinese submarine.

"Stay that launch order, Mr. Singh. Take damage reports from all sections," Courtenay said.

The XO lifted his hand away from the torpedo launch control and began calling all compartments, but the lighting came back on before he could report. Brunelli breathed again.

"No damage reported, Captain. All systems nominal."

"Helm, ahead slow; hold your depth, maintain your turn …" Courtenay said.

"Noise is clearing, I … I have the target," the sonarman said. "Bearing zero four seven, range 3 miles, speed … 4 knots, no, 3 … She's slowing."

Williams stood, bent over so he could still read his screen. He was hopping from one foot to the other as he read the text flowing down the screen. "HOLMES is in. He's paused the system reset. Now he's inserting our exploit."

Courtenay ran his hand through his hair and absently wiped his bloodied chin. "That is very good, Mr. Williams. I assume this means you will be able to order the Chinese boat to surface so the US Navy can take it in tow?"

Williams was still watching his screen. "Take her in tow? From what I can see, we can just tell her to sail herself to Hawaii, or San Diego for that matter. She's ours now."

The Battle of Hawaii: Makaha Ridge

"MULTIPLE CONTACTS, bearing two six zero," Kernow announced. "Uh, call it … 21. Twenty-one targets locked."

"All launch units reloaded and in position," Kennedy confirmed.

"Lock all targets," she told Kennedy. "Empty the pods."

Kennedy punched some keys. "Twenty-four missiles up. Ready to launch."

"Launch and reload," Baruzzi said.

"One through four, launching," Kennedy confirmed.

Even inside their Hawkei, the sound of the missiles rippling from their launchers so close by was deafening.

As soon as the sound died away, Baruzzi, Kernow and Kennedy were out of the command vehicle, doors open, standing on its chassis so they could see the effect of their attack with their own eyes.

"Yeah, two down!" Kernow yelled a moment later. "Three … four …"

Baruzzi had her binos up, sweeping them along the line of landing craft. They had hit the surf just offshore as her battery had fired, and she saw puffs of smoke from ahead of their fans, explosions along the US line of defense, as the big hovercraft fired smoke mortars and opened up with their autocannons. She was counting too, but to herself. "… *five … six …*"

Only six kills.

Fifteen or so landing craft still pushing in. Behind them, another two or three limping toward the coast, damaged but still moving.

Smoke blanketed the coast in front of the PMRF and airfield, both from the mortar rounds just fired and the still-burning convoy. TOW anti-tank missiles punched out of the smoke, slamming into the closest hovercraft. A couple developed a list as their air cushions were punctured, but momentum drove them up onto the beach anyway.

Others went straight through the surf, mortars firing again as they rode up onto the sands and disappeared into the smoke, their triple blowers sending it swirling around them.

"KAUA'I COMING over the horizon again," Captain Sally Hall said. She'd had 90 minutes to make peace with her demons.

All she'd had to do was remind herself how many people were dying across the other side of the Pacific, from missiles, bombs and a virus that caused you to drown in your own blood.

How many more might die on the islands coming into view.

And how fate had given *her* the chance to do something about it all.

'Tug' Boatt had his head in the Skylon's ISR systems menu, preparing for their second flight over the Sino-Russian fleet. He looked up. "Start the checklist." He looked down at his screen again, like it was just another day at the office.

He surprised her sometimes. She'd seen him tear up on movie night at Vandenberg, watching some stupid romantic comedy that ended in a wedding. But up here, in that seat, right now—he was a block of ice.

"Sentinel RV arm-and-launch sequence," Hall said. "Power to post-boost vehicle, check. Booster pre-ignition validation, check. Target data loaded, check. Dual-key launch confirmation, check ..." She reached forward to a console that sat between them and tapped the two physical keys sitting there. "Keys in safe position, check." She continued until she reached the end of the checklist. "MIRVs one through fourteen green. PBV systems nominal. Sentinel D6 armed and ready to deploy. Start launch countdown?"

Boatt checked their range to target. "Count it down," he said.

She tapped a button. "One minute five ..."

On the heads-up display ahead of them, a cross appeared in space with a dotted line linking them to it. Their trajectory. The cross: their Sentinel missile's automatically calculated launch point.

In the middle of the instrument panel in front of them was a small black panel with two red keys. The Doomsday Box, the groundcrew called it. She remembered one of the first things she'd been taught as a pilot — "if it's dusty, or red, don't touch it."

Until you have to.

They both leaned forward, Hall reaching out with her left hand, Boatt with his right. She gripped the key closest to her. They'd already input and validated the weapon launch confirmation codes released by the US President and relayed to them by the commander of USINDOPACOM.

"Arming RV," Boatt said, preparing to turn his key. "On three ..."

"Two ... three." She turned hers. "RV armed. Thirty seconds to launch ... *mark*."

Their cameras panned and zoomed across the Chinese fleet ahead of them. She could see it was in the process of reversing course, ships making white curving tracks through the water as they changed their heading from east to west.

All but three: the Chinese fleet tender, the carrier *Liaoning* and a *Renhai* cruiser on the southern flank of the fleet. Two were stationary, burning; one was just a stern in a pool of oil and lifeboats. There were no other ships coming to their rescue, Sally saw.

She felt their Skylon, 'Mako,' shake as its payload doors opened. The 2-ton payload inside was weightless in low earth orbit, and had to be kicked into space with compressed air jets. Hall watched the weapon deploy while Boatt compensated for the slight shove to keep them on-course.

"Clean separation," Hall announced. "Post-boost vehicle ignition in ... eight ... five ... four ... three ... two ... one."

The tail of the stubby missile burned brightly, but only for a few seconds. It only had to put itself onto a re-entry trajectory, after which the boost vehicle separated, tumbling behind the warhead as it dropped away and below their Skylon.

"I feel like I should say something Oppenheimerish," Boatt said.

"Silence is golden, boss," Sally told him. She looked away, over her right shoulder, at the rising moon.

THE SENTINEL was the missile born from the Ground-Based Strategic Deterrent Program to replace the aging Titan II ICBMs. The D6 version of the Sentinel was not land based. It was designed to be carried into space aboard a heavy-lift rocket like the Falcon 9, or in the payload bay of a Skylon. So it didn't need the first-stage booster rocket of a ground-launched missile, just the post-boost vehicle and re-entry vehicle containing the 14 warheads.

There were still treaties banning the positioning of nuclear weapons in space though, and the D6 was not a treaty breaker, because its 14 individually targetable warheads weren't nuclear. Each warhead was tipped with 500 lbs. of solid tungsten. Used over land, the tungsten warheads would hit like meteorites, cratering the ground, ejecting debris, starting fires with superheated air and causing widespread destruction with shockwaves. Over water, the effect was just as catastrophic, penetrating deep into the water before disintegrating due to the immense force and heat generated upon impact.

But they weren't nukes.

Knowing the Multiple Independently Targetable Re-entry Vehicles in the body of the Sentinel warhead weren't nuclear, but rather tungsten, had helped Sally Hall deal with her demons.

She hoped China would see the difference.

From the moment it broke free of its post-boost vehicle, the Sentinel warhead began homing on PLAN *Shandong*, riding in the center of the fleet, flanked by cruisers and destroyers.

Cruisers and destroyers that could not just engage enemy ships, aircraft and cruise missiles but that constantly scanned the outer reaches of the atmosphere looking for carrier-killer ballistic missiles.

Armed with HQ-19 anti-ballistic missile interceptors, two of the *Renhais* flanking *Shandong* detected the heat signature of the Sentinel warhead entering the atmosphere and locked onto it, shared intercept data and launched two HQ-19 missiles each.

The Sentinel warhead was still four minutes from impact, maneuvering as it fell toward the *Shandong* Carrier Strike Group at nearly five times the speed of sound.

As the four Chinese interceptor missiles neared the Sentinel, its nose cone split open, and 14 independently targeted re-entry vehicles speared into the atmosphere together with an equal number of unguided decoy warheads that fell faster and burned brighter.

The Chinese cruisers desperately launched 20 more interceptors as their first four slammed into the now empty, already disintegrating Sentinel MIRV carrier.

Four of Sentinel's 14 MIRVs were aimed at the projected position of *Shandong*—data that had been updated by Skylon's ISR systems milliseconds before the Sentinel separated from Mako. Ten aimed themselves at the largest of the warships sailing around the carrier in a wide honeycomb pattern that took in almost the full diameter of the fleet footprint, except for where the stricken *Liaoning* and her escorts were already stopped dead in the water.

The 14 hypersonic glide vehicles could guide themselves to their targets with great precision, despite the speed and violence of their re-entry. But their tungsten warheads didn't need a direct hit to kill or disable. Superheated air and water could also do that.

SALLY MIGHT HAVE developed a sudden interest in the moon and stars, but Tug Boatt felt compelled to watch the earth below.

He saw bright flashes in the atmosphere above the Chinese ships, probably impacts or near misses from interceptions on the Sentinel warhead. Had they hit it before MIRV separation?

He didn't need to wait long for the answer. More flashes, closer to the surface, as more interceptors began hitting MIRV warheads.

Ten of the 400-kilogram tungsten warheads hit the water like a shower of meteorites. Tug's wide-angle camera was centered on *Shandong*, and the scene looked at first like a shower of gravel thrown into a pond. Small white dots, white waves rippling outward from each.

His altitude from the surface, growing with every second, created an artificial separation between what he was seeing and what was really happening to the Chinese ships.

Obliteration.

Shandong disappeared. Vapor clouds climbed into the atmosphere across the breadth and depth of the fleet. One by one, the racing shockwave ripples of white foam spreading out across the target area merged, until they were a series of circular mini tsunamis, rocking the bigger ships at the outer perimeter of the fleet, overturning those closer in.

Slowly, the scene of the attack disappeared over the horizon. Tug let the cameras roll until the last Chinese ship faded from view over the curve of the sea, and shut down the ISR feed.

Hall hadn't spoken for several minutes. She had moved her gaze from the stars and was paging through systems menus, checking fuel and battery levels.

"It's done," Tug told her.

"Moving fuel from auxiliary to main tanks," she said, not actually acknowledging what he said. "Batteries at 80 percent. Doesn't look like anything shook loose. Good seal on payload doors."

"Uh … roger that. You can get some rest until we come around again in 90 minutes."

"Will do," she said. "Commander has the vessel." She pressed a button on her helmet, and her visor went black.

ALESSA BARUZZI WATCHED the battle on the beach with horror. They'd emptied their supply of missiles, but at least 15 of the landing craft had made it to shore. It was crawling with Chinese troops and armored vehicles. There was too much smoke to see if the American lines were holding … or if they had fallen.

"Grab your rifles and mount up!" she yelled to her people.

It was a 30-minute drive back down from the bluff to the beach. The battle could be over by the time they got there, but she somehow doubted it.

TAMMY BALLARD saw the Chinese "police officer" drop his grenade as he died and threw herself into the small room leading off the corridor, which turned out to be a tiny bathroom. When she gathered herself and looked outside again, she saw the grenade burning furiously on the wooden floor, and heavy flames licking up the plush curtains and wooden window shutters.

Incendiary, she thought. *No putting that out.*

She wanted to go in and pull the body of the Honolulu PD sergeant out, but the flames were too hot, and she could still hear firing downstairs.

Worry about the living, Tammy; the dead can take care of themselves.

She checked her ammunition and pulled a magazine out of the weapon of the man she'd shot on the stairs. Going down the stairs a step at a time, she reached the first floor and saw two Chinese police dragging Freeth through the rear doors with one of his arms around each of their shoulders. His head was hanging forward as though he was wounded, or unconscious. One of the Chinese cops stopped when he saw her, lifted his pistol and sighted on her. She froze. She thought about firing, but they had Freeth right between them. She wasn't that good of a shot. He squinted at her, then turned away, heading down the rear stairs with Freeth.

The T-shirt, she realized. *He thinks I'm one of the Alliance supporters.*

A "construction worker" with an assault rifle ran across the lobby before skidding to a halt on the wooden floor and pointing past her. "You! Get out the back. We're setting fires."

The hell you are, Tammy thought, and put two bullets in his chest.

A heavy burst of fire from outside the building smashed through the glass-paneled front door. A bullet caught her in the shoulder and spun her around. Her head hit the banister post as she fell, and she smacked into the wooden floor hard.

The last thing she saw before her eyes closed was flame, licking across the floor.

BARUZZI'S FOUR HAWKEIS drove through the state park at dangerous speeds, and straight into a firefight. Chinese armored fighting vehicles were trying to push through the smoke and fire of the ravaged coastal convoy and make a run for the Kaua'i capital, Lihue.

Baruzzi pulled her vehicle to a halt up at the Kekaha Lookout, jumping onto the vehicle's hood so she could see

497

south to Highway 50 on the coast. She could see fighting at the small bridge going over the channel at Waimea. Chinese light armor on the western side, cannons chewing at a motley collection of US Army and Marine squads on the eastern side of the bridge.

And armed civilians?

As she watched, two anti-tank missiles reached out from the American side of the bridge and slammed into Chinese armored vehicles. One exploded, turret flipping through the air. The other shrugged the hit off and inched forward, a platoon of Chinese troops tucked in behind it.

Baruzzi jumped into her vehicle again, pointing down the road, grabbing at her throat mic as the vehicle accelerated again. "Alright, weapons ready. The situation is: we will be coming down off this road behind a Chinese armored column. On my order, we will pull off, use our vehicles for cover and hit the enemy foot soldiers moving up with their armor. Eat dirt if we're engaged by enemy armor. They're trying to cross the bridge at Waimea, and that isn't happening today."

Kennedy, driving, reached out a fist to bump hers. "Hell no, Lieutenant."

Baruzzi checked her weapon.

And then it was *on*.

They came roaring down the winding road out of the foothills, past a hospital, ambulances lined up outside, lights flashing, already taking the first wounded …

Park on their right. Tracer fire. Marines engaged with enemy foot soldiers. Not the fight she wanted.

"Blow through," she told Kennedy.

He crouched down over the wheel, foot to the floor. Gunfire, hitting their vehicle behind them. She looked over her shoulder, saw the other four vehicles tucked in tight behind her. As they hit the Kaumualii Highway he swung the wheel left, the Hawkei went up on two wheels, and they were suddenly there … a hundred yards behind the Chinese troops moving up behind their armor.

Except it wasn't a platoon.

It was a *company*.

Kennedy didn't need to be told. A baseball pitch bordered by a waist-high stone wall ran along the left side of the road, and he pulled in beside it, leaving just enough room to open his door.

Baruzzi was out as soon as the vehicle stopped, climbing over the hood of the Hawkei, jumping over the stone wall and down as the Chinese troops reacted to their sudden appearance in their rear and opened fire on them.

She saw a line of bullets stitch along the top of the wall, heard Kennedy grunt. Looked down the wall and saw the rest of her unit dismounting, rolling and tumbling over the wall into cover. Her vehicle and four others—fewer than 20 men.

The incoming fire got heavier. *Keep moving, Alessa!* a voice told her. She reached for her tactical mic. "Command will move up the wall with Pod Two and flank, Pods Three and Four, covering fire. Now!"

Back along the wall, a half dozen men rose to firing positions behind the wall and began returning fire. Kennedy hadn't made it over the wall. No time to worry about him. Baruzzi looked at Kernow, lying flat on the ground. "You good?"

"Yes ma'am!" he said, rising to a knee.

"Let's move," she said, and began running at a crouch. The wall was a hundred yards long and ran parallel to the road. Bullets hammered at the wall beside and behind them as they ran, but nothing heavy caliber yet.

Then Baruzzi reached the end of the wall. She fell on her butt, back to the wall. No incoming fire here. Her men back where they'd dismounted were trading fire.

"Command, Pod Two, let's give 'em hell," she said. "On three. One ... two ..."

She barked the order and rose to one knee, sighting over the wall. She saw Chinese troops trying to rush her men back along the wall, charging, yelling. She'd gotten behind them.

Firing short bursts, she began walking her fire from the soldiers at the front of the charge to those behind them, then those closest to her. Kernow stayed beside her, doing the same. The men of Pod Two, further down, were firing into the mass of bodies too.

The Chinese charge faltered. Some of the Chinese soldiers dived for the hard bitumen of the road and tried to return fire. Others broke and ran across the highway to where there was a souvenir shop, a shaved ice place, a public library ...

Baruzzi heard her rifle bolt click on an empty chamber, dropped to her butt again and changed out the magazine. Waited a beat, then rose again looking for a target.

She saw a civilian in shorts, a singlet and sandals, standing between shops, pump-action shotgun at his waist, firing at running Chinese soldiers as fast as he could work the action.

Chinese soldier on the road, limping away, still carrying his rifle. She dropped him. Another two running for the shaved ice shop. Four rounds into their backs. Then movement to her left ...

She saw a six-wheeled Chinese armored vehicle backing up the highway in their direction. Turret with a rotary cannon on it swinging around toward her as it reversed.

"Enemy armor!" Baruzzi called out. "Everyone down!"

She threw herself forward as the stone above her head began disintegrating. Looking back over her shoulder, she saw dust and masonry flying as the enemy armored vehicle worked its fire along the line of the wall.

She looked around desperately. They couldn't fight a tank. Needed to withdraw, but where to? Road ahead of her, tennis courts across the baseball field to the left. Some kind of school on a rise, stone-backed earth embankment across the other side of the road.

But getting there would mean crossing open ground under the barrel of the Chinese tank.

Then she heard the thud of rotors high to her right, the *whoosh* of a missile, followed by an explosion that sent searing hot air across her back. Helicopter, pulling away to the north behind her.

Apache.

Kernow yelling. "Air Cav! Yeah baby! *Air Cav!*"

She risked rising to a knee again, looking over the wall. The Chinese armored vehicle was a smoking wreck. There was another burning farther down, toward the bridge. On the other side of the road, more Chinese troops running between shops and residences. Two more armored vehicles, popping smoke and pulling back.

Away from the bridge. Back toward their beachhead.

"Squad, up and engage the ground troops!" Baruzzi ordered, training her rifle on a running silhouette between buildings. "Take down as many as you can!"

THREE MINUTES LATER, it was over. Baruzzi stood, pushing her helmet back on her head.

Smoke drifted across the road, curling around fallen bodies. Some still alive, most dead. Ammunition cooked off in a nearby armored vehicle and she ducked, but it was down by the bridge.

Kernow had his helmet off and was standing there, rifle hanging loose in his hand, scratching his head. He gave her a wild-eyed look.

"Holy shit, ma'am," he said. "That was *insane.*"

She couldn't disagree.

State of the War Briefing

Transcript, Pentagon Press Office, July 3, 2038

LADIES AND GENTLEMEN, an update on events of significance from the last week.

The United States and its allies, in a major naval battle northwest of the Hawaiian Islands, has repelled an attempted invasion of Hawaii and destroyed the combined Chinese and Russian fleet that launched the invasion force.

No US Navy vessels were lost in this engagement, though we regret several aircraft and their crews gave their lives to ensure our victory. We are still completing our assessment of this engagement, but we are confident in our conclusion that all three Chinese aircraft carriers were sunk or put out of action.

The invaders attempted to land troops on Kaua'i Island on Hawaii and were repulsed by troops of the US Army, Coast Guard, Navy, National Guard and Marines. We need also to praise the people of Kaua'i who gave invaluable support to our troops during this action. Regrettably, China chose to indiscriminately deploy air-dropped anti-personnel and vehicle mines in its attack, and these have caused large numbers of casualties among both military personnel and civilians across the Hawaiian Islands. We will hold a separate briefing on demining operations and what precautions the civilian population will need to continue to take.

As I mentioned, Russian ships and troops were among the invasion force, and their losses were also significant. The US President is expected to make a statement about the role of

Russia in the invasion of Hawaii, and we will make no further comment on this.

China also attempted an invasion of Guam. This invasion force has been contained to the southwest corner of the island and is cut off from supply, and the surrender of Chinese troops is being negotiated.

Wake and Midway islands were also attacked. These attacks were repelled, and no Chinese forces remain on these islands.

Regarding our three key war aims: Taiwan has been ravaged by the Chinese bioweapon, but US forces on the island are secure and continue to offer vital support to the Taiwan government. Due to the significant losses suffered by Chinese forces in the Battle of Hawaii, the threat of invasion of Taiwan has been revised down from "high" to "medium." In the South China Sea, operations to demilitarize illegal Chinese installations were paused to allow US forces to respond to the attacks on Guam and other islands. This campaign will now resume. In relation to our objective to meet and defeat Chinese military aggression wherever it may be directed against the United States and its allies, we have had a resounding victory in the central Pacific, and we will continue to prosecute our goal of defeating China, and any of its Shanghai Pact allies that choose to join with it in war.

Epilogue

THE PERSONNEL at Naval Base Kitsap in Washington State had seen many things in this war already. But few to rival the arrival of two non-American submarines at Delta Pier. The British boat arrived first, gliding into the dock just under the water before slowing to a halt and then rising to the surface, its 20-foot sail nearly touching the canvas over the dock. But Kitsap's dock workers had seen *Astute* class boats at Kitsap before; what was more interesting was the company this one was keeping.

Sliding into the other arm of the wedge-shaped pier was a Chinese *Type 095* submarine. A party of armed Marines was there to greet it, just in case. And when it surfaced, to their surprise, the figure that emerged from a hatch on its foredeck was not Chinese but rather a chubby, bearded Caucasian geek in a hoodie.

Grinning ear to ear.

Taifun's systems all appeared to be responding to commands sent via ELF, but it had been possible that *Taifun* had destroyed part of its AI computing core before the hack went in, so Carl Williams insisted on being put aboard *Taifun* before they submerged and began sailing in tandem for the safety of Washington State.

Despite being uncrewed, the *Type 095* of course had maintenance hatches and walkways, and the stolen schematics NSA had managed to obtain told him exactly where to run once he got down the ladder into what had been the control room but was now a featureless room devoid of any kind of controls, instruments or displays.

He'd felt a moment of skin-crawling creepiness as he closed the hatch over his head and was suddenly alone with his laptop aboard the huge submarine. It was entirely in darkness—because why would it need internal lighting?

He had a flashlight, and his laptop, and HOLMES.

"Uh, HOLMES, does *Taifun* take voice inputs? Can I ask for lights?" he said, hanging onto the top rung of the ladder, earpiece in his ear connecting him to HOLMES.

It does, HOLMES said. *How good is your Mandarin?*

"Rusty," Williams said. "Send an ELF request via *Agincourt.*"

A couple of minutes later, amber safety lamps came on. They didn't help much, but he got to the bottom of the ladder without breaking a leg.

He'd run aft, flashlight in hand, scared of what he would find. Carl didn't do running, and he was glad no one could see as he stopped in a gangway to draw breath. The conical servers that made up the quantum computer core were in a box-shaped room on the same level as the conn, and he'd made straight for it, ignoring a million things that on another day, any other day, would have had him entranced for hours.

The entrance to the server room was hermetically sealed, and he went through the first door, closed it behind him, waited for the air to be replaced and then opened the second door, shining his light across the servers.

He saw a physical access panel with a simple optical fiber cable connection and connected HOLMES to it.

I reviewed the server logs, the AI said a couple of minutes later. *There has been no sabotage. I do not recommend we try to issue any commands from here though. Physical interference can trigger an auto-destruct routine. We should limit communication of orders to* Taifun *via the US ELF frequency it has now accepted as valid.*

506

He'd stayed aboard *Taifun* for days, even after a team of NSA and Office of Naval Research specialists came aboard and took over. Their main concern was to ensure *Taifun* could keep receiving data but would ignore any orders it might get from its former masters. It hadn't been easy to stop himself looking over their shoulders constantly and yelling "don't touch that!" but as they gradually peeled away *Taifun*'s many layers, the wonder that was the Chinese vessel lay exposed to him, and he could only marvel at the ambition of its creators.

And the hubris, to think it could not be hijacked and turned against them.

They were not complete fools. *Taifun* had been locked out of the PLA Navy battlenet the moment she had been hijacked. So the potential for using her to spy on the flow of data across the Chinese navy was still just a dream. It might one day come to pass, but unlike the German Enigma Machine, which was put to use immediately, the US Coalition wouldn't be using *Taifun* to listen in to PLA Navy coded communications anytime soon.

What they found buried deep in its code, though, was perhaps even more valuable.

Taifun had a latent ability to monitor not just PLA Navy but also PLA Ground Force, Air Force, Space Force, and, most critical of all, Strategic Missile Force communications. That latent capability had just not been enabled. Williams suspected politics had been at play, since in any AI learning system, more data was better. There was no practical reason to limit *Taifun*'s access only to navy data. But there were probably a million political reasons. The benefit to the hijackers was that because *Taifun*'s access across the other commands had never been enabled, it had apparently never been *disabled*.

The access to Chinese Strategic Rocket Force communications was most important of all, since it could give the US and UK advanced warning of any Chinese nuclear strike order.

With the flick of a few digital switches, *Taifun* began assimilating battlenet data from across every PLA command *except* Navy. HOLMES ordered *Taifun* by ELF to prepare hourly summaries of the data and forward it to him for analysis and distribution.

Taifun didn't seem to care that this was a strange duty to give a submarine; she simply did as she was asked. Nor did she question why she was now based at a pier in Washington State, USA, and not patrolling the Pacific anymore.

As long as her orders were authentic, and these seemed to be, hers was not to question why.

Soon intelligence on every element of China's war machine, from corps and air wing down to company and squadron level, was flowing into NSA in quantities no human analytical team could manage. HOLMES categorized, prioritized and distributed the data to other AI subsystems, after which the reports were passed for action to a dedicated unit inside NSA, appropriately called: MIDNIGHT. The intelligence they generated was given multiple cover code names, to hide its single source—some indicating it came from human agents, some from cyber interceptions, some Electronic Intelligence or Space Surveillance.

The Joint Chiefs were exposed to the intelligence being generated by MIDNIGHT and immediately decided any military action proposed as a result of MIDNIGHT intelligence had to be approved by the Chairman of the Joint Chiefs, for fear that if China became suspicious its communications were being read "in the clear," they would tear down and rebuild their battlenet.

NSA had no idea how long the MIDNIGHT access would last—but Williams had delivered. The US Coalition's Enigma Machine moment had arrived.

HMS AGINCOURT had not been allowed to spend very long enjoying the Washington State summer weather.

She went straight back out on patrol in pursuit of the remnants of the Sino-Russian fleet, which had been scattered to all points of the compass by the orbital weapon bombardment.

And after several fruitless days combing the Pacific, a sighting by a newly launched US satellite led *Agincourt* to the Russian *Ivan Gren* class landing ship, *General Oleg Tsokov*. It had been damaged in the US orbital attack and was limping northwest toward the Russian Kuril Islands at only 10 knots, in the company of a single *Steregushchiy* class corvette.

Until now they'd only come across ships that had already been destroyed: some capsized, others on fire, some with just their bow or stern sticking out above the water. Oil. Lifeboats. And bodies. So many bodies.

The *Tsokov* and his escort were the first vessels sailing under their own power that they'd identified.

"Corvette's position?" *Agincourt*'s captain, Courtenay, asked.

"Ahead of the *Tsokov*, more like it's getting ready to provide a tow than worried about executing an anti-submarine patrol," his sonar officer said.

"Helm, port two degrees."

Courtenay had already ordered four Spearfish torpedoes loaded into *Agincourt*'s tubes and armed.

The only reason he hadn't already taken the shot was that they had new orders, and he was awaiting permission from his base in Faslane, Scotland.

"What is taking them so long?" Singh asked.

"It can only be politics," Courtenay replied, frowning. "I suspect Downing Street is on the line."

"The Prime Minister?" Singh asked, surprised.

"And the War Cabinet," Courtenay replied. "The decision to sink the Argentine cruiser *Belgrano* in the Falklands War was made by committee, and I sense a committee at work in this delay."

"With respect to our political betters, this is a bloody funny way of running a war," Singh declared.

Minutes ticked by, measured only by the nervous fidgeting of personnel in the control room.

"Message on ELF from Faslane, Captain!" Courtenay's comms officer reported at last. "Message reads: *Trail at minimum safe range, but do not engage unless threatened.*"

With untypical violence, Courtenay slammed a palm against the armrest of his chair. "Helm, engines to ahead slow. Sonar, let me know the second the target changes speed, or if that corvette looks like it's heading our way."

"Someone got cold feet," Singh decided.

"It's one thing to attack Russian ships bearing down on an ally's territory, another thing to sink them as they are withdrawing to their own," Courtenay guessed. He gave McDonald a sour look and lowered his voice. "There must be someone in the UK government harboring the fantasy that Britain and Europe won't be pulled into this mess."

THE CALL FROM QINGDAO woke Chief Engineer Lo Pan at 0300 hours. No call that came at 0300 was ever a good one, in Lo's experience. This wasn't an exception to that rule.

"Chief Engineer," the voice of a PLA Navy liaison said. "I am to inform you that shortly after being ordered to attack an enemy submarine inside the Pacific Fleet line of defense, contact was lost with PLAN *Taifun*, and it is assumed destroyed."

"Attack an enemy submarine?" Lo said incredulously. "What idiot decided to use *Taifun* as though it was some kind of common attack submarine?"

There was an awkward pause at the end of the line. "Chief Engineer, I believe Admiral Li gave the order."

"Then I hope he will take the consequences," Lo said, and hung up the call. He sat himself up, then called his deputy. "Bad news. *Taifun* has been lost. The navy says 'destroyed,' but don't assume that. Download all data from the time we lost contact for two hours before, and send it to me. And remove its ID from PLA Navy battlenet servers so its login can't be used by anyone to send or receive." He was about to lay the cell phone aside when he heard the man was still talking. "What? Yes, navy servers. It wasn't active on army or air force. Navy, yes."

He lay his head down again. The loss wasn't catastrophic. Alright, he may have overpromised regarding *Taifun*'s capabilities in submarine versus submarine combat. It was, after all, only as good as the data it had been trained on, and China's submarines had precious little actual combat experience for it to learn from. This learning would go into the database though, for the next boat in the *Taifun* class, which was already on the slips, awaiting launch.

And the submarine that gave the class its name had more than proven its worth—piloted itself across 3,000 nautical miles of sea, evading and even disabling an enemy én route before singlehandedly launching a surprise attack on Hawaii to rival the Japanese attack in 1941.

With experience, even in death, his *Taifun* systems would only grow stronger.

TAMMY BALLARD was ready to climb out of her hospital bed and strangle the man sitting in the chair beside her.

Not that she had anything against him personally. He was just doing his job, but her family was waiting outside, and he was the only thing standing between her and them.

She'd spent the previous day and now the entire morning going over what she had seen, heard and done inside the palace with detectives from Honolulu PD's Criminal Intelligence Unit.

They were particularly concerned about Jonah Freeth's movements. Of course.

She tried to sit up in bed, wincing at the pain in her bandaged shoulder. The bullet that struck her had lodged against her collarbone, but hadn't broken it. Ironically, it looked pretty certain she'd been shot by Honolulu PD from outside the palace. "For the tenth time," she said. "Sorry. I can't tell you if Freeth was dead or alive when I last saw him. He was being dragged out the rear door between two Chinese in police uniforms ..."

"Not walking. His feet weren't moving?"

She closed her eyes, remembering. "No, he was being dragged, not walking. Look, I was shot. I'm tired. Why don't you tell me what you're trying to get to?"

The man closed his notebook. "We found the weapon we think killed Sergeant Cuccino," the detective said. "We just got back the forensics, and it has Freeth's prints on it. But if he was being dragged outside unconscious, it's hard to see him shooting Cuccino ..." The detective let that hang. "So it's an important detail."

"I saw him earlier," Tammy said. "When I first went inside. He didn't have a weapon I could see. But I can't tell you 100 percent if he did or didn't kill Cuccino, and I can't tell you if he was alive or dead when he was being dragged out that door."

What she did remember—she remembered the look from the Chinese cop, squinting at her down the barrel of his pistol. She'd just been a target to him. One he chose not to shoot, but it could so easily have gone the other way. She shuddered.

SERGEANT PAN TIEN had hijacked a vehicle from a woman who looked like a nurse, hauling her out by the hair when she stopped to avoid running over him, Freeth and the other scout.

He drove north from Honolulu at a sedate 55 miles an hour, to the safe house that had been bought for them by sleeper agents, on a farm off Highway 61 near Maunawili. He parked the car in the farm's old barn, and then the two of them carried Freeth inside. He left his man to watch the Alliance leader while he put the radio and television on and stood by his cell phone.

Over the next two hours, six more men arrived, in two vehicles, which they also parked in the barn. Six men out of 16. Fewer than he liked, but more than he'd expected after the violence of the police response at the palace. Then again, he wasn't surprised the Honolulu police had reacted the way they did. The brave sergeant had probably been a popular guy.

His man came into the room as they were watching a news report showing a slaughterbot being taken down by a rocket-propelled grenade, over and over. "He's awake," the man said. "I tied him to the bed."

Pan nodded and stood, stretching. He'd get this done, set up a roster for a watch, then grab a couple hours' sleep. He went upstairs to the bedroom where they'd dumped Freeth. He was bound hand and foot to the bed, and turned his head as Pan entered.

"Ah, Mr. Freeth. Congratulations on your uprising. Burning down the Capitol building was inspired. The Battle of 'Iolani Palace is on all the news bulletins too. I didn't realize the place had such significance to your people. I wish I had known; I feel quite embarrassed at the state we left it in."

"You feel nothing," Freeth said bitterly. "You used us."

"No, Mr. Freeth, we are helping you," Pan said. "You should be more grateful. I lost 10 men protecting you from the police at the palace. Ten brave men, martyrs to *your* cause."

"There would have been no fighting if you had not started it," Freeth said. He spat blood from his mouth. "The deal I made was ..."

Pan waved the words away irritably. "The deal, the deal ... The deal was we would support your uprising, and we did that. We are doing that still. That is why you are alive. Leader of the rebellion, Jonah Freeth, on the run. You are going to keep making your stirring videos while we go out and do the hard work for you. Sabotage, attacks on police and the Army: our people have been preparing this campaign for many years, and you will get to take the credit for all our labors." He checked Freeth's bonds, then patted him lightly on the cheek. "When we are done, you are going to be the people's hero, Jonah Freeth. Maybe even King, one day."

"Go to hell," Freeth said.

"Ah," Pan smiled. "The brave police sergeant said that too. And look where it got him. Think about that while I get some sleep, Mr. Freeth."

ALESSA BARUZZI and her unit were back on Unulau Ridge, protecting Kaua'i's Lihue Airport.

Lihue had been saved by the most disorganized, bloody-minded rabble of military personnel and civilians she'd ever witnessed on a battlefield. The carnage she'd been part of at Incirlik when the Syrians had dropped chemical weapons was nothing like the scene at Waimea.

There were Chinese dead everywhere. Burning armored vehicles, blackened crew members hanging out of hatches. Blood. Body parts. When the shooting was over, the American survivors were all standing there, unable to believe they were still alive. Army beside Marines, civilians with assault rifles and shotguns that looked like they'd been pulled from farmhouse walls, you name it. Baruzzi saw a Kanaka kid with a slingshot standing in the middle of the highway, eyes wide, blood running from his ear.

The media called it the Battle of Waimea Bridge.

The next day, though, the Chinese were still dug in on the other side of the island, like ticks. The same ditches and canals that had prevented them from breaking out of their beachhead were also making it hard to dislodge them. They were pounded day and night for the next 48 hours by precision long-range fires, but the Chinese force responded with counter-fire and anti-air, even launching the occasional missile of their own at Lihue or O'ahu.

Hawaiian Joint Forces Commander, Major General Reg Samuels, called on the Chinese commander to surrender, but there was no response. Most of the infrastructure at the PMRF had already been destroyed in the Chinese landing, so six B1-B Bones of the 419th Flight Test Squadron dropped 200 2,000 lb. JDAM-ER bombs on Barking Sands, delivered from 50 miles out to sea into an area only about three times the size of New York's Central Park.

Baruzzi and her MML crew had watched it from their position back up at Makaha Ridge. They'd lost Kennedy at the bridge, which cut Baruzzi like a knife in the gut, but it could have been worse. A lot worse.

Even though she knew the direction from which the Bones' attack was going to be delivered, and approximate timing, she didn't hear the B1-Bs or see the bombs arrive. The *sound* of their arrival hit Baruzzi first, a rippling peal of thunder that continued for nearly half a minute, the last bombs still arriving even as the pressure wave from their detonations drummed against her chest, 6 miles away.

Black, brown and gray columns of smoke rose a half mile into the air and then began spreading out to sea. Like a volcano had erupted right underneath the PMRF.

"Those poor bastards," Kernow said in a low voice. "I don't care who they are. They were sent here on a one-way trip to hell."

"If there's anyone still left alive after that, I hope they have the sense to surrender now," Baruzzi said.

There was, and they did. The smoke was still rising into the sky when the first Chinese soldiers came walking, limping or crawling out, led by soldiers carrying white flags.

On their way back to Lihue, Baruzzi's battery drove slowly past a column of prisoners being marched over the bridge out of Waimea, the farthest point of their advance. One of them regarded her with curiosity as she passed. He had a broad, flat face and snub nose, covered in blood turned brown. His eyes were bloodshot, but bright and curious, and he seemed to be taking in every detail of their vehicles as they passed.

He didn't look like a man who realized they had been beaten ... yet.

Because they had been. You couldn't argue that. People were comparing the Battle of Hawaii to Midway, or Leyte Gulf. Turning points in the last Pacific War.

The US battlenet was being restored. China's Northern Fleet had been decimated. They'd pulled back from the Central Pacific, from Wake, from Midway. Guam was like Kaua'i, just a matter of time until Chinese troops surrendered. There was even momentum on Taiwan—microdrone swarms taking down the slaughterbots as soon as they landed, their president and his new premier rallying their armed forces again, US Marines moving out of Keelung and setting up a Forward Operating Base on the west coast at Taichung Port for the first time.

The virus though. Baruzzi hadn't lost any of her crew yet, knock on wood. They'd been ordered to stay isolated, literally camping atop Unulau Ridge, their only physical contact with the outside world the food, fuel, water and ammunition drops

Navy delivered for them daily down by the Lihue harbor breakwater.

The Navy crews never hung around though.

The rumors said people were going down like flies across the islands and there was no treatment or cure. You got sick, Death rolled his dice and you either recovered or you didn't.

"AWACS alert," her new TCA, Sergeant Tracy Guerin, announced. Baruzzi still kept expecting Kennedy to swing into the Hawkei and drop his lazy ass into the seat next to her every time the door opened. But that wasn't ever going to happen again.

She'd told Kennedy's wife he'd been a big part of their victory, and he was. It was just that she didn't feel like celebrating until the job was finished.

And by that, she meant the job of putting the Chinese genie back in its bottle.

"Sub-launched missiles detected. Bearing two niner five, range 80, projected target: Kaua'i," Guerin said.

She sighed. "Alright, people, you know the routine ..."

SEVERAL DAYS had passed since she'd arrived back at Edwards AFB, and Carmen Carliotti had managed only two hours of sleep the previous night. She'd been flown off O'ahu as the Chinese hovercraft started coming ashore at Kaua'i, and she'd been following events across the Pacific closely from Edwards—from mopping up after the invasions of Kaua'i and Guam and the start of mine-clearing operations on installations across the Pacific to the continuing insurrection in Honolulu, plus meetings, too many to name. In the last 12 hours, she'd joined a meeting of the Joint Chiefs, chaired a meeting of the NSC ExCom, had a one-on-

one with HR Rosenstern and then fallen asleep in her makeshift Situation Room before being led to a cot in a corner and giving orders to be woken in two hours.

She was shaken awake by the ever-attentive Colonel Charles, with a strong cup of coffee, a toiletries kit and a towel.

"Ma'am, if you'd like to get ready, there is a meeting of INDOPACOM unified command chiefs in 30 minutes."

She swung herself into a sitting position and took the coffee. "Thanks, Colonel. What happened while I was asleep?" They'd already developed an understanding. Along with her coffee, he came armed with whatever was the latest intelligence on the hot topics she was following, and let her lead the way with questions as she drained her first mug. "Start with the sea war."

"Well, the good news. Updated damage assessment from the strikes on the Sino-Russian fleet: both carriers, *Liaoning* and *Shandong*, were sunk, along with several amphibious assault ships and supply vessels. Russia lost several vessels too. *Virginia* class subs, the Brits and Australians have been dogging the stragglers and claimed three more vessels overnight. The rest, a few cruisers and destroyers, are withdrawing northwest, toward the Russian Kuril Islands. Chinese submarines are still a big problem; fast as we can clear mines, they launch new cruise missile strikes and resow them. Your next meeting the Joint Chiefs will be discussing options for an intensive anti-submarine campaign, and updates on the situations on Guam and our Pacific bases."

"Civil unrest?"

"Hawaii or stateside, ma'am?"

"Hawaii first."

519

"Freeth is still on the run. His followers are claiming responsibility for a spate of attacks on military personnel, a bridge and a power station on O'ahu, and there have been similar attacks on Big Island and Maui. Hard to gauge public support at this time, but his call for a vote on independence is gaining traction."

"We need to show solidarity with the people of Hawaii now, more than ever. I want the names of any civilians, police or military personnel killed in these attacks. I'd like to speak with their families."

"Yes ma'am. FBI thinks Freeth's movement is getting help from the Chinese: arms, money, training …"

"Why am I not surprised?" She sighed. "Every rock we look under, China is there. Which leads me to the protests at home."

"The Defenders of Liberty marches were shut down in most capital cities. But they went ahead in Detroit, Montpelier, Birmingham, Saint Paul and … Houston, I think … There were reports of clashes with police and Guardsmen …"

"Anyone injured?"

"Yes, several shooting deaths, ma'am. One Guardsman."

"I want to speak with HR Rosenstern when I'm done with my shower."

Then they came to the topic she always saved for last. Charles had decided it was not because it was the topic she was least interested in, but because it was the hardest for her to hear since there was virtually nothing she could do about it—which was not a situation a US President was accustomed to.

"Pandemic numbers."

"Uh ... US mainland will hit 300,000 active cases today, a little ahead of expectations. Currently the death toll is just under 30 percent, 90,000 dead. Hawaii has 3,000 cases now, 800 dead. On Taiwan, the rate of infections and deaths has flatlined, but that's just a factor of how many have already been infected or died. Good news is first studies show high levels of antibodies in survivors, so the reinfection rate is lower than feared. But you've got a call with the Secretary of Treasury later. I was told the economic situation is ... grim. The healthcare system is collapsing, and Treasury is predicting a massive unskilled labor shortage as soon as next year ..."

Carliotti's eyes were getting colder as each new number fell on her ears.

"Postpone my attendance at the INDOPACOM meeting. I want an immediate video call with the Directors of CIA, DIA and the Commander SOCOM. I've reviewed their proposals for retaliation over the release of the bioweapon, and they do not go far enough across the Chinese Communist Party hierarchy and do not reach deep enough into their personal lives to do justice to the millions who will suffer from the pestilence and economic ruin they have unleashed on the world." Carliotti's coffee cup was shaking in her hand as she spoke. "You can put this in your memoir, Charles. Quote: 'As the president said these words, it became clear to me she meant to see every member of the Chinese Communist Party Central Committee rotting in hell before the end of this war.'"

"I ... Yes ma'am," he said. "But there's ... maybe it's not my place to tell you." He stopped, handing her a towel.

"You already are, Colonel," she pointed out.

He looked around, checking no one else in the war room was in earshot. "There's some good news on the virus, ma'am. Fantastic news maybe. A special operations unit on Taiwan was involved in an operation in Taipei ..."

She sipped her coffee, frowning. "Go on."

"Ma'am, it looks like they recovered a large sample of the Chinese vaccine."

She stopped sipping. Nearly dropped her cup. At NSC ExCom earlier, they'd discussed options for sourcing and then reverse-engineering China's H5N1c vaccine. High-risk options, involving agents operating behind enemy lines in China, Iran, North Korea or Russia. The intelligence community consensus was it could take months to just source the vaccine samples and smuggle them out, let alone begin producing a copy. She'd ordered them to set operations in motion and start building factories to manufacture it already, since vaccine production capacity was always a bottleneck in pandemics.

The advice of vaccine researchers who'd examined the H5N1c strains presenting on Taiwan and now in the US was that, even with unlimited funding, if they had to start from zero, a vaccine could take a *year* to develop. By which time hundreds of thousands, if not *millions*, would be dead, and China would have leverage over every nation willing to trade their allegiance for a vaccine.

"You're *sure?*"

"Yes ma'am. Heard it from the admiral, but also heard it from the Air Force captain who is flying the samples to Alaska via Japan right now. So I trust it."

"Colonel, you know what this means?" she asked. "Obviously, you do. This is ..."

"Freaking fantastic, ma'am?" He smiled.

"Does a high five fall inside your comfort zone, Colonel?" Carliotti asked.

He took the towel from her and held up a hand. "From the US President? Anytime, ma'am."

Putting down her coffee, Carliotti gave him a high five, then composed herself. She picked up her coffee again; her hand no longer shaking.

"I still want that meeting with CIA, DIA and SOCOM, Colonel," she said, voice cold again. "Vaccine or no vaccine, those responsible *will* pay."

FALANIKO 'NIKO' AKIU was paying. He'd lost part of his heel, and the doctors had taken some of his buttock for the graft. His brother had joked it was lucky he had a big ass, but Niko didn't think that was too funny.

Niko didn't think much was funny at all right now.

The guys from Fire Station 4 had been past to tell him he was going to get a medal, but they were still trying to work out if it would be a Fire Service medal or a Navy medal, like a Purple Heart or Bronze Star. It would depend if they decided the most important thing was the girls he saved or the slaughterbot he'd brought down.

"Or both, eh?" one of the guys said. "You *should* get a Silver Star, if they add both together. Except they probably won't give a Silver Star to someone who busted out of the brig."

Niko would have traded both his left ass cheek and any medal they might give him if he could just wind back time and stop himself dropping his weapon, or stop Presley Ortiz from jumping out that door. You ask Niko Akiu what he was thinking as he lay in his hospital bed staring out the window, usually he was thinking that.

Or he was thinking how, everything that happened, running from the slaughterbots, shooting one up and especially getting shot, you could keep that shit. He'd decided he wasn't cut out to be a firefighter, that was for sure.

But he'd surprised himself how he was around blood. Fixing up Presley's classmate, binding his own wounds, cleaning up the cuts and scratches the other girls got from flying glass and brick. He hadn't fainted, or puked, or panicked.

Niko had decided he was going to go back to A-school, go a different way. When he got back on his feet—literally—he was going to be a Navy corpsman.

NO ONE WAS going to give Outlaw a medal, so when the dust settled, Rory and Uncle got the crew together at Dillingham Airfield, took a magnum of Champagne, poured everyone a glass and poured the rest over the AC-130X's scarred black nose.

Then they drank the rest of the crate they'd bought, draining their glasses for every kill silhouette the ground crew had painted on the command module bulkhead inside the plane.

They'd been told only about 15 Chinese landing craft made it to shore, and though there was a lot of duplicate claiming between Air Force and Army and Marines, their LOCUST strike had probably destroyed at least five *Yaks* and damaged double that many. So they painted five hovercraft up there. *Liaoning* was just a partial, so they painted half an aircraft carrier up there too. The *Gorshkov* corvette they'd hit in the first days of the Battle of Hawaii would also have been borderline, since they only damaged it, but then they heard the USS *Tang* torpedoed it after the Skylon strike, so they called that a partial kill too. But they still drank a full glass of champagne for it.

That night, Rory had fallen asleep in his pilot seat in Outlaw's cockpit and snored right through to morning with no nocturnal visitor creeping into his sleep to terrorize him.

The next day, they'd flown 74 stretcher cases and the medical teams looking after them from Hawaii to San Diego for treatment. None had died on the way. And that had been a damn good feeling too.

They got back to Davis Monthan AFB in Arizona to find the base in quarantine lockdown, news bulletins showing lines outside banks and gas stations and supermarkets empty—but after what they'd been through, they couldn't help but feel the worst was behind them.

AFTER SEVERAL DAYS of missions broken only by mandatory eight-hour rest breaks, Tug Boatt, the pilot and groundcrews of the 615th Combat Operations Squadron, were finally being taken off the line.

Space Force now had enough hardware in space to cover basic ISR needs, which was just as well, because the crews of the two Skylons of the 615th had begun to treat critical system error messages as normal every time they went up.

Tiger and Mako, like their crews, needed some serious downtime.

Sally walked in on Tug reading news on a tablet PC in their mess at Vandenberg, spun a chair around and sat opposite him without speaking as she waited for him to look up.

"Russians put missiles on an island just 50 miles off the Japanese coast," Tug said.

"That's not very neighborly. They aren't technically at war yet, are they?" she asked.

"No, but they will be." He pointed to an image of a Japanese flag flying over a runway with a destroyed Russian helicopter on it. "Japan just went in, kicked the Russians off the island and claimed it back for Japan."

"It's a world war now, boss," Hall said. "Which ..."

He turned off the tablet and pushed it aside. "I know. A Group Captain Mainwaring from 1 Squadron, RAF Space Force, called me this morning. They want their pilot back."

Hall nodded. "The rumor is this is going to spread to Europe, whether we like it or not."

"Russia bought into this fight on China's side for a reason." Tug nodded. "And I doubt their ambition is limited to small Japanese islands."

Hall reached out a hand for him to shake. Her T-shirt today said, "*I fought the law and the law lost.*" He took it and shook.

"Thanks for everything, boss. It was fun," Hall said. "Until it wasn't."

AFTER ALL she'd been through, Jensen made sure Fi got VIP treatment when they reached the port. He told Corps Intelligence aboard the *Bougainville* that Fi was the one who tamed and delivered to them their first working slaughterbot and they should treat her as a high-value asset.

She was put in quarantine like the rest of them, but she spent most of her time being debriefed by cyber spooks wanting to know how she'd done it.

There had been a lot less fanfare about the case of mysterious vials Jensen had delivered. It had been picked up by two guys in MOPP gear and whisked away, and he never saw or heard about it again. He'd convinced himself that the case hadn't been the thing that got Xu and Jackson killed, which was just as well since no one seemed to think it was important.

He and Chang had both received personal letters of thanks from the Taiwanese president though. They had also been delivered to him in quarantine by a man in MOPP gear wearing a black suit and red tie underneath, sweating profusely. He stayed only long enough for Jensen to read the letter before he took it back again.

"I don't get a copy?" Jensen asked.

"No," the man said, as though that should be obvious. "This letter does not exist."

"Well, then, I figure I've at least earned the right to ask a small favor," Jensen said.

"What favor?" the man asked suspiciously.

The president and vice president had been on TV after their release from house arrest, announcing the death of the premier in a Chinese slaughterbot attack. There was even shaky camera phone footage, showing two slaughterbots firing into the premier's compound and his security detail bravely fighting back.

After 10 days of quarantine, Jensen was waiting for Fi to get her release too. He met her in the infirmary galley for breakfast.

She beamed when she saw him and came over and sat down as he pushed a bowl across the table to her.

"What's this?" she asked.

"Congee," he said. "With sweet potato. I got the kitchen to make it special for you."

"Yuck," she said, pushing it away and looking around. "Don't they have pancakes?"

He'd been expecting that. Got her settled with juice, pancakes, eggs, hash browns, syrup and bacon and sat, quietly impressed, as she forked it all down. When she was done, he pushed a small folder over to her. His "favor" had come through.

"OK." She looked at it suspiciously. "And what's this?" She opened it, pulling out some documents. "A plane ticket? Passport?"

"Taiwanese passport, since you didn't have one," he said, opening it to an inside page. "US Visa. Letter from your guardian, your uncle, saying you can travel. Plus a USAF flight requisition: Taipei to Tokyo, then San Diego. Open date, since you'll probably want to say goodbye to people and who knows when we'll be allowed off this island paradise of yours, anyway."

She looked at the papers, wide eyed. Then she heard what he said. "We? You said *we*."

"I'll go back with you," he said. "Make sure you get there OK, get you settled in. Or my sister will. You'll be staying with her."

"What? Where?"

"Quantico, Virginia. That's where the lab is."

"What lab?"

"US Marine Corps Warfighting Lab: Robotics Division," he said. "I've been assigned there, to evaluate Fluffy, your pet slaughterbot. You'll work with me, help pull it apart, show us what makes it tick."

"You don't need me," she said, not believing him.

"Well, the lab decided they want me on this project, and I convinced them I need you," he said. "You'll still have to go to school. What grade are you anyway?"

"Upper secondary, year 10, but I …"

"So that's a sophomore? They might start you as a freshman, you know, year nine—because of your English."

She stuck out her jaw. "My English is good. And I don't want to go to a stupid American school."

"That's the spirit." He smiled. "Off to a great start."

She went back to looking through the papers. "Is all this real?"

"Well, there's a catch."

She looked up, suddenly wary. "What catch?"

Jensen turned around, put two fingers in his mouth and whistled. From a wall of the galley, a familiar form came limping over and then sat beside Jensen.

"You remember Squirt?"

"Yeah?" She looked at the LS3. Jensen had replaced the sonic drill headpiece with a camera attachment that someone had painted eyes on. It didn't make him look friendlier.

"He's your job interview," Jensen said. "Ever since the thing with the premier …"

"What thing with the premier?" she asked, deadpan.

"The … oh, I see what you did there. You've been warned. Very good," Jensen nodded. "Ever since that thing that didn't happen, he's been glitching. Has these 30-second blackouts. Techs insist it's not a hardware problem. We've done a complete power down and reboot, reinstalled his OS, but he still glitches."

She pointed to some fluid dripping on the deck from a rear leg joint. "And leaks."

"No. Or yes, but I call that a design feature. I can't send him back in the field if he's glitching, and I don't want to bring him to Quantico like this. Can you have a look at him?"

"I guess," she said. She absently flipped open a panel on his back as she chewed on some bacon, and pulled away some wires to look at a diagnostic screen inside, wrinkling her nose at what she saw. "Maybe. How much does it pay, this lab job of yours?" she asked, without looking up.

"See if you can fix the damn dog first," Jensen said. "Then we can talk about hourly rates."

THE VOICE at the end of the call HR had been told was from a journalist was not a journalist.

Rosenstern had been preparing himself with the same set of answers he'd already given to a dozen media outlets in off-the-record briefings. Yes, the US President was on Taiwan. Yes, key members of the administration had isolated themselves in a central location, in line with the US President's Pandemic Control Executive Orders. No, he would not say where it was. No, he couldn't tell them what the military situation was on (pick a country, island or atoll). They should wait for the next Pentagon briefing. No, he had nothing to add to what the president had already said regarding the pandemic restrictions.

But, oh, man. Let me off the leash, and I would have more than a few things to say. Humiliated by being thrown off Air Force One and buried under the ice in Greenland, HR Rosenstern had been relegated to dealing with the fallout from the flurry of Executive Orders putting the National Guard on the

530

streets, restricting travel, restricting gatherings, granting extraordinary powers to Homeland Security, the Health Secretary, the Director of Immigration and Customs Enforcement ... you name it. His cell phone had been running hot with calls from outraged Congress members, senators, governors, civil libertarians, lobbyists, billionaire donors and ... journalists.

And he thought he was about to have to blow off another one, a journalist from a liberal blog he detested. But one with a huge following.

How would they all react if they knew the architect of every one of the president's Pandemic Executive Orders was HR Rosenstern? That knowledge was the only thing that kept him from walking out onto the ice and shooting himself with a walrus harpoon.

"Hey, Alan, hope you're doing alright?" he said, trying to inject a little energy into his voice.

"Mr. Rosenstern, this is not Alan Carlton," the voice said.

He froze. "You can't be on this line," he said, resisting the temptation to get up and look out into the corridor. The door to this conference room was shut, but that meant nothing.

"I can be on any line I choose, Mr. Rosenstern," the voice said. It was deep. Verbal mahogany. It had been digitally modulated, but it was the Principal's voice. "And be assured, the line is secure."

"What do you want?" HR asked. He felt his heart beating faster. Were there any loose ends he hadn't attended to? Raven Rock, the Joint Wargaming Council? No, he'd dealt with them both. He'd put the president where she was supposed to be, when she was supposed to be there. It wasn't his fault the Raven Rock operation went sideways. And the Raven Rock investigation had been diverted into a fleet reporting only to him, which he'd put on hold as soon as the president had declared war on China. Following the unfortunate death of another JWC Director, Julio Ramirez, he'd disbanded the JWC. It had outlived its usefulness, both to ExCom and to HR. The Executive Orders? Had they gone too far? Not far enough?

No, he'd done exactly as he'd been asked.

"I want to congratulate you for recent developments, Mr. Rosenstern," the voice said. "I see National Guardsmen outside my office. Protesters on the streets. Armed rebellion. States threatening to secede from the Union ..."

No, you didn't call to congratulate me. You need something, Rosenstern was thinking. And his next thought was, *You can leverage this, Rosenstern.*

"Thank you. I've done the best I could in the circumstances," he said. "Is there anything more ...?"

"Ah, so modest, Mr. Rosenstern," the voice chuckled. "But our work isn't done, is it?"

"No?"

"No. We have tilled the soil; now it is time to sow the seeds of change."

Tilled the soil? HR had known that the rebirth of his nation was going to be a messy affair. He'd been among the first to see that the coming crisis would be the perfect crucible for revolution. He hadn't expected that he personally would have to play the role of midwife, bloodied hands guiding the newborn America into the world. But so be it. He was ready for whatever came next.

HR was no wiser about the purpose for the call though. "And, how can I help?"

"I'm told your time at the top in the White House is over. You've been 'put on ice' so to speak."

HR blanched. He'd started to see the signs too, but to hear another, to hear The Principal, put it into words was a knife in the heart. And the man intimated he knew exactly where HR had been evacuated to. His access to top secret intelligence was unfathomable. If he'd heard rumors of HR's imminent fall from grace, then it was just a matter of time.

HR stared bleakly at the desk phone. "If what you say is true and my usefulness to the cause is over," he began. "I am grateful for…"

"Don't write your own obituary too soon, Mr. Rosenstern," the voice said. "I have another role for you to play. One that is even more important. As soon as you can extract yourself from your icy prison."

BUNNY O'HARE was stateside again. When 68th Aggressor had been pulled back to Luke AFB in Arizona, she'd taken Touchdown's "recommendation" to grab a few days leave before Meany's memorial service and been granted permission to leave the base as long as she complied with lockdown directions: no unauthorized cross-border travel, no gatherings over 20 people, seven-day quarantine when she returned to duty.

She'd also been required to revisit the combat report from her attack on *Liaoning* before she took leave. Meany Papastopolous had been nominated for an Air Force Cross (posthumous) for delivering the strike that destroyed *Liaoning*, but there was apparently some confusion over whose missile had hit the carrier first. "Not only was it Captain Papastopolous' missile that struck the carrier first: his sacrifice in drawing enemy escort fighters to him allowed me to complete my attack." Bunny wrote. "However, he doesn't deserve an Air Force Cross. He deserves a Medal of Honor."

"Air Force is promoting you to Captain," Touchdown said as she was leaving, and before Bunny could speak, held up her hand. "My recommendation. You'll stay with the 68th, and you can't refuse. We're being brought up to squadron strength again, and you'll command our Widow pilots. I will keep Raptor responsibilities. And I want you giving more input in mission planning. Your strategy for taking out *Liaoning* worked. Your plans, don't ask me how, usually do. You'll still be Aggressor Inc.'s Uncrewed Combat Training Lead, but as long as we're at war, I want you as a flight leader, giving input on how to win it. No more cruising."

She hadn't said yes, but she hadn't said no.

She'd packed a bottle of bourbon, a case of beer, some pot noodles, apples and a book, and driven her pickup south of Buckeye to a cabin she owned down on the Gila River.

Coast Guard, out looking for Chinese lifeboats, found Meany's body two days after he went down. They'd all kept hoping that by some miracle he'd make it back to them again, so it hurt twice as much when they were told he wasn't going to. Was he dead or alive when he hit the water? If he was alive, for how long? Bunny had a lot of questions, but she didn't want to know the answers.

She spent three days drinking, reading and doodling on a notepad. She had no TV at the cabin, but the radio was talking about the Battle of Hawaii like the USA had already won the war and the pandemic was the bigger problem now. She couldn't blame them. It was hard to see how China could come back after losing all its carriers, most of its Northern Fleet, and with the surrender of its troops on Guam just a matter of time.

Except ... Bunny knew China had three fleets, not one. And the South and East Sea Fleets were still largely intact. Wake and Midway were unusable. Pearl Harbor-Hickam and most Hawaiian air bases too. The civilian casualties from proximity mines were horrific. She'd tuned her radio to a channel that had no news bulletins.

On the day of Meany's memorial service, she sent a simple message to Touchdown: *Won't be there today. O'Hare.* Instead, she drove into Buckeye, to the Ponderosa Ink Emporium. When she handed her sketch over to the tattooist, he looked at it skeptically.

"That supposed to be a robot?" he asked.

"No," she said. "Exoskeleton, with, like, a Terminator head."

"That's ... different," he said, frowning. He got out a book of sketches, and flipped through until he found the page he wanted. "Something like this?"

"Sure," she said, taking off her T-shirt. She pointed at something that was close to her sketch.

"Uh, OK, where you want it?" he asked, looking her over. "There's not a lot of real estate left."

Bunny had thought about it. Who would be a good companion for Meany? He might have to live on her skin for a while, she wouldn't want him feeling too crowded. He didn't like crowds, liked to have room to move since he wasn't so light on his feet. And she didn't want him stuck next to someone he wouldn't get along with. Then she had it.

She pointed to a spot under her ribs. "Can you put it here?"

He bent over, squinting. "Yeah, sure. Now, colors ..."

"Is there room to put a fish beside it?"

"A fish? Have to be small."

535

"That's fine. A small fish."

Meany had never met the gnarly Taiwanese fisherman, Lin Zhiwei, but they both had a never-say-die approach to life. She smiled as she remembered the old guy picking up his blunderbuss, thinking nothing of trying to take a pot shot at a slaughterbot. He'd be good company for the British pilot, and she didn't have a tattoo to remember the fishermen by yet.

She agreed the details with the tattooist, lay back while he made his stencils, closed her eyes and tried to remember the first time she met Meany. A joint forces mission they'd flown during the Russian orbital weapon crisis.

"OK, this is not going quite as I intended," Meany had said, staring down the video link at her as she was laying out how she saw their upcoming mission.

"I get that a lot, Flight Lieutenant," she'd said. "And we may be in different armed forces, but I am flight lead for this mission." An RAF Lieutenant and USAF Captain were equal in rank and it felt like he didn't realize that. A rank she later lost, but that was another story.

"Apologies, Captain," Meany had said, but not like he meant it. He pronounced it *Cap'n*. She'd loved his Welsh lilt.

"I just need you along for your missiles, Flight Lieutenant," O'Hare had told him. "Otherwise, this is a USAF mission, and you will be under my command."

Not exactly a great start to a beautiful friendship. But he'd turned out to be one of the few in Bunny's life who could put up with her. Had her back in combat, had it on the ground. Saved her more than once from doing something really, really stupid.

"OK, we good to go?" the tattooist said, showing her the stencil.

Bunny lifted her head to look, then lay back again. "So good," she said. "Don't be afraid to make it hurt."

/END

Author note

Thanks so much for following the Aggressor series. I hope you are enjoying reading it as much as I enjoy writing it!

The premise of MIDNIGHT was simple—what if China took the current US Pacific warfighting strategy of "area denial" and used it against the USA? Not a war of conquest, but one of denying the US the ability to use its possessions in the Pacific to project power.

In MIDNIGHT, this strategy only partially succeeds. The impact it has will be explored in Volume V of the Aggressor series, FULCRUM.

A quick note on the insurrection subplot in this book and the actions of the 'Hawaiian Freedom Alliance': this is an entirely fictitious organization and bears no intentional resemblance to any of the several independence or sovereignty movements that do exist on Hawaii. These movements to date have only employed peaceful means to lobby for sovereignty or independence, and there is no evidence of Chinese interference in their activities.

This book simply speculates on how China *might* do so, in the context of total war.

The situation in which military commanders on Hawaii find themselves—under-resourced and scrambling to put together the assets needed to mount a defense of the islands when most INDOPACOM resources are forward deployed—is not exaggerated. US strategic defense planners have put a lot of faith in the belief that an amphibious attack of the type foreseen in MIDNIGHT would be impossible for an enemy to achieve.

And there is that word, "impossible."

Skylon provides a solution to this challenge in MIDNIGHT, but the same impact on an enemy fleet could have been achieved with tactical nuclear weapons, submarines and standoff strike aircraft if they were available, or hypersonic ballistic or cruise missiles if the US has deployed these by 2038.

The choice of an orbital bombardment weapon in this novel was prompted by the claim by US lawmakers in 2024 that Russia was planning to deploy a nuclear weapon in space, and speculation that, if not nuclear, the weapon could be a Kinetic Energy Projectile or orbital bombardment weapon.

For a more complete exploration of the implications if this became a reality, just read *Orbital*!

Which leads me to this … what is next for the Aggressor series?

FULCRUM will be the last episode of the series, and I want to do it right. It will feature all your favorite (surviving) characters from the first four books, and be the most ambitious of the series, covering multiple theaters and spanning multiple years.

Final release of Vol V, FULCRUM, is planned for **September 2024**.

But don't despair. I will release a preview of the first few chapters of FULCRUM during summer 2024 FOR FREE. Just go to www.fxholden.com and sign up for my mailing list to get the preview.

And, did I say … FREE?

Go to www.fxholden.com now and subscribe!

FX Holden, Copenhagen, March 2024

FULCRUM: Coming July 2024

Volume 5 of 5 in the Aggressor Series

fulcrum /fool'kram/
noun
The point or support on which a lever pivots.
An agent through which vital powers are exercised.

In FULCRUM, US Coalition Allies and the Shanghai Pact face off in an epic global battle for survival, spanning the Pacific, Asia, Europe, and the USA.

The Sino-Russian Pacific fleet has been destroyed. Does it mean the end of China and Russia's ability to project power in the Pacific, or does it still have the means to continue the fight?

The US Coalition has its 'enigma machine.' What effect will it have on the course of the war?

A terrible toll has been taken on the 68th AGRS Aggressors. Can they rise again or is the USAF's most lethal squadron out for the count?

Get an early preview of Fulcrum for **FREE** this summer 2024 by joining the mailing list at www.fxholden.com or enjoy the anticipation of the full and final volume of the Aggressor Series coming September 2024.

Glossary

For simplicity, this glossary is common across all FX Holden novels and may refer to abbreviations or systems not in this novel. As such, it is useful as a reference beyond this book! Please note, weapons or systems marked with an asterisk* are currently still under development or speculative. If there is no asterisk, then the system has already been deployed by at least one nation.

3D PRINTER: A printer which can recreate a 3D object based on a three-dimensional digital model, typically by laying down many thin layers of a material in succession.

AC-130X*: a variant of the AC-130 series of special operations aircraft and follow-on to the AC-130J Ghostrider. Stripped of all heavy weapons to make room for two Rapid Dragon* palletized ordnance dispensers, it is envisaged as a signals and electronic intelligence, surveillance and reconnaissance aircraft with drone and standoff strike capability.

ADA*: All Domain Attack. An attack on an enemy in which all operational domains–space, cyber, ground, air and naval–are engaged either simultaneously or sequentially.

AI: Artificial intelligence, as applied in aircraft to assist pilots, in intelligence to assist with intelligence analysis, or in ordnance such as drones and uncrewed vehicles to allow semi-autonomous or even fully autonomous decision making.

AIM-120D: US medium-range supersonic air-to-air missile.

AIM-260* Joint Advanced Tactical Missile (JATM), proposed replacement for AIM-120, with twin-boost phase, launch and loiter capability. Swarming capability has been discussed.

AIS: Automated identification system, a system used by all ships to provide update data on their location to their owners and insurers. Civilian ships are required to keep their transponder on at all times unless under threat from pirates; military ships transmit at their own discretion. Rogue nations often ignore the requirement in order to hide the location of ships with illicit cargoes or conducting illegal activities.

AIR TROPHY*: 'Trophy' is an Israeli-made anti-projectile defense system using explosively formed penetrators to defeat attacks on vehicles. It is currently fitted to several Israeli and US armored vehicle types. In 2023 the US Navy announced it was testing the Trophy system for naval defense. Use as an air defense system is speculative.

AGGRESSOR/ADVERSARY: Fighter squadrons that provide training against adversary aircraft are known as 'Aggressor' squadrons. The US Air Force has several in-house No. 9 Squadrons (including F-16s and F-35s) which it uses to train fighter pilots and joint tactical air controllers. In the US Marines and Navy these are known as 'Adversary' units. In 2022, the USAF confirmed that Aggressor aircraft in Alaska had been used to intercept Russian aircraft off the coast of Alaska, and No. 9 Squadrons had been used to backfill regular USAF squadrons deployed overseas. Many air forces including the USAF and RAF, also use private contractors to provide these services, and several large private military aviation contractors exist, fielding recently retired F-16 and F-18 fighters. The most advanced private air force in the world, Air USA, claims to be able to field three No. 9 Squadrons including 46 ex-RAAF F/A-18 Hornets.

ALL DOMAIN KILL CHAIN*: Also known as Multi-Domain Kill Chain. An attack in which advanced AI allows high-speed assimilation of data from multiple sources (satellite, cyber, ground and air) to generate engagement solutions for military maneuver, precision fire support, artillery or combat air support.

AMD-65: Hungarian-made military assault rifle

AN/APG-81: The active electronically scanning array (AESA) radar system on the F-35 Panther that allows it to track and engage multiple air and ground targets simultaneously

ANGELS: Radio brevity code for 'thousands of feet.' Angels five is five thousand feet.

AO YIN: Legendary Chinese four-horned bull with insatiable appetite for human flesh

APC: Armored personnel carrier; a wheeled or tracked lightly armored vehicle able to transport troops into combat and provide limited covering fire

ARMATA T-14: Next-generation Russian main battle tank

ASFN: Anti-screw fouling net. Traditionally, a net boom laid across the entrance of a harbor to hinder the entrance of ships or submarines. Can also be dropped from a fast boat, or fired from a subsea drone to foul the screws of a surface vessel.

ASRAAM: Advanced Short-Range Air-to-Air Missile (infrared only)

ASROC: Anti-submarine rocket-launched torpedo. Allows a torpedo to be fired at a submerged target from up to ten miles away, allowing the torpedo to enter the water close to the target and reducing the chances the target can evade the attack.

ASTUTE CLASS: Next-generation British nuclear-powered attack submarine (SSN) designed for stealth operation. Powered by a Rolls Royce reactor plant coupled to a pump-jet propulsion system. *HMS Astute* is the first of seven planned hulls, *HMS Agincourt* is the last. Can carry up to 38 torpedoes and cruise missiles, and is one of the first British submarines to be steered by a 'pilot' using a joystick.

AUKUS class submarine*: AUKUS is a trilateral security pact between Australia, the United Kingdom, and the United States announced on 15 September 2021 for the Indo-Pacific region to counter China's influence. The AUKUS submarine deal signed in 2022 will provide Australia with access to nuclear-powered submarines, which are stealthier and more capable than conventionally powered boats. The total cost of the deal is estimated to be $100 billion, making it Australia's biggest defense spend. According to media reports, Australia will first buy US-designed *Virginia* class submarines as a stopgap, before acquiring a future UK-designed boat under a multi-billion-dollar deal. The UK-built submarines are currently in the design phase and are set to replace the *Astute* fleet. The *AE1* featured in this novel is speculative.

ASW: Anti-Submarine Warfare

AWACS: Airborne Warning and Control System aircraft, otherwise known as AEW&C (Airborne Early Warning and Control). Aircraft with advanced radar and communication systems that can detect aircraft at ranges up to several hundred miles, and direct air operations over a combat theater.

AXEHEAD: Russian long-range hypersonic air-to-air missile, identifying code R-37, designed primarily to shoot down large aircraft at long ranges. Used in combat in Ukraine. The Royal United Services Institute stated: "The Russian Air Force fired up to six R-37Ms per day during October 2022. The extremely high speed of the weapon, coupled with very long effective range and a seeker designed for engaging low-altitude targets, makes it particularly difficult to evade." The

Ukraine Air Force disputes this assessment. The Axehead effectiveness is therefore assumed high, but impossible to verify.

AUTONOMOUS vs SEMI AUTONOMOUS: In drone warfare, an autonomous drone is one which can conduct its mission completely independent of human interaction once launched. This reduces its vulnerability to jamming as no signals pass between its operator and the drone which can be jammed. A semi-autonomous drone is one which relies on a wireless/radio/satellite link for communication with its operator but can make some decisions on its own if contact with the human operator is lost or unnecessary. Due to the reliance on a communication link to the operator, such drones are susceptible to jamming.

B-21 RAIDER*: Replacement for the retiring US B-2 Stealth Bomber and B-52. The Raider is intended to provide a lower-cost, stealthier alternative to the B-2 with expanded weapons delivery capabilities to include hypersonic and beyond visual range air-to-air missiles.

BARRETT MRAD M22: Multirole adaptive design sniper rifle with replaceable barrels, capable of firing different ammunition types including anti-materiel rounds, accurate out to 1,500 meters or nearly one mile

BATS*: Boeing Airpower Teaming System, semi-autonomous uncrewed combat aircraft. The BATS drone is designed to accompany 4th- and 5th-generation fighter aircraft on missions either in an air escort, recon or electronic warfare capacity.

BATTLE-NET: Generic name for tactical data sharing systems such as the US The Tactical Targeting Network Technology (TTNT) system; a high-bandwidth, secure data sharing network that enables real-time sharing of targeting and situational awareness data among aircraft, ground vehicles, and command centers, allowing for faster and more effective decision-making on the battlefield.

BELLADONNA: A Russian-made mobile electronic warfare vehicle capable of jamming enemy airborne warning aircraft, ground radars, radio communications and radar-guided missiles

BESAT*: New 1,200-ton class of Iranian SSP (air-independent propulsion) submarine. Also known as Project Qaaem. Capable of launching mines, torpedoes or cruise missiles.

BIG RED ONE: US 1st Infantry Division (see also BRO), aka the Bloody First

BINGO: Radio brevity code showing that an aircraft has only enough fuel left for a return to base

BIRD-DOG*: An 'autonomous foraging drone' or uncrewed aerial vehicle which can locate its own sources of power resupply and operate completely independently of human interaction when ordered to.

BLACK WIDOW (P-99)*: *Artist impression above.* Several companies were competing in 2023/4 for the Next Generation Air Dominance (NGAD) air superiority initiative. The Black Widow is a purely speculative platform combining what is known about the requirements issued and the designs in testing. NGAD is described by the USAF as a "family of systems," with a stealth fighter aircraft as the centerpiece of the system, and other parts of the system likely to be uncrewed escort aircraft to carry extra munitions and perform other missions. In particular, NGAD aims to develop a system that addresses the operation needs of the Pacific theater of operations, where current USAF fighters lack sufficient range and payload. The successful NGAD aircraft is therefore unlikely to resemble current US stealth fighters such as the F-22 Raptor or F-35 Panther.

BLOODY FIRST: US 1st Infantry Division, aka the Big Red One (BRO)

BOGEY: Unidentified aircraft detected by radar

BRADLEY UGCV*: US uncrewed ground combat vehicle prototype based on a modified M3 Bradley combat fighting vehicle. A tracked vehicle with medium armor, it is intended to be controlled remotely by a crew in a vehicle, or ground troops, up to two miles away. Armed with 5kw blinding laser and autoloading TOW anti-tank missiles. See also HYPERION

BRO: Big Red One or Bloody First, nickname for US Army 1st Infantry Division

BTR-80: A Russian-made amphibious armored personnel carrier armed with a 30 mm automatic cannon

BUG OUT: Withdraw from combat

BUK: Russian-made self-propelled anti-aircraft missile system designed to engage medium-range targets such as aircraft, smart bombs and cruise missiles

BUSTER: 100% throttle setting on an aircraft, or full military power

CAP: Combat air patrol; an offensive or defensive air patrol over an objective

CAS: Close air support; air action by rotary-winged or fixed-wing aircraft against hostile targets in close proximity to friendly forces. CAS operations are often directed by a joint terminal air controller, or JTAC, embedded with a military unit.

CASA CN-235: Turkish Air Force medium-range twin-engined transport aircraft

CBRN: Chemical, biological, radiological or nuclear (see also NBC SUIT)

CCP: Communist Party of China. Governed by a Politburo comprising the Chinese Premier and senior party ministers and officials.

CENTURION: US 20 mm radar-guided close-in weapons system for protection of ground or naval assets against attack by artillery, rocket or missiles

CHAMP*: Counter-electronics High-power Advanced Microwave Projectile; a 'launch and loiter' cruise missile which attacks sensitive electronics with high power microwave bursts to damage electronics. Similar in effect to an electromagnetic pulse (EMP) weapon.

CHONGMING CH-7 Rainbow*: A stealthy flying-wing uncrewed fighter aircraft similar to the US F-47B, with a 22-meter wingspan and 10m length, and a maximum take-off weight of 13 tons. Reportedly able to fly at 920 km/h or 571 mph, with an operational radius of 2,000 km or 1,200 miles. Can carry air-to-air or air to surface missiles in an internal bay. Prototypes have been photographed and production was due to begin in 2022 but deployment has not yet been confirmed.

CIC: Combat Information Center. The 'nerve center' on an early warning aircraft, warship or submarine that functions as a tactical center and provides processed information for command and control of the near battlespace or area of operations. On a warship, acts on orders from and relays information to the bridge.

CO: Commanding Officer

COALITION: A US-led Coalition of Nations.

COLT: Combat Observation Laser Team; a forward artillery observer team armed with a laser for designating targets for attack by precision-guided munitions

CONSTELLATION* class frigate: the result of the US FFG(X) program, a warship with advanced anti-air, anti-surface and anti-submarine capabilities capable of serving as a data integration and communication hub. The first ship in the class, USS *Constellation*, is expected to enter service mid-2020s. USS *Congress* will be the second ship in the class.

CONTROL ROOM: the compartment on a submarine from which weapons, sensors, propulsion and navigation commands are coordinated

COP: Combat Outpost (US)

C-RAM: Counter-rocket, artillery and mortar cannon, also abbreviated counter-RAM

CROWS: Common Remotely Operated Weapon Station, a weapon such as .50 caliber machine gun, mounted on a turret and controlled remotely by a soldier inside a vehicle, bunker or command post

CUDA*: Missile nickname (from barraCUDA) for the supersonic US short- to medium-range 'Small Advanced Capabilities Missile.' It has tri-mode (optical, active radar and infrared heat-seeking) sensors, thrust vectoring for extreme maneuverability and a hit-to-kill terminal attack

CYBERCOM: US Cyberspace combatant command responsible for cyber defense and warfare.

DARPA: US Defense Advanced Research Projects Agency, a research and development agency responsible for bringing new military technologies to the US armed forces

DAS: Distributed Aperture System; a 360-degree sensor system on the F-35 Panther allowing the pilot to track targets visually at greater than 'eyeball' range

DEWS*: Directed Energy Weapon Systems. Various laser and microwave energy based systems are in development or have seen experimental use by militaries including US, UK, Japan, Russia, China, India and South Korea. The US Navy has deployed the 60+ kilowatt HELIOS laser system on several vessels, which is claimed to be capable of long-range Intelligence, Surveillance, Reconnaissance (ISR) and Counter UAS operations, including optical infrared jamming. The US Army has announced the BLUEHALO 20-kilowatt anti drone system will be mounted on light tactical vehicles and a 50 kilowatt MSRAD (Maneuver Short Range Air Defense) laser on Stryker vehicles. It is also experimenting with a truck mounted 50 kilowatt HEL-MD (High Energy Laser Mobile Demonstrator) laser for cruise missile and artillery defense.

DFDA: Australian armed forces Defense Forces Discipline Act

DFM: Australian armed forces Defense Force Magistrate

DIA: The US Defense Intelligence Agency

DIRECTOR OF NATIONAL CYBER SECURITY*. The NSA's Cyber Security Directorate is an organization that unifies NSA's foreign intelligence and cyber defense missions and is charged with preventing and eradicating threats to National Security Systems and the Defense Industrial Base. Various US government sources have mooted the elevation of the role of Director of Cyber Security to a Cabinet-level Director of National Cyber Security (on a level with Director of National Intelligence), appointed by the US President to coordinate the activities of the many different agencies and military departments engaged in cyber warfare.

551

DRONE: Uncrewed aerial vehicle, or UAV, used for combat, transport, refueling or reconnaissance. Militaries and manufacturers twist themselves in knots to avoid using the word 'drone.' For example, 'loitering kamikaze drones' such as the Switchblade and Lancet have been described by the UK military as 'One Way Uncrewed Aerial Attack Vehicles.' Let's just call them drones.

ECS: Engagement Control Station; the local control center for a HELLADS laser battery which tracks targets and directs anti-air defensive fire

EMP: Electromagnetic pulse. Nuclear weapons produce an EMP wave which can destroy unshielded electronic components. The major military powers have also been experimenting with non-nuclear weapons which can also produce an EMP pulse–see CHAMP missile

ETA: Estimated Time of Arrival

F-16 FALCON: US-made 4th-generation multirole fighter aircraft flown by Turkey

F-22: The F-22 fighter is a stealth aircraft with low radar cross-section (RCS), long range, and high weapons payload capability, introduced in 2005 and currently planned to be retired in the 2040s. Though intended primarily for air-air combat it is capable of carrying a variety of air-to-air and air-to-ground weapons, including missiles, bombs, and rockets, with a maximum weapons payload of approximately 2,000 pounds.

F-35: US 5th-generation fighter aircraft, known either as the Panther (pilot nickname) or Lightning II (manufacturer name). The Panther nickname was first coined by the 6th Weapons Squadron 'Panther Tamers'. There is much speculation about the capabilities of the Panther, just as there is about the Russian Su-57 Felon. Neither has been extensively combat tested, though the F-35 has reportedly been used in combat by the Israeli Air Force.

F-47B (currently X-47B) FANTOM*: A Northrop Grumman demonstration uncrewed combat aerial vehicle (UCAV) in trials with the US Navy and a part of the DARPA Joint UCAS program. See also MQ-25 STINGRAY. The Fantom is used in these novels as an example of a possible uncrewed combat aircraft, and should not be taken to reflect the actual capabilities of the X-47B.

FAC: Forward air controller; an aviator embedded with a ground unit to direct close air support attacks. See also TAC(P) or JTAC

FAST MOVERS: Fighter jets

FATEH: Iranian SSK (diesel electric) submarine. At 500 tons, also considered a midget submarine. Capable of launching torpedoes, torpedo-launched cruise missiles and mines

FELON: Russian 5th-generation stealth fighter aircraft, the Sukhoi Su-57. There is much speculation about the capabilities of the Felon, just as there is about the US F-35 Panther. Neither has been extensively combat tested. Unlike the F-35 however the FELON has not entered large scale production and few flying production airframes exist. Capabilities discussed in these novels are speculative.

FINGER FOUR FORMATION: a fighter aircraft patrol formation in which four aircraft fly together in a pattern that resembles the tips of the four fingers of a hand. Three such formations can form a squadron of 12 aircraft.

FIRESCOUT: an uncrewed autonomous scout helicopter for service on US warships, used for anti-ship and anti-submarine operations

FISTER: A member of a FiST (Fire Support Team)

FLANKER: Russian Sukhoi-30 or 35 attack aircraft; see also J-11 (China)

FOX (1, 2 or 3): Radio brevity code indicating a pilot has fired an air-to-air missile, either semi-active radar seeking (1), infrared (2) or active radar seeking (3)

GAL*: A natural language learning system (AI) used by Israel's Unit 8200 to conduct complex analytical research support

GAL-CLASS SUBMARINE*: An upgraded *Dolphin II* class submarine, fitted with the GAL AI system, allowing it to be operated by a two-person crew.

G/ATOR: Ground/Air Oriented Task Radar (GATOR); a radar specialized for the detection of incoming artillery fire, rockets or missiles. Also able to calculate the origin of attack for counterfire purposes.

GBU: Guided Bomb Unit

GPS: Global Positioning System, a network of civilian or military satellites used to provide accurate map reference and location data

GRAY WOLF*: US subsonic standoff air-launched cruise missile with swarming (horde) capabilities. The Gray Wolf is designed to launch from multiple aircraft, including the C-130, and defeat enemy air defenses by overwhelming them with large numbers. It will feature modular swap-out warheads.

GRAYHOUND: Radio brevity code for the launch of an air-ground missile

GRU: Russian military intelligence service

H-20*: Xian Hong 20 stealth bomber with a range of 12,000 km or 7,500 miles and payload of 10 tons. Comparable to the US B-21.

GYRFALCON, J-31: The Shenyang FC-31 Gyrfalcon, also known as the J-31, is a Chinese prototype mid-sized twinjet 5th-generation fighter aircraft developed by Shenyang Aircraft Corporation. It has a length of 16.9m, height of about 4.8m, and a wingspan of 11.5m. The aircraft has a maximum speed of 1,200 knots, a combat range of 670 nautical miles on internal fuel or 1,042 nautical miles with external tanks, and a service ceiling of around 65,616 feet3. It has a maximum payload of 8,000 kg (four missiles in internal bays and six missiles or bombs on external hardpoints) and a maximum take-off weight of 28,000 kg. The first prototype took flight on October 31, 20121, and reached operational capability in 2020. It is being made available for export and is expected to replace the J-15 Flying Shark as China's dominant carrier aircraft.

HACM*: Hypersonic Attack Cruise Missile. A two-stage missile with solid fuel first stage boosting the missile to supersonic velocity after which a scramjet engine takes over to drive the missile to speeds of Mach 5 and above. The contract to develop HACM was awarded to Raytheon in September 2022.

HARM: High-speed Anti-Radar Missile; a missile which homes on the signals produced by anti-air missile radars like that used by the BUK or PANTSIR

HAWKEYE: Northrop Grumman E2D airborne warning and control aircraft. Capable of launching from aircraft carriers and networking (sharing data) with compatible aircraft.

HE: High-explosive munitions; general purpose explosive warheads

HEAT: High-Explosive Anti-Tank munitions; shells specially designed to penetrate armor

HELIOS*: Laser weapon. See DEWS

HEL-MD*: High Energy Laser Mobile Demonstrator) laser. See DEWS.

HELLADS*: High Energy Liquid Laser Area Defense System; an alternative to missile or projectile-based air defense systems that attacks enemy missiles, rockets or bombs with high energy laser and/or microwave pulses. Currently being tested by US, Chinese, Russian and EU ground, air and naval forces. The combination of HELLADS with HPM defense systems is logical but speculative. See also DEWS.

HIMARS: High Mobility Artillery Rocket System is a highly mobile artillery rocket system developed by Lockheed Martin Missiles and Fire Control that offers the firepower of MLRS on a wheeled chassis. It carries a single six-pack of rockets or one long range GPS guided ATACMS missile on a 5-ton truck, and can launch the entire MLRS family of munitions. It has a shoot-and-scoot capability that reduces the enemy's ability to locate and target it.

HMD: Helmet Mounted Display. Rather than a Heads Up Display or HUD which is projected on the windscreen in front of the pilot, the HMD is projected onto the visor of the helmet and thus follows the pilot's vision as they turn their head.

HORDE*: Drones, missiles or smart bombs with onboard AI and the ability to coordinate their actions with other drones while in flight, either autonomously or using preselected protocols. 'Horde' tactics differ from 'swarm' tactics in that they rely on large numbers to overwhelm enemy defenses. See also SWARM

HPM*: High Power Microwave; an untargeted local area defensive weapon which attacks sensitive electronics in missiles and guided bombs to damage electronics such as guidance systems. Chinese weapons developers using a pulse-HPM or EMP weapon were reported in 2023 to have brought down an uncrewed aircraft flying at 5,000 feet. The US Air Force Research Laboratory's (AFRL) Tactical High Power Operational Responder (THOR) system is a shipping-container-sized HPM weapon designed to bring down drone swarms. All HPM systems can currently be regarded as prototypes, and squad level or miniaturized HPM systems do not yet exist.

HSU-003*: Planned Chinese large uncrewed underwater vehicle optimized for seabed warfare, i.e. piloting itself to a specific location on the sea floor (a harbor or shipping lane) and conducting reconnaissance or anti-shipping attacks. Comparable to the US Orca.

HUD: Heads Up Display - an image projected on the windscreen in front of a pilot to show vital information about the aircraft and its systems so that they don't need to take their eyes off the outside environment. See also HMD - Helmet Mounted Display.

HYPER-LONG-RANGE ARTILLERY (HLRA)*: This is a projection of capabilities currently in development in various armies. In 2021 the US Army began testing rocket assisted long range artillery. The M1299 Howitzer is armed with a new 155 mm L/58 caliber long, 9.1 m gun tube, XM907 gun, designed by Benét Laboratories that can fire the XM1113 rocket-assisted round. This gives it a range of over 70 km (43 mi) – much greater than the 38 km (24 mi) of the M109A7 Paladin. In December 2022, the XM907E2 cannon fired an XM1155 sub-caliber projectile out to 110 km (68 mi). China is also exploring this concept, coupled with AI, to enable precision targeting of targets on Taiwan by mainland-based artillery shooting across the Taiwan Strait. Projected 15 years into the future it is expected HRLA systems will be able to hit targets 200km or 120 mi away.

HYPERION*: Proposed lightly armored uncrewed ground vehicle (UGCV). Can be fitted with turret-mounted 50kw laser for anti-air, anti-personnel defense and autoloading TOW missile launcher. See also BRADLEY UGCV

HYPERSONIC: Speeds greater than 5x the speed of sound. Often used in relation to missiles. Ballistic missiles are by nature hypersonic. Examples in use include the Russian Kh-47M2 Kinzhal, or "Dagger" in Russian: a Russian hypersonic air-launched ballistic missile that is claimed to have a range of 2,000 km (1,200 mi) and Mach 10 speed. It can carry either conventional or nuclear warheads and can be launched by Tu-22M3 bombers or MiG-31K interceptors. It has seen use in the Ukraine conflict with US forces claiming a 100% interception rate using the PATRIOT missile defense system (unverified).

ICC: Information Coordination Center; command center for multiple air defense batteries such as PATRIOT or HELLADS

IED: Improvised explosive device, for example, a roadside bomb

IFF: Identify Friend or Foe transponder, a radio transponder that allows weapons systems to determine whether a target is an ally or enemy

IFV: Infantry fighting vehicle, a highly mobile, lightly armored, wheeled or tracked vehicle capable of carrying troops into a combat and providing fire support. See NAMER

IMA BK: The combat AI built into Russia's Su-57 Felon and Okhotnik fighter aircraft

IONIC BOUNCE: a technique used by air defense radars to detect stealth aircraft by bouncing radio waves off the boundary to the ionosphere, striking the aircraft on their larger upper surfaces.

IR: Infrared or heat-seeking system

ISIS: Self-proclaimed Islamic State of Iraq and Syria

J-7: Fishbed; 3rd-generation Chinese fighter, a copy of cold war Russian Mig-21

J-10: Vigorous Dragon; 3rd-generation Chinese fighter, comparable to US F-16

J-11: Flanker; 4th-generation Chinese fighter, copy of Russian Su-27

J-15: Flying Shark; 4th-generation PLA Navy, twin-engine twin-seat fighter, comparable to Russian Su-33 and a further development of the J-11. Currently the most common aircraft flown off China's aircraft carriers.

J-11 AI variant*: *Zhi Sheng* (Intelligence Victory); 4th-generation, two-seater twin-engine multirole strike fighter. In 2019 it was announced a variant of the J-11 was being developed with *Zhi Sheng* Artificial Intelligence to replace the human 'backseater' or copilot.

J-20: 'Mighty Dragon'; 5th-generation single-seat, twin-engine Chinese stealth fighter, claimed to be comparable to the US F-35 or F-22, or Russian Su-57. Aviation experts believe it would have a larger cross section than its western counterparts, not just because of its larger size, but also because it employs nose-mounted canards. The first operational squadron of J-20 fighters was stood up by China in 2018. As many as ten squadrons exist today.

J-31: See Gyrfalcon.

JAGM: Joint air-ground missile. A US short-range anti-armor or anti-personnel missile fired from an aircraft. It can be laser or radar guided and has an 18 lb. warhead.

JASSM: AGM-158 Joint Air-to-Surface Standoff Missile; long-range subsonic stealth cruise missile capable of fielding multiple warhead types (e.g. electronic warfare, high explosive, cluster, anti-armor.) JASSM-ER is the Extended Range variant which can travel up to 580 miles or 930 kilometers. JASSM-E is an electronic signature attack version designed specifically to attack enemy command, control and intelligence targets. Other variants include electronic warfare and anti-radar capabilities.

JDAM: Joint Direct Attack Munition; bombs guided by laser or GPS to their targets

JOE*: "Joint Outcome Evaluator." A natural language learning system (AI) used by the DIA to conduct sophisticated analytical research support. The DIA has publicly reported it is already using AI for analytical support and to explore machine learning potential, but the JOE system in this novel is speculative.

JLTV*: US Joint Light Tactical Vehicle; planned replacement for the US ground forces Humvee multipurpose vehicle, to be available in recon/scout, infantry transport, heavy guns, close combat, command and control, or ambulance versions

JTAC: Joint terminal air controller. A member of a ground force–e.g., Marine unit–trained to direct the action of combat aircraft engaged in close air support and other offensive air operations from a forward position. See also CAS

K-77M*: Supersonic Russian-made medium-range active radar homing air-to-air missile with extreme maneuverability. It is being developed from the existing R-77 missile.

KALIBR: Russian-made anti-ship, anti-submarine and land attack cruise missile with 500kg conventional or nuclear warhead. The Kalibr-M variant* will have an extended range of up to 4,500 km or 2,700 miles (the distance of, e.g., Iran to Paris).

KARAKURT CLASS: A Russian corvette class which first entered service in 2018. Armed with Pantsir close-in weapons systems, Sosna-R anti-air missile defense and Kalibr supersonic anti-ship missiles. An anti-submarine sensor/weapon loadout is planned but not yet deployed.

KC-135 STRATOTANKER: US airborne refueling aircraft

KINZHAL: Russian air launched ballistic missile. Deployed in Ukraine conflict. Claimed to fly at Mach 10, Russia asserts the Kinzhal is both hypersonic and impossible to intercept. Ukrainian Patriot missile crews claim the Kinzhal travels only at Mach 3.6 (not hypersonic) and has been successfully intercepted. It is impossible to verify these competing claims.

KRYPTON: Supersonic Russian air-launched anti-radar missile, it is also being adapted for use against ships and large aircraft

LAUNCH AND LOITER: The capability of a missile or drone to fly itself to a target area and wait at altitude for final targeting instructions

LCS: Littoral combat ship. In the US Navy it refers to the *Independence* or *Freedom* class; in Iran, the *Safineh* class; in other navies it may be considered equivalent to a frigate or corvette class. Has the capabilities of a small assault transport, including a flight deck and hangar for housing two SH-60 or MH-60 Seahawk helicopters, a stern ramp for operating small boats, and the cargo volume and payload to deliver a small assault force with fighting vehicles to a roll-on/roll-off port facility. Standard armaments include Mk 110 57 mm guns and RIM-116 Rolling Airframe Missiles. Also equipped with autonomous air, surface and underwater vehicles. Possessing lower air defense and surface warfare capabilities than destroyers, the LCS concept emphasizes speed, flexible mission modules and a shallow draft.

LEOPARD: Main battle tank fielded by NATO forces including Turkey

LIAONING: China's first aircraft carrier, modified from the former Russian Navy aircraft cruiser, the *Varyag*. Since superseded by China's Type 002 (*Shandong*) and Type 003 (*Fujian*) carriers, the *Liaoning* is now used for testing new technologies for carrier use, such as the J-31 stealth fighter.

LIBERATOR II*: Also known as the 'Liberty Lifter.' The Liberty Lifter is a concept for a long-range, low-cost seaplane that can carry heavy loads across oceans by flying close to the water surface using the ground effect. The concept was launched by DARPA in mid-2022 to develop a new plane that could combine the speed and flexibility of airlift with the runway-independence and endurance of sealift. The concept aims to revolutionize heavy air lift for maritime operations and logistics. DARPA awarded contracts to two teams, Aurora Flight Sciences and General Atomics, in February 2023 to design their own versions of the Liberty Lifter. The final designs are expected by mid-2024, and the winning design will proceed to build and test a full-size prototype. DARPA hopes to have the Liberty Lifter flying within roughly five years

LOITERING MUNITION: A missile or bomb, able to wait at altitude for final targeting instructions. Example: The AeroVironment Switchblade is a miniature loitering munition, designed by AeroVironment and used by several branches of the United States military. Small enough to fit in a backpack, the Switchblade launches from a tube, flies to the target area, directed wirelessly by an operator and crashes into its target while detonating its explosive warhead.

LONG-RANGE HYPERSONIC WEAPONS (LRHW)*: A prototype US missile consisting of a rocket and glide vehicle, capable of being launched by submarine, from land or from aircraft.

LONGSHOT*: Air launched drone, first flight expected 2024. According to manufacturer "able to be launched by crewed fighter jets, transports or other aircraft and capable of venturing deep into hostile airspace to effectively engage enemy targets. Able to conduct a fighter sweep ahead of a strike wave and join human-crewed aircraft on a mission, effectively bolstering the firepower of the forces."

LRASM: Long Range Anti-Ship Missile is a stealth anti-ship cruise missile developed for the United States Air Force and United States Navy by the Defense Advanced Research Projects Agency (DARPA). It is a precision-guided missile designed to meet the needs of US Navy and Air Force Warfighters against maritime capital ship targets, with a long range that enables target engagement from well outside the range of direct counter-fire weapons.

LS3*: Legged Squad Support System–a mechanized dog-like robot powered by hydrogen fuel cells and supported by a cloud-based AI. Currently being explored by DARPA and the US armed forces for logistical support or squad scouting and IED detection roles.

LTMV: Light Tactical Multirole Vehicle; a very long name for what is essentially a jeep.

M1A2 ABRAMS: US main battle tank. In 2016, the US Army and Marine Corps began testing out the Israeli Trophy active protection system to provide additional defense against incoming projectiles. Improvements planned for the M1A3 are to include a lighter 120 mm gun, added road wheels with improved suspension, a more durable track, lighter-weight armor, long-range precision armaments, and infrared camera and laser detectors.

M22: See BARRETT MRAD M22 sniper rifle

M27: US-made military assault rifle

MAD: Magnetic Anomaly Detection, used by warships to detect large artificial objects under the surface of the sea, such as mines, or submarines

MAIN BATTLE TANK: See MBT

MALD: The ADM-160 MALD (Miniature Air-Launched Decoy) is an air-launched, expendable decoy missile developed by the United States. It uses gradient-index optics to create a radar cross section that simulates allies' aircraft in order to stimulate, confuse, and degrade the capability of missile defense systems. Later variants (MALD-J) are additionally equipped with electronic countermeasures to actively jam early warning and target acquisition radars.

MANPAD: Man portable air defense missile, such as US Stinger, Chinese Crossbow or UK Starstreak.

MASS*: Marine Autonomous Surface Ship, or autonomous trailing vessel. Not to be confused with Uncrewed Surface Vessels such as kamikaze drone boats, which have already seen action in Ukraine.

MBT: Main battle tank; a heavily armored combat vehicle capable of direct fire and maneuver

MEFP: Multiple Explosive Formed Penetrators; a defensive weapon which uses small explosive charges to create and fire small metal slugs at an incoming projectile, thereby destroying it. As used in the Israeli Trophy armored vehicle defense system.

MEMS: Micro-Electro-Mechanical System

METEOR: Long-range air-to-air missile with active radar seeker, but also able to be updated with target data in-flight by any suitably equipped allied unit

MIA: Missing in action

MIKE: Radio brevity code for minutes

MIL-25: Export version of the Mi-25 'Hind' Russian helicopter gunship

MML*: Multi Mission Launcher. A further development of the NASAMS concept. The MML is the first major development program successfully undertaken by the US government industrial base in more than 30 years. The Miniature Hit-to-Kill Missile was developed by Lockheed Martin specifically for the MML. Intended to fill the C-RAM role this approximately 2.5 feet (76 cm) and 5 pounds (2.3 kg) missile fits six to a MML pod. Multiple missiles have been integrated and tested with the system including FIM-92 Stinger missiles, AIM-9X Sidewinder and AGM-114 Hellfire and Naval Strike missiles. Expected deployment 2025.

MOP: Massive ordnance penetrator. A 30,000 lb. bomb with a hardened steel casing using GPS guidance to enable precision targeting. It can be launched at 'standoff' ranges and glide to its target.

MOPP: Mission-Oriented Protective Posture protective gear; equipment worn to protect troops against CBRN weapons. See also NBC SUIT

MP: Military Police

MQ-25 STINGRAY: The MQ-25 Stingray is a Boeing-designed prototype uncrewed US airborne refueling aircraft. See also F-47B Fantom. Already in service.

MSRAD: Maneuver Short Range Air Defense laser. See DEWS.

MSS: Ministry of State Security, Chinese umbrella intelligence organization responsible for counterespionage and counterterrorism, and foreign intelligence gathering. Equivalent to the US FBI, CIA and NSA.

NAMER: (Leopard) Israeli infantry fighting vehicle (IFV). More heavily armored than a Merkava IV main battle tank. According to the Israel Defense Forces, the Namer is the most heavily armored vehicle in the world of any type.

NAMICA: The Indian NAMICA (NAG Missile Carrier) is an Infantry Fighting Vehicle (IFV) equipped with a 30 mm automatic cannon, a 7.62 mm machine gun, and a launcher for anti-tank guided missiles, designed to provide fire support and transport for infantry troops.

NATO: North Atlantic Treaty Organization

NAVAL STRIKE MISSILE (NSM): Supersonic anti-ship missile deployed by NATO navies

NBC SUIT: A protective suit issued to protect the wearer against Nuclear, Biological or Chemical weapons. Usually includes a lining to protect the user from radiation and either a gas mask or air recycling unit.

NORAD: The North American Aerospace Defense Command is a United States and Canadian bi-national organization charged with the missions of aerospace warning, aerospace control and maritime warning for North America. Aerospace warning includes the detection, validation and warning of attack against North America whether by aircraft, missiles or space vehicles, through mutual support arrangements with other commands.

NSA: US National Security Agency, cyber intelligence, cyber warfare and defense agency

OFSET*: Offensive Swarm Enabled Tactical drones. Proposed US anti-personnel, anti-armor drone system capable of swarming AI (see SWARM) and able to deploy small munitions against enemy troop or vehicles while moving.

OKHOTNIK*: 5th-generation Sukhoi S-70 uncrewed stealth combat aircraft using avionics systems from the Su-57 Felon and fitted with two internal weapons bays, for 7,000kg of ordnance. Requires a pilot and systems officer, similar to current US uncrewed combat aircraft. Can be paired with Su-57 aircraft and controlled by a pilot.

OMON: Otryad Mobil'nyy Osobogo Naznacheniya; the Russian National Guard mobile police force

ORCA*: Prototype US large displacement uncrewed underwater vehicle with modular payload bay capable of anti-submarine, anti-ship or reconnaissance activities

OVOD: Subsonic Russian-made air-launched cruise missile capable of carrying high-explosive, submunition or fragmentation warheads

P-99 Black Widow (Pursuit Fighter)*: Concept aircraft. Several companies were competing in 2023 for the Next Generation Air Dominance air superiority initiative. The Black Widow is a purely speculative platform combining what is known about the requirements issued and the designs in testing. NGAD is described by the USAF as a "family of systems," with a stealth fighter aircraft as the centerpiece of the system, and other parts of the system likely to be uncrewed escort aircraft to carry extra munitions and perform other missions. In particular, NGAD aims to develop a system that addresses the operation needs of the Pacific theater of operations, where current USAF fighters lack sufficient range and payload. The successful NGAD aircraft is therefore unlikely to resemble current US stealth fighters such as the F-22 Rapiére or F-35 Panther.

PANTHER: Pilot name for the F-35 Lightning II stealth fighter, first coined by the 6th Weapons Squadron 'Panther Tamers' due to the unpopularity of the official name 'Lightning II'. There is much speculation about the capabilities of the Panther, just as there is about the Russian Su-57 Felon. Neither has been extensively combat tested.

PANTSIR: Russian-made truck-mounted anti-aircraft system which is a further development of the PENSNE: 'Pince-nez' in English. A Russian-made autonomous ground-to-air missile currently being rolled out for the BUK anti-air defense system.

PARS: Turkish light armored vehicle

PATRIOT: An anti-aircraft, interceptor missile defense system which uses its own radar to identify and engage airborne threats

PEACE EAGLE: Turkish Boeing 737 Airborne Early Warning and Control aircraft (see AWACS)

PENSNE: See PANTSIR

PERDIX*: Lightweight air-launched armed microdrone with swarming capability (see SWARM). Designed to be launched from underwing canisters or even from the flare/chaff launchers of existing aircraft. Can be used for recon, target identification or delivery of lightweight ordnance.

PEREGRINE*: US medium-range, multimode (infrared, radar, optical) seeker missile with short form body designed for use by stealth aircraft

PERSEUS*: A stealth, hypersonic, multiple warhead missile under development for the British Royal Navy and French Navy

PHASED-ARRAY RADAR: A radar which can steer a beam of radio waves quickly across the sky to detect planes and missiles

PL-15: Chinese long-range radar-guided air-to-air missile, comparable to the US AIM-120D (though with longer range) or UK Meteor.

PL-21*: Chinese long-range multimode missile (radar, infrared, optical), comparable to US AIM-260

PLA: People's Liberation Army

PLA-AF (PLAAF): People's Liberation Army Air Force, comparable to the US Air Force, with more than 400 3rd-generation fighter aircraft, 1,200 4th-generation, and nearly 200 5th-generation stealth aircraft

PLA-N (PLAN): People's Liberation Army Navy

PLA-N AF (PLANAF): People's Liberation Army Navy Air Force, comparable to the US Navy Air Force and Marine Corps Aviation, it performs coastal protection and aircraft carrier operations with more than 250 3rd-generation fighter aircraft, and 150 4th-generation fighter aircraft. There is speculation the PLA-N AF is considering the J-31 Gyrfalcon* (a prototype stealth fighter) for its aircraft carriers.

PODNOS: Russian-made portable 82 mm mortar

PUMP-JET PROPULSION: A propulsion system comprising a jet of water and a nozzle to direct the flow of water for steering purposes. Used on some submarines due to a quieter acoustic signature than that generated by a screw. The most 'stealthy' submarines are regarded to be those powered by diesel electric engines and pump-jet propulsion, such as trialed on the Russian *Kilo* class and proposed for the Australian *Attack* class*.

QHS*: Quantum Harmonic Sensor; a sensor system for detecting stealth aircraft at long ranges by analyzing the electromagnetic disturbances they create in background radiation.

QING* class submarine (Type 032): A class of diesel-electric submarine currently undergoing testing in China's People's Liberation Army Navy. It is said to be the world's largest conventional submarine, at a submerged displacement of 6,628 tons and is able to submerge for a maximum of 30 days. It features torpedo and vertically launched missile tubes and is believed to be capable of firing nuclear armed ballistic missiles. Only one of this class is known to have been deployed. It is speculated China built only one of this type of submarine because it was struggling at the time to build small nuclear reactors, having relied on Russia until this point to supply nuclear submarine power plants. This may also be why China's aircraft carriers are not nuclear powered.

RAAF: Royal Australian Air Force

RAF: Royal Air Force (UK)

RAPID DRAGON*: Palletized Munition Deployment System, in testing with USAF. A disposable weapons module which is airdropped in order to deploy flying munitions, typically cruise missiles, drones or glide bombs, from unmodified cargo planes such as the AC-130J Ghostrider.

REUNION* (Operation): Secret Chinese project to develop the Tianyi (Wing of Fate) armed autonomous drone and associated deployment technologies such as the TLV drone mothership and launch sites. Equivalent in scope to the US Manhattan project to develop the atom bomb, it is intended to supplant traditional invasion by ground forces, allowing control of enemy territory without the massive cost and risk of a conventional invasion.

ROCAF: Republic of China Air Force. The air force of Taiwan.

ROE: Rules of Engagement; the rules laid down by military commanders under which a unit can or cannot engage in combat. For example, 'units may only engage a hostile force if fired upon first.'

RPG: Rocket-propelled grenade

RTB: Return to base

SAFINEH CLASS: Also known as *Mowj/Wave* class. An Iranian trimaran hulled high-speed missile vessel equivalent to the US LCS class, or the Russia *Karakurt* class corvette

SAM: Surface-to-Air Missile; an anti-air missile (often shortened to SA) for engaging aircraft

SAR: See SYNTHETIC APERTURE RADAR

SCREW: The propeller used to drive a boat or ship is referred to as a screw (helical blade) propeller. Submarine propellers typically comprise five to seven blades. See also PUMP-JET PROPULSION

SEAD: Suppression of Enemy Air Defenses; an air attack intended to take down enemy anti-air defense systems; see also WILD WEASEL

SENTINEL*: Lockheed Martin RQ-170 Sentinel flying wing stealth reconnaissance drone

SIDEWINDER: Heat-seeking short-range air-to-air missile

SITREP: Situation Report

SKYHAWK*: Chinese drone designed to team with fighter aircraft to provide added sensor or weapons delivery capabilities. Comparable to the planned US Boeing Loyal Wingman or Kratos drones.

SKY THUNDER: Chinese 1,000 lb. stealth air-launched cruise missile with swappable payload modules

SKYLON*: With capabilities similar to the US re-usable space drone the X-37B (see separate entry) and a modular payload Skylon is designed to take off and land like a normal aircraft. The vehicle design is a hydrogen-fueled aircraft that would take off from a specially built reinforced runway, and accelerate to Mach 5.4 at 26 kilometers (85,000 ft) altitude using the atmosphere's oxygen before switching the engines to use the internal liquid oxygen supply to accelerate to the Mach 25 necessary to reach a 400 km orbit. The high temperature test of the Reaction Engines – Rolls Royce precooler took place in 2019. Testing of the core engine components and pre-burner took place during 2020 and 2021. Uncrewed test flights in a "hypersonic testbed" (HTB) are planned for 2025.

SLR: Single lens reflex camera, favored by photojournalists and enthusiasts

SMERCH: Russian-made 300 mm rocket launcher capable of firing high-explosive, submunition or chemical weapons warheads

SOSUS: Sound Surveillance System. A chain of underwater listening posts located across the Arctic and Pacific Oceans. Used primarily for detection of submarines. US Navy recently announced it was upgrading SOSUS into the Deep Reliable Acoustic Path Exploitation System (DRAPES)* which is expected to have active low frequency sonar and magnetic anomaly detection capabilities added.

SPACECOM: United States Space Command (US SPACECOM or SPACECOM) is a unified combatant command of the United States Department of Defense, responsible for military operations in outer space, specifically all operations above 100 km above mean sea level

SPEAR/SPEAR-EW*: UK/Europe Select Precision at Range air-to-ground standoff attack missile, with LAUNCH AND LOITER capabilities. Will utilize a modular 'swappable' warhead system featuring high-explosive, anti-armor, fragmentation or electronic warfare (EW) warheads.

SPETSNAZ: Russian Special Operations Forces

SPLASH: US Navy and Air Force Radio brevity code showing a target has been destroyed. In artillery context splash over means impact imminent, splash out means rounds impacted.

SSBN: Strategic-level nuclear-powered (N) submarine platform for firing ballistic (B) missiles. Examples: UK *Vanguard* class, US *Ohio* class, Russia *Typhoon* class.

SSC: Subsurface Contact Supervisor; supervises operations against subsurface contacts from within a ship's Combat Information Center (CIC)

SSGN: A guided missile (G) nuclear (N) submarine that carries and launches guided cruise missiles as its primary weapon. Examples: US *Ohio* class, Russia *Yasen* class.

SSK: A diesel electric-powered submarine, quieter when submerged than a nuclear-powered submarine, but must rise to snorkel depth to run its diesel and recharge its batteries. Examples: Iranian *Fateh* class, Russian *Kilo* class, Israeli *Dolphin I* class.

SSN: A general purpose attack submarine (SS) powered by a nuclear reactor (N). Examples: HMS *Agincourt*, Russian *Akula* class.

SSP: A diesel electric submarine with air-independent propulsion system able to recharge batteries without using atmospheric oxygen. Allows the submarine to stay submerged longer than a traditional SSK. Examples: Israeli *Dolphin II* class, Iranian *Besat** class.

STANDOFF: Launched at long range

STINGER: US-made man-portable, low-level anti-air missile

STINGRAY*: The MQ-25 Stingray is a Boeing-designed prototype uncrewed US airborne refueling aircraft

STORMBREAKER*: US air-launched, precision-guided glide bomb that can use millimeter radar, laser or infrared imaging to match and then prioritize targets when operating in semi-autonomous AI mode

SU-57: See FELON

SUBSONIC: Below the speed of sound (under 767 mph, 1,234 kph)

SUNBURN: Russian-made 220 mm multiple rocket launcher capable of firing high-explosive, THERMOBARIC or penetrating warheads

SUPERSONIC: Faster than the speed of sound (over 767 mph, 1,234 kph); see also HYPERSONIC

SWARM: Drones, missiles or smart bombs with onboard AI and the ability to coordinate their actions with other drones while in flight, either autonomously or using preselected protocols. 'Swarm' tactics differ from 'horde' tactics in that swarms place more emphasis on coordinated action to defeat enemy defenses. See also HORDE

SYNTHETIC APERTURE RADAR (SAR): A form of radar that is used to create two-dimensional images or three-dimensional reconstructions of objects, such as landscapes. SAR uses the motion of the radar antenna over a target region to provide finer spatial resolution than conventional beam-scanning radars.

SYSOP: The systems operator inside the control station for a HELLADS battery, responsible for electronic and communications systems operation

T-14 ARMATA: Russian next-generation main battle tank or MBT. Designed as a 'universal combat platform' which can be adapted to infantry support, anti-armor or anti-armor configurations. First Russian MBT to be fitted with active electronically scanning array radar capable of identifying and engaging multiple air and ground targets simultaneously. Also the first Russian MBT to be fitted with a crew toilet. Used in combat in Syria from 2020 and claimed by Russia to have entered combat in Ukraine (but not verified independently). Very few examples are believed to exist and the last time they were paraded in public, three were seen, but one broke down and could not complete the parade.

T-90: Russian-made main battle tank

TAC(P): Tactical air controller, a specialist trained to direct close air support attacks. See also CAS; FAC; JTAC

TAIFUN*: Speculative iteration of the Zhu Hai Yun class drone mothership. The Zhu Hai Yun, launched in 2022, is the world's first drone carrier vessel, capable of launching and recovering up to 50 autonomous uncrewed vehicles.

TAO: Tactical action officer; officer in command of a ship's Combat Information Center (CIC)

TCA: Tactical control assistant, non-commissioned officer (NCO) in charge of identifying targets and directing fire for a single HELLADS or PATRIOT battery

TCO: Tactical control officer, officer in charge of a single HELLADS or PATRIOT missile battery

TD: Tactical Director; the officer directing multiple PATRIOT or HELLADS batteries in ground air defenses, or interception operations aboard an AWACs aircraft.

TEMPEST*: British/European 6th-generation stealth aircraft under development as a replacement for the RAF Tornado multirole fighter. It is planned to incorporate advanced combat AI to reduce pilot data overload, laser anti-missile defenses, and will team with swarming drones such as BATS. It may be developed in both crewed and uncrewed versions, and a version for use on the two new British aircraft carriers is also mooted.

TERMINATOR: A Russian-made infantry fighting vehicle (see IFV) based on the chassis of the T-90 main battle tank, with 2x 30 mm autocannons and 2x grenade or anti-tank missile launchers. Developed initially to support main battle tank operations, it has become popular for use in urban combat environments.

THERMOBARIC: Weapons, otherwise known as thermal or vacuum weapons, which use oxygen from the surrounding air to generate a high-temperature explosion and long-duration blast wave

THUNDER: Radio brevity code indicating one minute to weapons impact

TIANYI (Wing of Fate) autonomous drone*: A speculative design based on the TIKAD/SMASH DRAGON prototypes; gyro stabilized flying gun quadcopters which can be fitted with automatic weapons or 40 mm grenade launchers.

TIANGONG: Chinese space station launched in April 2021 and currently comprising 3 modules. Planned expansion to 5 modules by 2025, the station is seen as a step toward a crewed Mars mission. With the International Space Station (ISS) due to be decommissioned in 2031, China will have the only functioning space station. There have been no discussions about international missions involving Tiangong, primarily because China was excluded from ISS participation by the USA.

TLV: Tianyi Launch Vehicle, a supersonic drone mothership launched by maglev, which glides to its target before engaging an electric engine and dispersing a swarm of autonomous Tianyi (Wing of Fate) drones.

T-POD*: Trauma-Pod battlefield medical assistant. A speculative merger of ongoing research into battlefield trauma treatment which aims to enable AI assisted rapid diagnosis and stabilization of the most common battlefield injuries (blast injury, projectile weapon injury, cardiac failure).

TOW: US wire-guide anti-tank missile, fired either from a tripod launcher by ground troops or mounted on armored cavalry vehicles

TROPHY· Israeli-made anti-projectile defense system using explosively formed penetrators to defeat attacks on vehicles, high-value assets and aircraft. It is currently fitted to several Israeli and US armored vehicle types. Use in aircraft is speculative.

TSIRKON*: (aka Tsirkon), scramjet powered anti-ship missile claimed by Russia to be capable of Mach 9 or 9,800 km an hour. Because it flies at hypersonic speeds within the atmosphere, air pressure in front of it forms a plasma cloud as it moves, absorbing radio waves and making it difficult for radar to detect. Russia claims to have deployed the missile on its Admiral *Gorshkov* class frigates but it has not been observed in use e.g. in Ukraine. Seel also Zmeyevik (air launched variant).

TUNGUSKA: A mobile Russian-made anti-aircraft vehicle incorporating both cannon and ground-to-air missiles

TYPE 054, TYPE 055: Chinese fleet defense destroyers. The Type 054 destroyer is a multi-role frigate equipped with anti-ship missiles, air defense missiles, torpedoes, and a 76 mm gun based on the old Soviet *Sovremenny* class; while the Chinese Type 055 destroyer is a more advanced guided missile destroyer with a more powerful armament that includes advanced air defense systems, land attack cruise missiles, anti-ship missiles, torpedoes, and a variety of guns, similar in role to the US Arleigh Burke class.

TYPE 95*: Planned Chinese 3rd-generation nuclear-powered attack submarine with vertical launch tubes and substantially reduced acoustic signature to current Chinese types

UAV: Uncrewed aerial vehicle or drone, usually used for transport, refueling or reconnaissance

UCAS: Uncrewed combat aerial support vehicle or drone

UCAV: Uncrewed combat aerial vehicle; a fighter or attack aircraft

UDAR* UGV: Russian-made uncrewed ground vehicle which integrates remotely operated turrets (30 mm autocannon, Kornet anti-tank missile or anti-air missile) onto the chassis of a BMP-3 infantry fighting vehicle. The vehicle can be controlled at a range of up to 6 miles (10 km) by an operator with good line of sight, or via a tethered drone relay.

UDV: Underwater delivery vehicle. A small submersible transport used typically by naval commandos for covert insertion and recovery of troops.

UGV: Uncrewed ground vehicle, also UGCV: Uncrewed ground combat vehicle

UI: Un-Identified, as in 'UI contact.' See also BOGEY

UNIT 8200: Israel Defense Force cyber intelligence, cyber warfare and defense unit, aka the Israeli Signals Intelligence National Unit

UPWARD FALLING PAYLOADS (UFP)*: A DARPA research project of the 2020s, now shelved, to develop deployable, uncrewed distributed systems that lie on the deep-ocean floor in concealed containers for years at a time. These deep-sea nodes could be remotely activated when needed and recalled to the surface. In other words, they "fall upward." Payloads could include sensor packages, canister-launched aerial drones, mines or torpedoes.

URAGAN: Russian 220 mm 16-tube rocket launcher, first fielded in the 1970s

U/S: Un-serviceable, out of commission, broken

USO: United Services Organizations; US military entertainment and personnel welfare services

V-22 OSPREY: Bell Boeing multi-mission tiltrotor aircraft capable of vertical takeoff and landing which resembles a conventional aircraft when in flight

V-280* VALOR: Bell Boeing-proposed successor to the V-22, with higher speed, endurance, lift capacity and modular payload bay

V-280* VAPOR: Concept aircraft only. AI-enhanced V-280 with anti-radar absorbent coating, added rear fuselage turbofan jet engines for additional speed, and forward-firing 20 mm autocannons

VALKYRIE (XQ-58)*: an experimental uncrewed stealth fighter designed and built by Kratos Defense and Security Solutions to support a USAF requirement to field an uncrewed wingman cheap enough to sustain losses in combat but capable of supporting crewed aircraft in hostile environments. In January 2023 it was announced the USAF had purchased two Valkyrie demonstrators for $15.5m USD, shortly after which the US Navy announced it had done the same.

VERBA: A Russian-made man-portable low-level anti-air missile with data networking capabilities, meaning it can use data from friendly ground or air radar systems to fly itself to a target

VIGILANT CLASS COAST GUARD CUTTER: The *Vigilant* class Coast Guard cutter is a medium-endurance cutter with a displacement of approximately 1,000 tons, a sensor suite that includes radar, sonar, and electronic surveillance equipment, a weapons system that includes a 25 mm Mk 38 chain gun and various small arms, as well as a flight deck and hangar capable of supporting helicopter operations for search and rescue, law enforcement, and other missions.

VIRGINIA CLASS SUBMARINE: e.g., USS *Idaho*, nuclear-powered, fast-attack submarines. Current capabilities include torpedo and cruise missiles. Planned capabilities include hypersonic missiles.

VORTEX*: 'Quantum Radar' technology that generates a mini electromagnetic storm to detect objects. First reported by Professor Zhu Chao at Tsinghua University's aerospace engineering school, in Journal of Radars, 2021. A quantum radar is different from traditional radars in several ways, according to the paper. While traditional radars have on a fixed or rotating dish, the quantum design features a gun-shaped instrument that accelerates electrons. The electrons pass through a winding tube of a strong magnetic fields, producing what is described as a tornado-shaped microwave vortex.

VYMPEL: Russian air-to-air missile manufacturer/type

WIDOW*: P-99 Black WIDOW (Pursuit Fighter). Concept aircraft. Several companies were competing in 2023 for the Next Generation Air Dominance air superiority initiative. The Black Widow is a purely speculative platform combining what is known about the requirements issued and the designs in testing. Envisaged is a long range 'missile truck' able to carry 12 medium range and two short range air-to-air missiles in an internal payload bay, or a mix of air-to-air and air to ground weapons e.g. cruise missiles. NGAD is described by the USAF as a "family of systems," with a stealth fighter aircraft as the centerpiece of the system, and other parts of the system likely to be uncrewed escort aircraft to carry extra munitions and perform other missions. In particular, NGAD aims to develop a system that addresses the operation needs of the Pacific theater of operations, where current USAF fighters lack sufficient range and payload. The successful NGAD aircraft is therefore unlikely to resemble current US stealth fighters such as the F-22 Raptor or F-35 Panther.

WILD WEASEL: An air attack intended to take down enemy anti-air defense systems; see also SEAD

WINCHESTER: Radio brevity code for 'out of ordnance'

X-37C*: A successor to the US X-37B uncrewed re-usable space craft, itself a scaled down version of the X-40 space shuttle intended to put small payloads in orbit. First observed in 2010, it set a record for the longest time in orbit for a re-usable spacecraft in 2022, with a flight of 908 days. The X-37C is a conceptual armed variant that will carry a 250kW High Energy Liquid Laser to enable it to conduct satellite interceptions.

X-95: Israeli bullpup-style assault rifle. Bullpup-style rifles have their action behind the trigger, allowing for a more compact and maneuverable weapon. Commonly chambered for NATO 5.56 mm ammunition.

XLUUV*: Xtra Large Uncrewed Underwater Vehicle. Several navies have XLUUV prototypes in development, with the US and China the most advanced. These submarines are commanded remotely and because they are uncrewed, can travel larger distances underwater without requiring replenishment. Most designs being explored include modular payloads that can be switched out depending on the mission, from special forces insertion, to the launch of missiles or laying of mines.

YAKHONT*: Also known as P-800 Onyx. Russian-made two-stage ramjet-propelled, terrain-following cruise missile. Travels at subsonic speeds until close to its target where it is boosted to up to Mach 3. Can be fired from warships, submarines, aircraft or coastal batteries at sea or ground targets. Claimed to be operational but has not been seen in use in the Ukraine conflict.

YPG: Kurdish People's Protection Unit militia (male)

YPJ: Kurdish Women's Protection Unit militia (female)

YUAN WANG class tracking ships: Ships of 18-21,000 tons displacement, used for tracking and support of ballistic missiles and satellites, aircraft and for signals interception.

Z-9: Chinese attack helicopter, predecessor to Z-19

Z-19: Chinese light attack helicopter, comparable to US Viper

Z-20: Chinese medium-lift utility helicopter, comparable to US Blackhawk

ZHU HAI YUN class vessel: Aka Zhuhai Cloud (pinyin: Zhu Hai Yun) is described by China as an autonomous 'oceanography research vessel' designed for uncrewed operations in open waters and as a mother ship for uncrewed vehicles. It has been described in media as the first Chinese "drone mothership" and the first "uncrewed aircraft carrier."

It is capable of hitting a top speed of 18 knots (about 20 miles per hour) and can carry 50 flying, surface, and submersible drones that launch and self-recover autonomously. A semi-submersible variant which can launch surface to air missiles is speculative.

Zmeyevik: air launched near-hypersonic ballistic missile. See also Tsirkon (Zirkon).

Made in the USA
Columbia, SC
08 April 2024

34116139R10317